WICKED Heat

NEW YORK TIMES BESTSELLING AUTHOR
J. KENNER

All rights reserved.

No part of this publication may be sold, copied, distributed, reproduced or transmitted in any form or by any means, mechanical or digital, including photocopying and recording or by any information storage and retrieval system without the prior written permission of both the publisher, Oliver Heber Books and the author, Julie Kenner except in the case of brief quotations embodied in critical articles and reviews.

PUBLISHER'S NOTE: This is a work of fiction. Names, characters, places, and incidents either are the product of the author's imagination or are used fictitiously. Any resemblance to actual persons, living or dead, business establishments, events, or locales is entirely coincidental.

Wicked Heat Copyright 2024 © Julie Kenner

Release Me excerpt Copyright 2013 © Julie Kenner

Cover design by T.M. Franklin

Cover art by depositphotos.com, ©epic22, ©stokkete

Published by Oliver-Heber Books

0 9 8 7 6 5 4 3 2 1

Wicked Nights
(Stark World standalone novels)
Sometimes it feels so damn good to be bad.

Wicked Grind

Wicked Dirty

Wicked Torture

Wicked Heat

Wicked Fortune

Dear Reader:

I wrote *Wicked Heat* as a standalone title that can be enjoyed even if you've never met Damien Stark or any of the characters in Stark World. But for those of you who know the world well, this book falls chronologically about four months after the events in *Interview With The Billionaire*.

If you haven't read all of the Nikki & Damien Stark books, you may notice a few spoilers, especially with regard to Ash, Bree, and the characters and circumstances in *Lost With Me* and *Enchant Me*. While I've tried to limit spoilers as much as possible, sometimes the little devils just insist on being on the page.

Finally, if you're new to Stark World, please be aware that the books set in this world have dark undertones and tend to revolve around people overcoming trauma on the way to finding love and their HEA.

XXOO
JK

P.S. – if you're ever in the Los Angeles area, be sure to check out the Ripped Bodice! It really is an awesome store!

PROLOGUE

You can't truly know anybody. Not your friends. Not your neighbors.

Not your lovers.

Not even yourself.

I learned the last one the hard way. Harsh? Maybe. But once you truly understand how brutal the world is—how quickly the ground can be ripped out from under you—the easier it is to get from one day to the next.

You keep a tight lock on your heart.

You hold your secrets close.

And you look out at the world from behind a wall of glass bricks, so thick it's almost shatterproof.

Almost.

That's the tricky word. The hard lesson that nearly broke me.

Because despite everything I thought I knew—despite every rule I'd set for myself—I let him in. I let him get close. A man whose hands have caressed me. A man I fear I don't know at all. Who may have betrayed me in the most brutal of ways.

He is a mystery, and yet I let him hold my heart in his hands.

Now, I am fully at his mercy. And all I can do is hope that he is truly the man of my dreams... and not the tormentor who still hides in my nightmares.

ONE

My cheek muscles are sore from smiling so much, but I don't care because—hands down—this is the absolute best day of my life. "Do you want it signed to you?" I ask, taking the copy of *Reveries at Dusk* from the outstretched hand of the last reader in line—a wide-eyed blonde in a UCLA tee.

"Are you kidding? Of course." She pushes a lock of hair out of her eyes, then spells her name for me. Her copy of my first—and so far, only—book is already open to the title page.

It's now fifteen minutes past closing time, and while there are a few people still mingling in the store, she's the last person in line. As for me, I may look like I'm seated, but I'm really floating on a cloud, not quite able to believe that so many readers had come to The Ripped Bodice—an incredible bookstore in Culver City—to meet me and get a signed copy of the book.

And not just that. Before settling at the table stacked with copies of *Reveries*, I'd done a Q&A in front of dozens and dozens of readers.

Seriously—Best. Day. Ever.

Even better than the day my agent called to tell me my

book, a steamy women's fiction novel with magical elements, had made the top ten of the *USA Today* bestseller list.

I finish my inscription, then sign my name—Bree Bernstein—below where it's printed on the title page.

When I pass it back, the smiling blonde hugs it to her chest. "Thanks so much. I've read it twice already, and I can't wait for the next one. I have to know if Ace comes back." She holds a hand over her heart and swoons.

I know how she feels. Ace is far-and-away my favorite character. Not too surprising considering who I modeled him after. But that little authorial tidbit is meant only for me.

I offer a benign smile. "Ace died."

She cocks her head. "Please. There's no way Bethany is letting death keep her from her love."

"Is that what he is? What about Dirk?"

She presses her fingertips to her temples and groans. "Oh, man. You're killing me."

I laugh. "I promise it's not meant to be torture. Thank you," I add. "It means a lot that you love them as much as I do."

We chat a bit longer, then she asks for a pic with me before heading over to the counter to pay for the stack of books she's collected in the store—with mine right on top.

I wait until she's done, then hurry to the checkout area and start spewing out my thanks to the owners, Leah and Bea, even as I tell them that I hope I was okay. This was my first ever Q&A as a published author.

"You did amazing," Leah says.

"Fantastic," Bea adds.

A small part of me fears they are just being nice—Did I stumble over my words during my talk? Did I give away too much of the plot?

But mostly, I believe them. Today felt good. Like it's the second half of my job. The first part's where I sweat out the book in blood. The second part's where I feel the love and know it was worth it.

I spend another fifteen minutes chatting with the store staff, but I know they probably have things to do in this last hour before the shop closes. So I repeat my thanks, then gather up the ridiculously amazing goodie basket from the store. A few fans also brought gifts, and those are piled in the basket, too. A mix of candy and wrapped packages and homemade bookmarks and other trinkets that I treasure.

The summer sun is low in the sky when I reach the door, and it's hitting the glass in a way that turns it into a mirror. I pause for a moment, just looking into my own brown eyes, my long, almost-black hair hanging loose around a face that is lit up with so much joy I barely recognize it as mine.

I turn back to my hosts. "Thank you both so much. Today was a keeper."

Leah grins. "That's what we like to hear."

"Thank you again for coming," Bea says at the same time. She glances at the clock. "Are you going to be late? I should have cut questions off a few minutes earlier, but it was going so well."

"Oh. No. Not a problem." I feel my cheeks go red. During the Q&A, someone asked how I was going to celebrate after the signing. Since *head home and stream a romcom* sounded lame, I concocted a party in Burbank. "They know I'm coming from over the hill, and my arrival time is a moveable target." A total lie, but, hey, I write fiction.

Leah grins. "Have fun."

"And pop in next week," Bea adds. "We'll have more stock for you to sign."

"Will do," I promise as I head out, giddy all over again at the idea. It doesn't get much more author-y than that.

He shouldn't have come.

As far as Ash was concerned, that was a given. Axiomatic. As true a truism as ever there was.

He should have left Los Angeles two days ago, right after his breakfast meeting. He should have canceled tomorrow's interview, then hopped the first flight back to his Austin office. He could be kicked back at his desk, reviewing the most recent test results on the INX-20. Or prepping for his upcoming meeting in Vegas.

Or, hell, he could be chasing typos as he proofread next week's shareholder report.

Anything—*anything*—other than sitting parallel parked in a red zone while he waited for a woman who hardly knew he existed to step out of a bookstore and into his line of sight.

No. That wasn't true. She felt the tug of attraction as much as he did. He was certain of it.

She knew him.

She wanted him.

She'd pushed him away.

And wasn't that a hell of a thing?

She wasn't the first woman to reject him, of course. But he had ego enough to remind himself that it didn't happen often. Still, she was different. With her, the rejection had stung.

When they'd met, that first glimpse had felt like a punch in the gut. Albeit a pleasant—hell, *arousing*—punch. But he hadn't pursued anything. Wrong time. Wrong place. Wrong vibe.

Wrong man.

Back then, he'd been angry—drenched in hate for Damien Stark, the father he thought he understood, and on a mission to destroy a family he'd resented.

The nanny for his father's kids, Bree had merely been part of the scenery, and yet she'd pulled his focus without even trying. But the last thing he'd needed was the distraction of a woman, no matter how much he'd craved that distraction.

Even later, after the dust had settled and he was back home, she'd pop into his mind. Hundreds of miles between them—and much fewer words exchanged—and yet there she was. The beautiful girl with the haunting eyes who'd made his cock go hard with nothing more than a sideways glance.

That soft skin. That adorable smile. That sharp mind and stunning body he was certain would fit perfectly against his own. A body he shouldn't desire. But he did, and in his fantasies, they'd make love sweetly under the sun, her bare skin glistening with sweat as he thrust inside her. As she whispered that she knew him. That she believed in him.

That she wanted him.

But that was all just his fantasy. Why the hell would she want him? Not after what he'd done.

He might have fooled the press. They'd gone from calling him reckless, to praising his determination and skill, to telling the world that he never backed down. That he was the man who went after what he wanted and wrote his own damn rules.

He was Ashton Fucking Stone, and when he set a goal, he achieved it.

That's how the media spun it, anyway.

But Ash knew better than anyone that those reporters were morons.

Yup, Ashton Carrington Stone was a walking, talking lesson in the decline of journalism. Because he wasn't the man they described. Not really. Maybe he could toss them a bone in the context of business. But in the personal?

Not even close.

But—damn him—four months ago, he'd let himself believe his own press. He'd spent a few days in his father's house, and once again, Bree was there.

That's when he'd seen it. That flicker of heat in her eyes. More, he'd felt it. The way the air had sizzled when they stood close. When he'd caught her arm as she'd stumbled on the stairs.

It had been late—well past two in the morning—and she'd been wearing a tank top that accentuated her figure and baggy sweats that suggested she didn't care how she looked. Her long hair had been pulled into a messy bun, and when she'd met his eyes, hers were dark and heated.

More than anything, he'd wanted to fall into that fire with her. To lose himself in the heat of her touch. The warmth of her kisses.

So, yes. He'd leaned in. Then his little sister had called out, and Bree had bolted.

Disappointing, but probably for the best.

A few days later, both their flights had been canceled and they'd ended up together at the airport hotel's bar.

She'd been right beside him, their hands had brushed, and that simple touch had sent a riot of lust and longing racing through his veins. And in that moment, he'd been certain that she wanted him as much as he wanted her.

He'd never been so wrong.

He'd given her his spare key, then waited for her, pacing his room as he sipped Scotch, but tasted anticipation.

She'd ripped his guts out. Left him hanging.

It had taken him two drinks to realize the truth. A sad testament considering how much the press praised his intellect. Apparently, that only applied to math and science. Because she never showed, and he hadn't seen that coming. Why would he? Ashton Fucking Stone hadn't been stood up before. Not one single time.

He didn't much like the feeling.

He'd called, of course. But she didn't answer her phone. And the only thing that finally quelled his rising fear and certainty that something had happened to her—because surely she wasn't intentionally staying away—was the flashing light on his room phone. And the message she'd left on the hotel's voicemail.

I can't.

Two little words.

Two tiny, throwaway words from a woman he barely knew, and yet they'd hit him with more force than a Formula One race car crashing into the sidewalk.

It had been a definitive message. A solid goodbye. More than that, it had been a firm *go away*.

The woman didn't want him.

So why the hell was he now sitting outside a bookstore some four months later, hoping to talk to her? Did he really think he'd be able to change her mind? Or that he'd be satisfied just being friends?

Better to walk away, but he couldn't make himself do it. There was desire on both sides, he was certain of it. And one way or another, he was going to make Bree Bernstein his. He was Ashton Fucking Stone, after all. What was it the press was always saying? That he never backed down? That when he set a goal, he achieved it?

They were right. He got what he wanted. Always.

Everything except Bree.

"You're an idiot, Stone. And you've got one hell of an ego."

Fuck that.

He turned the ignition key, firing the engine and fully intending to pull away. He even went so far as to put the car into gear and give it a little gas. Then he spat out a curse, slammed on the brakes, and shifted back into park before killing the engine.

And then, as he had for the last ninety minutes, Ashton Stone sat in the borrowed Mercedes... and waited.

TWO

The night air is cool against my bare arms as I cross the asphalt to where I parked Maisy, the adorable Mini Cooper convertible my parents got me as a congratulations present when I sold *Reveries*. I guess they'd been paying attention every time I mentioned how much I love my former boss's car.

Now I open the passenger door and put the basket in before circling back to the driver's side. I hesitate only a moment, then climb in and start the car. I consider putting the top down, but it's been raining on and off all day, so I leave it up and maneuver my way onto the street. But I don't go to Burbank. Not yet.

Instead, I pull into the first coffee shop I see. I'm already over-caffeinated, but I order a latte at the drive-through anyway, then slip into one of the parking places so I can sip it while I rummage in my goodie basket. Because, hey, why wait to see what else is in there? It's not like I'm in a hurry to get to my imaginary party.

I roll my eyes at my own self-pity. After all, technically, I'd had plans. They'd just gone kablooey. My bestie, Aria, with her screwy work schedule. And Kari with whatever emergency kept her from coming. She hadn't said. Just called the bookstore and asked Leah to pass along the *sorry see-you-soon* message.

To be honest, that was fine by me. That little emotional factoid twists in my stomach. After all, Kari was the first friend I made after moving to LA, and we've always vibed. But I can't deny that there's been some distance between us ever since—

No.

The word blares out like a foghorn in my mind, because no way am I letting my thoughts go there. Not on such a great day. Hell, not ever. Not ever, ever again.

Raindrops.

Roses.

Whiskers.

Kittens.

It's a stupid mantra, but I learned the hard way that my mom's advice to channel Julie Andrews really does work. And with every repetition, I push the approaching darkness back just a little bit more. Then, for good measure, I text Kari and tell her I'm sorry she had to bail, but that I'd probably see her tomorrow at Upper Crust, the cafe/bakery where she works.

I take another sip as I glance around, then frown when I notice the burly forty-something man standing a few feet from the coffee shop's door. He's wearing sunglasses, so I can't see his eyes, but it looks like he's staring right at me.

I think back, trying to figure out how long he's been there. *Yes.* He'd been there when I pulled into the space. He's still there. Is he watching me?

Why would he be watching me?

Panic courses through me, turning my body to ice, and I clench the steering wheel, forcing myself to do the breathing exercises that my therapist taught me in those long months after the kidnapping when every little glitch seemed to set me off. A sideways look from an unfamiliar man. A car behind me following the same route to the grocery store. A stranger asking to share a table in a coffee shop.

A man staring at me for no reason.

Stop.

Deep breaths. I remind myself to take deep breaths. And once I'm calm, I'll get the hell out of there.

Then I see him extend a hand as a well-dressed woman approaches. They hug, he leads her into the coffee shop, and I slump in my seat, relief and irritation rushing through me. *I'm past that. I'm fine.*

Or, at least, I'm trying to be.

I take another sip of my latte, forcing myself to stay right here in the parking lot to prove the point. And since I now need a distraction, I turn my attention back to the gift basket. In addition to a Ripped Bodice tee and a card thanking me for coming to the signing, there are goodies from fans, including a pair of earrings that have little covers of the book and a framed print that has a romantic quote from Ace done in beautiful calligraphy. When I find a box of pralines, I remember the woman who'd insisted her family take a detour in their journey from Louisiana to Disneyland so she could come meet me at the signing.

After I've looked at everything, I arrange it all back into the basket—albeit not as neatly. I'm about to start up the car again when I notice the envelope tucked in between the decorative purple tissue paper and the wooden weave of the basket itself.

I pluck it out and can immediately tell there's a gift card in there. Probably for the store, and since my reading habit is voracious, I'm grinning when I rip open the envelope.

It's not from the store, but I'm still smiling when I see the QR code stamped on one side of the light green plastic and the words SCAN ME in giant black letters on the other. As I follow that order, I make a bet with myself that it's either a fan doing a reading from my book or a video of a book club discussion.

At first, all I see is a completely black screen. Then words appear.

Watch.

Listen.

No incoming calls.

No incoming texts.

No distractions at all.

Your full attention is required.

I roll my eyes at the antics of whoever put this together, and I upgrade my guess to a dramatic reading. Maybe even a scripted version of Chapter One. I settle back in my seat and watch the letters fade.

As the screen returns to black, I hear a crackle and background noise. The hum of an air conditioner, maybe? I'm not sure, but something about the sound is familiar.

I turn up the volume, then stiffen when I hear a choking gasp.

No. Please, no.

Every cell inside me turns ice cold, and I start to shake, making that same choking, terrified sound that's coming out of my phone.

No. No. Please not again. Please, no.

"Strip." The filtered voice is all-too familiar, and my throat seems to close. It's getting harder to breathe. I want to pull my feet up onto the seat and curl into a ball. I want to disappear.

I want to close this webpage and get away from this voice out of my nightmares.

I can't.

Even if my hands weren't shaking so much, I still couldn't close the site. I want to scream, to toss my phone into the street. To drive away and never look back. But I can't.

Somehow, I have to be brave.

Tears stream down my cheeks as the voice speaks again. "Strip or I'll strip the little girl."

The words are coming through the phone—I know that. But I'm hearing them almost seven years in the past. In the memory that is playing in my head. A lost, dark memory of those long, horrible hours.

Taken. Held against my will, helpless and terrified and completely unable to protect the sweet baby girl who was my charge. Little Anne, not yet two, who'd been snatched along with me.

Everything inside me wants to close this screen. To stop the voice. To block the images that will surely come. But I can't. Because the people who would do something like this are the kind of people who mean what they say. I don't know what they want from me, but I know they want something. And if I want to protect Anne—to protect myself—I have to keep watching that horrible black screen. I have to wait for the next words.

I taste saltwater and realize that I'm crying. The screen is still entirely black. That voice is silent. But I hear Anne calling out for me, her words woozy and soft.

My entire body is shaking from the inside, as if I'm naked in a freezing room, and the only thing I can hold onto is the knowledge that right now Anne is healthy and happy and safe with her parents on a private tropical island. That, and the absolute certainty that she remembers nothing of the kidnapping.

I do, though.

I remember being locked in that room. Fighting the urge to sleep and knowing that they had drugged me. Battling the ice-cold terror that the drugs would kill me. Struggling to stay awake to comfort Anne.

Failing, and then spiraling down into a dreamless pit of darkness, as hollow and empty as death.

For years, I've told myself that nothing happened in those missing hours. That they kept me knocked out so that I wouldn't fight or scream. But now, listening to that message and staring at my phone screen, I know that I'd fed myself a lie. Things happened.

Bad things. Horrible things.

And I'm terrified I'm about to finally meet the ghosts that have haunted me ever since.

THREE

I fight a wave of nausea as I wait, certain more words will appear. Either that or the voice will return. Or the black will fade into an image of the room where we'd been held. But there is nothing except a silence that seems to last an eternity.

By the clock it's not even been thirty seconds.

Then I hear a whimper. *It's me.* "Please." My voice is thick, the words slurred. "Don't hurt her."

"Strip, bitch." It's that familiar, filtered voice again. "Strip, or I'll play with the little girl instead."

I start to shake. *I don't remember that.* The voice is mine, but I don't remember the threat at all. My mouth has gone completely dry, and my hand is holding the phone with such intensity it's a wonder the damn thing doesn't shatter.

This is a nightmare. It can't be real. How can this be real?

But it is, and I don't understand what's going on, and when the sound finally dies and the screen flashes a new message, I cry out in a freakish mixture of horror and relief.

One hour. Scan again.

The words disappear, replaced by others, then still more after that.

No police. No law enforcement or private security. Disobey, and there will be consequences. Dire consequences.

I draw a tremulous breath.

This is our little secret, Brianna.

Set a timer and scan in one hour. Fail to do so, and you will know the full meaning of regret.

One second. Then another. I set the timer on my phone for fifty-nine minutes. Then I glance at the clock. Eight-seventeen. I make a mental note just in case the timer fails me. I have to do this right, have to follow the rules. Whatever they want, I must do it.

Then I just sit there, holding the phone, terrified it's going to ring. Equally afraid that an hour will pass, and I'll never hear from my tormentor again, and that horrible recording will one day be played for the world. And when it airs, there will be video, too.

Just the thought makes my stomach curdle.

I'm trying to control my breathing when the message fades, the white letters swallowed by blackness until I'm left staring at an inky black webpage.

It's over.

Except, of course, it's not. This is merely a break. A reprieve. And the only thing I'm truly certain of is that it's going to get a lot worse.

I don't even think of ignoring the command to scan the QR code again in an hour. And I'm sure as hell not going to the police. Not yet, anyway.

But I'm also not going to just sit here like a terrified victim, even if that's what I am.

Instead, I force myself to draw one breath, then another. I need to calm down. I need to stop my hands from shaking. A much harder task than it sounds, and it takes all my effort to force my trembling index finger to tap my phone screen so that it pops back to life. And then there I am, staring at that completely black page again.

Grimacing, I get on with my task, tapping to highlight the URL in the address bar at the bottom. I click copy, then drop the address into my Notes app, feeling just a little smug. I have no idea if that will help me at all, but at least I'm doing something.

Now, what else can I do?

Okay, I think. *You can handle this. Step one: quit shaking. Step two: get home. Step three: scan the code again. Step four: focus. Who could be behind this? Who would do this to you when everyone involved in the kidnapping is dead?*

At least, I think they are.

I don't have any answers. But I tell myself it must be a joke. Some horrible, vile, in-very-bad-taste joke.

Unfortunately, I don't believe that at all.

With great deliberation, I force myself to simply sit there and breathe and try to calm myself enough so that I get home before the hour is up. And without crashing my car in the process.

At the moment, confidence is low.

Somehow, I manage to keep my hand steady as I start the car. And in the exact moment when the engine turns over and my music blasts on, a hard rap lands on my window. A scream rips out of me as I thrust myself sideways, banging my ribs on the armrest.

Outside the window, I see a man's torso. Then he bends down, and I gasp with recognition as he speaks. "Oh, hell, Bree. I'm so sorry. I didn't mean to scare you."

Ashton Stone.

For a moment, I can only stare. This is the man I'd seriously —albeit secretly—crushed on when I first met him. A man who'd come to Los Angeles about two years ago with a plan to destroy his father, my boss.

A man with a famous temper and a reputation for facing down danger. For being reckless.

For being brilliant.

A man with the kind of mind that can make millions and the kind of face that dark angels envy. A chiseled face, framed by raven-dark hair, and highlighted by deep blue eyes that conjure thoughts of long, lazy days on a Caribbean beach.

There's something magnetic about him, and every time I'm near him, I feel that tug pulling me closer.

But he's not safe. Not for me. Maybe not for anyone. And the last time we bumped into each other, I'd run far and fast out of nothing more than an instinct for self-preservation. An act of cowardice on my part that undoubtedly pissed him off.

All of which begs the question of why I now want to throw open my door and launch myself into his arms. To tell him the horror story that this fairy tale night has morphed into.

But I can't.

I don't truly know him.

I can't really trust him.

And I damn sure can't break the rules for him.

And as my fingers remain tight around my phone, I can't help but wonder what he's doing right here. Right now.

His brow furrows as the corners of his mouth curve down. "Bree?" He taps lightly on the glass again. "Brianna, are you okay?"

Shit.

I sit up straight, then I do the hardest thing I've ever had to do. I roll down the window and smile at Ashton Stone. "I'm fine. I was just...lost in another world."

I try to swallow, but my throat's too dry. *What is he doing here? Surely, he's not the one who—*

"No." I say the word with such force in my head that it actually comes out of my mouth.

Immediately, his eyes darken. "What is it? What's wrong?"

A wave of confusion rushes over me, then I realize that he thinks I was answering his question. "I—no. I meant to say that I'm fine. Nothing's wrong."

As if to prove that all the press about him being a genius is true, he cocks his head and says, "You sure about that? Because I'm not convinced. What can I do?"

"Nothing. It's just a fight with my boyfriend." That's a lie, but I'm hoping he'll not only drop the subject, but that the fact that I have a—very fictional—boyfriend will ensure he doesn't set his sights on me again.

He says nothing. Just makes a low noise like, *mmmm*.

I wait for him to say goodbye and head into the coffee shop. Instead, he continues to stand there.

I clear my throat, then glance at the clock. I still have time to get home before the deadline to scan the code, but I want a very big window. I can't miss that scan, and the idea of getting the next message in another parking lot doesn't sit well at all.

I aim a perkier fake smile at him. "Listen, it's wild seeing you here, but I really should get going." I shift Maisy into reverse but keep my foot on the brake.

"You sure you're okay?"

"I told you I am," I snap.

He still doesn't move. And my irritation level climbs as he keeps standing with his hand on the door so that I can't raise the window without coming off as a total freak. There's something dark in his demeanor. Something that makes me shiver. It's not fear, though. Not that tight, cloying coldness I'd felt watching the video.

Instead, it's a quiet wariness. The worry that, despite my

better judgment, I might give in and succumb to whatever he asks. After all, that's happened before.

Or, at least, it almost happened.

I feel my cheeks heat, and I cut my eyes away to focus my hands, now clenched on the steering wheel as if it's a life preserver.

"I was hoping we could go inside," he says. "Talk over a couple of coffees."

I'm tempted to do that very thing. To sit close together at a table in the back and tell him everything I just saw. To beg him to help me.

Because I know that he would do exactly that.

Instead, I hold up my cup. "I've already got one."

"Then we're halfway there. Join me inside. Or invite me into your car and we can hit the drive-through." He flashes a little half-smile that's sexy as hell... and makes me wish I could teleport out of there. "I figured we could commiserate. We're both walking into the lion's den tomorrow. It's going to seem like old times."

The lion he's referring to must be Maggie Bridge, a reporter who had interviewed us both about four months ago as part of a feature on Damien Stark. As far as I'm concerned, Maggie is the spawn of Satan. "She's doing an interview with you, too?"

He nods. "Apparently she's fascinated with the INX-20."

"Well, who wouldn't be?" I force a smile, pretending I know what he's talking about. Since this is Ash, I assume he's referring to a race car or an engine or something else related to really fast cars. But since I need him to be gone, I don't ask for clarification. For that matter, I don't say anything at all.

My silence doesn't seem to bother him in the least. He just flashes his trademark half-smile. The one that's slow and sexy and full of temptation. "Maggie mentioned she was interviewing us back-to-back, and I figured it would be easier if we endure her questions together."

"Together?" It takes me a moment to process, then I sit up straighter. "Wait, what? She's interviewing us at the same time?"

His brows rise. "I thought it was one of my more brilliant ideas. Don't tell me you were looking forward to facing Maggie alone?"

God no. But I'm also not sure I want to face you, either.

I don't have the nerve to say that aloud. Instead, I say, "But what do the INX-whatever and fantasy romance have to do with each other?"

He grins and holds my eyes a second too long before saying, "Not a damn thing. Guess Maggie'll have her work cut out for her."

I manage to hold back a laugh, surprised to realize that despite whatever horrible prank some asshat is pulling on me, I'm enjoying this strange back-and-forth. "You're an idiot, Ashton Stone. You know that, right?"

The insult doesn't faze him at all. "Most people have an entirely different assessment."

"Then most people are idiots, too. She's not going to alternate questions about my book with questions about your latest automotive innovation. She's going to talk about you personally. And she's going to pump me to talk about Nikki and Damien and about..."

I trail off with a shudder, then shake my head. He knows about the kidnapping. And he must know I have no desire to open up to Maggie Bridge about it.

"We'll keep her in line," he says.

"How?"

"Trust me."

I roll my eyes.

He chuckles. "Thanks for the vote of confidence."

"Don't kid yourself. There are no parameters where that woman is concerned."

"There will be," he assures me with so much confidence that I'm glad he's hijacking the interview, even though I always sound like a tongue-tied fool when I'm around him.

"I thought you and I could stay behind after the interview," he adds. "Have a coffee. Catch up."

My insides go cold, because I know perfectly well that *catch up* really means *finally hear why you ghosted me when everything seemed to be going so well*.

To be honest, I'd pretty much decided that he'd let that go. It's been months since I bailed on him at the airport Hilton, and while it's true that he hasn't been around much, when we have crossed paths, he hasn't cornered me for an explanation.

Apparently, times are changing.

That, however, is the least of my problems.

"Bree?"

Once again, I tighten my hands around the steering wheel, but manage to tilt my head so I'm looking right at him. "It's a moot point," I say. "This whole conversation. I won't be at the interview tomorrow. I have to cancel."

"Do you?"

I smile, all sunshine and innocence. "One of those last-minute conflicts."

"Lucky you." His eyes linger on mine a second too long. "But too bad for me."

I shrug, making a mental note to call and leave a message about canceling as soon I get to the house. Because even without adding Ash to the mix, after today's unexpected dose of hell, there is no way I'm sitting down with that viper again.

I look pointedly to where his hands are still on my open window frame. "I need to get going."

"I still think we should grab a coffee. After all, you owe me."

I stiffen. "Owe you?" There's an edge to my voice. If he's talking about the hotel....

"Leaving me to face that woman alone? Yeah. I mean, I thought we were friends."

My entire body relaxes. Apparently, he's not going to press me about standing him up. Not now, anyway.

"It's a huge debt," he continues, "but I'd be willing to negotiate down to one coffee and half an hour."

The tiny smile that touches my lips feels pretty good, and that's almost enough to make me agree. Because right then I want to be with someone who can make me laugh. Who can make me forget the nightmare I've tumbled into.

Except I can't forget it.

Not ever.

And I sure as hell can't tell Ashton Stone—Anne's uncle—anything about what's going on.

"Bree?"

"I really have to go." I don't quite meet his eyes. "I'm meeting someone." Since Aria's probably home by now, that's technically not a lie.

He studies my face with an intensity that makes me fear he can read my thoughts. Then his expression seems to clear, and he lifts one shoulder. "Right. Well, Okay."

He looks so dejected, I almost change my mind. It's not an expression I expect on the face of a guy like Ash. He—like his father—is a certified Master of the Universe. The kind of guy who knows what he wants, goes after it, and succeeds. The kind of guy who always comes out on top.

Always.

Except with me.

I sit up a little straighter. Suddenly, I'm not so worried about his dejected expression. Maybe it makes me small, but considering all the shit that's happened to me in the last hour, I'm feeling pretty good about having the upper hand.

His brow furrows as he studies my face. "Are you sure you're okay?"

"What the hell?" I snap, done in by the gentleness of his voice. "I don't want to have coffee with you, and that must mean my world is off kilter? I'm in a hurry. Just like I told you. I don't owe you a dissertation on my life."

I don't mean to, but as I speak, I meet his eyes.

And that's when I realize what it is, this unexpected sensation that is coursing through me, firing my senses, igniting that fight or flight response.

It's not confusion or fear or irritation, though I wish it were.

Instead, it's anticipation. And, so help me, it's desire.

FOUR

Sixteen months Ago—Bree (Las Vegas)

"This is exactly what I needed," I say, leaning back on the cushioned chaise. I'm snug as a bug in one of the roomy poolside cabanas on the VIP deck at the Stark Century Hotel & Casino in Vegas, surrounded by a flurry of beautiful people and even a few Hollywood A-listers. Best of all, my lifelong BFF came with me on this vacation, and she's snuggled in right along with me.

"I get it now," Aria says. "The allure of your job," she explains, when I roll on my side and shoot her a questioning glance. "It's the perks."

I prop myself up on my elbow—the better to swat her with one of the cushions—then flop back down. "Yup. This is what all nannies do during the day. Lounge about drinking fruity cocktails and gossiping. And when the kids get restless, I just order them a Manhattan from the live-in bartender."

"Seriously?" She sits up, the black tips of her spiky red hair standing out against the delicate white drapes that make up the sides of the cabana. "Why the hell am I working my ass off in New York?"

"You're not for much longer," I tell her. Not if I have any say in it. I've been trying for ages to convince her to move to LA with me. And since I'm about to buy a fixer-upper in Burbank, I think I've pretty much convinced her.

She flashes a wicked grin. "If that very superior ass is one of the perks, I'm moving tomorrow." She nods toward a cluster of loungers on the far side of the pool where Bryan Raine, a megastar on the way to going super nova, is holding court.

"He's a total prick," I say, careful to keep my voice low. "But you're dead-on right about the nice ass."

Ari's eyes widen. "You've met him?"

"Once," I say, "and he was perfectly polite. Total smiling for the fans moment. But I've heard stories. Several stories." Technically, I've *over*heard stories, but I don't mention that. That's one of the perks—and dangers—of my job.

I've been working on and off as a nanny for Damien Stark's family for years, ever since their littlest girl was only one. She's going on eight now, and to say it's been a roller-coaster ride would be the understatement of the millennium. I love them, though. And not just the kids, but Nikki and Damien—and omg, how long did it take me to get comfortable using their first names?

It had been weird at first, working for the most well-known and respected billionaire in the universe. And scary, too. Especially since there'd been a time when I wasn't sure they liked or trusted me—a terrifying, painful time after the kidnapping that I make a point of *not* thinking of because—*shit*.

Not. Thinking. Of. That.

Bottom line, being in a household like that, you see and hear all sorts of things that could screw up a business deal, be sold to some horrible gossip rag, or get loose on social media and totally blow up. And, yeah, there'd been a rocky period when I was afraid they were looking at me like a time-bomb. But now I know with absolute certainty that they not only like me, they trust me.

Best of all, they truly think of me like family.

How do I know?

Partly, because they tell me. But also because they do sweet things like letting me pivot to part-time and live in their guest house so I can focus on writing my second book. And things like this—sending the kids to relatives so that I can have a relaxing long weekend in Vegas with my BFF at one of Damien's hotels while he and Nikki are off to Europe.

"Now I really want to meet him," Aria says, her eyes shooting once again toward Bryan Raine. "Asshole actor? Might be that's just his Hollywood persona. Get me close and I can check out his aura."

I force myself not to roll my eyes. There are times when Aria's a little too woo for my taste. But at the same time, her first impressions are usually right.

"There will be no aura-checking today," I tell her.

"Party pooper."

"That's me."

"Pretty please?" She makes prayer hands. "We'll just wander over to that side of the pool. I'll be your bestie."

"You already are."

"I could call ABC rules," Aria says, making me scowl. We established the ABC Club way back in second grade. A for her. B for me. C for *chain*. Because the rule chained us together as Best Friends for Life. No request too big. Always having each other's backs.

"Fine," I say. "But just remember, he's an asshole. And if I introduce myself, it will surely get back to the Starks, and I'm going to look like the jerk who used this lovely weekend they gave me to toss my friend in front of celebrities."

I cross my arms and stare her down. "But if that's what you want me to do...."

"Oh, hell yeah," Aria says. "I mean, I'm your bestie. Stark's just a paycheck."

I shake my head, roll my eyes, then settle back onto my chaise. "Bitch," I mutter, making her crack up. I reach for my Cosmo, only to find the glass empty. And though I could signal a waiter, I sit up, stretch, then stand, albeit a little unsteady after two—no, three—drinks. "I'm going to hit the ladies' and order another round. Same for you?"

I'm unsurprised when she eagerly agrees. After all, this trip is all about sluffing off, getting drunk, then crashing in our suite and spending the next two nights talking and trashing every bad movie we can find before she flies back to New York on Tuesday.

There's an entrance to the lounge off the pool, so it only takes a second to pop by the bar and put in the order. Then I shift course to the nearby ladies' room, which is about as elegant as Buckingham Palace. When I come out, the bartender signals to me, and I head his direction, curious as to what he might need.

"One of our guests offered to buy your current round of drinks. I told him they were already comped, but I thought I should let you know."

I stand up a little straighter. "Really? Well, that was nice of him. Can you point him out?"

"He's already left the lounge, but his name is Ashton Stone. I believe he's checking out tomorrow."

"Oh." A dangerous heat spreads through my body. "I, um... Thank you." My voice sounds thin, and my pulse has kicked up its tempo. I want to ask if he knows where Ash went. Did he exit to the outside? To the lobby? To the pool deck?

But I say nothing.

Instead, I force a thank you past my suddenly dry mouth, then hurry back to the safety of my bestie and our snug little cabana.

Except it's not safe.

As soon as I settle onto my chaise, I see him. *Ashton Stone.* A man who could be the role model for all those bad boy cliches. Tall. Dark. Definitely dangerous. I'd first met him at the Starks' Malibu home when he'd shown up out of the blue, cloaked in secrets and drama.

I'd seen the tension between him and Damien.

And, yeah, I'd felt a different kind of tension between him and me.

Worse, I'd liked it. Probably too much. The sensation of those eyes roaming over me like a caress. The nights imagining what those hands—so famous for working on sleek, fast cars—would feel like on my skin. He's a man who, like his father, walks through the world like a magnet drawing in power and control and passion, so that it all seems to swirl around him in a heady, intoxicating mix. But there is no way I can allow myself to get drunk on Ashton Stone.

I Won't.

I can't.

I just... can't.

Except there he is on the far side of the pool, and though I know I should look away, I don't. As if he's heard a siren's call, he turns his head, and his eyes lock on mine. He takes one step forward, then another until I almost believe he's going to walk across the water to my side. But then he stops at the edge, his eyes still on mine.

I try to look away, but don't. I can't seem to break the spell.

"Bree?"

Jarred back to reality, I turn to see Aria cocking her head toward the waiter who is holding out my drink. When I take it,

Aria catches my eye, and I realize that she's noticed Ash, too. She raises a brow, but I just shake my head. One tiny fraction of an inch.

That's all I need to do, and in true BFF fashion, Aria slides off her chaise, goes to the front of the cabana, and closes the drapes to block our view of the pool.

And just like that, Ash is gone.

I tell myself that's the way I want it, but as I take my first sip of the Cosmo, I can't help but wish that it was Ash making my blood buzz, not vodka. But that's never going to happen.

No matter how much I might sometimes think I want it to.

FIVE

I blow out of the coffee shop parking lot so fast, it's a wonder I don't roll over Ashton's toes, and I keep my eyes on the road except for one quick peek into the rearview mirror.

He's still standing there, and even though I'm quite a few yards away, I can see his frown, his brow furrowed as if I'm a total mystery to him.

I hit the gas and watch in the rearview until Ash disappears into the distance.

Gone. And that's just fine with me, so long as Ash doesn't decide to track me down and force an explanation as to why I blew him off at the airport hotel four months ago.

A squiggle of guilt curls in my belly. I'd left a total cop-out message for him instead of calling and actually talking to him. I know I should remedy that. Pull up my big girl panties. Dial his number. Explain that I can't be what he wants.

Hell, I can't even be what *I* want. There's certainly no way with Ashton. We can't even be "just friends." Not knowing the way he makes my heart beat faster. The way my skin tingles when I'm around him. The way he makes me smile.

If I were any other girl with any other history, maybe I could tell him my reasons for staying far, far away. Bree Bernstein, though? She hides her secrets deep. And that's as it should be. Because open or closed or slightly cracked, that door is best left untouched.

The bigger problem is that, whether I want to or not, I'll be seeing him in less than twenty-four hours. Because as much as I want to avoid talking to that snake, Maggie Bridge, I know I can't really cancel. My friend Evelyn Dodge—a semi-retired agent who knows everyone who's anyone—jumped through a zillion hoops to set up the interview, to my editor's great delight. "You may not like Maggie Bridge," my editor had said, "but she's got one hell of a readership. Evelyn Dodge is a goddess."

Since that was one-hundred percent true on all counts, I'd agreed to the interview. And even though I hate that Ash is going to be on the perimeter, I have to suck it up.

As if I didn't already have enough to deal with.

I grimace, realizing that, if nothing else, my mental side-journey into All Things Ash got that horrible message and website out of my head for at least a couple of minutes.

But it's back now, and if I let it in, I know it will overwhelm me. I need to get small. To go inside myself the way I learned to years ago. Even if only for the forty-some-odd minutes I have left before hell rains down on me again.

My hand is shaking when I plug in my phone and order up a classic rock playlist. I crank up the volume and let the Rolling Stones, Queen, and AC/DC fill the car so there's no room for thinking at all.

Except it doesn't work. The terror of that message swirls inside me with too much force, and my mind is a raging storm of fear by the time I reach Burbank and my two-bedroom fixer-upper.

For a moment, I sit in the driveway, the car turned off, but my hands still tight around the steering wheel. I don't know what to do. I need help. I need the police. Or a private investigator. *Someone.*

But the rules...if whoever is doing this found out I broke the rules....

Fuck.

With a determined swipe, I brush away the tears that cling to my lashes. Then I throw the door open, grab the gift basket and the fucking QR card that tainted it, and head for my front door.

"I was wondering when you'd get—" Aria begins, looking up from the sofa as I stumble inside. Her short hair is rumpled and her long, lean body is decked out in Snoopy leggings and her NYU tank top. She has the expression of a person with nothing more than chilling on her mind.

Then her expression changes, her pale blue eyes narrowing as she tosses her book aside and stands up. "What's wrong?"

The worry in her voice causes a fresh round of tears to rise in my throat, but it's the fact that she knows me so well that twists my heart. And without any warning, all the pain and fear and confusion and—dammit—memories burst out of me in a torrent of sobs and sniffles and hot tears that trail down my cheeks to tease the corners of my mouth.

Aria's at my side so fast she might have teleported, and before I know it, we're both on the lumpy garage sale sofa we bought two months ago after Aria finally left New York to move in with me. "Hey," she whispers. "Hey, it's okay."

Her arms are around me, wrapping me up in love and comfort. Aria gives the best hugs on the planet, which she says is because she's hugging with all eight of her arms. Her given name is Ariadne, because her mom thinks spiders are the coolest of creatures, and, yeah, it suits her.

Right then, I don't care why her hugs are amazing. All I know is that I want to stay like that, letting my best friend comfort me until all the horror is washed away in a torrent of tears.

But that's not going to happen. It's not going away—in fact it's coming back in just minutes—and crying won't do shit for me.

With a massive effort, I ease free, then lean forward and bury my face in my hands. Aria knows not to keep holding me, but she grabs my favorite wearable blanket off the back of the sofa and puts it over my shoulders. I shove my arms through the sleeves, then pull it tight around me as I order myself to breathe. No crying allowed. Just. Freaking. Breathe.

"Was the signing terrible?" Her voice is overly calm. It's the same tone she uses with the spooked animals who come to the clinic where she's been working for the last ten days. "I'm sorry I couldn't come. Dr. Kay wanted me to stay with Beyonce-the-bull-dog since he's been so—"

She cuts herself off with a sharp shake of her head. "Doesn't matter. You want to talk about it?"

I don't.

I don't want to think about it, talk about it, write about it.

All I want is to erase it. I want to turn on some magical tap and wash it away, leaving everything clean and shiny and safe.

But bad shit doesn't go away on its own. That's another one of those lessons I learned the hard way.

"Bree?" She slides off the couch and crouches right in front of me, her hands on my knees. "Come on, girl. You're starting to freak me out."

I choke back a sob that's part laugh. *Freak out?* Understatement of the century. Then I shift on the sofa, pulling away from her to scrunch into the corner with my knees pulled up and my feet on the biggest lump of this lumpy wreck of a couch.

I check my phone. *Twelve minutes.* That's all the reprieve I have before the horror starts all over again.

"Br—"

"Whiskey," I say, and her brows immediately rise. I hardly ever drink at home, and when I do, it's usually wine. "Please."

She studies my face, and her wide, full lips curve into a frown. I think she's going to argue, but she crosses the very short distance to our tiny kitchen. I can see her over the pass-through bar. Pulling down a glass. Adding ice. Disappearing for a moment as she squats to grab the whiskey from the lower cabinets where we keep the hard liquor.

When she returns, she's carrying two glasses. "I don't know what's up," she says, passing me mine, "but I have a feeling I'm going to need this, too."

She takes a sip, then sits on the coffee table in front of me. I don't sip. I gulp. Then I cough because my throat's on fire. "I don't know where to start," I say when I can talk again.

"The signing—"

"Was awesome."

Aria tilts her head in a silent *seriously?*

"It was. Everyone at the store was great, and I didn't freeze up during the Q&A, and the readers were so into it I felt like a celebrity, especially once I started signing books. But after..."

I close my eyes as I trail off, because I really, really, *really* don't want to talk about it. Not even to Aria, who knows me inside and out, just like I know her. We've been friends since birth—like literally. Our moms were besties, and Fate must have been feeling mischievous because not only were they pregnant together, but they gave birth on the same day. To me at 12:01am and Aria at 12:59 pm. Freaky, but we figured if the universe wants us to be friends, why fight it?

Now, there's no one in the world I'm closer to. We've been through parent drama, boyfriend drama, high school jealousy, fashion nightmares, college terror, work angst, and everything else on the Girl Grows Up checklist. I know all her secrets. She thinks she knows all of mine.

She used to. She doesn't anymore. Nobody does. And I really, really, *really* don't want that to change.

But it's going to. And that one simple, horrible certainty absolutely terrifies me.

Aria's brow furrows as she studies my face. "You're scaring me. Just spit it out. The truth can't be worse than what I'm imagining."

"Yeah," I say. "I think it can."

"Bree—"

"I know." The words come out sharper than I intended. "Sorry." I hold up a finger to keep her quiet as I draw a deep breath. I don't want to tell her. It's not that I don't trust her to keep quiet. It's that I don't want *anyone* to know, not even me. I want the whole nightmare to be locked in the past, hidden inside the thick, steel vault of my mind. And never, ever, ever coming out.

But since that's not possible, I also selfishly want my friend. So I take another deep breath and start talking, telling her first about finding the QR code in the goody basket. "And when I scanned it..." I trail off with a shudder but force myself to go on. Tears stream down my face, but I ignore them as I tell her what the written message said. Then what I heard on the recording. "*Strip.*" And, "*Strip or I'll strip the little girl.*"

For a moment, she's totally silent, her face going pale under her makeup in a way I'd thought was just a figure of speech. She looks like a ghost, and I reach for her hand and squeeze it.

Two big tears trail down her cheeks as she squeezes back, so tight I may have to pry her free. "Strip," she whispers, repeating the word my kidnapper had said.

I nod, then release her hands as I draw my knees in closer, then hug my legs tight enough to cut off circulation.

"But you told me nothing happened to you. You said they kept you and Anne in a room. Drugged so that you wouldn't remember anything."

I nod. That's what I'd said, all right.

"Then—" She cuts herself off with a shake of her head. "Okay. I probably wouldn't have said anything to me, either. But you shouldn't be ashamed. Come on, Bree. You know that whatever happened in that room, none of it's your fault."

Logically I do know that. But I was the one with Anne when she was taken, and me along with her. I was the one who inadvertently led the prick of a kidnapper to her. So, yeah, knowing's one thing. Believing's something completely different.

"Not. Your. Fault," she repeats, clearly reading my mind.

I shrug. "Also not the point." She starts to speak, but I hold up a hand and continue. "I didn't keep it from you," I tell her. "I didn't know."

"You—wait. What?"

"I only remember him saying *strip*." I've had dreams though. Horrible dreams where I'm touched. Caressed. Dreams that have me fighting my way back to wakefulness cold and shaking—and reminding myself that it's only a dream. Only a dream.

Except now I know it wasn't. And some part of me has always known the truth and kept it locked up tight. A secret even from me.

"You're serious?" Aria presses, pulling me back from my thoughts. "You don't remember the rest of what he said?"

"Nothing." I blink back tears. "What else don't I remember?" The tears flow in earnest now, and I hurl one of the couch pillows across the room. "*Dammit!*"

I have to calm down. *I have to.* I can't fall apart because I can't fuck up.

Whatever they want, I have to do. And that means I have to breathe. I have to settle.

I have to think.

"You don't remember..." Aria's words aren't a question, but they're not really a statement, either. They're just a remnant of thought as her mind tries to wrap itself around all of this.

"I didn't," I tell her. "Not at all. Now, though...." I shudder. "Now, I think I'm starting to."

I'd told her before how our kidnappers watched us through cameras. At the time, I'd believed the kidnapper was alone. I've since learned that wasn't the case. There were two of them and at least one more who knew but may not have participated. All three are dead, including Rory, the vilest of all of them, because he's the one I knew and trusted.

The one I'd slept with. The one I'd dated. The one I'd thought maybe I could even love.

I cringe, not for the first time wondering about my own judgment. If I fell for a man like that, what does that say about my perception? My choices? And if it wasn't just me—if the whole world looked at him and saw a good person—how do you ever know anyone at all?

"Bree?"

I realize I've zoned out. "I'm okay," I assure her. "It's just..."

"Icky?"

I almost laugh. "Yeah. Icky sums it up pretty damn well."

For a moment, she's silent. Then she moves to sit on the coffee table and faces me. "I don't get it. Everyone involved in the kidnapping is dead, right?"

I nod.

"Then who...?"

"I don't know," I say, and that gaping hole in my knowledge

terrifies me. "There must have been someone else involved." I force myself to keep my voice steady, but it's hard. For years now, I'd believed that nightmare was dead and gone. Now I think it's come back to life, and I fear that, like a vampire, this time it will be even harder to kill.

"Did you recognize the voice?"

I shake my head. "It was filtered. Just like before. But I think it was Rory. A recording, I mean."

"Fucker," she says, the word coming out harsh and fast. "I almost wish he were alive so I could kill him all over again. Whoever shivved him in jail deserves a pardon. That's all I'm saying."

I don't disagree.

He was the one who'd shoved the first dose down my throat, thrusting me into a drug-induced nightmare where the world went wonky. Where I'd half-sleep, half-dream. I'd float in a non-reality that was, at least, slightly less terrifying than the reality in which I'd been trapped. It had seemed like forever, but it really wasn't that long. Little Anne they kept longer. Another factoid on which I balance my many mountains of guilt.

They'd kept Anne drugged, too. I'd been so scared that the drug had hurt her that after we were free, I interrogated every doctor I could. I learned that they used a drug called Versed on both of us. It's oral and it relaxes you down to the bone. It's used a lot with children to calm them down before surgery.

Because of the amnesiac effect, Anne has no memory of the kidnapping at all. She doesn't even have bad dreams. But maybe they didn't get my dose quite right. Because even though I don't remember, for years after the kidnapping, I had nightmares.

Horrible nightmares that felt so damn real. Dreams where I'd wake up in that room naked. Dreams where fingers caressed me so gently, only to then slap me with a force so hard my body lurched in pain. Dreams where my legs were parted. Where fingers teased me. And where, to my horror, those same fingers aroused me, too.

I've had no dreams that any of the men sexually penetrated me, thank goodness, and the doctor I went to afterward found no evidence that I was raped that way. But that's cold comfort. I was violated, and as much as I want to believe my dreams are only a dream, I know that's not the truth.

I want to tell Aria about the nightmares. About how I think —how I *know*—that they're really memories. My therapist, Teresa, assures me that talking about it will help me deal. But I can't do it. They say that time heals all wounds, and that's what I'm counting on. But as far as I can tell, time is a fickle bitch, because even though I've learned to fake it, today has made crystal clear that I'm not healed at all.

"I'm so sorry," Aria says, her voice gentle as she tucks a lock of hair behind my ear.

I lift a shoulder in a tiny shrug. "I'm okay."

I see her mouth twist and know she's thinking the same thing I am. Physically, I may be okay. But I left that room with a shit load of issues, all of which I want to shove into a deep, dark closet and close the door forever.

Honestly, I thought I had.

Not at first. For a year after the kidnapping, I'd hated even being alone in a room with a guy. But with time and therapy, that got better. I even went on a few dates. Even kissed a sweet writer I'd met at a conference. But there was no want or need. On the contrary, there was only a numbness I dared not push aside, because I knew damn well that what hid behind that fog was cold, hard fear.

Teresa told me not to rush it, so I didn't. And the more I healed, the more I thought I'd be able to get close again. After another year, I tried to date again. A guy I met through a friend. We didn't click, but at least I tried.

Or, okay. Maybe I didn't. The truth is that the guy was a total cutie with a great personality and the kind of quirky sense of humor I love. But I felt nothing. No spark. No desire. And I was okay with that. After all, I'd reminded myself, the last man I'd dated locked me in a room.

The truth is, I hadn't felt desire for years after being taken, and maybe that's unhealthy as shit, but it felt safe. Like I was in a protective bubble.

But that bubble burst with Ashton Stone.

The first time I met him, I'd felt that spark again. And it had terrified me. So much, I'd even run from him.

Now here he is again, and I'm not sure if I should be happy, terrified, or both.

"Bree?"

I shake myself from my thoughts as she indicates my phone, the countdown now uncomfortably close to two minutes. "Do you have any idea who could be doing this? It's been what? Six years? Who could have that recording now? They caught everyone who was involved, right? It's over. That's what you told me."

She's right—that's what I told her. I'd thought it was true.

I'd moved on, telling myself that no kidnapper was going to leap out from behind a tree and drag me back. But people get it wrong all the time. Bad things really do come back. And monsters rarely die.

"I think I was wrong." The words are heavy on my tongue. "I think maybe it's starting all over again."

"*No.*" Her voice is fierce. "No, fucking way. And you are *not* logging back into that URL. Fuck them."

I open my mouth to argue, and that's when my timer chimes, making us both jump. I don't bother to respond to Aria, and she doesn't even try to stop me from scanning the code. On the contrary, when I snatch up the phone, she moves to sit right beside me so we both can both see the screen.

We might *think* Fuck Them, but disobey? Not happening.

As soon as the site pulls up—totally black once again—I have to force myself not to push her away. Whatever the video will show—and, yeah, I'm sure this time it will be video—I don't want her to see it. Hell, I don't want *me* to see this.

But then she puts her arm around me, and I snuggle closer, grateful for the comfort.

As before, there's nothing but black. But this time, no words appear.

This time, the black fades revealing an all-too familiar room. I hear Aria whimper and realize that I'm holding her hand so tight I've probably crushed a few bones. "Sorry," I whisper, then try to force myself to relax as I watch Video Bree, naked and unconscious on the floor.

Then *he's* there. One of my captors. Probably Rory, but I can't tell for sure. He's dressed all in black, his face hidden and hair covered. He kneels and puts his hands on me. Intimate. Invasive. "No," I whisper, as if words can will it so. "Please, please, no."

"Oh, God," Aria says, and I squeeze her hand even tighter. I want to look away, but I can't. I can't move. I can barely breathe as I watch this sick fuck's hands roam all over me.

"I don't remember." My words are seasoned with the taste of tears. It's exactly what I was afraid I was going to learn. Exactly what—deep down—I'd always feared. "I don't remember any of that."

It's horrible. Infuriating. Vile. An assault on everything decent and right, and as relieved as I am that I was unconscious, part of me wishes I'd been awake through the whole thing, because I would have scratched the bastard's eyes out.

Then I realize I haven't seen the worst of it. Because right there in the center of the screen is Anne sitting in her cute little play outfit and surrounded by a ring of toys. She's dopey from the Versed, and I know she doesn't understand what's going on, but it doesn't matter. This is Damien Stark's little girl, and from the way the shot is framed, it looks like some horrible bastard is putting on a show especially for her... and using my body as the stage.

SIX

Anne.

All I can think of is that little girl. A sweet kid who may have started out as my professional charge but has become part of my family.

"She's older now," I whisper. "If that video's released, she'll know it's her." The last word is broken by a sob as I lift my head and look at Aria through tear-filled eyes. "She won't understand all of it, but she'll know people are watching her. Pitying her. I can't let that happen. I have to—"

My frenetic thoughts are interrupted by a high-pitched tone coming from my phone, followed by that terrifying, filtered voice. "And now a word from our sponsor." The voice is almost lyrical, the humor unmistakable underneath that tinny, canned voice.

"Remember the rules," it says. "You will not call the police or any sort of law enforcement official or private security company, team, or person. If you do, we will know. Break this rule and the videos will be released."

There's a pause, as if my tormentor is letting that settle in.

As if I need more time to understand how much the people I care about will suffer if those videos get out.

By the clock, the voice is silent for only a minute. In my heart, it's an eternity. When it returns, it's harder somehow. The danger even more palpable.

"If you want to protect the little girl—if you want to know the price to keep your own secrets hidden—if you want to know the price to make this all disappear—scan the code again in five minutes."

The image of me and the stranger and Anne freezes, then turns to black. A beat later, a yellow smiley face emoji fills the screen, along with the words *See You Soon* in a comic-style font.

"Fucker," Aria whispers.

I say nothing. I'm too numb. Too scared.

"Bree—"

I hear the catch in her voice, and I lift my head to look at her through tear-filled eyes.

"You have to tell Mr. Stark."

Ice floods my body. "I can't."

"They said *price*. And I'm pretty sure this house doesn't have enough equity to cover a blackmail demand. Besides, Anne's in the middle of it. He and Nikki should know."

She's right, but I just shake my head. "I can't. They've finally healed from the kidnapping. They're on a family vacation. I'm not even sure where to find them." That's not actually true. They own an unpopulated private island in the Caribbean, and they've gone there for a family getaway. Damien took his satellite phone for emergencies only, but I'm not about to track down the number and call.

Aria gives me the look that says she knows perfectly well that I could get in touch if I wanted to. "Oh, well, then, definitely let them come home to find this blasted all over the internet."

I sag, my whole body sinking into itself. "I can't do it to them. The family. How can I draw them back into this?" Just the idea makes me queasy, and hot tears are already pooling in my eyes.

"You don't have to," Aria says as she gently wipes away an escaping tear. "Just Damien. Tell him what's going on. Tell him that you have to pay to keep it quiet, and you need his help. You know he will."

I want to nod. I want to say that, of course, I'll contact him. After all, Aria's right that he makes the most sense, and he could have ransom money wired within the hour. But I can't make those words come to my lips. I remember only too vividly how broken he was. I'd been through hell, and they'd released me without Anne. I felt like I'd been turned inside out. Like I'd never be me again. Like the world was bearing down on me, and I was only half-living in my body.

When I'd looked at Damien, I knew he felt the same way, too. He hadn't been taken, but his little girl had, and the trauma had gone through him like acid.

"I won't," I whisper. "Not unless I'm a zillion percent certain there's no other way."

I can tell Aria wants to argue, but to her credit, she only nods. "Fine. You win." She groans with frustration. It's a strangled, rough sound, and she stands up, then runs her fingers through her choppy hair. When she starts pacing, my spirits lift. Not much, but a little.

The truth is, my bestie's pretty much a hot mess who's quit or gotten fired from every job she's ever held. She's edging up on thirty and still doesn't have a clue about what she wants to do for the rest of her life.

She's worked as a receptionist, vet tech, Uber driver, and more. She has a degree in biology and dropped out just shy of getting another in physics. She has a zillion trophies from gymnastics competitions, and she taught herself to speak near fluent French. She's worked as a runway and print model, and even did some background vocals for an indie record.

None of which has translated into a paycheck that lasted longer than five months.

But toss her in a pressure cooker? That's when she shines, and I feel the tiny, green shoots of hope start to push up through the black that has swallowed me.

"Okay. No Damien and no cops or security types," she says after a silence so long I'm afraid she's going to burn through our five minutes "So we put a pin in that while we listen to this next message, then we make a plan. Possible sources for the price they're demanding. And possible bad guys. I don't care how crazy, we write them down. And we figure out how that card got into your basket."

"I haven't got a clue about that," I admit. "The basket was on my table the entire time."

"Not before the signing, though. And I doubt you were paying attention when it was beside you. You were signing and talking to readers, right?"

I nod. "And some readers added their own gifts to the basket. They were all so sweet. I can't imagine any of them would..."

"Probably not," Aria says. "They'd have to be really ballsy. But one could have been a plant. Not one of your fans at all. Just someone pretending. Someone trained. Like a pickpocket. Or maybe someone slipped in from the back of the store. The basket was probably in a stock room or something before they gave it to you."

I shrug. My head is pounding, and I realize I've had nothing but coffee since my very early dinner. Before, I was too nervous about the signing. After, too scared. Now, I stand up and go to the kitchen for Ibuprofen. And—because I really need it—my emergency half-gallon of cookie dough ice cream. With two spoons, of course.

"Maybe the store has security cams," I suggest when Aria joins me at the table. "I'll ask in the morning."

Ari nods as she shovels a spoonful of ice cream into her mouth, then talks with her mouth full. "Good plan. Hopefully they'll have them, you get a pic, and this is all over in a jiffy."

Over. My stomach twists, but I nod. What Aria doesn't get—what I'm now absolutely certain of—is that all the shit that happened to me and Anne is never going to be over.

Ari stabs at the ice cream but doesn't take another bite. "Were you followed from the bookstore? Whoever sent this was probably watching you. I mean, they'd want to know you actually saw that first message, right?"

"Can't techie types tell that I was on the website?"

"I think they can see that someone is. But how would they know it was you?"

I hadn't thought about that. "I might have tossed the card thinking it could have a virus," I muse. "Or maybe the envelope fell out of the basket, and someone picked it up."

She taps the end of her nose. "Exactly. And since they need to be sure you got it, they must have been watching."

I glance around the spartan little house I bought for a song because it's in totally shit shape. I don't care, though, because I fell in love the moment I saw it. And the idea that someone could be hidden outside, watching and waiting, totally creeps me out. "Nobody followed me." I say the words firmly even as I try to think back. But the truth is, I wasn't paying attention.

When I left the bookstore, I was still on my book-signing high. Santa and his reindeer could have been behind me, and I wouldn't have noticed a thing.

And when I left the coffee shop, I was too wigged out. All I wanted was to get home. It hadn't occurred to me that someone might be watching. I don't mention the man who'd been waiting for the woman outside the coffee shop. Aria doesn't need to know just how jumpy I was. And still am.

"What about inside?" Aria asks. "Anyone standing too close when you ordered?"

"No, no. I wasn't inside at all. I went to the drive-through, then parked so I could check out the basket. If there was someone sitting in a car watching me, I didn't notice them."

That's true enough. The other man I noticed was standing right by Maisy's window without a covert bone in his body. For that matter, Ashton was about as overt as a man could be. *But why had he come over to talk to me? And why was he there in the first place? He doesn't even live in Los Angeles.*

Ari's eyes narrow to slits as she leans forward. "Dammit, Bree, tell me what you're thinking."

"Ash," I say. It's not him—I can't believe it could be him—but what if it's him?

"Ash," she repeats. "Ashton Stone? Damien Stark's son? That Ash?"

I nod feeling numb. "He was at the coffee shop. But it's not him. We're friends. Sort of. I mean, there's no way."

Ari's brow furrows. "And we're talking about the same Ashton Stone, right? The one who was all over the news for the shit he said when he crashed Stark and Nikki's vow renewal ceremony?"

She tilts her head as she stares me down. "The *friend* you almost got up-close and personal with at the airport four months ago?" She punctuates the word 'friend' with air quotes.

"*I did not.*"

"Well, yeah. That's my point. You left the poor guy with blue balls. Maybe he's pissed."

My skin prickles, as if I've just been doused with ice water.

"Bree?"

I barely hear her. My head's too full of protests. And fear.
It can't be him.

I lift my head and my eyes meet Aria's. "He's a good guy."

"He's a guy with a reputation as a hot head who blows off serious steam when things don't go his way. He's a guy with a death wish."

"The hell he—"

"Have you watched any of his races?"

"He doesn't race anymore," I say.

"Why are you defending him?"

"Because..." I trail off, uncertain. When he first burst into the Starks' life, Damien didn't trust him. Not only were there whispers of assault and a possible murder cover-up, but he'd called Ash reckless. A guy who had something in him that he needed to burn out.

But I know Damien doesn't feel that way now, and I've gotten to know Ash, too. He has an edge and a temper, sure. But a kidnapper? A blackmailer?

The thought is too horrible to even consider. I can't believe it. I won't believe it. "He had nothing to do with the kidnapping," I say firmly. "He wouldn't have those tapes."

And even if he did, he sure as hell wouldn't be tormenting me.

Would he?

SEVEN

"How much do you really know about him?" Aria asks, putting a gentle hand on my knee.

Nothing, I think, but I'm saved from answering when the timer goes off. Although "saved" isn't the right word at all.

"Should I stay?" she asks as I start to scan the QR code again.

In a flash, I reach out and grab her hand. "Yes. Please, yes" My mouth feels dry, and I know my palm is sweating. I regret the words as I say them, but I don't want to take them back. There's horrible stuff on those recordings—I know that. Even though I don't remember it, I *know* it.

And maybe I don't want her to see the horrible stuff. But she's my best friend, and I think I need her to. I think if I'm going to see it—if I'm going to start remembering it—I need someone who'll share the burden. And that someone is, always has been, and always will be Aria.

She meets my eyes. Just one small nod, and I know she understands.

On the phone screen, nothing's happening. Just that spinning wheel that suggests a bad connection. Aria and I look at each other, panicked, and I'm about to reboot the Wi-Fi when the screen turns solid black and white text pops up again.

$3,000,000

That's all it says. Then the number starts to flash, and an obnoxious Woody Woodpecker-style laugh comes through the speaker. But it's not a joke, as the voice soon tells me. A low, distorted voice that I'm certain is computer generated.

"Three days, Brianna," the voice says as Aria opens her phone and taps an app to start recording. "Three days to gather three million. And because we are true gentlemen, the clock will not begin to run until noon tomorrow."

A low, tinny laugh rolls out. "You think we are not gentlemen, but you would be wrong. We give you these extra hours. And we give you our word. The money in exchange for these videos deleted from the web, the hard copies delivered to you for either safekeeping or destruction. Three million for the certainty of peace for you. The promise that this little blip in your past will not come back to haunt you or the pretty little Stark princess again.

"We could renege on this promise, but we won't. As we have said, we are gentlemen. And the rules are the rules. And one of those rules is that you must abide as well. Stray from the path, and you will pay a severe price."

I wince. Not from the words so much as from the way Aria's grip is squeezing the bones in my hand together. And from the panic that's racing through me. *Three-million dollars?* How the hell am I supposed to get three-million dollars?

"In case you doubt our sincerity, we take our lead from your very own Glindeon Brotherhood. That will be *your* price."

Beside me, Aria gasps. The Glindeon Brotherhood is pure fiction. More than that, it's fiction I created. An alliance of elf-demon hybrids who operate as a magical mafia that's a constant threat to the heroine, Bethany. And the price they exact from anyone who crosses them is always high.

"As for the little girl's payment for your failure...." The speaker trails off, that tinny, inhuman voice now fat with menace. "I'm sure the world will be more than interested to see what she witnessed. What she was part of. What you did in front of her."

I hear myself whimper, and Aria squeezes my hand.

"No," I whisper, my mouth so dry I can barely utter the words. "No, please, no."

But the voice can't hear me. It just drones on. "Defy us in any way and we shall blanket the media with videos and photos. Believe us when we say that the one we have already revealed to you is tame."

I blink, forcing back tears, desperate for this voice to shut up, shut up, *shut up*. But it just drones on and on in that cold, brittle, heartless cadence.

"Perhaps that is what you want," it continues. "After all, you would be thrust into the spotlight, too. Such notoriety would surely cause your career to soar. Who wouldn't want to buy a book from a woman under such a spotlight?"

I sit up straighter, the heat of anger and fury forging me into steel.

"Isn't notoriety the path to fame? Didn't your former employer ride that pony to his billions? Haven't you profited from the vile fruits of his labors? Perhaps you want more. Perhaps *this* is what you want. Perhaps you won't pay us because you want the videos released. And when they hit every news channel in the world, perhaps you will even thank us."

"Don't listen," Aria hisses. And for the second time in my life, I know that if push comes to shove, I really do have it in me to kill.

"But the little girl?" Now, the voice is almost pleasant. Or as pleasant as the computer-altered voice of a totally sick fuck can be. "If those images and videos come out, dear little Anne will spend her life not as Damien Stark's spoiled brat, but as the poor, pitiful little girl who was kidnapped and tormented. A little girl who will come to understand that someone is still out there who knows what happened to her. Someone who, one day, might take her again. And that next time she won't be drugged. Won't simply sit in the background rocking herself in a haze of dreams. She will be you. Touched. Violat—"

"*No!*" I actually scream the word, as if whoever sent this recorded message can hear me.

"We won't let that happen," Aria says, our hands locked tight together.

"Today, you preened," the voice continues. "You strutted and crowed, thinking you had created something wonderful. When you look back, remember that it was you who gave us the way to ensure your compliance. Defy us, and we will become the Brotherhood personified. We will release your shame to the world.

As I tighten my grip on Aria's hand, the three-million-dollar figure disappears, replaced by a date and a time. Noon, Pacific Time. Three days from tomorrow. "Keep track of our appointment card. You may scan any time after six a.m. Pacific time for instructions as to where to transfer the funds. Once you scan, you will have fifteen minutes to comply. The latest you may scan is noon.

"Three million and we disappear forever. Less, and you will find the penalty to be very stiff indeed. And in case you need further incentive, from now until the money we are due reaches our account, you may amuse yourself by scanning the code to reveal your Greatest Hits—a curated collection of all the videos and images that will be released if our demands are not met."

And then it's gone. That tinny voice. But the low static that had buzzed behind it continues, edging through the silence that seems to fill the house. I want to hurl my phone across the room and make that horrible buzzing stop, but I know I can't. I can't close that page until I'm sure the message is over.

Then the static snaps off, and that fucking happy face appears on the black screen above three words written in lovely calligraphy: *Enjoy your evening!*

Finally, the screen goes blank, and I'm left wondering how the hell I'm going to get my hands on three million dollars.

Then I lurch forward and vomit all over my and Aria's shoes.

EIGHT

My phone is my lifeline now. And I fear that's not a metaphor.

So instead of smashing it, I start to pace, not even caring that I reek of vomit, as I try desperately to come up with someone—anyone—who isn't Damien and might have three million dollars.

"*Bastards.*" Aria grinds out the word. "None of this is on you, Bree. Do you hear me? Not one single, fucking thing. Tell me you know that. Tell me you believe it."

I just shake my head. "That doesn't matter. All that matters is the money. Where the hell am I going to get that kind of money?"

"Damien," she says. "I know you don't want to, but you have to," she adds at the same time that I snap, "No!"

I can't bear the thought of hurting Damien and Nikki this way. There must be another solution. I consider asking Evelyn—but she's known Damien for almost his entire life, and I'm terrified that she couldn't keep the secret. Not only that, but she and her husband are in the middle of building a new house, and while she's well-off, I don't think she could spare as much as I need.

Maybe banks have good interest rates on *So you're being blackmailed* loans.

I bark out a twisted-sounding laugh, realizing that I may be a little hysterical right now. Then Aria is in front of me, holding my shoulders and ordering me to take deep breaths.

Raindrops. Roses. Whiskers. Kittens.

By the time I hit *tied up with string*, my mind's clearer. But I still don't have a plan.

Ari sighs. "We just have to make a list and—"

My phone rings, interrupting her and making me jump as it vibrates in my hand. I glance at the screen. "Five-one-two area code."

Ari scowls. "Where the hell is that?"

"I should answer it," I say, even though I want to toss the phone—and the horror it's delivered to me—far, far away.

"No." She makes a grab for the phone, but I pull back. "Dammit, Bree," she says as it rings again. "Just let it go to voicemail. Give yourself time to think."

I almost agree, then I shake my head. "What if it's them?"

The thought sends a wave of nausea crashing over me.

Ring!

"It isn't them," she says. "Probably a telemarketer."

"You don't know that."

She cocks her head and stares me down in that Aria way she has. "Like they'd let you see their number."

"Duh. They're calling from a burner phone."

Another ring.

"I have to," I whisper, terrified I'll get punished if it rolls to voicemail.

Her shoulders sag a little. "Put it on speaker," she orders. "We're in this together now."

I blink back tears as I comply, hating that she's been dragged into this mess, but thankful that she's got my back.

"Hello?" My mouth is so dry that my voice is little more than a croak.

"Bree? Is that you?"

I stiffen at the familiar voice.

Beside me, Aria mouths *who?*

Ash, I mouth back, realizing that she wouldn't know his voice. Though I've talked about him *ad nauseam*, they've never met in person. And even though he's been interviewed by many an on-air reporter, Aria's unlikely to have caught a broadcast about racing or engines or whatever else Ashton Stone has going on in his burgeoning empire.

"*Bree.*" His voice has an urgent edge now. "Are you there?"

"I'm here," I say, my voice mousy and strange. I clear my throat and try again. "What do you want?"

If he notices the ice I've managed to edge into my voice, he doesn't mention it. "I just wanted to check on you."

Beside me, Aria's brows rise as she mouths—very clearly— *What. The. Actual. Fuck?*

"Check on me? What am I, a kid? Are you my daddy?"

"Do you want me to be?" His voice drops in tone, and I immediately regret my words.

"No. Ick."

He chuckles. "Never understood the appeal of that one, either."

"As fascinating as it might be to know we have that in common, why are you calling? And why did you call from another number?"

"Another number?"

"You didn't pop up. I got some 512 number instead."

"Pop up? You mean, I'm in your contacts?"

I silently curse. "Nikki put you in."

"Oh." I can practically hear the frown in his voice.

"Is that a problem?" I snap.

"What? No. God, no. I was only wondering why."

Because I asked her to.

I don't tell him that, though. "A college friend had her wedding in Marfa."

He chuckles. "Those famous lights."

"It really was pretty," I say, remembering the stunning night sky of that small, Texas town. "Anyway, Nikki said you were in West Texas that week, too. Nearby at some test track. She thought I should have your number in case I needed help or, I don't know, whatever."

More accurately, I had suggested Ash as my emergency contact, and Nikki had thought that was a stellar idea. I don't tell Ash that part. Especially since I never got up the nerve to call him.

"She probably gave you my personal number. I'm calling from a work line. Is *that* a problem?" he adds, mimicking my earlier question.

"Nope. No problem."

"The wedding would have been, what? A couple of months ago?"

"Yeah." A bit more than that, actually. Why?"

"Just that it's a shame you didn't ring me up."

"Oh." My chest is suddenly very tight. And, yeah, I'd thought about calling him at least a dozen times. And each and every time, I'd chickened out.

"I would have taken you for a spin."

Oh. "A spin." My mouth is far too dry. "Because those test tracks just go around and around in circles."

"Not exactly what I had in mind," he says, his low voice as soft as a caress.

I feel my cheeks heat as Aria crosses her arms and mouths O.M.G.

I shift, putting more of my back toward Aria. Somehow, I have lost complete control of this conversation.

"At any rate," he continues, "I'm flattered you still have my number."

"Yeah, well, I never think to cull them. You'd be surprised how many people are in my contacts that I've totally forgotten exist."

"In that case, maybe I didn't need to call after all."

I have no idea what he's talking about, and I shift back to look at Aria, who's standing there with her brow furrowed, like she's focused on a jigsaw puzzle she can't put together.

Just hang up, she mouths when I shoot her a questioning look.

I really should. But instead of taking the upper hand, I take the bait. "What do you mean?" I ask Ash. "Why would you need to call?"

"That's the question of the hour, isn't it?"

Ari throws her hands up, then stomps to the table by the door where we keep the mail. I watch as she scribbles something in Sharpie on the back of an envelope, then shows it to me: HE'S PLAYING WITH YOU.

I wish I could argue, but I think she's right. More, I think the game he's playing is dangerous. I'm just not sure what kind of danger.

"Dammit, Ash. I'm not in the mood. Tell me why you're calling or I'm hanging up."

"That's why I'm calling," he says, his voice firm, but gentle. "Your mood."

"Excuse me?"

"There's something going on with you. Right now, you're edgy. And earlier you seemed off. And I'm not arrogant enough to think it's just because of what happened at the airport."

"I'm not edgy," I snap at the phone. I'm not proud of the

way I bailed on him that night, but I sure as hell don't want to get into it now. "And I wasn't *off* at the coffee shop. I was tired. I'd just come from a two-hour talk and book signing. And then you popped up at my car and startled me, and—"

"And that's all it was? Being startled?"

Something twists inside me. Something dark and a little dangerous. I meet Aria's eyes, and she shakes her head slowly.

I hesitate, then I take the phone off speaker and shift away from her. But not so much that I miss her exasperated expression.

"Listen," I tell him, "I'm fine. Thanks for checking on me, but I'm peachy keen. Really."

"Very glad to hear it. I'm in North Hollywood at the moment. I was supposed to grab a drink with a friend, but he had to bail. Why don't you come join me? Or I can swing by and pick you up. I can't be more than twenty minutes away."

I glance sideways at Aria, who cocks her head in a way that makes me think she knows exactly what Ash just proposed. I turn away again, not wanting her to see the temptation I'm sure is all over my face.

"Sorry. Gotta say no."

"Because you don't want to have a drink with me? Or because I spooked you?"

The words hang there, cold and terrifying. Is Aria right about him? Is this all a game, and this call is his way of never letting me know for certain—even while he drops hint after hint —that he's behind the videos?

"I'm not in the mood for games," I say. "And my mood is fine. Just because I didn't go all gooey when you pounced on me at my car doesn't mean that something spooked me out of my senses."

Except, of course, that's exactly what it means.

"Fine," he says. "You weren't spooked, and you aren't acting strange. All of that is entirely in my imagination."

"Glad we're finally on the same page."

"In that case," he says, "it must be me."

A chill races through me. Surely he's not saying...

I force the thought away. "What are you talking about?"

"You're flat-out rejecting me tonight. You shoved me away outside the coffee shop. You stood me up at the hotel a few months ago. And now I learn that you didn't reach out to me in Texas. As you may be aware, I've got a reasonably high-IQ. I can do the math."

"Can you?"

"Indeed. And my quick wit and superior reasoning skills have concluded that the only possible remaining reason why you won't have a drink with me is, well, me."

"You really may be as smart as they say." And even as the words pass my lips, I realize that I'm flirting. My entire life is crumbling around me, and I'm actually flirting.

More, I don't know if that's a good thing or a bad thing.

All I do know, in fact, is that I should hang up. I should just end this cat-and-mouse game right now. Even if he's not responsible for the videos—and I really, *really* don't want to believe he is—I do not need the distraction of playing mental footsies with a guy like Ashton Stone. Not when hell is nipping at my toes.

Except...

"We're meeting with Maggie tomorrow," he says before I can gather my thoughts.

I cringe. "I told you I was cancelling."

"Yeah. You said that. But Evelyn pulled strings for that interview. You're not bailing."

Since he's right, I say nothing. I just scowl, which is ridiculous since he can't see me.

"We should meet up before. Talk about how we'll handle all the questions she's not supposed to ask but will anyway."

"I can manage on my own."

"Even better. That means we'll have plenty of time to sit and chat about non-Maggie things while we have our coffees."

I manage not to laugh. "You have absolutely no clue how to take no for an answer, do you?"

"No."

This time, I don't bother to muffle my laugh.

"What happened, Bree?" This time his voice is soft. "I thought—before, I mean—I thought there was something there. At my dad's house. Later at the airport. We've never talked about that."

I swallow. "I left you a message."

I hear the low huff of breath. "Yeah. A message." Silence wells between us. "Come on, Bree. I thought we—Was I just wrong?"

My chest goes tight. Suddenly, it feels like I can't breathe. "We're friends, Ash. Can't we just leave it at that?"

And eternity seems to pass, and I think that I'm going to fall into the abyss before he answers the question. Then he says, very softly, "Of course. If that's what you want, then, of course."

I close my eyes as a confusing wave of relief mixed with disappointment washes over me, and I know right then that I'm a Class A Liar. After all, I've gotten away with lying to myself for years.

When I open my eyes again, Aria's right in front of me, watching with a furrowed brow.

I look away, not wanting to see the confusion—and concern —in her eyes.

I'm attracted to him—there's no denying that—but nothing's ever going to happen. He could be the fairy tale hero who saves me from the scary monster, and it wouldn't matter. I walked—

okay, *ran*—away from him before because I had to. And, yes, it was hard and painful and disappointing. But I did it.

And since I already did it once, I know that next time will be even easier.

I just hope he won't put me in the position of forcing a next time.

For a moment, silence hangs on the line. When he speaks, his voice is both firm and gentle. "If that's really what you want," he repeats, "then I won't argue. Not now, anyway. But let's be clear. It will be a lie. There's something more than friendship between us, Bree. There has been from the beginning. And I think there still is."

Panic bubbles inside me. "No. You're wro—"

"And Bree," he continues, talking right over me. "There's something you might not know about me. I'm a man who's very good at two things. Solving puzzles. And getting what I want. And just so we're clear, what I want is you."

NINE

"Flirting?" Aria crosses her arms and glowers at me, and I swear she's going to start breathing fire at any moment. "He was freaking *flirting* with you." She stalks toward me. "And you were flirting back," she adds, emphasizing each word with a hard poke of her finger to my chest.

"*Ow*, and I was not.

"The hell you weren't."

"I *wasn't*," I insist. "And neither was he." I don't care what the evidence shows, I've already decided that I don't want him to be flirting because I don't want to go down any path where flirting might lead.

Well, *want* is a relative term. *Can't*. I can't go that route. Not with anyone, but most definitely not with him. He's too close. Too tied in with the Stark family. Too connected to all the memories I don't want. And to the ones I don't have...but am terrified will come back some day—and not only in my nightmares.

I don't, however, tell Aria any of that. Instead, I just stand with my arms crossed and stare her down.

"He's tied in with this somehow," she says.

I shake my head. "No. No, I know him. He would never do that. Anne's his little sister."

Ari cocks her head and gives me her *you know nothing, Jon Snow* stare.

"Sister," I repeat. "Sweet little girl. He adores her. He would never."

"And let's review the timeline, shall we?" She taps her index finger to the corner of her mouth. "Back when you and Anne were kidnapped, Damien knew all about his secret son and things were all snips and snails and puppy dog tails between them."

She cocks her head as I scowl. "Oh, wait," she continues. "That's not quite right. Damien didn't have a freaking clue. And as for your boyfriend—"

"Dammit, he is not—"

"—he was off working to become another Master of the Universe, with his primary motivation being to make enough money so that he could basically flip Damien and his entire family the bird by jamming that middle finger down into Stark's life and totally nuking that family's happy little existence."

She's not wrong. Over-the-top, but not wrong.

"In other words," Aria continues, "he wasn't exactly feeling warm and fuzzy to the Stark family. Was he?"

When I continue to say nothing, she takes a step toward me. "Was he?"

"If you ever decide to settle on a career, you should really look into being one of those scary professors you always see in movies."

"He hated Damien," she continues, completely ignoring my snark. "Like *hated* hated. Damien may have been clueless about Ash, but Ash knew all about Damien. He grew up watching this man—this freaking billionaire—live his amazing life with his kids and his beautiful wife. I mean, resentful much?"

Again, she's not wrong. But—as I very reasonably point out—they mended fences. Ash knows why Damien never knew he existed. "They're good now," I say. "They're a family now. He wouldn't do that to them."

"Maybe not now. But back when you were taken..."

I shiver. "No. It's just not possible."

"You're being naive," she says.

"You don't know them," I tell Aria. She's only ever talked to any of them in passing. "You have to take my word on it. Ash isn't someone who could—"

I cut myself off with a shiver. No way did Ash have a hand in what happened to me and Anne. No way at all.

Are you sure?

The snarky voice in my head is my own.

Aren't you forgetting Rory? You trusted him, too. You would have made this same speech for him, wouldn't you? But he took you and Anne. He locked you up. And you're only now learning what else he did.

"Bree?"

I snap my head up. "What?"

Her eyes are wide and a little scared. "I don't know. You zoned on me."

"I'm fine." I shake off the memory. "Ash isn't Rory. He wouldn't do it." I say the words firmly, but this time I'm not sure if I'm trying to convince Aria or myself.

For a moment, she stays perfectly still. Then she nods. Shrugs a little. "Okay, you say you're sure. I won't argue. We'll assume that he didn't have anything to do with the kidnapping. But that doesn't mean he's not involved now."

I settle into the corner of the couch and rub my temples, fighting a building headache. "Why are you so determined to think that Ash is part of this?"

"You really believe it's a coincidence that he was at the

coffee shop?"

"Yes," I say. But I have to admit there's a tiny, tiny part of me that wonders.

"Well, I don't think so," Aria says. "Especially when you consider everything."

I cross my arms and glare. "Everything?"

She starts to pace. "Just hear me out, okay?"

"Fine. Whatever." My head is about to explode. I don't have it in me to keep arguing.

"He's a bad boy, right? I mean, that's his rep. A guy who lives hard and drives fast. Fucks around just like most guys with his looks and his money, but he's never been in a relationship. Not really. Maybe one. But she died, so we can't ask for her opinion. And you know the rumor is he killed her."

I gape at her. "What are you? His biographer? And there is no way he—"

She holds up her phone. "I've been poking around online. There's a lot about him. But it's all very surfacy. Guy doesn't seem to like doing interviews.

"Oh, like that's the mark of evil. Guess I've got horns, too," I say, "because I can't stand being interviewed either."

"Why are you defending him?"

"I'm not. Why are you trying to vilify him?"

"I'm just laying out the facts."

"Whatever." I'm too mentally exhausted to argue. "Lay 'em out."

"Right." She starts to pace, her hands moving as she talks. "The guy's got a bad boy reputation. And the whole world knows there was bad blood between him and Stark. And since the world is always more interested in scandal than in hugs and puppies, it's probably fair to think that most folks still assume that Ash isn't a Damien fan. Right?"

I shrug. "Maybe. I don't know."

She twirls her hand as if egging me on. "Just go with me, okay?"

"I'm going. Get on with it."

She nails me with a very Aria look before plunking her butt down on the coffee table in front of me. "Let's say he had nothing to do with the kidnapping."

"Excellent. Can I go now?"

"Isn't it still possible that he got his hands on those vids? Hell, maybe whoever made them went to him. Offered them up, knowing they'd fuel whatever coals still burn."

"Coals?"

"You can believe all you want that Ash is rah-rah Daddy Damien now, but at least keep an open mind. Ashton Stone is smart, right? And that means he's smart enough to play the dutiful son when he really wants to tear it all down."

I shake my head. This conversation is just too much. "Why are you working so hard to make me distrust him?"

"Me?" Her blue eyes go wide. "Why are you so keen on defending him? The man was right there in that parking lot, probably standing where he could see your face when you first scanned that QR code today. You are not a stupid person, Bree. At the very least you have to suspect him."

"Ash isn't stupid either. And it would be nuts to be on site like that. To approach me like that."

She nods slowly. "You're right."

"Thank you."

"He's smart enough to pretend to be stupid. To hide in plain sight. To do the unexpected."

I consider banging my forehead against the wall, but since that would require getting up, I just stare at her. "You are trying way too hard."

"I'm not. You're just not listening."

"Oh, I'm listening. I'm just hearing gibberish. And again I

say, if he needs money, he's just going to ask Damien. There's zero reason to stick me in the middle of it."

She moves from the table onto the couch next to me. "You're not stupid, Bree. Don't start being stupid now."

"I'm not."

"The guy's got pride. He doesn't want to ask Daddy Dearest. He wants to twist the knife. So he goes to you because you'll go to Damien. And you know Damien will ask to see the images. And even if Ash had nothing to do with the kidnapping, that's going to twist the knife in Daddy's gut just a little."

"Ash isn't like that. I don't think he would ever be that vile, but he certainly wouldn't be now. He and Damien are close. He and Nikki, too. And he loves those kids to pieces."

She shrugs. "Maybe he does, maybe he doesn't."

I can only shake my head. "Why don't you like him?"

She snorts out a laugh. "Are we back in junior high? Dammit, Bree, the guy just lost about three mil. You must look like a damn easy way to refill that coffer by getting cash from Damien without Ash having to lose face by asking Daddy himself."

"Wait, wait, wait. Lost three million?" I'm completely baffled. "What are you talking about?"

"I've been talking about it for a millennium now."

"Three mil? You never said that."

"Sure, I did." Her brow furrows. "Didn't I?"

That banging-my-head-on-the-wall thing is looking pretty good. "Just tell me now."

"Some investor backed out a few weeks ago. I don't know the details, but it's a big deal. Now some other investors are threatening to pull out, and that would totally screw up his company going public. Or make him lose some other lucrative contract. I'm not sure. I just know that the loss is what they call a Big Freaking Deal for him."

I try to follow, but my idea of high finance is keeping a balanced bank account. Still, I've spent enough time around Damien to grasp the general concept. "Is this one of the things you read on the internet two minutes ago?"

"No. At the clinic a few days ago. Guy who came in with a sick ferret left the *Wall Street Journal* in the waiting room." She shrugs. "I grabbed it to read while I was watching Beyonce-the-bull-dog. What?" she adds when she sees my expression. "I don't only read gossip mags."

Despite the entire fucked up situation, I smile. *That's* my bestie. Then I actually process what she's saying, and I frown.

She points at me and nods. "Yeah, see. You get it. Whatever fell apart set him back big time." She cocks her head and purses her lips. "He needs to get that money."

"He's not like that," I insist. "Besides, from what I've overheard, he can afford to lose a few mil."

"Overheard?"

I shrug. "I'm pretty much invisible when I'm doing the nanny thing. I hear stuff. Ashton Stone is doing just fine financially."

"Maybe," she says. "But that doesn't mean he wouldn't be pissed about the loss. I mean, the guy could be rich as Midas and still want to refill the coffer."

"Like I said, Damien would give him the money in a heartbeat."

"Sure, but Ashton Stone is the kind of guy who'd be too proud to ask. So he sets this up knowing you'll go to Damien. Because how else are you gonna get the money?"

And isn't that the question of the hour? At the moment, Damien really is my best bet, but I just can't bring myself to ask him.

I take a few deep breaths as I gather my thoughts. "Look, maybe Ash is pissed about whatever fell apart. But pissed is one thing. Getting his hands on kidnap tapes and then blackmailing me is something entirely different. And stupid since, hello, I don't have millions, and there's no guarantee I'll rush to Damien. And Ash isn't a stupid guy."

Ari shrugs. "Okay, so, maybe it's not about the money. I mean, we've already said that this blackmailing bastard must know you don't have any. Maybe it's about the danger. He's not racing professionally anymore, right? Guy like that probably misses it."

"Not him," I say, knowing that she's going to call me an idiot. And she'll be right. Because from what I've seen and heard, Ashton definitely still chases the thrill.

"Dammit, Bree."

I shake my head. "Topic closed."

"You can't just—"

"Topic. Closed."

She presses her lips tight together, and I know she's counting to ten. "Fine," she says when she breathes again, and a noisy, uncomfortable quiet fills the air between us. She starts to say something else, then shakes her head.

"What?"

"Nothing. You'll hate it."

"What?" I repeat.

She hunches into her shoulders and looks at me sideways. "Why not ask him for the money?"

I frown, not quite able to compute her words. "I don't—what?"

"Ash. Ask him for the three million."

I gape at her.

She shrugs. "You said yourself that the millions he just lost haven't really hurt him. He can probably liquidate at least that much for you. If he cares about Anne and Damien—and you said he does—then he'll give you the money."

"But I can't—"

"Why not?"

"Because...."

I flounder for a reason, trying to put the mixed-up jumble of reason and emotion into words. "I—I don't want to tell him what's on those tapes. And he's only been in their family for like five minutes. I can't just dump this on him. Besides, the voice said no law enforcement or investigator types. What if he pulls someone in?"

"If you tell him not to, would he? Because if you don't trust him about that, you shouldn't trust him for any of it."

I slump, my mind desperately trying to come up with another alternative.

"Look," Aria says. "I adore those kids, too. And Nikki and Damien are the coolest. That's why you want to protect them, right? And if you had the money lying around, you'd pay out of your own pocket, wouldn't you?"

I nod. Even knowing that paying might not make it go away—blackmailers don't exactly radiate trustworthy vibes—if I had three mil lying around, I'd pay it in a heartbeat.

"Well, Ash loves them, too. That's what you've been telling me, right? You don't think he'd want to help?"

I stand up and start to pace, because that's what I do when I need to think hard—I move. Plotting books. Pondering real estate purchases. Deciding what to do about a blackmailer.

I'm even in constant motion when I'm writing. Ear pods in and my music playing while my fingers clack over the keys and my body starts to move with the characters. Aria says she can tell where I am in a book—action scene, love scene—just by watching my shoulders and back move with my imagination.

Most of the time, I don't even know I'm doing it. I guess that's because when I'm writing, I'm not really me.

As if reading my mind, Aria asks how I'd write this.

"What do you mean?"

"If you got a wild hair and decided to write a thriller. Where would the heroine get the bucks? Stark's brother? His best friend? His close business associates?"

I know those people, and they'd jump to help. But I've already decided that I can't go to them. It could get back to Damien. Or to law enforcement. I trust them all—I do. But I don't trust them more than myself.

"Ash is his son," I say. "It's a hell of secret to foist on him."

She cocks her head and smirks. "We already know that Ash can keep shit from Damien."

"Five seconds ago you were practically accusing him of being the blackmailer."

She shrugs. "Maybe he is. Doesn't mean you can't ask him for the money. Unless you've got a better idea."

The truth is, I really don't.

I draw a breath and pace some more. "If he is involved—and he's not," I say, though I'm not sure I mean it, "then he'll either say no so that he can watch from afar as I scramble for the money. Or he'll say yes because he knows that's what Innocent Ash would do."

"It'll be door number two," Aria says.

"And if he's *not* involved," I continue, railroading my words over hers, "then of course he'll pay. So long as he knows it's to protect Anne."

"He'll have it," Aria says. "I bet you a million—ha, ha—bucks that he either has that kind of money or can get his hands on it super quick."

I scowl because that's probably true. *So what would I have Fictional Ash do?*

I twirl a strand of hair around my finger as I try to parse this out. "Either way, he's going to pay, even if he has to borrow from some rich friend. That just makes the most sense. But that doesn't tell me anything. If both Guilty Ash and Innocent Ash pay, I'm still screwed. Because that means this won't ever be over."

Ari shakes her head. "No, no, no. Don't you get it? If he's really Innocent Ash—and if the real bad guy sticks with the deal—you pay, and the videos go away."

"A big *if*."

"Not so much. Because if they try to hit you up again, they increase their chances of getting caught. Once they get their money, they'll go away for good. I think," she adds with a shrug.

Honestly, she's probably right. "But if he's Guilty Ash?" I hate even thinking that.

"He still goes away. Because he's smart enough to know that's what a bad guy should do."

"Even though he didn't get his three million?"

She shrugs. "He can't risk pulling the same scam again. Not after you've paid. He either forgets about the three mil altogether or he blackmails someone else. But he can't go back to your well."

I draw a deep breath, my head aching from thinking about all this. From being scared. And from the harsh reality that's now staring me in the face: It doesn't matter if he pays or if he walks away, I won't know the truth. Not ever.

"I thought you trusted him," Aria says when I tell her as much.

"I do," I say, but she and I both know it's a lie. Right now, I don't trust anyone except Aria. And she doesn't have three mil to spare.

TEN

Four Months Ago—Bree (Upper Crust Bakery & Cafe)

One thought fills my head as I speed from the Starks' Malibu mansion to the Upper Crust bakery: *Maggie Bridge is a royal bitch.*

Yup. After careful study and consideration, that is my final opinion. And I should know. After all, I graduated from NYU with a degree in journalism, then topped that off with an MFA from UCLA. Which means I'm watchful. I know how to ask questions and how to write a damn good article.

It also means I know a hack when I see one. And Maggie Bridge is a hack in reporter's clothing.

Bottom line? I really don't like her. Especially after sitting in the Starks' beautiful house while enduring her inane questions and innuendoes for what felt like a century, but in reality didn't even hit the half-hour mark. Yeah, it was *that* painful.

Bitch.

I tap Maisy's brakes lightly as I take one of the many curves on this section of Pacific Coast Highway, then sigh. Maggie Bridge is *definitely* a bitch. But I was probably an idiot to agree to the interview in the first place. I mean, it wasn't like she even needed to talk to me.

She'd come to the Stark house to interview Damien and his family for what was supposed to be a fluff piece celebrating Damien's life and career. It's not like anyone's going to be flipping the pages of the magazine in their rush to read about me.

Then again, I *was* kidnapped along with Damien's daughter. So there's that.

"Idiot, idiot, idiot." I bang my fist on the steering wheel for good measure. Honestly, what was I thinking when I agreed to let her ask me about the kidnapping? Especially after Damien had made it clear that I could flat out decline.

But noooo. I'd had to go and be all gee-I'm-a-girl-so-I-want-to-please-of-course-I'll-do-your-stupid-interview-you-annoying-bitch.

Really. Don't. Like. Her.

At least I scored points for having the foresight to say I'd cut the interview off if it got too personal. But that attempt at putting up limits backfired because, hey, kidnapped.

And that's personal by definition.

Despite all that, it could have been fine. Except it was Maggie Bridge. And she poked and prodded and insinuated stuff about Damien and the kidnapping and guilt and all sorts of bullshit until I wanted to race out of that room and have a shower. And—yay me—that's exactly what I did.

I let her get under my skin.

I put myself out there, and she dredged it all up again.

Idiot.

At least I learned one thing. I'll never sit down for an interview with that woman again.

With a firm nod, I push Maggie Bridge out of my head as I accelerate into a sweet curve that straightens out right in front of The Upper Crust's parking lot. I'm going faster than I should, but Maisy can handle it, and I don't even skid as I make a hard right out of the curve, practically soar onto the lot, then glide into a parking space that fate put there especially for me.

I'm grinning when I kill the engine. That's one way to erase the lingering stench of Maggie Bridge.

"You look happy," Kari says once I'm inside and at the counter. "You sounded annoyed when you called."

I shrug. My flight's a red eye, so I'd hung around to watch over the Stark girls until after Maggie was out of the house. Then I called Kari as I was leaving to tell her that I was on my way, and that I needed the biggest, most chocolatey cookie in the place, along with a giant latte. Sadly, the Upper Crust doesn't sell the alcohol I desperately need. I figure I'll get that at the airport.

She's already got my order ready, and she passes it to me, then holds up a finger for me to wait while a broad-shouldered god with sun-blond hair slips up beside her. He puts his hand on her waist as he leans in to ask her a question. When he does, I notice his ginormous class ring. At least, I think it's a class ring. It's hard to get a good look at it because he's using his thumb to spin it around on his finger.

Nervous habit, I think, and then I smile as I look between him and Kari.

She nods, then blushes, turning back to me only after he slips away, then parks himself at the cash register further down the counter.

"Martin Street," she says when her attention returns to me. "New hire."

"And what does he work besides the register?" I ask, adding a salacious little lilt to my voice.

"You have a dirty mind," she says. "Let's just say he's a very... hard... worker."

"He likes working with you," I say, and she goes beet red.

"What makes you say that?"

I just shrug. No sense mentioning the ring. Poor guy hardly needs Kari focusing on that when they're out together. But when a guy's nervous like that around a girl, *like* is very much on the table.

"You really think so?"

"Yes, dufus," I assure her, then roll my eyes when she fans herself, first looking around to make sure no one else is listening.

Kari's a manager at the popular hangout, and we've become pretty good friends. Good enough that she'll show her true colors to me... but will otherwise try to be professional.

Try being the operative word.

We met because my cookie addiction meant that I was popping in every day. We started out with small talk, then started hanging out together when she got off shift. After a few months I realized that she'd mostly filled the gap I'd created when I'd moved to Los Angeles without Aria.

A wave of melancholy washes over me. I love Kari—I do. But I miss Aria, and I'm beyond excited that she's picking me up at JFK in the morning when my red-eye lands—*that* is a seriously true friend. Then we're spending almost the entire day together in Manhattan. After that, I'm going out to dinner with my parents before crashing in the house I grew up in.

"Want me to put a dozen in a to-go box?" Kari asks as she turns back to me. "My treat."

"Have I mentioned lately how much I love you?"

"Too bad I don't go for girls," she says. "Because considering the guys we both attract... and are attracted to...."

She'd dated Rory before I did, and now she acts like that's all a big joke. I can barely conjure a smile.

She may not feel like she constantly needs a shower after having gone out with that piece of shit, but Rory tainted me. So much that I haven't even been attracted to anyone since him.

Liar.

The word flashes in my mind like neon, and I try to shove it down, but all that does is conjure pictures of *him* in my mind.

The one man who has caught my eye.

The one man who has snuck into my fantasies.

Ashton Stone.

But that's not attraction. Not really. It's just a reaction to an exceptionally good-looking man. After all, I barely know him. I mean, yes, we've talked in the months since he crashed Nikki & Damien's celebration. I'd thought he was an asshole then—albeit a ridiculously hot asshole. But he'd redeemed himself, and I'd been glad. Not for selfish reasons, though. I was glad he'd come out on the non-asshole side of the equation for Damien's sake. Not mine.

Sure, we shared a few glances. But that's normal, right? I mean, we were the only twenty-somethings in the house. It's not like I had any illusions about Ashton Stone, a guy who goes through women the way someone with a cold goes through Kleenex. Anyone who pays attention to celebrity gossip knows that.

Even if he weren't a major player, there's no way a guy like that—a guy who'd started from nothing and built a fortune—would be interested in the family nanny. Not even one on her way to being an author. That was the stuff of romance novels and Lifetime movies.

And my life was about as far away from a fluffy romcom as the earth is from the sun.

My happiness in learning that he isn't a total jerk had nothing to do with him. On the contrary, I was simply grateful that Nikki and Damien and the kids didn't have to suffer through another asshole in their already asshole-filled family tree.

I wouldn't even go so far as to call him a friend. He's an

acquaintance. I like the guy. He's polite. He's interesting. And he hasn't been a shit to me.

But I'm not attracted to him. Not at all.

Not even a smidge.

Truly.

I haven't been attracted to anyone in years.

Sometimes, I wonder if I ever will be.

And the truth is that I hope I won't. What would be the point? Getting involved is terrifying enough even if all you're worried about is whether the two of you will mesh. Toss in my baggage, and the thought of starting out in a relationship is enough to send even the sanest person running into a closet and curling up in a ball.

And I'm not the sanest person. Not anymore.

Not by a long shot.

"You should have just jumped him."

I jerk my head up to find Kari back in front of me with a box filled with cookies. "What? Who?"

She cocks her head as she raises her brows. She doesn't say a word, but I get the message anyway: *Girl, do not even.*

"A, I don't know what you're talking about. And, B, I have no interest in getting involved with anyone, least of all Ashton Stone."

I say this last part in a whisper so low she has to lean forward to hear me.

"Who said anything about getting involved? Besides, from what I've read, Ashton Stone doesn't do involved. But you, my friend, need some touch. No, hear me out," she adds when I take a step backwards, my fingers in a cross to ward off evil.

Kari just rolls her eyes and barrels on. "It's like you're stuck in the mud. Take a leap. Take control. Sleep with Ash. Hell, sleep with any guy. Enjoy it. Then move the hell on."

"Kari..."

"You know I'm right. Teresa said pretty much the same thing, didn't she?"

I scowl, but I don't answer. Teresa's a good therapist. I, however, am a lousy patient. And besides, Teresa didn't tell me to fuck around. She told me to open my heart to possibility. Frankly, neither option works for me.

I cross my arms as I push the thoughts away. "You about ready?"

She glances at the mounted clock, then nods. "Give me another fifteen. Lisa will be here then," she adds, referring to another manager. "We've got plenty of time, right?"

"Oh, yeah." My flight isn't until eleven-thirty tonight, and it's barely seven. Kari's driving me to LAX in Maisy, and I'm letting her borrow the car for the three weeks I'll be doing the Manhattan pilgrimage since hers is in the shop.

"Cool." She takes my cookies and hides them away under the counter.

"Hey!"

"Oh, please. You'll get them back. Come on," she adds, coming around the counter and nodding her head for me to follow.

"Where are we—?"

"While you wait, I figured you could plug all the holes." She pushes through the glass door that opens onto a lovely beach-front patio.

"The holes?" I am totally confused. "What are you talking ab—"

I gasp, stopping cold as the far-corner table comes into view.

Maggie. Fucking. Bridge.

She's sitting right there, a yellow pad on the table in front of her and her fancy quill pen between her fingers.

"What?" Kari asks, her brow furrowed as she turns to face

me. "She said there were still some things to cover, and I thought—"

But I'm not listening anymore. Instead, I toss her my keys. She misses, and they clatter onto the wooden decking. Across the patio, Maggie looks up, sees me, and starts to wave. I turn my back on her and head inside.

Kari's right behind me. "What's wrong?"

"That woman is vile," I say. "Why would you set this up? How do you even know her?"

"I don't. I mean, I know she's a reporter, and she said she wanted to get some more details about—"

"I'll catch an Uber."

"What? No. I'm driving you. I just need to finish up, and you can talk with—"

"I'm catching an Uber," I repeat, but my shoulders sag a little despite my fury. "It's not you," I say. "I just need to go. And you can't leave now, so..."

"But—"

I lift my hand. "I'll call you tomorrow. I'll explain." Irritation dances like a snake in my gut because I shouldn't need to explain. She shouldn't be railroading me with reporters. But I know she was just trying to do me a favor, and how's she supposed to know that Maggie is a pain in my ass?

"Okay. If you're sure." Her voice is low. Steady. Like I'm a bomb and any change in tone will set me off.

Who knows? It might.

"I'm sure," I say, then offer her a half-smile. "Can I still have the cookies?"

The relief that spreads over her face is palpable. "Of course. Hang on." She trots back to the counter, then returns with the box. "Try not to eat them all on the way to the airport."

I roll my eyes like she's joking, but she's not. I'm a stress eater, and Kari knows it. And while I'm now certain she didn't do it on purpose, we both know that I'm now totally stressed out.

"I'll save one or two for the plane."

"Out of two dozen? Sounds about right." She grins, then moves in for a hug, which I gratefully return. Yeah, I'd freaked out on her, but I know she didn't mean to throw me under the bus.

"See you in a couple of weeks," I tell her, then hurry out the door, juggling the cookie box in one hand and trying to pull my phone out of my back pocket with the other. Easy enough, but I have to put the box on Maisy's hood in order to find the rideshare app. I put in the order and am relieved to see that the driver's only a couple of minutes away. So I grab my suitcase from the backseat, sling my purse over my arm, and curl my fingers through the very handy handle built into the top of the cookie box.

It takes me no time to cross the lot to where the entrance to the parking area intersects Pacific Coast Highway, so I'm surprised when a car glides to a halt in front of me. The surprise turns almost immediately to fear, though, because in that same instant, I realize that my rideshare driver is in a Toyota. And the cherry red sedan in front of me is a bright and shiny Mercedes.

I take a step back, then another. It's still plenty light outside, but you just never know.

I'm about to turn and hurry back into the cafe when the passenger-side window glides down. "Hey, Bree."

I tremble a little at the familiar voice, half-sure I'm imagining him. It wouldn't be the first time, though my fantasies aren't usually set in parking lots.

"What are you doing?" he asks at the same time that I bend over so I can see into the car.

It's Ash, all right. He has one hand on the wheel as he leans toward me, those wide shoulders seeming to fill the space as his body covers the center console.

"I thought you were heading to the airport."

That's what I'd told him when I'd left the Stark mansion after our interview together.

"I... well, Maisy." I sound like a total dufus, so I cough and try again. "I'm leaving my car with Kari. I'm waiting on my Uber."

"Get in."

I lift my phone. "No, it's ok. It's on the way." I point down PCH. I think that might be him right now."

"Get in," he repeats. "Cancel the ride." He pushes a button and pops the trunk. "I'll give you a hand."

"No, I've got it." The words are out before I even realize that I've decided to take him up on his offer. I'm traveling with only a carry-on, so it's easy to lift into his trunk to set beside his. I start to slide the cookies in, too, then change my mind. Not only might they get squashed if the suitcases slide around, but I want them close in case a cookie emergency should come up.

It could happen.

Soon enough, I'm settled in the passenger seat, the cookies at my feet and my phone in my hand.

"I didn't realize it took so long to cancel a rideshare," he says a few minutes later as we're speeding south toward the airport.

"Oh. I—sorry." I put my phone away, then immediately regret it, because now I have nothing to do with my hands. I drum my fingers on my jeans and sneak a sideways glance. His profile is all hard lines and angles, and sexy as hell, especially in contrast to the way his undoubtedly finger-combed dark hair brushes his forehead and the top of his ears.

From this angle, it's even more obvious how long his lashes are. I'm battling a bit of jealousy, actually, when he turns to look at me, those lashes now framing eyes of Caribbean blue.

I sigh a little, and desperately try to cover it with a cough.

"I have throat lozenges in the glove box," he says, and the words are so casual that I'm positive he knows I don't need a lozenge at all. Of course, I take one. "You?" I ask after I've popped mine in my mouth. Honey lemon. My favorite flavor. Honestly, I could eat lozenges like candy.

"I'm good. Thanks."

"Probably not good payment for the ride, anyway," I say. "After all, you're saving me about fifty dollars. More when you add in the tip. And they're your lozenges."

He turns to look at me again. "Does that mean you don't intend to pay me for services rendered?"

"I—oh." Despite the lozenge, my mouth has gone completely dry, and I squirm in the seat a little, other parts of me going decidedly damp as the first few wisps of a lovely fantasy start to play out in my mind.

Really not the time.

More important, not something I want. Fantasy is one thing —my very active imagination satisfies in more ways than just writing books that pay the bills—but that kind of reality's not part of the How Bree Copes In the World plan.

"Cookies," he says.

I look up at him, thrown by the unexpected word.

"That box at your feet. I've seen it before. That's the box the Upper Crust uses when you buy two dozen cookies." His mouth quirks up. "Sweet tooth?"

"Yes," I admit. "But I didn't buy them. Kari loaded me up. I'm going to share with my parents."

"Too bad for me." He taps the steering wheel and looks straight ahead when he adds, "Then again, absent cookies, I'll have to think of another way to get paid. Cash is so last year."

I fight a laugh. "Would it be terrible of me to admit that I'm now tempted to withhold cookies, just to see what kind of pervy imagination you have?"

His brows rise. "Pervy?"

I shrug, enjoying the game despite myself. "I won't know until I know."

"Be careful what you wish for." He turns just long enough to meet my eyes, and when he does, it's genuine heat I see in his.

My stomach does a little flip, and I manage a weak smile as I force myself not to beg him to let me out so I can call another Uber. What was I thinking? Flirting with Ashton Stone? I am not a woman who lives dangerously, and he's about as dangerous as it gets.

I slouch lower in the seat, then shift so that I'm peering out the window, trying to look like someone enraptured by the cute-but-too-close-together houses that line this part of PCH and the peeks of ocean we get whenever there's a decent-sized gap between them.

"What if I'm just wishing for snickerdoodles?"

I frown as I turn to face him, totally confused. "Snicker-doodles?"

"For payment," he says. "I'm a very big fan of snicker-doodles."

"Oh." I wince a little. "I'm a chocolate chip girl. I haven't looked, but I'd lay money that Kari loaded me up with chocolate chip."

"I'm easy," he says.

I raise a brow. "Yeah, I've heard that."

He laughs, then puts one hand over his heart. "Ouch."

"Hey, you reap what you sow."

"You do," he says, his voice more serious than I'd expected. "You really do."

I clear my throat. "So, cookies?"

"I think the going rate for delivering a beautiful woman to the airport is three chocolate chip cookies."

"Then you get five," I say. "I'm a big believer in tipping well. Even drivers who try to up their tips by tossing out blatantly false flattery."

"Don't even."

"What?"

"Don't even pretend that you don't know how gorgeous you are."

"Ash." I've already slipped out of my sandals, and now I pull my feet up onto the seat and hug my knees.

"I'm just saying...."

"You're just flirting. And I'm not your target audience."

He keeps his eyes on the road, but he tilts his head in the slightest of nods. "Fair enough," he says, and I bite back a sigh of relief. "But if you can't flirt with your friends, who can you flirt with?"

ELEVEN

Four Months Ago—Ash (the airport)

She was, Ash decided, the most frustrating woman he'd ever been attracted to. So frustrating, in fact, that he ought to suck it up, rein in his ego and libido, and settle for being nothing more than her friend. At least that was true. Wasn't it?

He frowned, thinking back. The first time he'd met her at his father's house, they'd tiptoed around each other. Primarily because he'd been an ass then. But as he settled into a relationship with the father he'd come to know, the stepmother he admired, and those siblings he adored—well, he'd also settled into a casual friendship with Bree. She was the kids' nanny, after all. Or, she had been. Now she was both a tenant and the part-time nanny.

Either way, she was a fixture in the household, and the only one close to his age.

Of course, they'd become friends.

And that's how they should remain.

That would be the smart path to follow. And he was a smart man, wasn't he? That's what everyone said, and they'd been saying it his entire life, even in those early days when the fact that he was smart had seemed to turn everyone in his family against him.

And, yeah, he'd been smart enough to dial it down. To keep to himself and not flaunt his grades. To read only when he was alone and undisturbed, and to keep his books in the back of his closet behind his dirty laundry and hidden from Abigail, the great-aunt who'd adopted and purportedly raised him. If put-downs and regular beatings were the way to raise a kid.

He'd gone from being a quiet child who never got in trouble, to being the guy who knew how to draw attention for reasons other than his brains. He'd gotten into sports. Into cars. Anything that let him go fast. Anything that helped him outrun the thoughts that spun in his head like demons, telling him to go faster, faster, faster.

Maybe if he went fast enough he'd outrun the whispers and rumors.

Maybe he'd finally be able to catch up with the secrets that floated on air, but that he could never quite grasp. Secrets about Ashton Stone, whoever the hell that really was.

Maybe if he ran fast enough, he'd finally learn.

That, however, wasn't possible. And the fact that he'd realized as much early on was one of the downsides of being smart.

So, yeah, he had kick ass reasoning skills, a seriously impressive head for science, and a pretty solid grasp on psychology.

Right then, every single synapse of his well-praised mind was telling him that the smart thing to do was to walk away from Bree. To drop her at her terminal, then drive on to the parking area and use the next few months to push her very firmly out of his mind.

That would be the smart thing.

But apparently, he wasn't as smart as his PR suggested. Because instead of dropping her off, he heard himself suggesting that, since they were both early, they could spend the time before their flights in the first class lounge.

"They've got a decent buffet," he added as an extra incentive. "Although I think those cookies would be better than anything they'll be offering for dessert."

"Even without snickerdoodles, you still want to spend time." She pressed a hand over her heart. "I'm honored. Truly. Of course, I'll join you."

"You just don't want to sit in those horrible gate chairs where you have to buy your own coffee."

"Don't be silly," she said as he pulled into the valet parking lot. "I'm not remotely interested in coffee. But I've heard those hoity-toity lounges have an open bar."

Her smile—and her voice—had a flirty lilt that he assumed was unintentional even as he hoped otherwise. A hope for which he then chastised himself. Over the years, he'd spent far too much time casually shaking off the shackles of friendship as she slid into his fantasies.

In reality, though, he'd hold his secret close, and maybe she'd never have to know how twisted he'd been or the horrible things he'd done, because he damn sure wouldn't tell her. He wasn't that man anymore. But he would spend every day for the rest of his life paying penance for all the mistakes the fucked-up version of Ashton Stone had made.

An hour later, they were tucked away in a U-shaped booth where they'd been talking, sipping their drinks, and snacking on a variety of food from the excellent-as-advertised buffet. As predicted, though, the cookies in the box out-did everything the dessert buffet had to offer.

They'd already split a snickerdoodle—a pleasant surprise for both of them when she opened the box and saw that it contained a mix of four flavors: chocolate chip, snickerdoodles, oatmeal raisin, and white chocolate macadamia.

But what really impressed Ash was the fact that Bree tried all four along with him, making her the first woman he'd met in Los Angeles who actually ate dessert. Most declined because they were "too full," or simply pushed it around on the plate, as if that would trick him into thinking she'd both eaten and enjoyed the treat.

Why not just say no? Why the pretense?

Or, better, why not dig in with gusto as Bree had?

He knew it shouldn't bother him, but he'd grown up in a household that spent more time trying to shift reality than living in the moment. It had made him a cynic in things both large and small.

"A Tic Tac for your thoughts."

He looked up at her. "What?"

"I don't have a penny."

"My thoughts aren't worth even that much. I was just thinking about dessert."

"What? My cookies aren't good enough for you?"

"Your cookies are amazing."

"I should hope so. I spent hours not slaving over a hot stove. And as for dessert, I'd split another cookie with you. I was thinking about getting another glass of wine, too. But I probably shouldn't." She checked the time on her phone's lock screen. "I'm boarding soon."

He glanced up at the monitor. "Looks like a lot of flights are starting to get delayed or canceled," he said. She'd been closing the top on the cookie box, but now she twisted to face the screen.

"I'm still okay for now," she said. "Hopefully we'll both get where we're going."

He nodded, pointing at the TV displaying the Weather Channel on another wall. "Those are some nasty storms all through the center of the country. I'm going to Texas.

You're going to New York. The odds aren't good for either of us."

She tilted her head to study the monitor herself, then looked back at him. "I'm going to channel the critically ill eternal optimist that lives deep inside me and say that we're both going to be just fine."

He leaned back in his chair, wondering at her tone. There had been a touch of humor in it, but it was underscored by something he recognized as pain. He didn't know what had happened to her during the kidnapping, but as far as he was concerned, she was more of an optimist after going through such an ordeal than he would ever have been. She was a damn strong woman. And he wasn't sure she realized it.

"—for the lounge."

"I'm sorry. Mind wandering. What?"

She flashed that darling smile of hers. "I said thank you for the lounge, for bringing me in here, I mean. I've never actually flown first class. Well, not since I was a little girl, and they don't serve alcohol to five-year-olds. It was really nice of you to share."

"You're heading out?" He felt like she'd just tossed cold water all over him. "Don't you want to wait to see if we actually have any place to go?"

"Eternal optimist, remember? Or eternal optimist in training," she amended. "I kind of fell off the wagon a few years ago. Pushed off, actually. And I ended up more than a little broken when I hit the ground."

He wanted to pull her close and comfort her. To ward off her memories. But all he did was meet her eyes as he said, "Maybe you did crack to pieces, but you're strong. You're back together now."

"Ash..." She looked down at the dregs of her drink, but she didn't take a sip. After a moment, she stood. "I should get going."

"I'll walk you."

"No, please, I'm fine. You still have more than half your drink left, and I need to hit the ladies' room on the way."

He wanted to kick his own ass. His father had told him she didn't like to talk about the kidnapping—and, really, who would? He should have kept his mouth shut.

He cleared his throat, suddenly feeling awkward in a way he hadn't experienced since high school. "Well, anyway, enjoy spending time with your parents."

"It'll be nice to see them. Mostly, I'm going to do the theater thing." She kept one hand on the handle of her wheeled bag, then slid the other into the pocket of her jeans. "Enjoy Texas."

"Yee-haw."

She rolled her eyes. "Work on that."

"Yeah, well, I'm based in Austin. Very tech-heavy city. And more like LA than cattle country. I'm not sure I'll ever get that twang down."

"But I bet you look good in the hat."

He had to laugh. "Actually, I do."

She grinned. "Has anyone ever accused you of modesty?"

He pretended to think. "Now that you mention it, no." He knew he was stalling and wondered if she was, too.

In time with the thought, he stepped closer and pressed his hand to her cheek. He bent in, then gently kissed her forehead. He felt the tension go through her like a snap, and she stepped back, stumbling against her wheeled bag and knocking it over.

"Bree, shit. I'm sorry."

"No. No. You just—I mean—I wasn't expecting, and—"

"And I was an ass." Shit, she looked like a cornered rabbit. "I'm so sorry. Blame it on the open bar."

"Totally," she's said, the color coming back to her face. "Open bars are such troublemakers. Damn your frequent flyer perks."

He wanted to flog himself, but there was never a whip around when you needed one. "So, we're okay? Because if I—"

"We're fine." Her voice was end-of-discussion firm. "The judges have ruled, and it turns out forehead kisses are not only appropriate but also common among friends. I shouldn't have jumped out of my skin."

He wanted to say something else. Something witty that would erase the awkwardness. "If the judges say so," was the best he could do.

"Totally. Completely by the book." She straightened her bag, then cocked her head. "I'll just, you know, head on out. And, um, I guess I'll see you the next time you're in LA. Thanks again for the lift and the peek into high society. "She reached for his hand, then squeezed it. "Despite the Morning of Maggie, this turned out to be a good day, Ashton Stone. Thanks."

"A very, *very* good day," he agreed.

Then she gave him one final smile before leaving the lounge with her purse and her carry-on.

But she left him the box of cookies.

Four Months Ago—Bree (at the airport)

As far as I'm concerned, rolling suitcases are the greatest invention of all time, far surpassing not only fire (more discovery than invention, but who's counting?) but also waterproof mascara and buy-one-get-one-free sales.

I'm clutching the extended handle of my rolling bag in one hand, my purse is snug on top, and I'm strolling along like I don't have a care in the world.

That, of course, is an illusion. Right now, I'm totally weighed down with care.

And what I'm caring about is Ash.

Caring about. Worrying about.

Thinking about.

Yeah, I'm thinking about him far too much. So much that it had taken all of my willpower to decline his offer to walk with me. Honestly, I'm not sure where that resolve came from. Some reservoir of strength I didn't even know I had, I guess. Because the truth is, sitting there with him in the lounge, sipping our drinks and talking about nothing and everything, was one of the best times I've had in a long time.

I'm not sure if that makes him an interesting raconteur or me a very easy audience. All I know for certain is that I had to get out of there. Because if I hadn't, that silent, throbbing thing growing between us might have ended up going somewhere. And I really don't want it to.

Liar.

Except I'm not. I'm not a liar at all. I don't want his kisses. I don't want his touch. I don't want to close my eyes and feel his fingertips on my naked skin.

I don't... and I do.

But it's *don't* that's going to win. It'll win because it has to.

Thankfully, I've reached my gate, and that puts an end to the Circle of Ash Angst that's going round-and-round in my head. I check the monitor, thrilled to see that we should be boarding in half-an-hour. Then I take a seat and pull out the book I'd grabbed for the trip. I'm two chapters into an Eve Dallas mystery, when I hear the people around me start shuffling and muttering. Since that's never a good sign, I glance up at the monitor, then groan as a voice over the PA announces what I've just learned: the flight's been canceled.

Well, shit.

Like everyone else, I get up and stand in line, hoping that

they'll be able to put me on another flight or at least get me out in the morning.

As a rule, airports are not super fun places for waiting. They're even worse when you're waiting in line. I spend the time bouncing from foot to foot, irritating the people standing near me, and poking around on my phone as I try to find out for myself if there's any other way I can get to Manhattan today.

From what I can see, there's not.

Apparently, I have picked the most popular day in the entire year to travel. Ironic, since there's literally nothing special about today. Except that it's the day I want to travel on.

Two hours and many chapters into my book later, I finally reach the help desk. The woman behind it looks almost as frazzled as I feel, but her smile is genuine. "We're so sorry for the delay. Rest assured that we're going to get everyone to their destinations. Is your final destination New York?"

"Yes," I say. The flight terminates at New York, but it has a stop somewhere in the middle of the country along the way. I don't even remember where.

"Okay. It looks like we can get you on tomorrow's eleven-fifteen flight. Will that work for you?"

It's not ideal, especially when she tells me the arrival time, but since I don't have a choice, I conjure my best smile and tell her that it's just fine and dandy. She looks relieved. I have a feeling I may be the easiest customer she's had all day.

"So, question for you," I begin, then continue when she flashes that perky smile again. "Is there some place to sleep in the airport?"

"We've booked a room for you at one of the nearby hotels. There'll be a shuttle taking you there, and a shuttle picking you up in the morning. It's all in this material," she says, as she bends down, gathers some papers off a printer, and sticks them in a folder. I take it, grateful to have a place to crash. I flip through the pages to make sure everything's there, then give her one final thank you.

And that's that. My luggage and I are on our way to a free night at an airport hotel. Let the good times roll!

By the time I'm on the airport shuttle, I regret my snarky sarcasm. It turns out that waiting around with a billion other people for an airport bus is not jolly good fun. By the time I get to the hotel, get checked in, and get to my room, I don't want to do much more than shower off the LAX grime, then crash on the bed and watch whatever happens to be streaming on the television.

Except, of course, there's nothing decent streaming. They have on-demand shows, but none of them appeal to me, and while I could watch something on my iPad, I can't seem to get motivated.

I'm not a big drinker—my afternoon with Ash notwithstanding—but right now I want to be around other people. Since the entire hotel is probably filled with travelers stranded because of the weather, I decide to go downstairs and have a drink in the lounge with other sympathetic humans nearby. Maybe I'll even grab some nachos. Nachos are messy enough that I rarely eat them, but they sound like the perfect food to pair with the occasion.

Decided, I wrestle a fresh pair of jeans and a faded My Chemical Romance concert tee out of my bag, then head to the door, not even bothering to put on makeup.

Soon enough, I'm sitting at a two-top pretending to check my phone as I scope out the people sitting at the bar. Because *writer*. It's character research.

I see two couples who are clearly traveling together. There are six other women and four other men. The men are hitting on the women. I watch, amused, because it's clear to me that none of those men are going back with any of those women.

And when the waitress brings me my glass of wine, I lift it in a silent toast to the men for at least giving it a try.

I take a sip, feeling a little bit sorry for myself. I won't be going back to the room with anyone either. Then I remind myself why that's a good thing.

A few minutes later, the harried waitress returns, this time with her tablet so that she can take my order. "Just nachos," I say.

"Oh. We don't have nachos." She nods at the menu that's on the table. I hadn't bothered to look at it. What bar doesn't have nachos?

"Just give me a second and I'll pick something else."

"No problem," the girl says. "I'll be right back." But I know she won't be right back, and I start to ask her to wait because I don't want another hour to pass before she comes around again.

But before I can get a word out, a familiar voice from behind me says, "She'll have cheese fries, two orders, and the crispy Brussels sprouts. And a second glass of wine. Plus, a double shot of Macallan 18. One ice cube."

The waitress actually titters as she flashes the kind of gooey smile that I imagine Ash is very familiar with. Then he walks around the table, and when I see the way he's smiling at me, I can't blame her for tittering at all.

"Can I join you?"

"It's a little late for that, especially since I'm making you pay. You ordered a hell of a lot more than I planned to."

"I don't want you going hungry."

I press a hand over my heart. "He cares."

"He does," Ash says, only his voice doesn't have the same goofy quality as mine.

I run my finger over the rim of my wine glass because otherwise I might look up at him. And I really don't want to look up at him. "I assumed you got out okay," I say to my Pinot Noir. "I figured you'd be in the clear heading south-ish."

He pulls out the chair opposite me and sits. Which means I can see most of him whether I want to or not. I take a sip, put down my wine, and give up the charade.

He grins, but whether it's because of my wine machinations or something else, I don't know.

"Apparently the storm is moving like a wall from one side of the country to the other. I was irritated at first. Now I'm kind of happy about it."

I lean back and study him. "Let me guess. You want to add tornado chasing to your repertoire of dangerous hobbies."

The corners of his mouth turn down as he slowly nods. "Interesting. I think I will add that to my list of possibles. Thanks for the suggestion. You'll have to go with me, of course."

"Why's that?"

He leans forward, then puts his hand on mine, his fingers making a V around the stem of my wine glass. "Because I think you'd like it. The speed. The chase. The danger."

I yank my hand back, leaving him with the wine. "You think wrong."

My pulse has kicked up tempo and I tell myself it's a panic attack.

It's *not* a panic attack. Although maybe I am panicking. Just a little.

"My mistake." He flashes that smile again. "I mean, who doesn't love chasing wind tunnels that can lift an entire bus and throw it a mile? I just assumed."

I'm saved from answering by the arrival of our order. But he's redeemed himself with me. A little, anyway.

We chat as we eat, and he scores even more points when he doesn't give me the eye when I polish off most of a basket all by myself. Over the years, I've noticed a horrible trend with LA guys, food, and women. As in, if you eat like you enjoy it, they get a look of fear in their eyes. One background actor I was set up with actually told me that if I wasn't careful, I'd "balloon" from a six to a twelve by the end of the date.

I told him I was an eight, and that pretty much ended our relationship right there. If I were to track down his Tinder profile—because I'm sure he has one—he probably only dates twos and fours.

All of which is to say that Ash seems entirely non-plussed by my appetite—which is only partially driven by my stress-eating tendencies. Mostly, I'm just having a good time. That, and the fact that I really like his food selection.

We don't talk much—it's been a long day for both of us. When he smiles, I smile back, but I'm not big on flirting, so I don't try. It's not necessary, anyway, because Ash is easy to talk to even though today is the first time we've had an extended conversation.

We've seen each other on and off for the last few years, but our verbal exchanges at the Stark home mostly consisted of me telling him how to work the espresso maker or asking him to watch the kids while I took a phone call. Nothing special. Not that someone could see, anyway.

But there was something underneath. At least, there was for me. And I liked to think there was for him, too. I especially liked to think that at night, when I couldn't sleep and would pass the time imagining that he'd slipped into the guest house. And then into my bed. He'd touch me in a way that kept the nightmares at bay, and I'd break apart under his touch before sliding into a blissful sleep, secure in the knowledge that nothing could hurt me in the strong, safe circle of his arms.

And now, as we sit here with each other chatting away like old friends, I force myself not to think about that familiar fantasy.

Instead, I tell myself that I'd been right about the bigger picture. That we got along. That he was easy to talk to. And not in an icky sycophantic way, but in a click sort of way. As in *we click*.

It'd felt the same earlier today in the lounge, too. But now is the icing on the cake, because I feel as comfortable with him as I do with Aria.

She just fits. And so does Ash.

And two hours, two drinks, and a shared brownie sundae later, my assessment stands: Ashton Stone is great company.

"So what time is your flight tomorrow?"

I jump. "Sorry, mind wandering. What?"

"Tomorrow. When do you leave? Crack of dawn?"

I shake my head. "I have to be at the gate at ten-forty-five. So it's not bad at all. Apparently, the shuttles run every 15 minutes, so it should be easy enough to get back. You?"

"Eleven-fifteen."

I nod. "Nice not to have to get up with the sun," I say. "Especially since it's been a long day. A long day with alcohol," I add.

I see the way he's looking at me, his head slightly tilted. A slow smile tugging at the corner of his mouth. My mouth is suddenly dry, and I take a sip of wine before saying, "I should probably get some sleep."

"Probably," he says, his finger tapping on his second whiskey glass as he continues to look at me. "Or you could be bold and stay up a while longer."

His voice flows over me like warm honey.

"Oh." Once again, I lift my glass, only to find it empty. "Um, do you want to order something else?"

"Actually, yeah. How about ordering a movie?"

"A movie?" I consider that, not sure if it's relief or disappointment I'm feeling.

"I've got a suite with an insane entertainment system plus a wet bar. Seems a shame not to use it."

"You have a wet bar in your room? Then why are you down here?"

He finishes off the last of his drink, his eyes never leaving my face. "Full disclosure?"

I hesitate, then nod.

"I saw that the planes to New York were grounded. I thought you might be down here."

"Oh." I'm flattered. And in the kind of way that makes my skin tingle. "You have my number. You could have just called."

"Ah, but that's not a meet cute."

I laugh at his deadpan expression. "And cheese fries are?"

"Number one ranked meet cute according to IMDB. Trust me on that. So, movie?"

I'm biting back laughter even as I duck my head so he can't see my eyes. Going to his room would be a bad idea. A very bad idea.

I draw a breath and force myself to look at him, fully intending to decline. What comes out is, "A movie sounds great."

His grin broadens as he pulls out his wallet and puts two hundred-dollar bills on the table. "I don't feel like waiting for the check. I think that should cover it."

"Either airport drinks are insanely expensive, or you're an incredible tipper."

"Go with whichever makes me seem more interesting."

"Done," I say, then laugh when he twirls his hand in a *tell me* gesture. "No way," I say. "I keep my assessments to myself." I give him my best smile. "Wouldn't want you to get an inflated ego."

"It's too late for that," he says as he stands. "Shall we?"

"Sure. But I need to run by my room first." I have no idea

what prompts me to say that. Except that I need a minute by myself. To settle this strange, rumbling feeling in my gut.

"All right. Let's go."

I shake my head. "Just give me your room number. I won't be long."

"I'll do better than that." He pulls the hotel's little paper key holder from his pocket and tugs out one of the two keys. Then he eases over to the empty table beside us and takes the Sharpie off the bill tray that the waitress had left. He writes his room number on the card, blows on it so the ink won't smear, then hands it to me.

"Perfect," I say.

"Don't take too long. I'm going to order wine and popcorn."

"Hotels deliver popcorn?"

"They better. Or I'll be having harsh words with the management."

A laugh bubbles out of me and I'm struck by how easy it is to be with this man. More than that, I see a little bit of his dad in him. A man used to getting what he wants because he has the personality and the means to make it happen.

Right now, he wants popcorn and a movie with me.

And damned if that isn't exciting... and downright terrifying.

TWELVE

I look down at the room key in my hand.

A simple hotel card key, but there's nothing simple about the room number scribbled on it.

I want to go. Right then, I think I want to go to that room more than I've ever wanted anything in my life. So much I can feel my feet starting to lead me in that direction. But I have to slow down. I need to stop and think. Because right now is not the time to be stupid.

So that's what I do. I stop dead in the middle of the lobby, ignoring the curses from other waylaid travelers forced to go around me. Then I let my eyes roam up and down the huge lobby, taking in all the other passengers who've been shuttled here. Some in family groups. Most alone. Like me.

Except I don't have to be alone.

Lightning flashes outside the windows, a rare sight in Los Angeles, and I watch in awe as the sky glows and the walls rumble. It's fabulous and beautiful and strange. And I don't want to be alone. Or maybe that's just an excuse.

I don't know. All I know is that I want what this card key can give me.

I want. And I hate myself for it.

My self-loathing isn't strong enough to stop me, however. There's something about him that pulls me in. That makes me *need*.

Without even realizing I've made a decision, I hurry forward, and the crowd parts for me like the Red Sea, as if everybody in this hotel knows that I have somewhere to be, and that I need to get there before I lose my nerve.

As I approach the elevator, I look at the key again, surprised to see that the number is still there. Why hasn't it disappeared? Why hasn't everything gone wrong? How is it that this weird, strange day could have turned out so right, and now I'm walking into the promise of something even better?

Ashton Stone.

Something like panic washes over me, leaving my skin feeling prickly and strange. I think that I should stop this nonsense. That I should turn around. But I don't. Instead, I mentally flip my panic the bird, then step into the elevator.

I watch, feeling removed from myself, as my finger rises and stabs the button for the fourteenth floor. Then I look around.

I frown.

When I'd stepped into this small box, I'd thought it was empty. Now it's crowded, and I shake my head at how lost I must have been in my thoughts. I squeeze into the corner, realizing that I'm the only single person here. Everyone else is coupled up, arms around each other. Some look frustrated. Others look happy to have this unexpected break in their travel.

All are looking at me.

I see approval in some eyes. I see contempt in others. I realize I don't care. I want what I want. And what I want is Ash.

I'm hyper-aware of my own body as I step out of the elevator on fourteen. Immediately, I lose my nerve, and I turn around to slide back into the elevator. But it's gone. Not just closed, but gone. I shake my head, realizing I've already walked down the hallway toward Ash's room.

Clearly, I should have stuck with Diet Coke.

I keep walking, looking for the number that is scribbled on the key: 1451. I walk the perimeter three times, but never find it. How the hell is that possible?

I start to worry that this is all a joke. That Ash wrote down the wrong number. That he doesn't really want me there at all.

As soon as the thought enters my head, I'm sure it's true. Tears well in my eyes, and I'm so certain of his duplicity, I start to run. Start to bolt back to the elevator. I can see it in the distance, only it seems to get farther and farther away with every step I take. I struggle on, though, and just as I'm about to reach out and punch the button, I hear my name.

Him. Not ten feet away and standing on the threshold of room 1451.

He holds out his hand, and I go to him.

"You look spooked? Are you okay?"

"I—I think I drank too much. I'm feeling a little off."

"Come on in," he says, urging me inside. Then he shuts the door and puts his hands on my shoulders as he studies my face. "You look fine," he says. Then he leans forward and gently kisses my forehead.

I feel my body stiffen. I know why I came here. I know what I want. Sex has been so hard for me since the kidnapping. As in, I haven't quite managed to even get that far.

With Ash, though... well, I'd come thinking it would be easier with him. But I hadn't expected this. True gentleness. Genuine caring.

I don't know what I'd thought he'd be like. A dream, maybe. Something I'd walk away from and never be sure it was real. And the not knowing would make it be safe.

I can handle fantasy. It's reality that twists me up.

But that single kiss on my forehead feels real, and now I don't know what to do.

"Hey," he says, using the pad of his thumb to brush away a tear. "What is it?"

"I didn't expect this," I admit, shocked I can tell him even that much.

He takes me by the hand and leads me to the couch. We sit, and he draws me in close. "Expect what?"

"You. I never expected you in my life. I never expected you to be like this."

"What's this?" he asks.

"You know."

"Yes," he says, simply. "I do."

And then I'm in his arms. His mouth is on mine, his hands on my shoulders, then sliding down so his thumbs can stroke my breasts.

Now we're in bed, and I'm naked, and I don't even remember getting here, which makes me sad, because I do not want to forget a single moment of this. He is everything I've wanted since the first moment I saw him, and I never even knew it.

How can I have been so aware of this man for so long, but every time I thought too hard about him, I talked myself out of it?

It's a stupid question. Because I know exactly how I kept that distance. And I know why, too.

The thoughts have opened a door, and dark wisps like demon fingers slip into my mind, whispering... whispering.

I try to block the voice. I don't want it in my head. All I want is Ash. The way his body feels. The way he's touching me.

I roll over, using my hands to push his shoulders back as I straddle him. "Please," I say, "please, please just make me forget."

His brow furrows, full of gentleness and concern. "Forget? Forget what?"

"Everything," I say. "Everything but you."

He doesn't smile, but the heat in his eyes says it all. He reaches up and cups the back of my head. Then pulls me down into a kiss that is so deep and so passionate that it's practically a substitute for sex.

His hands roam over me, firing every cell in my body. I'm on my back looking up at him and drowning in the ocean of his eyes. The corner of his mouth twitches, not in humor, but as a promise of what's to come.

Then he's kissing me, his body hard against mine, his hands on my wrists holding my arms wide, his tongue teasing and taking as he explores my mouth.

He's naked now, too, though I don't remember him undressing, and he breaks the kiss long enough to pull back and look at me before he starts to move down my body, painting my skin with a trail of kisses.

Lower and lower. His hands teasing my nipples as his tongue laves my clit, his mouth working a magic that has me grinding against him as I fist my hands in his hair and silently beg for more.

Then his hands are on my hips, and I'm lost in the wildness of his ministrations. His mouth. His tongue. His fingers moving from my hip to my core.

"Yes," I whisper. "More," I beg. I'm close, so close, and those red-hot coils of passion tighten inside me like a spring ready to explode. I've never in my life been so turned on, so aware of a man. Never so desperate for a touch.

Never so raw and uninhibited between the sheets.

He's done something to me. He's fixed me somehow. And I have to tell him so. He has to understand how important he is to me.

I open my eyes, needing him to feel, see, and hear the connection when I tell him how much this night means to me.

Then he lifts his head, his mouth leaving my pussy, his lips still wet with my desire.

And that's when I see it. See *him*.

Rory.

Right there between my legs.

I'm not in bed with Ash at all. I'm in bed with Rory.

I'm in bed with the monster.

THIRTEEN

Cold panic crashes against me, and I yank my legs up as I scramble backward until I'm scrunched against the headboard. But he's still there, his lips glistening in some sick perversion of satisfaction, and all I can do is scream and scream and scream until Rory disappears.

Until the hotel room disappears.

Until the entire world seems to disappear around me, shifting and changing until Rory is only a shadow haunting me from the grave.

But I don't stop. I keep screaming until my throat aches, until my head feels like it will explode.

Panic rises like bile. I don't know how to stop. I don't know how to make it stop!

Bree! Bree!

I feel hands on my shoulders shaking me. Another shake, then another.

Bree! Bree! Bree!

Nothing gets through until I feel a sharp sting across my cheek. Then I fall back, my skull slamming against the headboard. I cry out, then look around, trying to make sense of what's happening.

Aria is right there. Sitting close, but not touching me. "You're okay," she says. "It's me. It's Aria. You had a bad dream."

And just like that, I'm in my bed. My familiar, comfortable bed. I'm in Burbank, not an airport hotel. The storm and the airport hotel happened four months ago.

I never went to Ash's room. I'd chickened out, and I didn't see him again after he gave me his key. Not until he showed up beside my car window yesterday.

And Rory...I shudder as I look down at the tangle of sheets that have trapped me. Rory was—and is—long dead.

"It was him," I tell Aria, my voice gasping. "It was Rory. It started out as Ash, but then it was Rory."

"Shh. Hush. It's okay. It was just a bad dream."

I want to argue. To say it was more than a dream. It was need and want and passion.

And, oh, how I'd liked it. I'd wanted it. I'd so desperately wanted it.

I want to say all that, but I'm ashamed. Because it was Rory touching me. Rory turning me on. It was him, not Ash. Not the man I'd believed was touching me.

"Hey, hey. It's okay," Aria continues as I try to breathe through my gasping sobs. "It's just a dream."

Except it's not just a dream, and I can't tell her the truth. It was Rory. My ex. My kidnapper. It was him.

And I liked it.

Worse, it's not the first time.

After the kidnapping, my mind had been filled with nightmares of Rory touching me. So many nightmares that I'd finally worked up the courage to tell my therapist. Teresa had told me it was normal. That it was my mind working through fear and grief. My fear of getting close to someone warring with my desire for physical comfort.

Maybe she's right. Maybe it is normal. But now I can't help but wonder if my subconscious equates Rory with Ash. If deep down I know that Ash is just as dangerous as Rory, and by asking for his help, I'm walking straight into the lion's den.

Beside me, Aria strokes my hair the way our moms used to. "Rory is dead. He's not here. He'll never, ever hurt you again."

I take a deep breath, then another. "Ash," I finally manage to say. "He was Ash. And then he turned into Rory."

"You were dreaming about Ash?"

I nod, then scrub my hands over my face. "I'll be right back."

She tugs on my fingers, keeping me from walking away after I've swung off the bed. "Where are you going?"

"To the bathroom. I want to splash some water on my face."

I can tell she doesn't want to leave me alone even for that, but finally she nods. "I'll make you some cocoa," she says. "Meet me in the kitchen?" She looks me up and down as if she's afraid I'm going to flush myself down the toilet to escape. But I'm back now. I'm myself again. At least, I think I am.

"Really. I'm fine. Just a little shaken. I'll be okay."

She hesitates a moment longer, then releases my hand. She follows me to the bathroom, and I think I'm going to have to push her away to keep her from coming in. But when I step over the threshold, she hesitates only a moment before continuing to the kitchen.

I sigh, then close the door. I stare at myself in the mirror, wondering who I am. It's not the first time I've wondered that since the kidnapping. I don't know why, but I haven't quite felt like me since it happened. Teresa said it was because I'd been stripped of my autonomy. That I didn't have any will of my own, and even though it wasn't a long kidnapping, it still messed with my head.

She prescribed time and therapy, and the truth is that I am better. Not perfect, but better. I know my triggers. I understand what to avoid.

I should have avoided Ash.

Of course, the fact that some maniac is harassing me about the kidnapping and gaslighting me with video from those horrible days, could have something to do with it. But that's not what I want to think about, even though I know that I should.

I look at my reflection one more time. "It's not going away," I tell myself. "You know that. You have to think about it. You have to do something about it. And you need to ask Ash for the money."

That's the kicker, isn't it? That the only person who can help me is a man I don't really know. A man I'm wildly attracted to. A man I stood up. A man who just today told me flat out that he wants me even though for months I'd been sure that he hated me.

And why wouldn't he after the way I ghosted him at the hotel?

Except none of that matters because he's also a man who will give me the money. I'm certain of that. But I'm equally certain that he'll want something in return. And whatever it is, I'll have no choice but to agree.

Since that's not something I want to think about right now, I splash water on my face, ignore the fact that I've drenched the front of my sleep shirt, then pad barefoot to the kitchen where Aria's made cocoa for both of us.

She's perched on one of the stools that sit at our passthrough bar. Or what will be a bar after I finish studying YouTube videos to figure out how to finalize the wooden frame of this project that was abandoned by the previous owners.

After that I'm going to have to figure out how to tile the whole thing.

Right now, that's really not high on my to-do list.

Aria takes another bite of her bagel as I take my first life-giving sip of cocoa, then put a bagel in the toaster for myself. As the bagel heats, I gulp down a bit more of the warm treat, then top off my mug with what's left in the saucepan.

Aria watches me silently through the ritual. She knows me well enough to wait until I've had a few sips before engaging in any social niceties.

"You're talking to Ash today?" she asks as I rummage in the fridge for the cream cheese. "Also, I had the last of it."

I poke my head out. "Seriously?"

"There was barely a tablespoon left. I'll make a grocery run later. Have butter or jam and don't change the subject."

"Fine." I pull out the tub of margarine and a jar of strawberry jam.

"Bree..."

"He's crashing my interview. Of course, I'm talking to him."

She cocks her head. "I mean about the money."

"I know what you mean."

She looks at me.

I don't answer.

"Fine. Whatever. But if you don't ask him, you better have a Plan B in place. Can you talk to your parents?"

I gape at her, my bagel only an inch from my mouth. "Are you nuts? You know they don't have that kind of cash."

"They could get it."

I grimace. She's right. My parents aren't cash-rich, but they do have a ton of equity in a very snazzy Manhattan brownstone which has been updated to the hilt. It's worth a fortune... but it's also my parents' only asset. No way am I asking them to take out a loan. They'd do it—they'd justify it by saying that one day it will be mine—but I can't ask.

"I'm not going to ask them," I say. "Even if I wanted to let them know about all this shit, you know I can't ask them. They need that money."

"Hopefully not," she says, her voice gentle.

I stare into my mug and shrug. My dad's been showing signs of Alzheimer's. It's not bad yet, and the doctors are optimistic. But if he needs special care, that equity is what will pay for it. And even if it weren't a health issue, I want my parents to be comfortable in their old age. And that equity is the bulk of their retirement.

That's not all of it, though. As important as it is to me that my parents are comfortable as they grow older, it's even more important to me that they never learn the truth. They know I was kidnapped. Hell, the whole world knows that, though it's the Stark name that really gets the attention, leaving me—thankfully—in semi-anonymity.

But they don't know about the rest of it. The touching. The drugging. The things on that tape. Things I've been dreaming. The dreams that I now think are memories.

"You should talk to them," Aria says when I remind her of that. "They love you. They won't judge you. And you quit talking to Teresa. You have to talk to someone."

"I talk to you," I say, ignoring the elephant in the room. The one that's painted with Aria's mantra that I should go back to weekly therapy. But I don't want to. Teresa's on my speed dial for emergencies only now, and she'd agreed that if I was comfortable with that, it was a good step.

My bestie isn't so sure.

"Talking to me is great," Aria says. "You know I'll always be here for you. But I'm not a shrink."

"Neither are my parents. And I don't want to tell them. It

was hard enough telling you. And there is no way on earth I would ever ask them for money without giving them a reason."

"Say you're starting a business."

"Dammit, Aria!"

"Fine. Sorry. I get it." She puts her mug down and sighs. "They probably couldn't help, anyway. I mean, the money's in the real estate, not a safe. They'd have to get an equity loan, and that takes time."

"Yes," I say, relieved she's taking my parents out of the equation.

"But that leaves you with only one option."

Ash.

Neither of us say his name, but I can see it hanging mid-air between us in a crazy neon font, like the focal point of some thirty-second ad spot for a really crappy new soft drink.

I sigh. "I'll ask him for the money," I tell her. "Just as soon as I figure out how I'm going to bring it up."

I look up from my bagel to see her frowning. "Oh, what now? You're the one who just said he's the only option."

"I didn't actually say—"

"And the clock starts running in less than an hour," I add, cold fear rushing through me with that pronouncement. "Noon, remember?"

"Of course, I remember," she says, as I look pointedly at the clock mounted on the wall in the kitchen. *Eleven-fifteen.*

Seventy-two hours and forty-five minutes.

That's all the time I have to gather three million dollars.

I look to Aria with panic. "What am I going to do if he says no? I can't raise three mil by myself. It's impossible. It's—"

"He won't say no." Her words are firm. As if she's giving an order to the world.

It's ridiculous— Aria has no more insight or power than I have—but her certainty calms me.

"You'll talk to him after the interview," she says firmly. "You'll commiserate about what a bitch Maggie is, and you'll ask him for this one teensy favor. Then it's like we already said—if he's innocent, he'll help you out because that's who he is. If he's guilty, he'll help to hide his guilt and keep you close so he can watch you squirm." She shrugs. "Either way, you'll have the money."

Somehow, that doesn't make me feel better.

FOURTEEN

As soon as I pull into the lot at Upper Crust, I see the red Mercedes. The same one in which he'd driven me to the airport four months earlier.

Ash.

I close my eyes and breathe, trying to extinguish that spark of fear that has risen inside me.

It could be him. Ashton Stone really could be my blackmailer.

I don't want to believe it, but I have to at least consider it. I can't trust my own judgment. I know that. Wasn't Rory proof enough that I'm a fool where men are concerned? And Ash sent a text this morning saying he wants to talk to me after the interview. Why? To harangue me for bailing on him back at the airport? To suss out whether I've figured out that he's my tormentor? To apologize for freaking me out at the coffee shop? For some other reason I can't even imagine yet?

I don't know. All I know is that I'm dreading being alone with him. Dreading asking him for money. And at the same time, I'm secretly, ridiculously happy that he's going to be beside me when Maggie Bridge starts in on my life.

Am I a mess or what?

"I know you don't like Maggie," Kari says when I pause at the walk-up counter to order a latte and a cinnamon roll. "But I can't wait for her article to come out. Your book sales are going to skyrocket."

I grimace. "You really think so?" Skyrocketing sales sounds great. A debt owed to Maggie does not.

"Hell, yes. Her column is syndicated. It's going to be printed all over the country. Maybe in Europe, too."

Her enthusiasm is infectious, and I decide to treat Maggie like the Bad Thing you take with the Good Stuff. You may have a broken ankle, but that means you can justify sluffing off and bingeing *Real Housewives of Outer Space*. Or whatever.

"Anyway, thanks for being excited for me."

Kari scoffs. "Are you kidding. Actors come to Upper Crust every freaking day. You're my first author. And, *bonus*," she adds with a perky air punch, "you're already my friend."

"I can't possibly be the first author to grab a muffin and a latte here."

She shrugs. "First I know of."

I nod sagely. "That makes sense. We authors hide under a cloak of anonymity."

"Huh?"

"No one recognizes us because we're not slathered all over screens and billboards," I say. "It's not like people pay attention to the tiny headshot on the book flap.

"You're right. I wonder why?"

I roll my eyes. Sometimes Kari can be a little clueless. "Wish me luck," I say, but before I can walk away from the counter, she grabs my hand.

When I turn back to look at her, she meets my eyes, her expression serious as she intones, "May the waters be calm and the skies always clear."

I press my free hand over my heart, genuinely moved. That's the motto of Bethany's family, and the last words she said before Ace headed off into battle and the book ended in a cliffhanger.

Even though my goal is Maggie Bridge, I'm smiling as I head toward the back of the cafe. Kari and I became friends simply because I'd spent so much time at the cafe. But when I gave her an early draft of the book to read, our friendship kicked up a notch on both sides. The bonus is that not only does she love my work, but she also gives great story feedback, and the fact that she memorized the quote makes my morning. I love those words, and my publisher even printed them on the back of the book, right under my author photo.

And how weird is that? Having my picture on a book is—

I stumble as the prattle in my brain slams up against the reality I'm trying to forget. My image. My picture. My secrets.

Caught on tape in the most horrible way.

Oh god oh god oh god.

Suddenly my heart pounds in my chest. Sweat trickles from under my arms down my sides. I stand frozen in place, trying to remember how to Just. Breathe. Normally.

It's harder than it sounds, especially since this came out of nowhere, and I am about to have a full-blown panic attack right here on the Upper Crust patio surrounded by the morning coffee crowd. *Fuck, fuck, fuck.*

Once again, I tell myself to just breathe, but it's hard to hear with the *fuck* mantra slamming through my head. Then I jump when reality breaks through in the form of a hand at my elbow.

"Hey, hey." The voice is calm. Soothing. "It's me."

I close my eyes as Ash makes a second attempt to take my elbow. This time, I don't freak out. "Are you okay?"

I take one breath, then another. Then I look around. No one

is staring at me. As far as I can tell, no one other than Ash even notices me.

I tilt my head and see the furrow in his brow. The worry behind his eyes. "Bree?"

I swallow. "I'm fine. I just—I was thinking about a character. I got lost. In the plot. You know."

"Sure. Happens to me all the time. Only I'm thinking about a car or an engine. And there is no plot. Otherwise, totally the same."

I hear the humor in his voice and meet his smile, grateful he hadn't called me out. Maybe he has no idea that I'd frozen, but I doubt it. There's not much that man misses.

I'm standing there grappling for something to say when another voice that is far too perky blasts into the moment. "You-hoo!"

I glance over to see Maggie Bridge wiggling her fingers at us from across the patio. A familiar looking blond guy in an Upper Crust tee is standing behind her, leaning over to point to something on the menu.

I want to melt on the spot, and I look up at Ash. "She saw my freak out, too, didn't she?"

"Just tell her you didn't eat breakfast and got light-headed." His eyes are hard on mine. "Don't try the character story on her. She won't buy it. And you can tell me what really spooked you when we talk later."

I nod. He's right about Maggie. And as for that last bit... I'm not sure if he's talking about what spooked me just now... or four months ago when I ghosted him at the airport hotel.

I shove the question aside for later. Right now, I have to deal with Maggie. And that's more than enough to take on.

Once again, I'm overwhelmed with regret that I didn't call and cancel. But my publisher had been so thrilled when Evelyn set this up, that I couldn't bring myself to do it.

And the truth is that an interview with Maggie really will be good for the book. As much as I hate to toss her kudos, Maggie's influence really has helped kick some books higher on bestseller lists and even get picked for celebrity book clubs and other cool things.

And as awkward as it is to be around Ash after totally ghosting him four months ago, his presence gives me a shot of courage. Besides, as much as it pains me to admit it, I need him. Somehow, someway, I'm going to muster up the courage to ask him for a boatload of money.

Bottom line? I can do this thing. Hell, I can do all the things.

"Darlings!" Maggie calls, as the blond guy passes us with a bus tub filled with dishes.

Martin, I think, then congratulate myself on remembering his name. I'll have to ask Kari if they're still—wink, wink, nudge, nudge—working hard together.

"Look at you both," Maggie squeaks. "I'm so excited that I'm getting two for the price of one!"

She stands up, arms out and ready to take me in. I parry, then take the chair across from her. The table is square, but Ash doesn't take a side for himself. Instead, he scoots his chair around and settles in beside me. I tell myself I should be annoyed that he's invading my personal space. In truth, I appreciate the solidarity and wish he'd take my hand under the table, too.

Maggie flashes an overly white smile. Everything about her is just a bit too much. Her hair is one shade too dark for her complexion. Her eyebrows too thin for her face. Her lips too plumped. And the overall effect is that she looks just as fake as she is.

I suppose that's appropriate.

"Look at you two." She releases a dreamy sigh. "Do I hear the tweet of lovebirds."

"No," I say scooting my chair away from Ash. He does the opposite and twines his fingers through mine. I scowl, trying to ignore the fact that two seconds ago I'd wanted him to do that very thing.

But then he sets our joined hands on the table as if he's presenting a prize to Maggie. I grimace, fighting the urge to stomp on his foot or elbow him in the ribs.

"Come on, Maggie," he says. "You know better than to ask that. Some things should stay off the record."

I pin him with The Gaze of Fire, but the bastard just chuckles.

"I've gotten used to the spotlight," he says, his knee nudging mine under the table. "Bree hasn't."

Maggie's already squinty eyes narrow even more, as if she's not sure if she should be buying any of this. I know exactly how she feels.

Finally, she grants us a slow smile. "Well, she'll have to get used to being the center of attention." She turns those beady eyes to me. "Sorry, dear. But I don't think your man here could stay out of the spotlight if he tried. It's in his blood."

"We're not an item," I say, because what the hell does Ash think he's doing, other than yanking Maggie's string? Which, now that I think about it, is something I wholeheartedly approve of.

Ash shakes his head. "That's her way of making sure you're not going to print anything earlier than we're ready to announce it."

I stomp on his foot. He barely winces, and I wish that I'd worn heels.

"I'm a professional, Ashton. You know that. And I'm honored you both trust me to not only share your stories with the public, but to act as guardian over what you don't yet want to be public."

She aims that obnoxious smile at both of us in turn. I conjure all my willpower and manage not to vomit.

"We'll just make this more of a conversation than a formal interview. In the end that's always more fun for readers anyway don't you think?"

"Absolutely," Ash says.

I smile, but I think it may come across more like the baring of teeth.

She makes a show of starting the recoding app on her phone, then leans back with a pen in her hand. A yellow pad is already on the table. Even upside down I can see the little flowers she's drawn in the margin.

"Usually, I'd say ladies first, but Ash, I'm dying to hear about the INX-20. What can you tell me?"

Ash sits up straighter, and this time it's true passion driving his words. "As most people in the industry know, I've been working on a motor that runs on atmospheric energy. It's revolutionary technology, but my team has made amazing progress. The INX-20 is the first incarnation of the motor that we'll actually be installing in test vehicles."

He goes on to describe a motor that sounds like something from a Sci-Fi novel, and each word is infused with pride in himself and his team. Honestly, I'm pretty damn impressed, too.

"We've surprised a lot of people," he continues, turning slightly sideways to look at me. "It'll be several more years before we can actually go to market, but once we get it dialed in, this engine will have a serious kick. You'll look at it and think there's nothing there. Too small. Too mundane. Whatever. Then you realize that it's got punch. That there's so much more under the surface."

He squeezes my hand as he speaks, then meets my eyes. "It'll take you wherever you want to go."

"What lovely words," Maggie says, and I sag a little when he breaks eye contact to look at her. She turns her attention to me. "And what do you think of this new engine, Bree? Are you proud of your man?"

"Last I checked, I didn't own him."

Maggie laughs. "Atta girl."

I seriously want to punch her. Even more so when she asks, "So you're unimpressed?"

"Are you kidding? How could I be unimpressed with an achievement like that? Ash is a lot of things, and I'd say impressive tops the list."

I meet Ash's gaze. Nothing in the interview so far is bad. But I know Maggie better than to think the article will be good. He lifts a shoulder, which I interpret as *wait and see*.

Maggie leans forward. "Runs a bit in the family, don't you think?" Her voice is low, as if we're two girls out for drinks and gossip. "Impressive men, I mean."

"I suppose so," I say, though I'm sure she'll twist my words.

"There's been a lot of scandal in Damien Stark's past," she says, starting right in on that twisting. "Not long before Nikki Fairchild rolled into town, there were rumors that he killed an ex-girlfriend."

I stiffen with anger on Damien's behalf. "Wasn't he totally exonerated for that?" I'd read the story when it came out, long before I worked for him. A horrible hit piece and none of it turned out to be true. I frown, wondering if Maggie wrote that article.

"I'm not suggesting we adjudicate the case." She practically *tut tuts* her words. "I'm simply pointing out the father/son similarities."

She looks at me while she speaks. I'm sure I look as clueless as I feel.

"Oh, I see. I just assumed you were aware." She bends toward me and lowers her voice to a dramatic whisper. "His former girlfriend. Delia Cornwell." Then she straightens before turning to Ashton, her tone turning blasè. "What were you dear? A grad student? And such a reputation for being a rebel. He had bit of a temper then, too," she adds, her attention turning back to me. "And a girlfriend who ended up dead. A fall, wasn't it? Did they ever determine if it was suicide or murder?"

When she finally shuts up, she's staring right at Ash, who's staring right back. I have no idea what happened with his girlfriend, but based on what I know about Maggie, I'm positive Ash didn't harm her.

"I'm here to talk about the INX-20," Ash says. "Not about my past or my family."

"I understand." She looks between the two of us. "I'll keep all of that as secret as your relationship."

Ash clutches my arm, and I know it's not to keep me silent, but as a crutch to tamp his own rising temper. "We're here to talk about the motor and Bree's book. Get back on target, Maggie, or we're done."

"I find interviews go better if we let the conversation flow," she says.

I can tell Ash wants to say something else, but she turns her attention to me. "It must be very exciting to have your first book receiving so much critical acclaim."

"It is," I say, grateful that we've moved to the safer realm of fiction. "Writing is so solitary, and most people don't realize how much that old saying is true."

"What saying is that?" she asks.

"That writing is easy. You just open a vein and bleed."

She nods, as if I've just said something brilliant when in fact, I've only ripped off someone else's wit.

"What I mean is that it's hard and it's personal. So, the praise and accolades feel especially good. They're validating."

"You're saying a good story has to come from the heart? You have to be able to empathize with the characters? To share their blood, as it were?"

I think about her question, searching for little hidden Maggie bombs. Since it seems innocuous enough, I nod. "Right. It's a lot like acting, I think."

She leans forward in that way she has, and I feel a tug of dread in the instant before she asks," So how much of your experience as a kidnap victim did you draw on in *Reveries at Dusk*? And the love interests? Ace and Dirk? I'm sure I'm not the only reader wondering if one or both of them weren't based on real people."

As she asks, her gaze shifts to Ash. I freeze, but my cheeks heat, and I very much want to crawl under the table.

"Maggie," Ash says, his voice as sharp as a blade.

I put my hand on his. "It's okay," I say, though I'm kicking myself for accidentally opening this door. But since I did, I have no choice but to walk through it. "Obviously, I was kidnapped. That experience helped me to write the scenes in which Bethany was taken by the Dragon Riders. But that doesn't make the book about me. Every writer draws on the real world. That doesn't make it non-fiction, much less an autobiography."

"Hmm," she says, and I have a feeling she's disappointed that she didn't get more of a rise out of me. I glance sideways at Ash, barely managing to fight a very smug smile.

"Those Dragon Riders you created are an interesting cabal. I applaud you for including a few women, but the men..." She trails off, fanning herself with the menu. "So virile. So domineering. Was that something that appealed to you before the kidnapping, or did being held —"

"Goddammit, Maggie." The fire in his voice could melt stone. As for me, I've gone completely cold.

"I'm so sorry, dear," she says as I remain frozen. "I'm not

trying to dredge things up. I just find those characters fascinating and you wrote Bethany with such beautiful longing and intensity, that—"

Tension seems to flow off Ash in waves. "Just move on... or we will."

Her mouth screws up with frustration. Right then, I could have kissed Ash.

"Let's talk about Ace," she continues. "He was the most powerful of the riders. A risk taker. And my goodness, those love scenes were hot. Were they modeled after anyone in particular?" Her voice is so sugary sweet I expect her to bat her eyes.

I keep my own eyes firmly on hers, but I can practically feel the heat of Ash's body beside mine. "No," I say flatly. "No one in particular."

"I've written a little fiction. It must have been difficult to dredge up those emotions."

Beside me, Ash tenses. I put my hand on his knee to still him. I can handle this.

"It's fiction. And as I tried to explain earlier, to the extent I draw on my own experiences, it's cathartic."

"Does that mean you're past the trauma of your kidnapping? That you've worked it out of your system?"

My heart pounds. Sweat pools under my arms. But I walked into this, and no way am I showing Maggie-the-Bitch that she's pushing my buttons. "What happened to me was very traumatic. I don't think I'll ever fully get past it. But I've learned to cope, and it gets easier every day." I lift my chin, hoping she won't call me out on that monstrous lie when she tosses the next hardball.

To my surprise, she turns her focus off me entirely, aiming that thin smile at Ash. "And what about your history of recklessness in racing? And the chance you're taking with this new kind of motor?"

His eyes narrow. "What about it?"

"Just that you have a history of taking risks. I'm wondering if that serves the same purpose for you as writing does for Ms. Bernstein. That it's cathartic, I mean."

"Yes," Ash says. One simple word that holds a lifetime of pain.

"Really? And what is it that you're so desperate to work out?"

My stomach twists with guilt, because while I hate that she's got her claws in Ash, I can't deny that I'm curious about that very thing.

He pushes back his chair. "We're done."

"I was promised a full thirty—"

"We're done," he repeats. He holds out his hand to me. *Come on, Bree.*

I take it gratefully.

Right now, he really is Ace. And I'm Bethany. And he's sweeping me out of harm's way.

FIFTEEN

"God, I hate that woman," Ash says as we cross the parking lot to the red Mercedes.

"Right there with you," I tell him. "But I think it went okay. Thanks for reining her in." As unpleasant as the whole experience was, Ash's strong hand was what made it bearable.

"I'm not sure anyone can truly rein in that woman."

"Amen to that," I say, then clear my throat. "Listen, can we talk?"

He realizes that I've stopped walking and turns to face me. "Sure. Actually, I've been wanting to talk to you, too. I was worried, you know."

"About Maggie?" I shudder. "You had reason to be. But we survived. Even if I do feel like I rolled around in poison ivy."

"Not her," he clarifies. "You. I was worried when you disappeared at the airport. I thought something had happened to you." He shrugs. "And then when I got your message, I worried that I'd done something to—I don't know—scare you off."

"Oh." I swallow. Since he hadn't brought it up earlier, I thought we were going to simply skip over that little blip. "I'm really sorry about that. It wasn't you. Truly. And, well, I should have realized that you—anyway, I'm sorry."

He nods slowly, then slides his hands into the pockets of his jeans as he studies the ground. I tense, waiting for his response. Polite, because that's who he is. But laced with hurt over what I did, and temper because I did it to him.

But when he lifts his head, all I see is the faint glint of humor in his eyes. "I get it. Probably best to avoid drunken weather-inspired sexcapades. They never turn out the way you expect."

"I—" I stop because I have no idea what to say. I can barely process his words, much less the fact that they convey understanding.

He looks at me with the tiniest hint of a smile. "Did you expect me to say you owed me a night?"

"I—well, no. But—wait. *Sexcapades?* I thought you invited me up for a movie."

He presses a hand to his heart. "A guy can dream."

My laugh is cut off when he grabs my hand and tugs me to him. Since my mind is currently running through a Technicolor reel of sexual acrobatics, I'm fully expecting him to kiss me. And I'm more disappointed than I should be when he mutters, "Damn drivers think a parking lot is a racecourse."

That's when I realize I'd been so caught up in thoughts of Ash, that I hadn't been paying attention to where I'd been standing. As in, right in the middle of the driveway. I take a step back, intending to move out of the circle of his arms, but he holds me in place.

"I'll admit to being disappointed that night," he says, his voice like a low rumble moving through me. "But you don't owe me a thing. I know what trauma can do to a woman."

My head snaps up, and I realize the fear on my face must be palpable when he loosens his arms and steps back from me.

"My mother," he says quickly. "I meant that I know how my grandfather destroyed her. Oh, Bree, no. What did you think I meant?"

I shake my head, feeling like an idiot, because of course I'd leapt to my kidnapping.

"I'm sorry," I say. "Maggie. She put me on edge. It wasn't about you. Really."

That's not entirely a lie. And I do feel ashamed. We'd been having a perfectly civil conversation, and one wrong word and my fight or flight instinct sprang into play. Because apparently, I'm the only person in the world that bad shit has happened to.

Except I know that's not true. Not by a long shot. I know more about Ashton Stone than I probably should, simply because I was there when he first showed up at the Stark home.

I know about Sofia, Ash's mother and Damien's lifelong friend. She and Damien had both been mentally and physically abused by Sofia's father, Merle Richter. So much so that Damien and Sofia had been forced together sexually when they were only children, barely into puberty. And when Sofia became pregnant, she'd been taken away to live with Abigail, Richter's half-sister and Ash's great-aunt, while Damien—oblivious to Sofia's plight—traveled the world and rose as a tennis star with Sofia's father as his coach.

Already mentally fragile, young Sofia hadn't understood what was happening to her body, and when she'd had the baby, her mind had snapped. Growing up, Ash barely knew her. Technically, she lived in Abigail's house, but she was rarely in residence. Instead, she spent most of her life in an institution. Instead of a mother, Ash was raised by Abigail, a cold woman who'd fed him lies and half-truths and insinuated that the way he'd been conceived made him the devil's spawn. As for a father figure, Ash hadn't had one. His grandfather spent most of his time on the road coaching Damien until he died from a fall when Ash was still tiny. As for Damien, until recently, he hadn't even known Ash existed.

I can't even imagine all the trauma that Ash experienced in a household like that, essentially alone with a woman like Abigail whispering in his ear.

Ash isn't perfect—I know that. But I also know that he's strong. Probably stronger than he believes. And a bit messed up, though probably less than he should be. However you slice it, he's broken.

So am I. But Ash grew up that way. He knows how to hide the cracks. I'm still learning where my fissures are, and what will make me shatter.

"I really am sorry," I say. "I didn't mean to suggest that you had anything to do with what happened to me."

I feel like a complete shit. And where before I was grateful that he'd come with me to meet Maggie, now I wish I was alone so I wouldn't feel so small and stupid that I could easily crawl under the nearest rock.

"It was just a knee-jerk—"

"—reaction. Yeah. I get that, too." He steps closer, then brushes his fingertips over my cheeks, an intimate gesture I'm not expecting, but which washes over me like sunshine.

I'm afraid I might like it a little too much.

"I would never hurt you or Anne," he says. "I hope you know that."

I want to tell him that I do. Instead, I say, "You wanted to destroy Damien."

His shoulders drop, and he nods. "I did. I really fucking did." He glances around the parking lot, then uses his fob to unlock the Mercedes. "Listen, I don't want to leave this hanging, but I need to hit the road soon, and I still haven't packed. Come with me and we can keep talking? I can drop you back here for your car later."

I swallow, strangely hesitant to be alone with him. And not because I think that he'll hurt me. Quite the opposite. Because despite still being wary, there's something about Ashton Stone that pushes all my buttons... and in all the right order.

But it's not my buttons that have me saying yes. It's the fact that I still haven't asked him for the money. And the clock is ticking down.

"Well, that wasn't what I expected," I say when Ash pulls the Mercedes under the portico at the front of the Starks' Malibu house.

He turns to me, his brow lifted in question.

"You have a reputation, my friend. And I think you drove here slower than my cousin who lives in Manhattan and doesn't actually know how to drive."

He looks me slowly up and down. "A woman with a need for speed. I'll keep that in mind."

I roll my eyes, fighting an amused smile. Not to mention a tiny little bud of lust, so small and fragile it could wither and die... or bloom and thrive. I want the latter. But I also know better than to go there. I'm fine with fantasy. I don't do so well with reality.

We follow the paved walkway around the house to the manicured backyard that includes a pool, a huge patio, and the guest house where I used to live. There's also a stunning view of the beach, a tennis court, and a small bungalow just off the water.

Just your average home for your average billionaire.

Despite being huge, the house is actually pretty cozy. The truth is that I've always loved this place. And even though I adore my fixer-upper, I can't deny that living in Malibu with a beach outside my door is something I definitely miss. Which is probably why I gasp with delight when we head straight across the patio to my former digs.

"You're staying here now?" I ask as we step inside the guest house.

"Just for this trip." He turns to look at me before opening a satchel and filling it with a laptop and the papers that cover the kitchen table. "I go to sleep every night thinking of you."

I smirk. "That's either the worst pick-up line ever or genuinely creepy."

"I was going for seductive."

"Missed it by a mile," I tease though my laugh dies in my throat when I see the heat in his eyes.

For a moment, he doesn't move. He just holds my gaze. Then the corner of his mouth quirks up in a smile and he nods toward the bedroom. "I need to pack."

"Oh," I say, then follow him like a puppy as he moves into that room. I hesitate at the threshold, my attention drawn to the huge, familiar bed. I shift, forcing myself to seem as blasé as Ash, who's pulled a duffel from the closet and is now filling it with clothes from the closet and dresser.

I clear my throat, and he tosses a handful of briefs into the bag and holds my gaze. My cheeks are on fire as I clear my throat again. "Um, listen," I finally say, turning my attention to my feet. "This thing I wanted to talk about. I need to ask you something."

When I look up, he's moved closer to me. "Ash."

"Hmm?" He takes another step closer, bringing him fully into my personal space, so close I can smell the lingering hint of soap mixed with a scent that is pure male and completely compelling. "So tell me. What did you want to ask?"

I shake my head, suddenly unable to latch on to a single thought. "I can't remember."

The corner of his mouth twitches as his fingers brush my arm, bare in my sleeveless blouse. "Maybe it's the same thing I want to ask you."

"What's that?" My words—little more than breath—are swallowed up by the sweetness of a soft kiss that ends far too soon.

"That," he whispers. "And this." He kisses me again, only there's nothing sweet about this second round. This kiss is wild and hot and full of decadent promise. The kind of kiss that heats blood and melts off clothes. The kind of kiss that teases hearts and kills reason, and I lose myself in it. I kiss him back, relishing the taste of him. Craving even more.

This is the kind of kiss I miss. The kind I let play out in nighttime fantasies. The kind I dream of, then wake up in a cold sweat, crying silently into my pillow.

"Tell me you want this," he whispers, pulling away all too soon.

I want to tell him that I do. That I want it desperately.

I want to beg him to touch me, but I can't escape the fear. The worry that I won't ever be strong enough to be intimate with a man again.

And the worry that Ash could be *him*. My blackmailer. Maybe even my kidnapper.

I don't really believe that, but it's a sticky sort of terror, like sludge that clings and won't ever wash off. So thick and tenacious that it won't allow that one key thought to take root in my mind: the possibility that Ash isn't a man to fear at all.

In fact, maybe Ash is the knight who can keep those horrors at bay.

"Bree?" I see the concern in his eyes, but I scramble backward, until my back is pressed against the doorjamb. "I'm sorry," I say. "That was nice. More than nice. But I can't. I'm sorry. But I can't."

"You don't have anything to be sorry about." His voice is as soothing as a warm bath. "Can I help? Just tell me what you need."

A shiver cuts through me as time seems to stop, and his words hang in the air.

What you need.

It's as if Fate has tossed me into this surreal moment and given me Ash as a gift. I don't even think before I blurt out the words.

"I need three million dollars. And I need it in less than seventy-two hours."

Immediately, he goes ramrod straight. He's still standing between me and the bed, but he seems miles away, and a cold wave of fear crashes over me.

I try to read his face, but I can't. I'm not surprised. I've spent more time than I care to admit reading articles about Ashton Stone. They all talk about what a brilliant businessman he is. About how he inherited his father's skill in a boardroom. That he never gives anything away, and that his capacity to never show his cards clears a path for him to get everything he wants.

It's all true. I know it because I can't read a single thing on his face. All I can do is hope.

"Ash?"

"Why?"

I shake my head. "No."

"And if I insist?"

I swallow, refusing to cry. Technically, I can tell him. But I don't want any of this to get back to Damien. If Ash were to contact the police or do anything to break the rules...

"Can't you just help me?" My voice is thick with tears. "I'll pay you back somehow. Right now, I just need the money." I hear the panic in my voice and hate myself for it.

"Are you in danger?"

"No. Not like you mean, anyway." Technically it's true. I'm not in physical danger. Just in danger of hell breaking loose all around me.

Slowly, he takes a seat on the edge of the bed, and I can practically feel the burn as he looks me up and down. The woman he wanted. The woman who pushed him away. "All right," he says softly. "I'll get you the money."

My entire body goes limp with relief, only to freeze when I hear his next words: "But I want something in exchange."

I swallow, trying to ignore the ominous chill that makes my skin prickle. "Sure," I finally say. "Anything."

Not the best negotiating tactic, but it's not like I have a choice. The clock is ticking.

"Then we have a deal," he says, rising from the bed to step in front of me. "In exchange for three million dollars, I get you."

SIXTEEN

"What the hell?" I skirt around him, only to stumble over my own feet and tumble onto the bed. What happened to the tender man who'd comforted me only minutes ago? The man who'd been starting to earn my trust, but has now shattered it, leaving hundreds of dangerous shards between us. "You can't possibly mean—"

"Let me be perfectly clear," he says. "You can have your three million, but it comes at a price. *You.*"

I scramble over the bed until my back is against the headboard. Then I grab one of the pillows and clutch it to my chest. I want to flay him with a hard look. I want to cut his legs out from under him with the power of my disgust.

I want to hurt him.

Or rather, I want to want that.

But I don't.

Because what I really want is what he's offering.

And that scares me to death.

"You're a fucking bastard," I say with as much vitriol as I can conjure.

"I like to think of myself as an astute businessman negotiating the terms of a deal, which, frankly, I'm going to find very, very satisfying."

His mouth curves into a cocky grin. I really want to punch it. Not so much because he's tossing out these unbelievable terms, but because I opened the door to it.

"Fine," I say. "Negotiate."

He nods. "In exchange for three million dollars—"

"Transferred exactly when I say and to exactly the account I identify."

He nods, then continues without missing a beat. "—I will own you, body and soul. I will kiss you, tease you, touch you. When I want. How I want. Body and soul," he repeats, "with only two exceptions. First, I'll stop when you tell me to, but you're only allowed to tell me to stop if you're not enjoying my touch."

He moves to the bed, then bends over and places his hands on the mattress, his full attention focused on my face. "You could lie. I'm giving you that power. I'm gambling you won't use it."

My mouth has gone dry, but I still manage to ask, "What's the second?"

His eyes lock onto mine. "I won't fuck you. Not until you beg me to. Not until you mean it. And when you do, my ownership ends. Do you understand?"

I nod, relieved by his promise not to fuck me. And, to my horror and shame, a little bit disappointed, too.

"As for more specific terms," he continues, "you will not deny me any desire, any whim, any prurient pastime." He looks me up and down, and in that moment, I'm certain that he can see through my clothes and the pillow I'm clutching. That he knows my nipples are hard and that I'm wet with desire.

What I don't know is if he can hear my blood pounding and my panic rising. I want to tell him. To beg him to back off because this is a deal that can't work for me. I may think it can. I may even want it to. But I know better—if he makes me agree to this, it will break me.

But I don't say that at all. Instead, I lift my chin, determined to not show weakness. "Why?"

"I could say it's because I want you, and that would be true. But it's also because I want you to feel powerful." He stands up straight, then motions for me to come toward him. I hesitate before putting aside the pillow and crawling over the mattress to kneel in front of him. As soon as I do, he cups one breast through my shirt. The material of my bra is thin, and my nipple is hard against it. His fingers find the spot and tease me in time with his words. "And because I want to own you," he continues, as threads of electricity zing through my body.

As if he knows about those fiery strands, he traces his fingertip down, lower and lower until he's cupping me over my tailored slacks. "Look at me," he demands, and I realize I've closed my eyes, lost in the gap between longing and fear.

I do what he says, and find myself gazing at his face, and the desire I see there is so palpable I feel it reverberate throughout my body.

"I want to pleasure you," he says, moving his fingers in a slow, deliberate circle, the sensations he's generating making it suddenly hard to breathe. "Mostly, I want to be the man who makes you beg. And I want to be the man who gets you over that wall of fear you've built up inside you."

These last words bring me back to myself, and I scoot backward, clamping my thighs together. "You really are an arrogant son of a bitch."

His slow grin is cocky as shit and wildly sexy. "That's what people say."

I grab up the pillow and hug it again, hating the fact that his touch is so damned arousing. That my body is still tingling. And that even though all I want to do is slap his face, if he were to pull me to him right then, I think I would come in his arms.

I almost beg for him to do exactly that, just to see if I really could go there.

But I say nothing. I'll hold tight to the fantasy. But the possibility of a new reality is far too terrifying.

I draw a breath, reminding myself that despite the way my cells are dancing, he is being an absolute shit. "You're really going to use sex as collateral?"

He simply shrugs, looking as innocent as a schoolboy. Which, frankly, pisses me off.

"I thought I knew you. And now you're using the fact that me and An—"

His brow furrows. "You and what?"

"That you're a little prick," I snap, furious at myself for being careless almost mentioning Anne. "A little man. A fucking wolf in sheep's clothing and I should never have let myself trust you. Not even a little."

A see a shadow on his face and feel a kick of guilt that I quickly shove down.

"Have you considered that I'm afraid to lose you, and this is the only way I know how to keep you?"

I cross my arms over my chest as I look at him, not at all sure where he's going with this. "Lose me? When did you ever have me?"

He nods slowly, looking cocky as hell. "Good point. Maybe you're right. Maybe I'm just a son-of-a-bitch who wants to see you squirm." He pauses, his eyes never leaving my face. "Doesn't matter, does it? Because you need me."

I lift my chin. "I'll find the money some other way."

"Good. I hope you do. My dad would give it to you in a heartbeat." He tilts his head and makes a show of looking me up and down. "Why haven't you asked him?"

"Maybe I will." I don't mention that I don't have the number for the satellite phone. Ash does, and if that's my only excuse, I know he'd give it to me.

He indicates the door. "You know your way around. Go give him a call while I pack."

"Fuck you," I snap, then slide off the bed. I want to race out of there, but I move slowly, as if I don't have a care in the world. Then I ease out of the guest house and hurry to the door that leads from the patio to the first-floor entrance hall.

Thankfully, the key code hasn't changed since my last time babysitting, and I'm inside in no time.

I'm not entirely sure why I'm here other than to be contrary. There is no way I'm asking Damien for three million dollars. Aria and I have already gone there, dismissed that.

Which means Ash remains my only shot, and the only reason I have for being in the house is to show him that I'm not a pushover.

Except I am. Because, of course, I'm going to go back to the guest house and agree to every one of his stupid terms.

His stupid, terrifying, enticing terms.

What the hell is wrong with me?

Raindrops.

Roses.

Whiskers.

Kittens.

I let the mantra fill my head as I climb the grand staircase that leads from the ground floor up to the third floor, which serves as the heart of the house. It boasts a huge living area, the master and other suites, and the family kitchen and dining area. It's not the actual kitchen—that's a massive restaurant-worthy space on the ground floor. Instead, this area was originally planned as a catering kitchen before it became Stark Dining Central.

Right now, I'm only interested in the coffee machine. As my latte finishes brewing, I realize I'm no longer channeling Julie Andrews. And, yes, I'm feeling decidedly less stressed.

With a sigh, I take my latte and head to the sitting area. I glance up at the portrait of Nikki before settling on the sofa. She started her business with the money Damien paid her for that nude portrait in a deal not dissimilar to what Ash has offered me.

Like father like son...

Shit.

With a sigh, I pull out my phone, then put a call in to Teresa, only to get her message that she's out of the country on vacation, but that if it's a crisis I can press nine for an on-call therapist. I start to do that but change my mind and call Aria instead.

"Tell me everything," she says without preamble.

I do, pretty much word-vomiting all over her. I leave nothing out. And when I've given her all the embarrassing, sordid, details, the first thing she says is, "There's nothing wrong with you for wanting to take the deal."

"I *don't* want to. That's why I'm calling."

"Oh. Right. Gotcha." She sounds unconvinced. I feel an uncomfortable squiggling in my gut. "Have you talked to Teresa?"

"I tried her first. Nothing personal," I add, making her laugh. "She's on vacation."

"Wanna know what she'd say?"

I hesitate, then sigh. Aria's damn good at reading people, and she's gotten to know Teresa pretty well over the years. "Sure."

"Same thing I'm going to say. Take the deal."

"Oh."

She laughs. "Do not even. You called because you're

attracted to the guy. You want to sleep with him, but you're scared to sleep with him. And now this guy is basically offering you baby steps and an out clause? It's a no-brainer."

I bite my lip. She's not wrong. "What if I freak out. What if I have a panic attack?"

"Oh, sweetie..." For a moment, there's just silence. Then she says, "For the record, I'm still not convinced that Ash isn't the creep who's blackmailing you in the first place. But assuming he's not, we already know he's attracted to you, right?"

She barrels on, not giving me time to respond. "And he said you could take it slow, which means he's clued-in to the possibility of panic attacks, also right?"

This time, I manage an affirmative sound while she takes a breath.

"Plus, you want him to fuck you."

"No. I—"

"Do not even. This is me. You want to get past it. I know it. You know it. Teresa knows it. You've been working on yourself for years, and now we know that there's some honest-to-goodness crap locked away in your brain because of what your fucking kidnappers did to you. If getting busy with Ash helps get you past that, then I say *Go, Pussycat, Kill, Kill*."

I actually laugh. "You are the weirdest person I know, and I love you to death."

"Back at you. And I'm serious. Honestly, I'm kind of jealous. A hot guy is pretty much offering to give you sex therapy. That's not something to walk away from."

Sex therapy. For some strange reason, thinking of it that way makes the whole thing seem less sordid somehow.

Still strange and sordid... just less so.

"You still there?"

"Yeah. Sorry." I push myself off the sofa and start pacing. "I'm telling myself you're right. But I'm still not sure I can—"

"You have one other option," she says, cutting me off. "I was about to call you, actually."

"What option?"

"Get the three mil from somewhere else."

"Come on, Ar. We already talked about that."

"That was before I talked to Caleb."

"Oh, please tell me you didn't really." Caleb's her cousin, and though the three of us grew up together—and he's had a lifelong crush on me—I really don't need him knowing my problems.

"Unless you've figured out how to scrounge up three mil, you do *not* get to bitch about me asking."

I vehemently disagree about that, but I just cross my arms and stare down the phone. Which is entirely pointless since this isn't a video call.

"His grandfather died."

"He was in his late nineties, right?" I'm sorry, of course, but I have no idea what that has to do with anything.

"Caleb inherited the brownstone, and he's already got an offer on it. More than thirty mil. Less after taxes and all that crap, but more than enough to keep him in style for a long, long time. He said he'd give you the money in a heartbeat."

"I wish you hadn't asked that."

"Why? He said yes."

It really is tempting, but Caleb's one of those people who expects something in return for everything. And, yeah, Ash is expecting sex, but that's different.

Except maybe it's not.

Maybe it's only different because I'm intrigued by Ash's demand. And I have no idea what Caleb would hold over my head.

"Tell Ash you thank him for the offer of his fabulous cock, but you just can't go there. And if taking money from Caleb really bugs you," she continues, before I can sneak a word in, "then think of it as a loan."

"Ari—"

"The money's there. All you have to do is call him."

"Okay, fine. Let me think about it. Will you call and tell him thanks for me, and I'll be in touch if I need it?"

"If?"

"Aria..."

"I'll tell him you'll call sometime tomorrow."

I start to argue, but then I remember who I'm talking to. Arguing is pointless.

"I am right, though," she says.

"About what?"

"Ash. Even if you don't take his money, you really should take the deal."

"Aria!"

"Love you! Bye!"

And then she's gone, leaving me standing there staring at my phone.

"Miss Bree."

I jump a mile, then turn to find the Starks' butler, house manager, valet, and all-around Go-To guy, standing behind me.

"Gregory. I'm so sorry to barge in. I was visiting Ash and—"

I cut myself off with a shake of my head. "Honestly, he pissed me off, so I decided to come get a coffee. I should have buzzed you. Old habits."

"Nonsense," he says as I bend to retrieve my latte from the table. "You're always welcome. Would you care for another?"

"Thanks." I clear my throat as I follow him to the kitchen. "Can I ask you a question?"

He stops in front of the coffee machine and starts it brewing. "Of course."

"Right. Thanks. So, I was wondering. What do you think of Ash?"

Gregory nods, as if organizing his thoughts. "I've found him to be a charming young man. Though I confess it took a bit of time to get there."

We share a smile. Gregory's old enough to be my grandfather, but we became friends when I was working as the Starks' nanny.

"But you've known him as long as I have," Gregory adds. "Is there a particular reason you need my judgment in addition to yours?"

Because I'm a little baby who apparently can't make her own decisions?

True, but I decide not to tell him that part. "I guess—well, I know him, but I'm not sure I *know* him. I take a seat at the table. "And, well, I have a problem he's said he can help me with." I swallow, then look down, talking to the tabletop instead of Gregory. "The thing is, he wants something kind of major in return."

Gregory puts the fresh latte in front of me, then settles himself across the table, his hands folded in front of him. "I see."

Clearly, he doesn't. Not fully. But I'm not inclined to enlighten him.

"Is he trustworthy?" I ask. "I mean, I know Damien considers him part of the family now. And I know that Ash has apologized for the chaos he dropped when he first showed up."

"He has indeed."

"I guess I'm wondering about his character in general. Will he keep his word? Can he keep a secret? Is he—I mean, is he a guy who keeps his promises?"

Gregory sips his coffee, then puts his cup back down, his fingertip tapping the ceramic. "I confess I was leery when he first showed up, but he has swept all my concerns away. You know about his family situation?"

I nod, then shake my head. "Sort of. I'm not sure I know all of it." Gregory, I'm sure, does know all of it. He's in the know about everything that touches this house. One of the perks of being both trusted and invisible.

"It's not my place to share that with you, but I think it's fair to say that Mr. Stone has overcome at least as much as both Damien and Ms. Nikki. And I would rank his character on par with theirs."

"Really?" That's high praise. "Even if he wants—" I silence myself with a firm shake of my head. The truth is, Damien wanted the same thing, didn't he? It was a huge scandal when the secret of his early relationship with Nikki came out. The fact that Damien wanted Nikki's portrait—nude. And he paid her enough money for the sitting to start her own business. But it wasn't just the portrait he wanted. For the time allotted to finish the painting, he wanted *her*, and that meant in every way possible.

Unconventional, but it sure worked out okay.

Gregory's brows rise as he studies my face. "Like father like son?"

I take a sip of my latte, certain my cheeks have gone crimson. "I should get going."

I can tell he's fighting a smile as he walks me toward the stairs. "There are secrets you keep, Miss Bree. As you should. But as you navigate whatever arrangement you are negotiating with our Ashton, keep in mind that you aren't the only one with a darkness in your past that you'd rather not share."

SEVENTEEN

Ash wanted to kick himself for being an ass and scaring her away. He knew better. Especially considering this was Bree. He knew what she'd been through. Knew all about how she'd been kidnapped with Anne, his little sister who—at the time—he knew existed, but had never met. Now that he did know her—and adored her—Ash would have happily killed the fucker—plural, as it turned out—who'd taken them. But someone else hadn't gotten there first.

He'd overheard Nikki and Damien talking one evening, so he also knew that Anne remembered nothing of the kidnapping and hadn't been physically abused at all. He knew less about what had happened to Bree, but he did know that although she'd been drugged for much of the time, she hadn't been raped.

That good news had been twisted up with the bad, though. Because the bottom line was that someone had stolen her control. Had ripped her away from her world and tossed her into his own. Had violated her. Abused her.

But hadn't broken her.

There was too much strength in her. He'd seen it. Felt it.

That bastard Rory and the others had smashed her up hard. Maybe she was cracked, but she never shattered.

Right then, all Ash wanted in the world was to be the glue that held her together. Ironic, considering he was pretty damn cracked himself. But he didn't matter. Only Bree mattered. She'd gotten under his skin in a way he'd never experienced before.

She'd become his North Star.

And so you try to coerce her into being your sex slave? Good one, dude.

Ash feared that his conscience—that annoying little prick—wasn't entirely wrong. Considering how she'd stormed out, he may have just made the biggest mistake of his life.

The woman had been robbed of her control. Taken against her will. And he—asshole that he was—had stepped in to say that if she wanted his help, then he owned her. That she would be his to do with what he pleased.

And given her a panic button, too. You're not forcing her to do anything. You're giving her all the control.

He ignored the voice in his head. He had a reputation for using and throwing away women, after all. For destroying them.

Hell, maybe he had. After all, try as he might, he'd never truly wanted them. Not even Delia.

But it had been different with Bree. From the first moment he'd seen her, she had filled his thoughts. His fantasies. And not just those moments when he was alone in the shower, the air heavy with steam and his hands slick with lather. He damn sure hadn't pushed those fantasies away, but those were just sex. Need. Hunger.

Delicious and wonderful, but the other fantasies were what he treasured. The ones where she'd pop up in calmer, sweeter times, unbidden and unexpected. Like when he was having coffee on his back porch on the Hudson Bend peninsula outside of Austin. Or sitting on his downtown penthouse balcony overlooking Lady Bird Lake. Or when he was driving through the Texas Hill Country or along PCH.

He'd tried to exorcise her. To tell himself that he'd never have her and might as well forget her. To convince himself that he preferred the amalgamations. The cardboard cut-out women who'd so eagerly fall into his bed.

But it wasn't true. How could it be when every single time he fucked another woman, he could feel Bree nearby? Her soft lips brushing his ear, asking him why he would do that. Why a man like him—a man with enough intelligence and self-awareness to know his own worth even if he didn't believe it—would get busy with a woman like that? A woman he didn't even want.

He never answered her. Hell, he pushed her away, practically begging her to tell him no in each one of those fantasies.

He should push her even further away tonight.

With a long, slow breath, he studied his face in the mirror. Yeah, He knew an asshole when he saw one.

She can still say no. You aren't the asshole yet.

Except she wouldn't. She obviously needed the money. And he would give her that. More if she needed it, no matter what hoops he had to jump through to pull together that much cash. He wanted her close. Wanted her to feel safe.

Mostly, he wanted her. And the frustrating thing was that he wanted her more than he'd ever wanted any woman. Not even for sex, though that was definitely high on his Want List.

No, what he craved was her heart. Her trust. He wanted to hold her and protect her. To support her. To be the man she turned to when the world became too much.

He wanted to be her refuge.

Refuge.

With a frown, he stood up then started pacing, trying to shake loose a recalcitrant thought. *Refuge. Help. Safety.*

She already had all of that. She knew as well as Ash did that Nikki and Damien would always be there for her. And Damien probably had three mil sitting in his dresser drawer.

Slight exaggeration, but not entirely out of the realm of possibility. So why hadn't Bree asked Damien for the money?

Unless she had?

But no. Ash was positive Damien wouldn't turn Bree away if she was in trouble, and he had the very distinct feeling that the three million she needed was to ward off something bad.

And yet she hadn't asked his father...

Sure, she'd called his bluff and headed into the house to do that, but he knew she wasn't calling. If she was really willing to ask Damien, that would have been the first call she made.

He let the thought hang there as he paced, trying to make sense of it. And he kept circling around to the same conclusion —the only reason to keep Damien out was if Damien was already at the center of it. If the money she needed protected Damien in some way.

But how?

The thought made him feel vaguely nauseous and he felt his pulse increase in tempo. Ash hadn't been a Damien fan when he'd first met his father, that was for damn sure. But things changed, mostly because Ash realized that the picture he'd had in his head of his father had been painted by Abigail, a woman who hated Damien Stark.

Ash didn't count himself in that group. Not anymore. Now, he loved the man as if he'd been there Ash's whole life. He didn't completely feel like Damien was a dad—though to be honest, Ash wasn't sure he knew what having a dad actually felt like—but he respected the hell out of the man. And that went double for Nikki. That woman had been through hell and back. Good lord, the whole family had.

With a wry grin, Ash thought of all the crap he'd been

through in his life. If that was the defining characteristic, then he was definitely a Stark. And as far as he could tell, Bree was practically an adopted child in the family, too.

So why would she need that much money so quickly, but not immediately go to Damien for help?

Was someone threatening to expose something about Damien? And if so, why wouldn't she tell Ash? Or maybe she had already asked Damien, and he said no. But that seemed very out of character.

He got up and started to pace, then decided that the only way to know the truth was to go to the source.

"Well, fuck it," he muttered as he crossed the room to grab his phone and send a text:

I know you're incommunicado with the world, but just wanted to check in. All OK?

A moment later, three dots appeared, followed by a reply: *Wonderful. Relaxing at the beach.*

Where exactly is this island?

Top Secret. Only Gregory knows.

My own father and he doesn't trust me ...

It felt good typing that. Hard to believe that not that long ago he would have happily seen Damien Stark dead.

What's up?

Not much. Has Bree been in touch?

Ash didn't think Bree had the satellite phone number, but Gregory could always patch her through. For a moment, there was no response. Then the text box popped back up.

No. Is something wrong?

Shit. Now he couldn't tell if she really hadn't reached out or if the delay in response meant that she had, but Damien wasn't telling.

Nothing wrong. We were talking about some plans for when

you get back. House party or something. We'll fill you in when you're back in California.

Tell her we all say hi.

Ash turned as he heard a tap at the door. As it opened, he typed out one last text: *Got to run. Give N and the kids my love.*

He closed the app then turned to see Bree standing in the doorway. Her long, dark hair was tucked behind her ears, and the afternoon's bright light silhouetted her in a way that made her glow like the ethereal creature she was.

"You're back." The pleasure at seeing her was palpable, a physical thing, and so unlike anything he'd felt for any other woman he'd known. "What's the verdict on my proposal? Am I the biggest asshole on the planet or just a fucked-up guy?" He said it with a smile, but he meant every word. If he could do the last hour all over again, he damn sure would.

She looked at him, her face entirely expressionless, and he felt his heart sink and his stomach twist.

"Why can't you be both those things? Fucked up and an ass?"

"You make a good point. I think that describes me pretty well."

"I'd say so." She stared at him for another beat, then another. Still that flat expression. Still, his heart continued to sink.

"Caleb offered to give me the three million."

"Caleb?" The name was bitter in his mouth. "He's your friend. Aria's cousin. The choreographer."

Ash had met Caleb once when the dancer had come with Bree and Aria to a Hollywood premiere party for a mutual friend. Ash hadn't much liked the guy, though he hadn't been able to put his finger on why.

He got it now.

He'd hated the poor son-of-a-bitch because Caleb was

attracted to Bree. Ash didn't think Bree had even noticed, but Ash certainly had. And maybe that really did make Ash the asshole, but he still hated Caleb for that same damn reason.

Not that he'd let Bree see as much now. Instead, he pasted on his usual boardroom expression, the kind that showed no particular emotion. "Good. That's a good plan. No strings. And no asshole—that would be me—to deal with."

"You really are the asshole," she said, punctuating her words with a slow grin. "But I'm taking your three mil, anyway."

It took him a second to make sense of her words. "You want to repeat that?"

"I'm. Taking. Your. Money." She smiled, then bit her lower lip, which, frankly, was sexy as hell. "If you're still offering."

"Oh." Every drop of blood in his body shot straight toward his cock, and right then it felt as if all the sunshine came back into the world. "I've never been happier to be out three million dollars."

She laughed, and he grinned back. He had no idea what was going through her head, but at least he knew she didn't hate him.

"And you're accepting my terms?"

She blushed but nodded. "With one condition of my own."

He cocked his head. "Are you in a position to impose conditions?"

She lifted her chin, her eyes never leaving his. "You don't get to ask me what the money's for."

His chest tightened. Whatever was going on—whatever had not only forced her to seek out three million, but had also led her to agree to selling herself—had to be some pretty bad mojo. He wanted to argue. Wanted to hold her close while she told him everything. And then he wanted to fix it for her. Whatever *it* happened to be.

But he did none of that. Instead, he nodded. "Agreed. Now

tell me why *you* agreed." She shrugged. "Gregory says you're not an ass. Generally, I think Gregory's a pretty smart guy. I'm not sure how he missed the boat on that one."

He took a step toward her. "It's because I buy him really great Christmas presents."

"I figured it had something to do with that." She stepped fully over the threshold, then shut the door behind her.

He moved a bit closer, feeling strangely tentative, as if he was approaching a scared kitten. "I'm paying a pretty stiff price," he said, purposefully letting his gaze roam over her. "I hope the merchandise is worth it." He *was* taking a risk, and he was on the verge of wishing he could call back the words when he saw the corner of her mouth twitch.

"Hey, *caveat emptor*," she said. "And as for that stiff price... thank you."

"You're welcome," he said, but in his head, he was leaping up and down, celebrating the fact that they had a deal. The news pleased him more than it should have. This was a sex-for-money deal. Purely transactional.

Just something to help him let off steam and justify giving the woman three million.

Except that was bullshit, of course. He didn't want transactional with Bree. He wanted real. And he knew better than most that real could be some very scary shit.

EIGHTEEN

"You have immediate access, right?" I ask as Ash comes back from the main house with a Louis Vuitton travel bag over his shoulder. "To the money, I mean. Because I need it by noon three days from now. And what are you doing with that?"

"Borrowing it," he says, as he plunks the bag onto the bed and unzips it. He pulls out a sundress and passes it to me. "I think it'll fit you."

"It's adorable," I say, which is true. "But money? Access? Hello? It has to be an electronic transfer, so you're set up to do that, too, right? Do you need to make some sort of arrangement with your bank? Should you call and let them know?"

He lifts his head, meets my eyes, then crosses to a chest of drawers.

I get the message—he's got it under control.

I start to ask if I'm right about that, then tell myself to stop. To trust him. "Fine," I say, after drawing a calming breath. Then I focus on the dress I've been carrying around. "Um, this?"

"We call that a dress," he says. "It's one I had *immediate access* to, so..."

I pick up one of the small throw pillows from the bed and

toss it at him. "It's Nikki's, right?" I ask as he laughs and dodges the pillow. "Why are you handing it to me?"

He looks me up and down in a way that erases all the pillow-throwing laughter. "Because, Brianna," he says in a voice laced with heat. "I want you in a dress."

"Oh." The change in the room's atmosphere is palpable, and I hope I sound casual when I glance down at the tailored slacks and sleeveless blouse I'd worn for the interview. "What's wrong with this?"

"Did you think I was bluffing about payment?"

My nipples go hard, and my cheeks heat as the pressure of need builds between my legs. I want what he's calling a payment, and the only thing that bothers me is that he damn well knows it.

I tell myself that's just fine. Yes, I ran from him in the past, but this time I won't. I can't because that's the deal.

Which means that by the rules of our deal, we'll both get what we want.

As if he's reading my mind, the corner of his mouth quirks up, making him look like a sexy anti-hero from an action movie. He takes a step toward me, a raw heat filling the space between us. He's going to touch me—I'm certain of it. Just as I'm certain that I'll melt in his arms when he does. This isn't a bargain. His terms aren't really payment at all. He's simply giving me the money and throwing himself in as a gift.

"Go ahead," he says, once again looking me over in that hard, hot way he has. "Strip."

The world shatters like ice.

Desire freezes in my gut, hard and painful, as a wave of fear washes over me. I reach out to steady myself, only to find that nothing is there, and suddenly, I'm tumbling to the ground, my knees unable to support me, my entire body turned limp and cold and afraid.

Strip.

That word. That voice.

Except it wasn't that voice.

I scoot backward, then draw my knees up and hug them, telling myself over and over and over that it wasn't *him* saying it. That I'm not trapped in a room. That I'm fine, I'm fine, I'm fine.

Through a tunnel a thousand miles long, I hear Ash's voice calling my name. Then his hands on my knees. I twist, turning away from him, mortified as reality crashes back over me.

"Hey, shhh. It's okay. Are you hurt?"

I don't understand, then realize I'd landed hard on my elbow. I focus on that. The pain. Not the memory. Not the horror.

And little by little, I use that pain to help me focus so that I can follow Ash's voice back to the world. Back to myself.

"I'm sorry." My voice is small, like a child.

He's crouching in front of me, and tentatively takes my hands. I don't tug them away. "You don't have a thing to be sorry for," he says.

I see both understanding and a question in his eyes, like a man who knows that the moon is up in space, but he doesn't have a clue how it got there. "Are you okay now?"

I nod, surprised that it's true. Right now, with Ash beside me, I really am okay. I wait, knowing he's going to ask me what happened. That's when *okay* will turn into *horrible*. That's when the nightmares will come dancing into the room despite the sun shining outside.

But he doesn't ask. All he says is, "You'll have your money. But I'm cutting the strings."

The words flow through me like warm whiskey, welcome and a little intoxicating. But still a crutch.

I tug my hands from his as I shake my head. "I need that money," I say, my eyes on the floor. "But I'm not taking charity."

Gently, he uses a fingertip to tilt up my chin. "Can you tell me what's wrong?"

I shake my head. Then I stand up. I roll my shoulders back and take a deep breath. I can do this. I was surprised, that's all. But I can do this.

I have to.

"Say it again," I demand.

His brow furrows, then he slowly shakes his head.

"That word. Say it again."

He's silent.

"Dammit, Ash. You had conditions. That's the deal I agreed to." I feel tears sting my eyes, and I will *not* cry. I will not let the way that my kidnappers tormented me fuck me up. I will do my part, and Ash is going to play his part, too, or else I'm going to kick his extremely fine ass. "*Say it.*"

He looks at me, and I can't read a thing on his face. The he lifts his chin, and his eyes lock on mine when he says it: "Strip."

I wait for it—the second rush of fear, of disgust, of loathing for what they did to me, and terror from all the rest I still don't know. I haven't even had the courage to look at those Greatest Hits yet, after all. But the rush doesn't come. I'm not in that room. I'm in the Stark guest house. It may not be my home anymore, but it's a warm, familiar place.

And I'm with Ash. A man with a wicked reputation and a past laced with more than a little danger. A man who plays with his little brother and sisters on the floor of their playroom. Who laughed with me over drinks in a socked-in airport.

A man who put sexual conditions on the three million dollars I desperately need. Who agreed not to ask me why I need the money.

A man who didn't hesitate to withdraw those conditions when he got his first look at my pain.

In other words, I'm safe.

Slowly, I peel off my shirt. I look at him, expecting to see victory in his eyes, but I don't. Like his father, Ash is an expert at hiding his emotions when he wants to. Right now, all he does is indicate that I should continue. I do, toeing off my shoes and then stripping off my pants. I don't bother trying to look graceful. These are terms. Not a seduction. And I'm left standing there in my lacy bra and hipster panties. Just one more commodity in the trade.

The dress is on the floor where I dropped it. It's pale blue and strapless, with a bodice made of stretchy material.

When I start to put it on, he shakes his head. "Take off the bra."

I almost argue, just for form. A bra doesn't work with that dress, after all. I was just keeping it on until the very last minute.

But that's not the real reason I stay silent. As much as I hate to admit it, even to myself, I like this game. Before, I felt like a victim, desperately scrambling for money. Now—even though I'm undressing at the whim of a man who's paying me to submit so that I can pay off a sick fuck who's blackmailing me—I feel powerful.

That probably makes me delusional. At the very least, it makes me screwed up.

But I figure that's better than terrified.

The bottom line is that I trust Ash. And considering the very big hoop he's making me jump through, that's pretty remarkable.

Once the dress is on, I move to where he's sitting on the bed and turn around, as if I'm in a fashion show. "Done," I say as I start to step into my sandals, but he grabs a chunk of the skirt and holds me in place.

"Not quite," he says, then starts to hitch up my skirt.

"What are you—"

"Shhh," he says, and I go quiet. It hardly matters. I know what he's doing. He's going to touch me.

And damned if I don't want him to.

He ruches the skirt up, and I feel the warmth of his touch as his hands go to my hips and the band of my panties. He tugs them down, sliding off the bed so he can take them all the way to the floor. "Step out," he says, and I do, closing my eyes in expectation of his palms caressing their way back up my calves, my thighs. Finding my core. And, yes, finding me already wet.

Except he doesn't.

Instead, he sits back down on the bed.

I turn, frowning. "What the hell?"

"The deal was immediate access. No panties, Bree."

"Oh." Apparently, I was three steps ahead of him, and now I feel like an idiot who's shown her cards. Except I haven't. As far as he's concerned, I'm just complaining about his little game. About going panty-less.

Then I see the way his brow furrows, followed by a quick, smug smile.

He says nothing, but I know he understands.

It's fifteen-love, and Ashton is winning.

NINETEEN

"What now?" I lean against the kitchen counter as I talk to the open door of the bedroom. My voice is firm and crisp, like I'm the one in control here. Which, of course, we both know I'm not. "I seem to recall a big speech about getting me past all of my baggage. And, oh yeah, getting me three million dollars in less than two-and-a-half days."

My stomach tenses as my mind comprehends just how short a time that is.

"That's the plan," he calls back, his voice perfectly pleasant even though my words were said with full-on bitch undertones. And not the accidentally bitchy tones that tend to pop up when someone else is being a prick.

No, that's not why I'm being bitchy. If Teresa were to ask—and I'm sure that she'd be very proud to know that I've mastered this bit of self-analysis—I'd tell her that I'm bitchy because I'm vulnerable.

Because I've shown him too much of me.

Because I'm a woman who had all her control ripped from her, and now I've gone and surrendered it again.

All true. All exactly what I would tell Teresa if she were here.

It's also a big fat lie.

No, the real reason I've slid into bitch-dom is that with each passing moment I'm more and more attracted to this man who continues to surprise me. And, frankly, that scares me to death.

With effort, I force myself to ignore my spinning thoughts and concentrate on Ash. *"That's the plan,"* I repeat. "Okay, fine. That part I got. But can you narrow it down a bit for me? Like, oh, what exactly is the plan? When will you show me—I don't know, an account balance so I can quit stressing? And—for the zillionth time—you do have immediate access, right? This isn't a *have to sell stock and wait for the trade to clear* kind of thing, is it? Because my deadline is really, really firm."

Now I've done it. Just saying all that out loud has sent panic shooting through me all over again. The same panic that had left the building when Ash promised he could help.

I guess it's moved back in.

He's silent when he returns to the combined kitchen and living area. He stops right in front of me, and I instinctively lean back so that when he moves even closer, I'm trapped between him and the counter. His fingers go to my thigh, and he slowly eases the hem of the knee-length sundress up. My breath quickens, but I say nothing, and when he meets my eyes, I hold his gaze, lifting my chin a little in defiance. Because I know what he's trying to do. He wants me to beg. Or break. I'm not sure which.

I'm not sure it matters. Right then, all that matters is the way his fingers have found the soft skin of my thigh. The way his hand is now under my skirt, sneaking slowly up my inner thigh. Higher and higher.

I force myself to breathe regularly. To keep my eyes open. To not moan or squirm or otherwise show that I want this. Oh, how I want this. I want everything I ran from at the airport. And more. So much more.

He's right there—right at the juncture of my thigh and my core, and I'm wildly aware of my clit, swollen and sensitive. Just one brush of his fingertip would send me over. And, oh yes, I want to go. I want to fall off that precipice and into his arms.

But his finger doesn't move. His eyes stay locked on mine. His mouth doesn't claim a kiss. But for one beautiful, painful, arousing, frustrating moment, he seems to be a part of me. "Immediate access," he whispers. "Absolutely."

Then he backs away, the slightest hint of a smile tugging at the corner of his mouth.

"Prick," I say, but it only makes him laugh. "You're torturing both of us, you know. And who's to say I won't excuse myself and take care of the situation on my own."

"No," he says, at my side again in seconds. "I won't make you promise, but you won't do that. And neither will I."

My mouth is dry. "Why not?"

"Anticipation," he whispers, then taps a kiss to my lips. It's close-mouthed and quick, like the perfunctory kiss of a relative. Yet in that moment it seems like the most erotic touch I've ever experienced.

"Are we clear?"

I nod.

"Good. Then it's time to go."

"Go? Wait, what? Go where?"

"Austin."

I stand up straighter, my sappy, dreamy demeanor hardening with confusion. "As in Texas? We're going to Texas? Why?"

"My office is there. And my accountant. We'll make a stop in Vegas. I have a meeting there tonight. We'll head to Texas after that, and then we'll have all day Thursday, so you don't have to panic. You'll have the money by your Friday deadline at the latest."

I gape at him. "*Tonight*. You have a meeting tonight?"

"Vegas doesn't sleep."

"So we're flying?"

"I build engines and race cars," he says, turning and heading back into the bedroom as I follow. "What do you think?"

The very idea boggles the mind. "We're driving... to *Texas*?"

"To Vegas. We'll decide about the rest of the trip once we're there." He heads into the bathroom and returns with a shaving kit, which he hands to me. "Toss that in the bag for me while I grab a few other things."

"Oh, sure. No problem. Sex slave and servant girl. Happy to oblige."

He ignores my snark and heads back into the bathroom. I take the kit to the bed and plunk it in the duffel. As I do, a pair of rolled up jeans shifts, revealing a glossy red that looks strangely familiar. I push the jeans aside, then suck in air.

My book.

It's *Reveries at Dawn*. Right there in Ash's bag. And from what I can tell by the bookmark, he's at least three-quarters of the way through.

I push the jeans back and make sure the shaving kit is covered. I'm not sure why I don't want him to realize that I know he's reading my story. Maybe I'm afraid he's ultimately not going to like it.

Except that's not it at all. In fact, it's the exact opposite. It feels like a bond between us, all the more potent because Maggie was right about one thing: the sexy anti-hero who Bethany falls for? Yeah, he was totally modeled after Ash.

"Ready?"

I leap backwards. "You scared me!"

"Yes, this is a terrifying home, full of unexpected dangers."

I cross my arms and look him up and down. "You already made that perfectly clear."

To his credit, he laughs. "You make a good point, Ms. Bernstein."

I roll my eyes. "And to answer your question, no. I'm not even close to ready, considering I didn't know I'd be traveling to freaking Vegas today. We need to go to my house so I can pack, and I'll need my laptop, and I want to make sure Aria will be around when the workmen show up tomorrow, and—"

"Are you on any meds?"

I blink at the non-sequitur. "No."

"Got your phone?"

"You know I do."

"Need stuff for your period you can't grab at a drugstore?"

"Ash! Jeez! I'm not on—No!"

"Then you can text or call Aria from the car. You can borrow my laptop to write if you're on a deadline—and don't even try to tell me you don't save your work to the cloud—and anything else you need we can get on the way or in Vegas." He flashes the same smile I've seen so many times in newspaper and magazines. "My money, my way."

"I already agreed to the terms to get your money," I remind him. "Those weren't among them."

"But to fulfill those terms, you have to be physically present with me. And I'm leaving. If you want my money, you'll have to come with me. If you've changed your mind, I'm happy to release you from the terms of our arrangement."

"A lawyer would have a field day with that argument."

"Probably. But by the time a court rules, your deadline would be long gone. I may not know why you need the money—though you're going to tell me—but I'm confident time is of the essence. So give it up, sweetheart. I've won."

"Fuck. You," I say, which only makes him laugh.

"That's definitely a possibility," he says. "But let's not get ahead of ourselves."

"Holy crap," I say, staring at the piece of automotive artwork parked in front of us. We're in the Bat Cave, otherwise known as Damien's massive underground garage. It's cavernous and houses I-don't-know-how-many cars. All I know is that there are rows and rows of them. This one shines brighter than them all.

"Sweet, isn't it?"

"It's gorgeous," I say, though the word is completely inadequate. The body is molded in waves of black and orange and what might be blue but could just be a trick of the light playing off the shiny black depths. Looking at it, I'd totally believe this thing came from outer space. Or the future. Or, I don't know, Car Heaven, maybe.

"It's a McLaren P1 GTR-18," Ash says to me, which might as well be gobbledygook. I do, however, get the general drift. Translation: This is one seriously amazing car. And probably cost more than, oh, a space shuttle trip around the globe.

"When did Damien get this?"

"He didn't. It's mine."

"As in you designed it?"

He shakes his head. "No, I bought it. Technically, it's a track car, but I've done some modifications to make it street legal and add in a bit of comfort."

"Just a fun new toy?"

He quirks a smile. "I like toys. And I wanted to get familiar with her."

I glance at him, then run a fingertip over the sleek body. I've never been someone who considers cars sexy, but this beauty has completely changed my mind. "You're working on a collaboration," I guess. "Pitching them your motor."

"Am I?"

I tilt my head, studying him. "Either that, or you're gunning to be a driver when this baby's entered in races."

"And wouldn't that be sweet?" he says. But I notice he doesn't deny it.

I frown. I don't know much about racing, but I do know that Ash is an excellent driver who really shouldn't be on a track.

He was the youngest driver ever to win the Daytona 500, but he quit racing because of repeated crashes and because he knew he was reckless.

And not just in a car. Where Ashton Stone goes, a story follows.

Some are pretty damn cool—like how Hollywood's approached him a zillion times over, but he flipped them off because he didn't want to get sucked into that life.

Some are bad—like the rumors of the dead woman in his past that Maggie had alluded to. I'd heard those whispers before—the hints of scandal. Of a police investigation. Of pay-offs. And I have to admit—if only to myself—that I wish Maggie had pushed the question. I want to know what really happened, because I don't see that kind violence in Ash, but I'm not sure if that's because it's not there or because I'm intentionally averting my eyes.

All I do know—though I don't even want to admit it to myself—is that I'm attracted to him. A man with a dark and reckless reputation. A man shrouded with secrets. A man who comes from a family that's about as fucked up as they come.

A man who's definitely not the safe and stable port that I need after all the shit I've been through.

And there it is—the reason why I'm certain that Fate is one

cruel bitch. Because the first man I'm truly attracted to is a man I shouldn't let anywhere near my heart.

TWENTY

As advertised, the car is one hell of a sweet ride, especially once we're out of the city and the highway opens up. "Too fast for you?" Ashton asks an hour or so later as he kicks the speed up over a hundred and ten.

I laugh and shake my head. "For me, no. For the highway patrol? Maybe."

"A woman who likes a fast car. I approve."

I give him *that* look. "Lots of women like fast cars. But if you really approve, you should let me drive. I bet I could give you a run for your money."

He takes his eyes off the road long enough to glance my way, and though our eyes meet only for a second, what I see there has my pulse racing as fast as that speedometer.

"I think you definitely could," he says. But I'm no longer sure he's talking about driving.

I take a sip of the coffee I've been nursing as a noisy silence hangs between us. A silence in which I hear his voice in my memory: *I will own you. I will kiss you, tease you, touch you. When I want. How I want.*

"Recline your seat," he orders, his tone as low as that voice in my head.

"It reclines? Isn't this a race car?"

"I mentioned modifications. That's one." He looks at me just long enough to offer a cool smile. "I want my passengers to be comfortable." He pauses, his eyes still on me as we fly down the freeway. "Recline your seat."

There's both heat and command in his tone, and I consider arguing again, but it would be only for show. I made a deal, after all, and this is the price for my three million dollars.

More, I want to.

I want the feel of his fingers on my skin. I want to be awake and aware and aroused.

I want to know that I can handle it.

Most of all, I want to like it.

With Ash, I know that I will.

"Eager," Ash says, once the seat is all the way back, and it's only then that I realize that I've uncrossed my legs. And parted my knees.

I fight the urge to slam them back together, reminding myself that this is safe. This is a deal that I made. That if I say stop, he will. That I have just as much power as he does.

So instead of closing my knees like a vise, I spread them even further. I turn my head as I do and catch him looking at me. I say nothing, but we both know that the way I hold his gaze is the silent equivalent of *yes*.

Because I *am* eager, and I'd be a fool to think I could hide that from him.

He puts his hand on my knee, then slowly teases the silky material of Nikki's dress up my thigh. The brush of material against skin is wildly sensual, but it's not what I want. He's touching me through the material, and while that leaves a modicum of safety, it's not safety I crave. Not now. Not while we're flying down the highway with his fingers creeping up my thigh.

"Close your eyes," he says.

"But then I'll miss the view."

He chuckles. Interstate 15 is not known for its view. "Close your eyes. Keep them closed."

This time, I obey without objection. There's no point in protesting. Ashton Stone isn't a fool, and there's no way I can hide my desire. My nipples are hard against the stretchy bodice. And if he ever finishes what he's started, I know he'll find me wet.

I want that. Hell, I crave it. The knowledge that I made this happen. That I'm not being forced. I agreed to these terms, and this journey is as much about what I want as about him. It's exciting. It's freeing.

And, so far, at least, the way his fingertips gently caress my skin isn't even remotely terrifying.

"Tell me what you're thinking." His voice is a whisper, but the command in it is palpable.

"I'm not thinking anything," I lie.

"You're thinking that you like this. Your legs spread. My hand on your skin. Your eyes closed. The motion of the car. It's visceral. Sensual. And you want to beg me to slide my hand up your thigh. To find your core. To tease and touch. To make you hot. To make you beg. And then, finally, to take you over."

I fight a whimper, then manage a soft whisper instead. "No." But it's a lie, and we both know it. I want exactly that, and my body is on fire simply from his words.

But I don't want it yet. Or rather, I want it all. Exactly how he described it. Slow. Sensual. *Safe.*

I want the sensation to build. I want to feel. I want to *want*.

I want to go over from the touch of a hand not my own. And when I do, I don't want to be afraid.

As the vibration of the car caresses me, his fingers do the same, easing higher and higher with such infinitesimal slowness that it feels as though we've traveled miles and miles before he's even close to my core. My whole body feels alive. Hungry. Desperate.

And safe.

Now, though, he pulls his hand away, and I can't help my low groan of protest. For the last several miles, I've been forcing myself not to beg him to slide those fingers higher. To tease my clit. To slip inside me. I'm so wet. So needy. And all I crave in the world right now is for his touch to take me over.

So why is he doing the exact opposite of what I want?

I open my eyes, knowing I'm breaking the rules, but not caring.

"Problem?" He takes his eyes off the road, his brows raised in question as amusement dances in those deep blue eyes.

"Nope," I say.

"Good. I need you to do something for me." His voice is casual, but before I can answer, he changes his tone, his words turning low and sensual when he says, "Put your seat back up. Then tug down your bodice."

"What?"

"You heard me."

An odd sensation courses through me. Arousal, yes. But fear, too. All mixed together in a cocktail of trust and longing and pure sensual need.

"Ash, no. Anyone passing on my side of the car will see."

I hadn't raised the protest before. The car's seat—and anything that might be going on down there—would be visible only to a trucker who rode right alongside us. And at the speed Ash is driving, the odds of a truck keeping up are slim. But this is different. My breasts will be right there in the window.

He takes his eyes off the road long enough to rake a heated

gaze over me. "So let them see," he says as his fingertip finds my clit, making me arch up in both arousal and surprise. "You're beautiful."

The pure need that races through me is so intense that I squirm against his hand, silently begging him to slip his fingers inside me.

"You're so wet, baby," he says with a tenderness that makes this moment seem truly intimate rather than porny and prurient. "Tell me you like this," he murmurs as he gently strokes my clit.

"Yes." The word is barely breath.

"Good." He slips two fingers inside me. "I like it, too," he says as I rock my hips, silently begging for him to take me over even as his touch steals my thoughts and my reason, leaving me a shell of lust and need.

"Now do what I asked," he murmurs. "The bodice. Down. I want to watch you tease your nipples."

"Ash, no." The protest is genuine, but even so, my pussy tightens around his fingers, my desire trying to win out over my fear. "That wasn't part of our deal."

"Wasn't it?"

"You touching me," I say. "That was the deal. There was nothing about me touching myself."

I can't tell if the small noise he makes is a laugh or frustration. But when he pulls his hand away, it's me who's frustrated.

"Fair enough." He returns his hand to the steering wheel.

I want to cry. Mostly, I want to laugh. I haven't been this turned on—or had this much fun with a man—since... well, since ever.

There were boyfriends before Rory, sure. But mostly there'd been school and work and just... dates. No sparks. No real heat. I'd liked sex, but it had never been like this.

"Fine," I say, hoping I sound perturbed rather than turned

on. I bite my lower lip, and then, slowly, I tug the bodice down to free my breasts. My nipples are hard and sensitive, and I close my eyes as I tease them, letting the sensations wash over me, waiting for his fingers to slip inside me again and send me tumbling into that sweet oblivion.

"Baby, you are making me so hard."

The words are like a caress, and I feel my core tighten, my body begging for more.

"Go ahead," he says. "You know what you want."

A whisper of fear washes over me, but I ignore it. Instead, I slide one hand down over the silky material of the dress. It's still ruched up high on my thighs, and I tease it up a bit more, then slide my hand over my shaved pussy until my fingertip finds my clit and my body trembles from the rush of pure, sensual electricity.

I bite my lower lip, then glance over at Ash. His body is tense, his eyes on the road, but he's adjusted the mirror so that it reflects me rather than the highway behind us. And the hand that had earlier been touching me is now slowly stroking his cock.

A wild needs cuts through me, so intense that I feel my core clench and my nipples tighten. I fight the urge to squirm. To find the release I'm craving.

"Don't fight it," he says. "Take yourself over."

"Ash." I'm sure he can hear the need in my voice. I'm lost in a sea of lust. I barely even know myself in this moment, and I'm not sure if he's tormenting me or saving me.

I want to do it. I crave the release.

And yet I see the truck approaching on the right, another one following close behind.

"Trust me," he says, the heat in his voice pushing back the tendrils of fear. "The way you look now is only for me."

"And how do I look?"

He turns his attention away from the road only long enough to skim a glance over me. "Powerful."

The word envelops me, somehow more sensual than any other word he could have chosen. And yet I still feel unsure. Inadequate somehow. "Powerful?" I whisper. "Not sexy or beautiful?"

I want to cringe from the neediness in my voice, but if he hears it, he makes no indication. Instead, he simply says, "Power is sexy. Power is beauty. You're both, Brianna. Don't you know that?"

I blink, forcing myself not to cry. I tell myself I'm just overwhelmed. There's a ransom on my privacy, after all. And I'm selling myself to pay for it. Of course, I'm stressed. Of course, tears will flow.

But the tears aren't stress, and I know it, even if I don't want to think it. The tears are joy. Because Ash sees me. All of me.

I gasp out a choked little sound as I realize that I now understand what Rory and his cohorts took away from me. That this is what I'd never had. And without Ash—without someone stepping in and taking control — I never would have understood that I want to surrender. Not because I'm forced to. But because I need to.

But only to the right man.

Right now, that man is Ash.

With a start, I realize that this may be the first time I've truly owned what I want. I'd had sex before I was taken, of course. But I'd always let the guy lead. Though perhaps *let* isn't the right word. There'd never seemed to be a choice.

With Ash, it's different. Because even though our deal is that he has me however he wants me, right now, I'm the one with the power.

And what an odd feeling that is.

For a moment, I simply look at him. He takes his eyes off the road long enough to glance my direction, one eyebrow raised in that sexy way he has. "I believe you have your orders."

I do. And as the trucks come closer and closer, I shut my eyes and slip two fingers inside myself.

I tease my clit and imagine it's Ash touching me. Ash kissing me. Ash fucking me.

"Bree."

My name is barely a whisper, but it sends sparks dancing over my body, his whisper of my name even more intense than my touch.

He cups his hand over mine, his fingers curling over to stroke my clit, and I groan. I'm so close. So very close, and I want to explode like this. His hand on mine as we careen down this highway, the power of this car humming all around us.

Instead, he gently pulls my hand away, then tugs down my skirt. "Top up," he says.

"Ash, I—"

He just points, and I maneuver the seat so that I'm sitting upright again. That's when I realize that the sun has already slipped behind the horizon, and we're pulling in front of the valet stand at the Stark Century Hotel & Casino.

"Ash! What the hell?" I'm beyond mortified, certain that every valet who works there and every person standing nearby had just gotten and up-close-and-personal view of me with my top down and my skirt up.

"My property," he says, and all my warm fuzzy feelings turn to ice.

"That didn't mean—" But I cut off my words as a valet opens the door and offers me a hand to help me out. I take it, then search the valet's face for a smirk or a leer. *Nothing.* Which means he wasn't paying attention or he's very well-trained.

Since it's a Stark hotel, I assume the latter.

But none of the guests mingling nearby are smirking either.

I'm not mollified, though.

Over the car, I see Ash say something to the valet before he circles the car to slide up beside me. As he hooks an arm around my shoulder, I elbow him in the side and step out of his embrace.

He just laughs.

"It isn't funny," I say, whipping around to face him, only to find him indicating the car, where I see the valet slide into the passenger side and close the door.

I frown. When do valets enter on the passenger side?

I scowl, trying to peer through the glass to see what he could possibly be doing, but I can't see a thing through the window tint. I turn to Ash, intending to ask what the valet is doing and what we're waiting for when the reality hits me with the force of a slap.

We're waiting for me to get a clue.

Ash wasn't exposing me to the world. The world couldn't see me.

The fear that maybe they had, though....

Some deep and buried part of me has to admit to feeling a little bit of a thrill from being on display.

I don't, however, have to admit it to Ash.

TWENTY-ONE

Considering Ash's father owns the hotel, it's no surprise when we bypass the front desk and go directly to the elevators. As we cross the lobby, I see a few people turning to gape, some even lifting their phones, presumably to take video or pics of Ash, just as they do when Damien is out in public. Soon, I know, the fact that he's here in Vegas will be all over the internet.

I glance at him, but he's as cool about the attention as his father always is. I'm not surprised. He'd garnered his own fame early on as a race car driver, so he was already used to it before that fame had multiplied exponentially when his relationship to Damien hit the press.

I, however, am not used to it at all, and I move even closer to him, relaxing only when the elevator doors close. As soon as they do, Ash punches in the code for the penthouse suite, then backs me into a corner, his arms and body blocking me in. Not that I want to move. Right there in the protection of his arms is exactly where I want to be.

Even so, I gasp as he tugs the top of my dress down, freeing my breasts. He bends over, laving his tongue over my hard nipple. "Ash, no." I'm amazed I can get the words out. I'm so turned on I can barely think, my body all ice and fire and need.

"Any time, any place." His fingertips replace his tongue, and as they tease my nipples, his eyes hold mine. "That was the deal."

"Cameras," I say, ashamed that the word is only for form. I'm still tingling from the drive, my body craving his. I don't know what he's turned me into, but right then I don't care what kind of a show we're putting on.

"Breaking our deal?" The whispered question tickles my ears as his hand slides up my thigh, taking the skirt with it. I'm going to be fully exposed soon, blocked only from the few angles where his body shields mine.

Three million. Technically, that's what he's paying for this moment in front of the cameras. But the joke's on him, I think as his fingers find my core. As his lips tease down my neck.

Three million, I think, and I stay silent and exposed. This is the trade I agreed to. The deal he proposed.

Does he really not know that I crave the way his fingers touch my clit, the way he thrusts them inside me? The way he kisses his way down to my breast so that he's no longer blocking my view of the corners of the elevator car where I know those cameras are mounted?

I swallow, more turned on than I can ever remember being as I look at the lens across from me. As his fingers slide in and out in a rhythm that's taking me close, but not taking me over.

Who am I?

More important, who am I with Ash? And is that who I want to be?

The answer comes fast, and I cry out his name, begging him to take me over, too turned on to care who might be watching, or who Ash might have to bribe to destroy whatever is caught on those cameras.

I want this. I want *him*. This man who erases my fears. Who will bury my nightmares. Who will pay a fortune to keep me safe.

And who plays my body like a finely tuned instrument.

He pulls away from my breast, then rises to take my mouth in a kiss that is long and deep and claiming. If there was any doubt in my mind that I'd become his property sometime during this trip, it's fully erased now.

I need the three million.

I want Ashton Stone.

And the real horror is that once the money is transferred, I won't be his any longer.

As the elevator slowed, Ash stepped back, letting the material fall against those slim thighs as Bree adjusted her top, her eyes not quite meeting his and her cheeks flushed pink.

He wanted to pull her close and kiss her hard, but he knew from experience that Mina and David, the housekeeper and concierge assigned to the penthouse, would be waiting in the foyer when the doors opened, ready to take on any tasks required for one of the Stark family or their guests. Better to just stand beside her as the elevator slowed even though all he wanted to do was touch her.

His body was still on fire from the drive. He'd never been with a woman as responsive as Bree. But it wasn't just the way she reacted to him. It was the way she trusted him. Maybe she knew that the Stark family code he'd entered for the penthouse also disabled the cameras, but he doubted it. Which meant that she'd fully submitted to him when he'd told her not to worry.

It humbled him that she trusted him with her body. With

her privacy. With the intimate knowledge of what turned her on.

Most of all, she trusted him to fix whatever horror was nipping at her toes. A horror that could only be slain by a three-million-dollar payment.

He didn't know the specifics of why she needed it, but he was certain it was some type of blackmail. Though what a woman like Bree could ever have done that was worth paying three-million dollars to hide, he really didn't know.

He intended to find out.

"Fiftieth floor," she noted as the elevator slowed. "I've never been up this high. When Nikki and Damien gave me a week here once, Aria and I stayed on the pool level. It was incredible." She tilted her chin up as she looked at him, the corner of her mouth tugging into the tiniest of smiles.

"That must have been fun." He remembered that weekend. He'd been in town, too, and though he usually didn't visit the pool deck—the penthouse had its own pool—he'd learned that she and her friend had reserved a cabana for the day. "I've been here myself several times and I often go to the pool deck just for the company. And," he added as his eyes skimmed over hers, "for the view. I've been known to meet friends there, too. Sometimes, I'll even offer to buy them a drink. Always a disappointment when they have to decline."

"Maybe you'll have the chance to make the offer again." Her eyes sparkled with humor. "Another drink. Or something else interesting. Maybe if you do, they won't turn you down."

The edge of heat in her voice teased his cock, and he wanted to ask what drink or activity this mystery friend might find appealing. But before he could, the elevator doors slid open, revealing the now-familiar entrance hall along with Mina and David, the staff he'd come to know over the last couple of years.

He let Bree step out first, then followed and introduced

them. He gestured for Bree to continue inside while he hung back to give Mina and David their instructions—essentially to not worry about them since it was just an overnight stay. Then he sent them off, promising to ring if anything more was needed.

"Wow," Bree said when he caught up with her on the balcony. "The view is amazing." She was hugging herself to ward off the October chill as she looked out over the sparkling lights of Sin City.

"Lovely, isn't it?" he said, his gaze skimming over those sharp cheekbones. Her kissable lips. Her silky hair tucked behind an ear he was tempted to caress.

And why not? He owned her, didn't he? For now, at least, the woman he'd craved for what felt like an eternity belonged entirely to him, and he stepped behind her, ready to claim what he owned.

Gently, he urged her forward until her hands closed over the railing that topped the clear panels surrounding this level of the balcony. He was already hard, and he heard her breath stutter as he moved close, his cock straining against his jeans and pressing against the small of her back.

He put his palms on her bare shoulders, then tilted his head forward, breathing in the floral scent of her shampoo.

"Whatever you want," she whispered. "However you want it."

"She remembers the rules," he said, slowly peeling down the top of her dress until she was naked from the waist up. Then he cupped his hands over her breasts. Her breath hitched, and his cock grew even harder.

He slid one hand down, teasing her pussy through the thin material, his cock straining against the denim as she whimpered softly, then shifted, pushing her ass back against him in what could only be a silent plea for more.

"Beg me for it," he whispered, as his fingers teased their way under the skirt. As he found her wet and wanting and ready. "Beg me to fuck you right here, standing at the top of this city."

"Is that what you want?"

"Desperately," he admitted. He couldn't remember wanting a woman more, and it wasn't just because he'd been denied her for so long. Wasn't because of the rules he'd set. He wanted her humor and her strength. Her sass and her smile.

Most of all, he wanted the way she made him feel. As if he was her hero. As if he had the power to slay all the monsters that haunted her.

And somehow, someway, he would do just that.

"Beg me," he repeated, longing to be inside her.

"If I beg, I'm free." The soft words were almost whisked away by the breeze.

He stifled a groan. He'd set the damn rules. "I want you, Bree," he said, and he couldn't remember ever meaning those words more. "Tell me you want me."

"Yes." The word was little more than a tremulous whisper, but he could hear the truth.

"Say it," he demanded, his fingers thrusting inside her, making her gasp and moan in a way that only made him harder. "Beg me," he ordered as he teased her clit and she made soft sounds of growing pleasure. "Beg me," he repeated.

But she stayed brutally silent.

Frustration as pungent as fire curled through him. He'd never wanted anything more than what he craved right then. To yank the dress all the way off. To lay her out on one of the oversized chaises. To spread her legs and fuck her as the lights of the city twinkled like fairy dust all around them.

He wanted to lose himself inside her. To take her up all the way to heaven, then send her crashing back down like the burning embers of a shooting star, only to land safe in his arms again.

"Beg me," he pleaded, but she only shook her head. "You want me," he whispered, his fingers stroking her clit.

"Yes."

"Then beg me."

She laughed, and he knew she saw it, too. The irony that he was begging her to beg.

He couldn't help but smile at the game they were both playing. She could drag it out, but in the end, he would win. He'd have her begging for him by sunrise. And when she did, he would be more than happy to oblige. As for now...

She moaned as he slid the dress down over her hips and thighs so that it fell to the floor, leaving her naked in his arms. "Cold," she whispered, and he gathered her closer, then bent his mouth to her ear.

"Will it sound too cliché if I tell you I'll warm you up?"

He felt her soft laughter against the palms that again cupped her breasts. "Maybe," she whispered. "But what's a little cliché between friends?"

"You make a good point." He kept his left palm firmly over her breast but went exploring with his right. Teasing her nipple. Feeling the weight of her breast against his palm. Trailing his fingers down her soft skin, then tracing a fingertip over the pattern of her ribs. Her body was perfect. Not so thin that he could injure himself on a bone. Not so athletic that sex felt like an Olympic try-out, but also not so soft that she had no stamina and was content to simply lay beneath him like a fuckable pillow.

On the contrary, Bree responded with an enthusiasm that made him ache even more. That seemed to fuel the desire for her that he'd tamped down for over a year. Her bare ass writhed against his denim-clad cock. Her hands closed over his as he teased her breast. Not to stop him, but to move with him. As if she couldn't bear to not feel what he was feeling. To need what he needed.

Her breath was shaky, broken by soft murmurs of *yes* and *please*, and the way she wriggled against him only made the torture more sweetly intense. It took all his strength not to bend her over and fuck her from behind. To tease her clit as he thrust his cock deep inside her. To make her explode in his arms, screaming his name so that it echoed out over all of Vegas.

But that was against the rules. He wouldn't fuck her until she begged.

And when she begged, this would be over.

Would it?

The question came unbidden, and he shoved it aside. Right now, he cared only about this moment. Right now, he only wanted to touch Bree.

With her ass nestled against his cock, he slid one arm around her neck, locking her in place. He felt her stiffen, and in the next heartbeat, he remembered who he was holding. The horror that she'd been through when she'd been taken.

He released his chokehold, then took a step back.

"Stay."

Her whisper was barely audible, and he froze.

"Not like that." He moved closer, his palms light atop her bare shoulders and her back against his chest. "I don't have to hold you like that."

"What if—what if I want you to?"

He closed his eyes, certain he should refuse, but also hearing the plea in her voice. As if this was a test. Not of him, but of herself.

Then, without a word, he put his arm around her neck again. She exhaled, one tight little puff of breath, then arched back, surrendering to him. Humbling him.

Slowly, he traced his other hand down, starting at her

breasts, then easing over her ribs, then over her flat belly until he reached the smooth, waxed skin of her pussy. She made a whimpering noise, and when she shifted her stance to spread her legs a bit more, the certainty that she wanted his touch as much as he craved her slammed through him with full force.

He stroked his hand down, his fingertips rejoicing in the feel of her smooth skin, his lips parting in a low groan as he went lower still and found her slick and wet and needy.

He didn't tease her. Didn't play with her clit or trace softly over her labia. Instead, he thrust two fingers inside her, then held her tight as her back arched and her core clenched around his fingers.

"That's it, baby. Tell me you want it."

"Yes," she murmured as her hips moved and her breathing quickened. She was so close, and he wanted to take her over. Wanted to be the man who made her explode.

But he wanted more, too. And he was damn certain that she did as well.

All she had to do was beg...

He withdrew his fingers, then slowly teased her clit as she murmured, "No, Ash, please. Don't stop. Please, don't stop."

He bent to whisper in her ear. "Tell me what you want, baby. Beg for it."

"Bastard." But the word was a breath, and he heard the humor under the frustration.

Once again, he thrust two fingers deep inside her, teasing that sensitive G-spot as she writhed against him, her body craving everything he had to give, and her cry of, "More, Ash, please more," sounded so wild and desperate they could probably hear it down on the strip.

"That's it, baby," he said as he stroked and teased, wanting to take her over. Wanting to hold her close as she exploded in his arms. He didn't know what had happened to her when she'd been taken, but he could imagine.

And he would make it his personal mission to burn her fear to the ground, then build her back up with nothing but pleasure. "Beg me," he whispered. "Come on, baby. Beg me."

"Ash," she murmured. "I want—"

Ping!

The sharp chime of the elevator startled them both, and as Ash spit out a curse, she broke from his embrace to scoot out of sight on the far side of the glass patio doors.

"Dammit, I'm so sorry." He held up a finger to indicate he'd be right back, then hurried through the open doorway intent on strangling David or Mina.

Except it was his own ass he needed to kick. He'd locked down the elevator for the evening, but he hadn't turned on the Do Not Disturb function. And absent that command, the staff was authorized to reactivate the elevator in order to deliver urgent mail or packages to the entryway table.

But who the hell would be sending him something tonight?

He'd know in a second, he thought, as the elevator doors parted, and David stepped out.

"Mr. Stone. Sorry to disturb, but this was delivered by a local messenger and was marked urgent."

As David departed, Ash opened the slim cardboard envelope with the local messenger service's logo. Inside he found a letter-sized envelope with Ash's name printed on the front and a handwritten notation indicating that the service had received the fax fifteen minutes ago, and the sender had identified itself as Stark International. But it was a stamp reading URGENT that took up much of the envelope's real estate.

Ash couldn't imagine why Damien or anyone at the company would use a messenger service as a middleman and not just send the fax directly to the hotel. For that matter, why not text or email Ash directly?

Frowning, he slipped a finger under the flap to open the envelope. As he did, Bree hurried toward him, the dress back on, but her feet bare. "What is it?"

"Something from my father. Or his office," he amended, pulling out the paper, then frowning as he unfolded it to reveal a fax copy of Stark International's letterhead with no signature and no text. In fact, all that was on the paper was a QR code, neatly centered on the page.

"What the hell," he began, but he choked on the words when Bree sank to the floor, then pulled her knees up and hugged them.

She tilted her face up, and the terror he saw there almost ripped his heart out.

"That's not from Damien," she whispered, her voice so soft that he could barely hear her. "And the message is about me."

TWENTY-TWO

Ash shoved down the fear as he got her settled on the sofa. He crouched in front of her, his hands on her knees as he tried to stay calm despite the dread that twisted in his gut.

She hadn't told him a thing yet, but he knew this must be tied in with the three million dollars.

Despite his horrible childhood and despite all the times his temper had landed him in the gossip pages, Ash had never wanted to actively seek someone out and hurt them.

He wanted to now.

He didn't have a clue as to what he would see when he scanned that code, but it didn't matter. He would find the person who sent it. Find them. Hurt them. Make them pay for hurting Bree. For scaring her.

For bringing so much darkness into the life of a woman whose smile was brighter than the sun and whose laughter sounded like rainbows.

That wasn't who she was now, though. Just seeing that code had sucked the life from her face and the light from her eyes. Had taken a strong woman and broken her down into a frail child, now rocking herself on the sofa.

Ash had never felt more helpless in his life as he knelt in front of her. "I have to scan it," he said. "I have to. But I'm going to go over there to do it." He pointed to the balcony. "You stay here, okay?"

He started to rise, but she grabbed his hand, her grip much tighter than he would have expected. "I don't want you to see it," she whispered.

"I don't want to, either. Not after seeing what it's done to you." He cupped her cheek with his free hand. "But this is what the three million's about, isn't it? And I think I have to do this."

"It's for me." She reached for the stationery.

He shook his head. "It was addressed to me." Even if that hadn't been the case, he would have insisted on seeing it.

A small part of him said he was invading her privacy. A bigger part of him said to fuck that—he needed information if he was going to protect her. And he was damn well going to do that. He'd see her safe, no matter what horrors he might have to stomach along the way.

"You know what's going on here," he said. "Will you tell me?"

For a moment, she said nothing. Then she whispered—her voice so low he almost couldn't hear it—"Bring me my purse."

He had it in seconds, and she pulled out her phone, then took off the case to reveal a hidden gift card. She held it up, showing him a QR code. "It was in the basket at my book signing."

"Where does the link go?"

"To hell." Her voice was so full of fear he was having a hard time controlling his temper. He wanted to lash out at who ever had done that to her. Barring that, he wanted to hurl something heavy and breakable.

Wanted to, but wouldn't. No matter what, he wouldn't do a

thing that might scare her. "Bree, baby, I have to know if I'm going to help you."

"I haven't asked for your help," she snapped. "Not like that. I just asked for—"

"The money. I know." He kept his voice soft. "But this is addressed to me."

Her tear-filled eyes met his. "Who's doing this? They're all dead. Everyone who—"

She cut herself off with a shudder, but he understood. His mind had already gone that direction. "This is about what happened to you and Anne. The kidnapping."

He kept his voice calm, but it was hard. He hadn't known his sisters or Bree back then. But he knew them now. The woman in front of him who had already stolen his heart. The little girl who laughed when he tossed her into the pool and sent him a letter at least once each month with a picture she'd drawn especially for him.

"Is it photos? Did that creep Rory take pictures of you?"

Her laugh sounded a little manic. "Something like that."

"I don't want to, but we both know I have to open this link. Maybe it's not about you at all. God knows there's enough shit out there that someone might think that blackmailing me is a good call."

He started to rise. "I'll do it alone. Then I'll tell you what I find."

"No."

The word was so sharp it made him jump.

"Here. With me. Please. I know it wasn't addressed to me, but I have to see. Not because they're making me. But I just need to." The words were barely audible.

He didn't want to agree. He wanted to protect her. But he could already tell that wouldn't be possible. Not fully.

So he simply nodded and said, "Of course," then moved to

sit beside her on the sofa. Whatever that QR code would reveal, he knew it was personal. And horrible. He forced his growing fury down—it wouldn't help right now.

"Ready?"

She nodded, and he scanned the code, then held his phone so they could both see the screen.

It was black. Silent.

Then he heard a slight buzz, the kind of ambient noise when a microphone goes live but no one is talking.

Then the voice. A filtered voice that Ash was certain couldn't be manipulated back to normal for a voice print. He couldn't even tell if it was male or female. Just vile.

"Mr. Stone. How chivalrous of you to insist upon helping Bree play our little game. And as for you, naughty girl, we are so disappointed that you haven't watched The Greatest Hits yet. Not even a single ping and bounce out of curiosity. And we went to so much trouble. You hurt our feelings."

Ash glanced at Bree. *Greatest Hits?* But she was staring at the phone, and the only sign that the words troubled her was the fact that she reached out and twined the fingers of his free hand with hers.

"A pity," the voice continued. "Those moments are so delicious. Perhaps it slipped your mind. But never fear. We knew you wouldn't want Mr. Stone to miss out on seeing them, too. But before we begin—and, yes, you must watch to the end for our full message—we must express some concern, too. Is spending time with that man really in your best interest? Not just the time, but when you consider his particular character?"

The black disappeared, and bile rose in Ash's throat when it was replaced by the photo of a woman's body being pulled from the ocean, and above the photo a news-style headline blared out the question: *Murder or Suicide?*

His stomach curdled and he wanted to lash out. To reach

through the damn phone and kill whoever was on the other side of that image and voice. Instead, he simply held onto Bree as grief and regret welled up inside him and the voice droned on.

"Poor, sweet Delia Gray. A young woman trying to put herself through school. What a stroke of luck for a girl like her to stumble into a relationship with your Mr. Stone. Too bad she got knocked up. And too bad your benefactor didn't want to pay for the abortion."

Ash's gut twisted, and he kept his eyes forward, not wanting to see the disgust that surely painted Bree's face.

"Perhaps he's learned his lesson and that's why he's helping you? Are you the payment for his sins? We are impressed with your resourcefulness. We assume that you have charmed him into paying the bounty required to keep your naughty little secrets safe. But we are concerned. You've gotten in bed with the devil, dear Bree. And perhaps the ransom will harm you more than the past you so desperately want to hide."

He tightened his grip on her hand, gratified when she didn't pull away. He still didn't fully understand, but he was getting the drift. And just the mention of Delia meant that whatever demons this voice had unleashed on Bree, he was fighting them, too. Not just for her, but because his own demons hid behind that code, and he'd do whatever it took to slaughter the lot of them.

He started to tap the screen and pause the message, aching to explain to Bree about Delia. But she pushed his hand back with a simple, "no," as the voice continued on.

"So be wary, lovely Bree, before you let the devil share your bed. A devil in his own right as we have already shown. But also its spawn. You need look only to his mother. Psychotic. Brilliant. Dangerous. But who can blame her? A child of abuse—yes, Mr. Stone, your grandfather was such a charmer—and a victim of Damien Stark, who once claimed to love her, then broke her. Ah, gentle Bree. They are the man and woman with whom your protector shares blood. Do you truly wish to trust your fate to one who is—pardon our French— so very fucked up?"

Fury cut through Ash, and right then, he was on the verge of becoming the man the recording described. A violent, crazed monster who would destroy this room in a fit of fury, all the more insane because every single word he would be lashing out against was absolutely true.

If he'd ever been unsure that he was strong, that moment proved him to be a fucking Hercules. Because he managed to stay seated. To not explode. To try to be the man that Bree needed.

He turned to look at her, to see if she could discern his struggle. But he saw nothing on her face. No emotion at all.

Nothing except the blank expression of a woman trying to hide inside herself.

"But enough chatter," the voice continued in a perky, almost clown-like voice. "If you have chosen a devil as your champion, then so be it. But every champion must fight for the honor of his lady fair. And it's just deserts that your noble Ash learn what you truly are. Pitiful. Lost. Used. And—dare we say it—broken."

The black screen turned into a swirl of color, then the colors melted into letters that spelled out GREATEST HITS.

"What the hell?" he muttered as Bree choked out a single word: "No."

He eased closer, releasing her hand so he could put an arm around her, but she scooted away. "Don't." Her voice was high-pitched and as taut as a wire. "Don't touch me."

Something hard and horrible twisted in his gut as he studied her face, but it wasn't pain or fear he saw. Not anymore. Now it was strength and fury.

He nodded, glad for the fury. In his experience that was one of the best fuels for a fight. And right then, he knew she was fighting hard to stay calm.

As he watched, the words faded. The screen was black again. No image. No sound.

Then he heard breathing. Shallow. Then a whimper. Only the slightest of sounds, but it tore at his heart. *Bree.* Even from that tiny, pained sound, he knew that it was her.

The next voice wasn't. It was hard and harsh and distorted. "Strip."

At the other end of the couch, Bree shuddered.

Then the screen popped to life. She was there, sprawled naked on the floor, presumably asleep or passed out. A man approached, or at least Ash assumed it was a man. He couldn't tell since the figure was covered in a black robe and ski mask.

The hand was gloved, but it came off before touching Bree.

Vile. Intimate.

Taking her all the way, her body responding. The rest of her hiding inside herself, locked in a drugged sleep.

Ash forced himself not to react. Not to lash out in fury or try to pull her close to him. He needed it—to touch her and know that she was safe.

But right then, he knew, his touch was the last thing she needed.

"I'll leave," he whispered. "I don't care if it was addressed to me. I'm invading your privacy, and—"

Her hand reached out, finding his fingertips, then she scooted minutely closer so that she could take his hand. She didn't look at him, but the single word she spoke went straight to his heart. "*Stay.*"

He nodded, and as the rest of the horror played out, she kept her hand tight around his.

Five incidents. All similar. Some with one robed tormentor. Some with two. Some touching her with fingers. Some penetrating with toys. And all with Bree in a drugged haze that was only broken by cries when her captors took her to orgasm, or whimpers when the drugs began to wear off and some semblance of reality teased at her before the cloaked figures hurried to force her to drink more of whatever they were dosing her with.

Then Bree was alone in the room, curled up on the floor and crying, appearing only half-conscious when one of the figures entered. "Looks like someone's coming to thank you for a lovely date night," the voice said to her. "Apparently your body paid your ransom. They let you go, didn't they? And you abandoned that poor little girl who they kept behind."

Then the screen popped to black. "Rivals anything out of Hollywood, don't you think?" the voice said. "Drama. Secrets. Heartbreak and pain. So riveting. So revealing. And now we must thank you for your patronage... and for the three million. We do hope you still have the original code and that you calendared our appointment. We'd hate for you to miss the transfer time. But if you do, the world will certainly be entertained. All this and more, Bree. All out in the world if the money is even a one second late. Goodbye."

It was over.

Bree yanked her hand back, then drew up her knees and hugged her legs.

He stood, then tossed his phone onto the coffee table as if the phone, not the link, was the vile and tainted thing.

He wanted to reach out to Bree. To hold her close and absorb her pain. To take it into himself and leave her only peace.

But he couldn't. He couldn't even reach out a hand for her. Not when she'd just pulled away. Because there was no way— no way at all—he was violating her personal space.

For that matter, there was no way in hell he was continuing this game they were playing. He'd give her the three million—

hell, he'd give her more if that's what it took to keep her safe from those tormentors—but that bullshit agreement he'd forced on her?

No fucking way.

"Bree," he began, intending to tell her exactly that. But she held up a hand and shook her head as she stood, tears streaming silently down her face as she lifted her chin and met his eyes.

She opened her mouth as if to speak, then just shook her head again before turning and hurrying into the smaller of the suite's two bedrooms, then shutting the door behind her.

Shit.

He took a step that direction, then stopped, knowing full well that she needed space, and going into that room now would be about helping himself, not her.

But, dammit, he really wanted to go to her.

Then again, it was probably better that he didn't follow her. The last thing she needed was to see him lose his shit. And right then, he was on the verge of losing it all over the damn place.

With a start, he realized his arm was already back, ready to hurl a small vase he hadn't even realized he'd picked up. *Dammit.*

As much as he wanted the satisfaction of throwing that thing and watching it shatter, he put it down gently, then snatched one of the decorative pillows off the sofa and hurled it toward the balcony door. It hit the glass with a soft thud, then fell to the floor.

Not satisfying. Not satisfying at all.

But at least it calmed him enough that he knew he could contain his shit when he checked on her. Assuming she'd let him in the room.

He tapped lightly on the door, then leaned close, listening for permission. *Nothing.*

He considered walking away, but he needed to see her. Needed to look at her to reassure himself that she was okay. And, yeah, he needed her to truly understand that his help didn't stop at the three million. He would give her whatever she needed.

Once more, he tapped the door, and this time when she didn't answer, he turned the knob. *Unlocked.* He told himself that was as much an invitation as anything, and slowly pushed the door open.

She was curled up on the bed, her head on one of the many pillows and her legs up near her chest. He moved to her, taking the afghan from the foot of the bed and covering her before settling himself on the edge of the mattress.

"Should I leave?"

She shook her head, and the relief that flowed through him was more powerful than any emotion he could ever remember feeling.

"I didn't want you to see that," she whispered.

He tucked a strand of hair behind her ear, the action camouflaging his desperate need to touch her. "I didn't want either one of us to see it." He drew a breath. "I never knew it was like that," he said, his voice still as soft as cats' paws. "The kidnapping. From what little Damien has told me, I thought you were kept captive. Not hurt."

"They didn't hurt me."

"The hell they didn't," he snapped, the words bringing a hint of a smile to her lips.

"I mean not physically," she said. "But they definitely fucked me up."

"Why—"

"Damien doesn't know," she said, anticipating his question. "Nobody does." She closed her eyes, then drew in a noisy breath as if gathering courage. "I didn't even know."

It took him a second to realize he was standing, thrust to his feet by the horror her words implied.

"None of it?"

"I've had nightmares ever since." One bare shoulder moved, the tiniest of shrugs. "Now I know why. Guess my tormentor saved me a little bit on my therapy bill, huh?"

"Don't joke."

"Better than crying. Believe me, I've cried enough to know it doesn't do shit."

"Bree." He sat again on the edge of the bed. Gently, he stroked her hair, relief coursing through him when she didn't cringe away.

He wanted to find the words that would make it all better. He wanted to promise her that he would find out who'd sent that video and kill them with his bare hands. He wanted kiss her and make it all better, just like the prince in a fairy tale.

But this wasn't a story, and he was no prince.

So, he did nothing but sit beside her, stroking her hair as she dozed, and hoping that the small gesture soothed her, even if only a tiny bit.

Ding! Ding! Ding!

Her eyes flew open as the alarm on his damn phone chimed.

She blinked at him, then her expression cleared. "Your meeting?"

"I'm going to cancel it. I should have already."

She reached for his hand, then squeezed it. "No."

"Bree..."

"I'm just going to sleep," she said. "That's why we came here, right? Because you had an important meeting in Vegas?"

"Not as important as you."

He saw the smile tug at the corner of her mouth, then fade. "That's sweet. But I don't want those bastards who are haunting me to fuck you up, too. I don't think I can deal if you don't go because you think you have to babysit me."

Shit.

He considered lying to her. Telling her he'd go, then closing the bedroom door and staying in the living room, close enough that he could peek in on her.

Except, knowing Bree, she'd probably get out of bed and go into the living room just to make sure he was truly gone.

And the truth was, this meeting was crucial if he was going to take the INX project to the next phase. "All right," he said. "I'll go."

And once that monkey was off his back, he could focus all his attention on protecting Bree—and tracking down whoever was behind that goddamn video.

TWENTY-THREE

I awaken as if pulling myself from an abyss, my mind full of nothing but darkness. No memories. No sense of time. Not even a sense of self.

I know that I'm in a bed, my head on a pillow, my body atop the covers, but under a soft throw. I blink and sit up, trying to force my fuzzy mind to make sense of this unfamiliar room.

And then the memories come.

That black screen.

That filtered voice.

Those horrible, wicked videos.

I shudder and look around for Ash, but he's not in the room. Since I don't know how long I've been asleep, I don't really expect him to be. Slowly, like someone recovering from surgery, I slide off the bed. My bare feet are warm against the plush carpeting, and when I open the drapes, I see that it's still dark outside, the lights of Vegas twinkling like a zillion Christmas trees.

When I turn back toward the room, I notice that the other side of the bed is still perfectly made, the spread not even wrinkled. I wonder if Ash is asleep in the other bedroom, and I assume that he is. The thought deflates me. It's probably foolish, but I want to picture him holding me long into the night, keeping me safe while I sleep, his strong arms battling back any darkness that tries to invade my dreams.

"Stop it," I say aloud, albeit in the lowest of whispers. I shouldn't think like that. He's not my boyfriend, and we're together only for this trip. Only because I need his help. And in about thirty-six hours, the money will be transferred, and this will be over.

It's a business transaction, no matter how unconventional the terms. And he's hardly obligated to hold me when I sleep.

Except I want him to.

That simple truth pops into my mind, and I can't deny it. I want him with me. Holding me. Ash is safety. Whether it's stupid of me to think that or not, that's how he makes me feel. Like I'm the tormented princess and he's the noble knight keeping me safe.

Even now, I feel like I'm inside that video, cursed by an evil witch who's trapped me in a nightmare. Helpless on the floor and any moment someone will come in to touch me. To shame me. Maybe even to hurt me.

I shudder, then hurry from the bedroom, my spinning thoughts making me more than willing to swallow my pride and wake Ash up for company.

But when I reach the open door to the master suite, I find that he's not there.

Tendrils of worry creep up my back, and I look around for a clock since I don't have my phone. I remember the timer on his phone going off earlier, and him saying he had to leave for a meeting. But that wasn't long after we'd arrived, and the ornate clock on the living room wall makes clear that it's well-past midnight now.

I tell myself this is a good thing. After all, by the terms of our deal, I'm that man's property. I shouldn't crave him. On the contrary, I should be relieved to have time to myself.

Except that's all bullshit. I'm not relieved. I'm lonely and I'm edgy, and I snatch up the phone by the sofa and call the front desk, only to be told that they have no more idea as to Mr. Stone's location than I do.

So much for the concierge service at the Stark Century Las Vegas.

A tendril of anger starts to weave through me. I need him. I'm numb right now, and I need him to bring me back to life. The thought makes me cringe, and I try to push it away, telling myself not to think that. Not to believe it.

Except it's true. I do need him. I think I've needed him for a long time. And right now, I'm angry that he doesn't know that. That he's not here beside me. That he left me.

Why would he have left me?

What I need to do is text him and ask that question, so I take a few moments to search for my phone, finally locating it between two seat cushions. I shudder, realizing I must have lost track of it while Ash and I were watching that horrible video on his phone.

That video.

I hug myself, trying to erect a mental wall to keep those vile images out of my head.

Raindrops on roses and whiskers on kittens.

I tap out a quick text as the memory of those images keeps coming like wildfire.

White copper kettles. Mittens. Packages. String.

Fuck.

My mantra is not soothing, and Ash isn't answering, and I need to pee.

Since the latter is the only problem I can actually address, I head to the bathroom in the suite where I'd been sleeping.

And that, of course, is where I find the note.

In case you wake and I'm not back, a quick reminder that I left for a meeting. Tried to push to the morning, but no go. Sleep well. I will probably be back before you wake up.

The note mollifies me. And suddenly, I'm relieved that he's not here. Because, as much as I want to be strong, I can't help but collapse under the weight of it all, crushing my shoulders, pushing me down until I'm on the ground, hugging my knees, and rocking as I struggle to soothe myself while tears stream down my face.

I tell myself I can deal with all of this. That the real reason I'm crying is because I'm embarrassed by what he saw in that horrible, horrible video.

And that's true. I hate that he saw me weak and vulnerable. Imprisoned and abused.

But at the same time, I'm glad. Because he wasn't disgusted by me. He was horrified *for* me. And he tried to be strong for me, too.

So, yes, I'm glad. But I'm terrified, too. And not just because I'm being taunted and blackmailed, or because someone is threatening to turn my entire world upside down by releasing those horrible videos.

No, what terrifies me is me.

The vulnerability I've shown Ash. The fact that I've started to rely on him.

And the horrible, awful fear that it's all a lie and he doesn't have three million to transfer at all and those videos will flood the world.

But even that horrible possibility isn't the worst of my fears.

The worst is that I want him, and that desire terrifies me on so many levels.

And the only thing that soothes me is the certainty that while we may have a deal, we can't possibly have a future.

And yet there is still that desire. That craving. It burns inside me, and like a fairy tale princess I wait for my godmother to deliver some magical key, and when I turn it, all the baggage I've been carrying since the kidnapping will fall away, and I'll be free.

Free to touch, to feel, to love.

Because despite this strange deal we're operating under, I feel safe with Ash. Safer than I've felt in a long time.

Maybe ever.

Maybe that's an illusion, but if it is, I don't care. Right now, I want the illusion. Right now, I just want to feel safe.

Right now, I want Ash.

But Ash is nowhere to be found.

TWENTY-FOUR

This was what he needed, Ash thought as the McLaren screamed down the back straight at two-hundred miles per hour. The speed. The focus. The concentration necessary to keep from spinning out. To maintain total focus on what mattered, and never lose sight of the ultimate goal. Not to chase the monster, but to ride it. To tame it.

The raw power of the V8 engine radiated through the carbon fiber chassis, and moonlight gleamed on the livery as the car sliced through the night. He rounded yet another curve, accelerating beyond safety, his muscles aching with the strain of controlling the beast as the G-forces pressed him into the seat and the turbochargers emitted a high-pitched whine.

Although he was a fifty-percent owner in the private track located just outside of Vegas, he hadn't planned to come here tonight. On the contrary, his only intent had been to meet with Clark Maxwell in the Stark Century VIP lounge to finalize the terms of Maxwell's stake in the INX project—a significant stake that would ensure the industry-changing project could not only move forward with research but also with a planned IPO.

After the stereotypical celebration of whiskey and cigars, Ash would thank Maxwell again, then bid him goodnight before returning to the penthouse.

And to Bree.

He wouldn't have left her at all if this meeting hadn't been on his calendar for ages, and if Maxwell's investment weren't so damn important.

Even so, if Bree had been awake, he wouldn't have come. But considering the horrific day she'd had, he expected her to sleep through the night. And, again, the meeting with Maxwell was key.

At least that's what he'd believed. Never once had he expected Maxwell to not only pull out of the project, but to stab Ash in the back by giving him absolutely no warning.

So, yeah, celebrating was off the table.

And now he was pushing the McLaren's limits as Ash burned off the frustration of having lost an investor... and the fear of not knowing how the hell he was going to get the financing he needed to move forward with the INX.

Except these laps weren't solely about the INX.

A columnist once wrote that he wore a death-wish like some men wore a blazer, and maybe that was true. He didn't like to dive too deep into self-analysis. Chasing the monster was one thing. Sitting down and having tea and conversation with it was something entirely different.

All he knew was that he wasn't out there because of frustration with the INX, though that was what he'd told himself ever since Maxwell walked away. He was here because of Bree. Because whatever monsters he'd once believed were nipping at his heels were nothing but smoke and mirrors compared to the very real monsters that haunted her.

She hadn't asked for that. She didn't deserve it.

Now, he was on his fifth lap, and his blood was still burning.

The fear and horror from what he'd seen on that tape with Bree was spilling out, magnifying the demons that had slipped out from hidden crevices when Maxwell had walked out that door. The demons that said Ash couldn't be trusted. That he truly was the tainted failure his great-aunt had always said he'd be. That any success was a fluke, a mirage. A mistake.

He'd grown up hating her and the stories she'd told. Hating her lack of sympathy for his mother, who as a child had been destroyed by her father—Ash's grandfather and Damien's coach.

Most of all, he hated her sneering condescension. She was his family. His great-aunt. His adoptive mother, though she had not one maternal bone. She was supposed to love him. To help him.

But never once had she believed in him.

The thoughts went round and round in his head in time with the McLaren itself as he whipped it around the track again and again, hugging the curves and driving too damn close to the walls.

He knew he was being reckless. Hell, he was riding that tight path on purpose, trying to see who would flinch first—him or the devil.

It would be so easy, he thought. The tiniest flinch, and at this speed, he wouldn't be able to correct. He'd slam into the wall with the force of a rocket. Just that one little muscle spasm and it would all be over.

Was that why he was here? Was that what he wanted?

No.

Dammit, *no*.

It was true that Ash often needed the speed. The rush. The chase. There were times in his life when he'd come close, but despite all the hell in his life, he'd always viciously, painfully, desperately wanted to live.

He'd wanted the thrill to underscore it, sure. But despite

what the press said, he wasn't chasing the reaper, he was clinging to life.

Now, he wanted it more than ever. And not for just himself. Because tonight it wasn't his monster he was chasing. It was Bree's.

Once again, he floored the accelerator, eyeing the tachometer needle as it flirted with the red zone. The car gained even more speed, and the outside world blurred into light and shadows as adrenaline surged through his veins, an intoxicating cocktail that dulled the lingering memory of what he'd seen on that tape. Concrete proof that the monsters he'd been outrunning all his life truly did exist.

For Bree's sake—for his own—he was going to slay them.

As if the thought of her had worked a magic spell, he caught a glimpse of her in the bleachers. Her presence was like a punch in the gut, and he slowed on the next lap, his mind spinning as he wondered why she'd come and how she'd found him.

He didn't care. All that mattered was that she was there, and as he approached the pit, he skidded to a halt.

His eyes scanned the empty stands, searching for solace in the solitude. He didn't see her, and for a moment, he thought that he'd only imagined her.

Then there she was.

Bree stood alone in the dim light, her silhouette outlined against the bleachers. The sight of her took his breath away. He could see the strain in her posture, the lingering shadows of her recent trauma etched on her face. And Ash knew he would flip this car right now if he thought it would set her free. It wouldn't, though.

He might not be his father, but he had money, fame, notoriety, connections. He had the skill to fight death. To say fuck you to the ghosts that haunted him.

But he couldn't vanquish Bree's demons.

He'd get her the three million, sure. Come hell or highwater, he'd figure that out.

But that was only a quick fix, not a solution.

The only way he could truly help her—could truly win the woman who'd filled his head for years—was to slay her monsters.

And he didn't have a single fucking clue how to make that happen.

My heart is pounding as he jogs up the stairs to where I wait in the stands. "I woke up alone, you bastard," I snap, then pound my fists against his chest as he comes close and gathers me up.

"You goddamn fucking bastard." Fear fuels my words, pushing them out, wanting to wound, and I scramble out of his embrace as I continue my verbal assault. "What the hell were you thinking?"

I'm revealing too much—I know that. I don't want this man to know that I care so deeply. That I've been standing here, terrified while I watched him circle the track at such a speed that he must have one hell of a talented guardian angel to still be alive. Either that, or he has some seriously mad skills behind the wheel.

It's the latter, I know. But somehow the extent of his talent doesn't calm my raging fear or crippling terror.

"Do you have a death wish?" Again, my voice is a shout, and I punctuate the question with a hard shove against his chest. "This is how you're going to help me? What? Did you update your will? You die, and I inherit enough to pay off my blackmailer? Are you fucking stupid?"

I leave him no room to respond. "The answer is yes, in case you can't tell," I continue. "You. Are. Fucking. Stupid. And an asshole for leaving me alone. And a prick because you have a goddamn stupid death wish and that's a fool's way out."

I'm breathing hard, fury blasting out of me like machine gun fire. Fast and harsh and more about the kill than about the aim.

"A goddamn death wish," I repeat, then shove my palms hard against his chest one more time as he tries again to pull me close and calm me down.

I am *so* not in the mood to be calm.

"That's what my shrink says." His words are so soft that I barely hear him, and it's only after I finally settle a bit and say, "What?" that I realize his tone might have been an intentional ploy to get me to throttle back.

"The death wish," he clarifies. "My shrink says I have one."

"Oh." I take a step back, suddenly unnerved. I'm not sure what I expected, but his easy agreement definitely wasn't on the menu. To be honest, I'm not entirely sure why I'm here at all, except that I when I woke up without him, I realized how much I wanted him, and finally found a valet with whom Ash had chatted, revealing that he was taking the McLaren to a nearby track.

And once I found him—once I saw what he was doing here—that desire to see him and touch him not only multiplied, it morphed into a horrific, visceral terror that I was going to lose him tonight in a fiery crash.

Before I can gather my wits and ask why he has a death wish, he brushes the pad of his thumb over my lips, the soft touch as soothing as his words are harsh. "I'm not supposed to be here," he says simply.

"The track, you mean?" I haven't a clue what he's talking about, but the fact that he *is* talking calms me. A little bit, anyway.

He shakes his head. "On this earth. I'm not supposed to be here."

My mind is spinning. "What are you talking about?"

"You know the story. My grandfather forced his own daughter and my father together. I mean, hell, my mom's closer in age to a sister than a parent. And she was institutionalized so much I never really knew her anyway."

"I know," I whisper, but he keeps talking, and I'm not even sure he hears me.

"Before my grandfather died, he abused Damien and my mother both. Fucked them up big time. And now here I stand, a child that shouldn't ever have been born. I mean, hell, my mother was so young and damaged she didn't even realize she was pregnant. There was force. Abuse. Then there was me, and I got stuck living with my grandfather's sister—after all, who wouldn't want to grow up with a creepy great-aunt who made no secret that she thought I was Satan's spawn?"

He pinches the bridge of his nose. "And my grandfather? The man who arranged it all? Dead. And damned if I don't wish I could have pushed him off that building myself.

"Ash." My voice is so soft I'm not even sure he heard me.

He runs his hand up and down to indicate his body. "*Persona non grata.* That's me. Just the accidental aftermath of my grandfather's twisted mind, and since I couldn't be tossed in the garbage, I got tossed to Abigail."

"Ash, no—"

"And that's why my shrink—one of them—says I have a death wish. That I live my life tempting the universe to self-correct."

I hug myself, my heart breaking for him.

"That's why I chase the monster. I give the universe every opportunity to wipe me out of existence, just the way it should be. Because I wasn't wanted here in the first place."

"I want you." I can barely get the words out past the pain that I feel on his behalf.

I see the change on his face. The spark in his eyes, and the tiny smile that touches his mouth as he reaches out to run a strand of my hair through his fingers.

"My shrink's wrong, you know." His voice is so soft it's almost swallowed up by the spectator stands that loom over and around us. "I don't have a death wish at all."

The words take me aback. Considering Ash's reputation and what he'd just confessed to me, I was expecting him to own the whole "death wish" thing. Especially considering it's so obviously true.

"Then why are you out here by yourself driving like a drunken teenager?"

He chuckles. "I'm pretty sure my skills are sharper than your average seventeen-year-old."

I blink back tears. "Dammit, Ash. You scared me to death."

"Oh, baby." He brushes the pad of his thumb gently under my eyes, erasing the tears I hadn't realized I'd shed. "I'm sorry about that. I didn't mean to. And as for death, that's not it at all. The doctor and all those idiot reporters have it all wrong."

"Wrong?"

"It's not a death wish, Bree. I have a life wish."

I have no idea what to say. So I go with the only thing that makes sense. "What are you talking about?"

"It's easy to die," Ash says, still stroking a lock of my hair. "But one hell of a lot harder to live. That's probably true for everybody, but some of us have the lesson forced on us pretty damn early."

I consider what else I know of his past. About how Abigail had told him over and over and over that as a boy, Damien had forced sex on Sofia while she was traveling with her father and the tennis team. About Ash finally learning the truth. A truth that proved just how strong a man he truly is, because he'd survived the blow of discovering that Damien wasn't at fault at all. Instead, he was as much a victim as Sofia. As Ash himself.

"A life wish," I repeat, reaching for his hand. "You're saying that when you drive like that, you're turning it around? Not craving death, but celebrating life?"

He nods. "As fucked up as it can be here on this earth, some things are wonderful. And definitely worth celebrating." My hair is twined around his fingers, and now he spreads them, letting the strands fall free.

I think about what I'd just watched—him going around and around the track so fast I was certain he'd spin into a wall. One wrong move in that car, and death would have grabbed him whether he'd invited her in or not.

"Find another way," I say, but before the words are out of my mouth, he's kissing me. It's warm and almost gentle, but that's not what I want. I want hard. I want deep. I want this man to claim me. I want him to make me *feel*. I want all the things that scare me—the things I've been trying to outrun just like he's been trying to out-drive.

"Bree. Bree, oh, god, Bree." His lips are roaming over my cheeks, my chin, my neck, but not my lips, and I hear myself begging for him to *please, please kiss me*.

I thrust my fingers into his hair, tugging his face down to me as I look up to him. My eyes flicker open, and our gazes lock. My heart skips a beat as I see what's hiding behind his eyes. It's everything I've wanted. It's desire and life and hunger. It's beauty and pleasure, sunshine and tenderness.

It's love. Or, at least, I want it to be. Maybe it's too soon. I don't know. All I know is that the things that scare me—the demons that haunt me—fade away when I'm with Ash. I don't know if I'm ready, but I do know that I want him.

"Ash." I shift my hips so that I'm grinding against his cock, the pressure at the juncture of my thighs sending pleasure racing through me like electricity.

"Beg," he says. "You know the deal. Beg for it."

My chest tightens. I want this. And as soon as I beg, I'm free.

I don't want to be free.

But maybe I want to be close.

"I don't beg," I say. "I just take what I want."

I see both humor and heat flash in his eyes as I peel off that damn dress. Soon, I'm naked before him, wearing only my sandals with their two-inch heels.

"You're beautiful." His voice is heavy with lust and awe, and I feel it between my legs as surely as if he'd cupped his hand there. "Are you begging me?"

I lift my chin. "Hell no. I haven't—" I begin. "Not since Rory took—Well, not since...." I finish, feeling more fragile now. After all, I'd wanted Rory, too. I'd trusted Rory. Maybe I'd even loved him.

At the very least, I'd believed he was a good man. How can I ever know?

You can't.

The words ping inside my head, but I'm not sure if they are a reason or a warning. All I know for certain is that I trust Ash, and that there is no fear nipping at my heels.

I want to succumb to this man. I want to see how far we can go before the nightmares push in, as they inevitably will.

But maybe—just maybe—Ash is the man who can keep the nightmares at bay.

Except I can't. We have a deal. And I need that money one hell of a lot more than I need Ash inside me. Even if right now, it really doesn't feel like that.

He cups my cheek as he pulls me close, and all thought flits from my head as he moves both hands to my bare ass. "If you're begging, we should go back. A room. A bed. Creature comforts."

"No," I insist. "Here." I turn my back to him, refusing all arguments. At the same time, I take one of his hands, then slide it between my legs. I look back over my shoulder, then grin with victory as his fingers start to tease me. "The Ash I saw on that track," I begin. "Power and control. I want that."

His fingers stroke me, and I moan. I'm so wet. So needy.

"Are you begging me? Are you desperate for me to fuck you?"

"Yes," I murmur as his fingers thrust inside. "I'm desperate. But I'm not begging."

He uses his other hand to swipe my hair off my neck, sending it tumbling over my shoulder where the soft strands tease my breast.

Then his mouth is on my neck, his kisses driving me as wild as the fingers I'm grinding against. His free hand cups my breast, and I arch back, wanting to lose myself in passion. In him.

"Tell me to stop, and I will in a heartbeat. You understand?"

"Yes." I barely recognize that passion-strangled voice as mine. "But I won't ask. I want everything, Ash. Everything except what I have to beg for."

I spin in his arms, then hook my hands behind his neck, pulling his mouth to mine. His hands are on my ass, and he tugs me closer so that I feel the bulge of his erection beneath his jeans. I slide a hand down, stroking him before my fingers find the button, then the zipper. He groans as I stroke him, as I urge him back to one of the stadium seats.

"Sit," I say, then watch his face. I expect him to argue. To be the one to claim control. But he doesn't. Instead, he holds my eyes as he settles into the chair, his slacks open and his very hard cock exposed.

His brow lifts in question, as if he knows how much I want him. How much I want to beg him to be inside me.

But I won't. I need that money. And I made this deal.

"Knees," he says, and I feel the reverberation of that order all through my body. I hesitate only a second, waiting for the inevitable twang of fear, determined to keep it at bay.

But it doesn't come. There's no fear. There's only longing. Genuine desire.

That tightening of my nipples. That heat between my thighs. I close my eyes, reveling in the moment, then jerk my head up when he brushes a hand over my forehead.

"Bree. Are you okay?"

The question warms me more than it should, and I shake it off, then lift my head to look at him. "Tell me what you want."

"You know."

I make a show of licking my lips. "Tell me," I repeat.

His brows rise almost imperceptibly, and I see a flicker of something that might be humor, but might also be lust, in his eyes. "Your mouth," he says. "On my cock."

I say nothing, but this time I kneel before him. I put my hands on his thighs, then lean forward and lick his cock from tip to balls before drawing him into my mouth and teasing him with my lips, my tongue, my fingers.

I don't close my eyes. Instead, I twist to peek at his face. I see passion. I see how far I'm taking him. Need. Desire.

I cherish all of it. I revel in it. This power over him. I want to take him over. To make him beg and cry out and need. And without thinking, I pull back, then rise, climb onto the stadium seat, and straddle him.

I'm so wet, and he's rock hard, and it takes all my control not to take him inside. To remain like this, grinding against him, but not letting him fill me even though it's very clear that both of us want exactly that.

I put my hands on his shoulders as I move back and forth. *Me* in control. *Me* making him moan. Making him cry out my name.

Then his hands cup my breasts before sliding down to my waist, to my hips. Now he's in control, moving me, rocking me. "I want you, Bree." His voice is low. Guttural. "I want all of you. Beg for it. Dammit, Bree, I want you to beg."

But I only shake my head, his need turning me on even more until it feels like I'm glowing with power, especially when his fingertip slides between us as he plays with my clit, when he thrusts those fingers inside and begs me to, "Come, baby. Go over. You're so close. Go over with me."

Then he leans forward and closes his mouth over my breast, and that's when I explode, his cock between my legs, his fingers playing me like a fine instrument. My core tightens around his fingers and in that instant, he arches back, groans, and comes as well.

And as I fall back to earth, rocking forward to put my head on his shoulder and simply breathe, only two thoughts are clear: *More* and *Ashton*.

For a moment we stay like that, half-naked with him now soft beneath me. Then I ease off and shimmy back into the dress before digging in my purse for tissue. I offer him a handful, and we share a smile as we clean up.

"I don't know what I was expecting," he says. "But it wasn't that."

"Good surprise?" I ask. "Or bad surprise."

"Terrible."

I laugh. "Yeah. Just awful."

He finishes putting his clothes together, then stands. "One important thing," he begins, and I feel myself tense, afraid that he's about to steal the joy from this moment. Because that's what always happens, isn't it?

But that's not what happens at all. Instead, he grins at me, then glances up into the stands. "The moment we're back at the hotel, remind me to log onto the track's computer and erase the security feed."

"Deal," I say, laughing as he brushes my hair away from my face.

He kisses me, this time soft and sweet. "On second thought," he says, nuzzling my ear. "I might keep that recording for myself."

TWENTY-FIVE

Since I'd taken a taxi to the track, I make the half-hour drive back to the hotel with Ash in the McLaren, my skin still tingling from the way he'd touched me. Held me. Made me his.

I sigh, letting my mind linger on the memory of the kisses he'd skimmed over my body. And from the words that had flooded through my soul with his touch. *Want. Need. Mine.*

Love?

Maybe, but I can't let that one into my head. It's too soon.

And far too scary.

"Tell me about your code," he says as soon as we're on the way. He's holding my hand, removing it only when he needs to shift gears. I don't have to ask for an explanation. I know he's referring to the QR code I'd pulled from my phone case earlier that evening.

That evening. Had it really only been hours since he'd seen those horrible images with me? Those vile "Greatest Hits?" I hug myself, hating that Ash knows what he now knows… but also glad that I have Ash to help me shoulder the burden.

I draw a deep breath to bolster myself. "I told you it was in the goodie basket from the book signing, right? Well, I'd just watched it when you knocked on my car window outside the coffee shop."

He turns long enough to meet my eyes, his own haunted. "No wonder you looked so spooked."

"We thought it might be you," I admit. "Aria and me. Mostly Aria. Like a criminal returning to the scene of the crime."

"And I came to your car because I wanted to see your reaction?"

"That was her theory."

"What do you think now?" he asks, turning to face me.

"I think you need to watch the road. And I think you're one of the most honorable men I've ever met. You wouldn't hurt me," I say, though some silent, inner part of me amends that statement to say that he'd never hurt me *like that*." I'm not sure about emotionally. I think about how haunted he'd looked when the image of that woman — Delia—had popped onto the screen. I don't know the whole story, of course, but I don't think either one of us has a decent track record where relationships are concerned.

"I would never hurt you." His words are as solid as the man himself, and if nothing else, I know that he believes them. But where hurt is concerned, intent isn't always what matters. Like smoke, hurt can sneak into crevices and wind through weak spots. Most of my life has been an object lesson in that particular theorem.

"Do you have any idea who sent these QR codes?"

His question pulls me from my dark thoughts about his dead ex to dark thoughts about my kidnapping and our suspect list. With a sigh, I hug myself and shake my head. "Everyone involved in the kidnapping is dead now."

"Everyone that you know of who was involved."

"True." I don't like it, but since someone got their hands on those videos, it's a fair guess there was someone else involved. Or someone who knew Rory or one of the other players behind the whole, horrific scheme.

"Involved at the time, or became aware later," Ash says, when I share my thoughts. "Also, maybe they weren't involved back then, but they were aware. Maybe someone who was personally involved with Rory or one of the other players. They knew about the kidnapping but wanted nothing to do with it."

"And now they're hard up for cash?" I suggest. "Found the old footage and decided to take advantage?"

"Could be," he says.

"The problem is we don't have anything solid to go on."

"*Yet*," he says. "We don't have anything to go on *yet*." His hands tighten on the steering wheel, his knuckles going white. "I swear," he adds, his voice as sharp as a blade, "I will figure out who's behind this."

I want to bask in his certainty, but I know better than to blithely believe. "How?"

"I don't know," he admits. "But I will. You can count on it."

I let his words wash over me, expecting frustration. Instead, I feel hope. Because something in his tone tells me that he won't rest until he figures it out, and through it all, he's determined to protect me.

"We'll start with the QR codes," he says. "We have two, and presumably they go to different URLs. That's a lead."

"I saved the link to the first URL my code sent me to. I'm not sure if that will help, though."

"Never rule out anything," he says. "That might be key. And in about thirty-six hours, we'll have instructions for transferring funds, which should help, too. Money has to go somewhere. And we should be able to trace it."

"You can do that? It has to be undetectable, otherwise

they'll release the images. And Ash, I really don't want those videos out there."

"They won't ever be. Not if I can help it." He reaches over and takes my hand, then gives it a gentle squeeze. "But you're strong, Bree. Stronger than you think. If they did get out, you'd survive. Hell, you'd do better than survive."

I manage a wan smile. "Thanks for the vote of confidence, but if it's all the same to you, let's concentrate on not letting them know we're trying to trace anything."

"Agreed. And I have someone in mind."

My stomach twists at the thought of having someone else see those images, and when he squeezes my hand and whispers, "Need to know only," I melt just a little from the simple fact that he understands me so well.

"Thanks," I say, certain beyond a shadow of a doubt that Ash wouldn't intentionally hurt me. And that means he'll protect my secrets.

It also means I can trust him with more than he already knows. So I take a deep breath, then say, "Anne's on my video, too."

His head whips around, a wild fury coloring his face. I hold up a hand as I shake my head. "No, no. Not like what you saw them do to me. As far as I know, no one ever touched her."

I go on to explain what Aria and I had seen, especially the vile image of me with Anne in the frame.

"Those fuckers," he whispers. "I swear, I will find who—" He cuts himself off, and I watch as he forces himself back to calm. "I have your back now, baby. No one is going to hurt you like that ever again. As long as I'm drawing breath, no one is going to hurt you, period. Not you. Not Anne. And if we can help it, not anyone else, either."

The passion and promise in his voice seems to fill the car. It certainly fills me.

At the same time, though, I squirm a little. He's making a vow to protect me. But he only knows part of Brianna Bernstein. The part I show the world, covered and carefully cloaked to reveal only some of the flaws in the sculpture.

Granted, I've pulled back the cover more for him than anyone else except Aria. But what he doesn't understand and can't know is just how many spidery cracks run through me. Far too many to let me get truly close to anyone. Because with so many fault lines, any direct impact could shatter me. And even the pressure of a hug could make me fall apart completely.

I want to tell him. I want to believe that Ash is the glue that can ultimately hold me together.

But I say nothing. Instead, I just slip out of my shoes, pull my feet up onto the seat, and hug my knees as the desert slips by and the lights of Vegas grow brighter outside the window.

"It could be coincidental," he says after a few more miles, "but I find it very interesting that they chose three mil."

"Because of your company? Aria said the same thing."

"Did she?" He takes his eyes off the road and looks at me. "What else did she say?"

"Something about an investor pulling out, and that puts you in the hole for about three mil." I run my palms down the jacket of his I'm using as a lap blanket. "She might still think you're behind all of this. I haven't talked to her since—well, since before the interview with Maggie."

I suddenly realize how fast everything has moved. The bullshit interview. The trek to the Stark mansion. And then we were on the road. I hadn't even called Aria, just sent her a text telling her that Ash is helping me. She'd replied with a wide-eyed emoji, but nothing else.

"That's why I was at the track," Ash says, pulling my thoughts from Aria and back to his three-million-dollar hole.

"What do you mean?" I keep my voice calm despite the fingers of dread now creeping up my spine.

"My meeting tonight. It was with another investor. Turns out he's not investing a dime, much less millions. I went to the track to take the edge off after getting slammed with that bit of bad news."

He takes his eyes off the road long enough to meet mine. "Aria was right."

My entire body goes cold. "You're saying that you—"

"Oh, hell no." His head whips around to look at me, and I'm certain the horror I see there is genuine. "You don't really believe that I would—"

"You just said so!" I hear the edge of hysteria in my voice.

"I meant that she's right about the deficit. But that's my company, not me. I've got personal holdings. Real estate I bought when I started making money. A significant stock portfolio. And if I'm desperate, I even have a trust fund that Damien set up for me, which I swore I would never touch, and he swore I could leave untouched until Doomsday, but as his son, it was mine."

That's right," I say, remembering. "He and Nikki set up a trust for all the kids. When Damien learned about you, they never even hesitated. You're his son. You got a trust fund."

He says nothing to that, but I can't help but notice the way his body stiffens just a little and the way his chin lifts. "They certainly kept you in the loop."

"More like I'm invisible when I'm in nanny-mode. I probably shouldn't have told you that. It's something I overheard, and not my business. To be honest, I had forgotten all about it until you mentioned it. Sorry. I don't' mean to get all up in your business."

"It's fine."

He still doesn't look at me, and unlike his usual ease while driving, he's holding the steering wheel as if it's a life-preserver on the Titanic.

"Ash? Are you okay?" I feel like I've said something horribly wrong, but I don't know what it could be.

"I'm great actually." His voice is thick with emotion. "The truth is, I haven't touched that trust. I always felt it was his way of buying me off."

"Are you kidding? He loves you. The whole family loves you."

"I know. But I didn't believe it at the time, and I think that early animosity tainted that trust fund for me. Your reminder that they love me removed that shadow."

I hug myself, hating that he'd ever felt even the tiniest bit alienated from the people I knew genuinely loved him.

"I am a part of that family, now," he says. "It's a strange kind of miracle, but Damien truly feels like both my father and my friend. And Nikki feels more like an older sister than a stepmom. And those kids—I'd give my life for those kids, but they're so much younger they seem more like nieces and nephews than siblings."

"I get that."

"But none of that matters because at the end of the day, they're family, no matter what label I use. It took me a long time getting here. And a long time believing that Damien felt the same. And honestly, I don't think I knew until this moment how quickly he really did pull me into the family."

He reaches for my hand. So, thank you again," he says again, and it's only when I try to respond and can't that I realize my cheeks are wet and my throat is clogged with tears.

He lets go, then gently brushes my cheeks. "At any rate, the point is that Aria's right about the facts, but not about her conclusion. I've got enough assets to free up the three mil for you. And even though I'd rather go the OPM route, I've also got enough to bankroll the INX project if I need to."

"OPM?" I have no idea what he's talking about.

"Other people's money," he says with a grin. "Definitely the preferred way to go. But I have assets I can liquidate and add to what I've already invested in INX if it comes to that. Not the most astute financial decision, but it's doable. With plenty still there for you."

I nod with relief and understanding.

Or, I think with a frown, *mostly* understanding. "I understand the OPM thing," I tell him. "I've watched enough financial news and hung around the Stark house enough to know that diversification is good. But I also remember overhearing Damien talking about the INX-20. How he thinks it's going to change the industry. And how he wanted to invest, but you asked him not to."

"True."

"But why?"

Ash doesn't turn to look at me. "If I can't find another investor, I'm the one who'll fill that gap. Not Damien."

"Again, why? You just said that would make your position too large. That it wasn't the most financially sound decision."

"I'm willing to invest in myself if I need to."

I know I should let the subject drop, but I just don't get it. "But you don't need to. Damien would happily invest. He's already told you he wants to. And the man's a tech genius. If he says he wants to invest, it's because he means it. Because of the INX, not because of you."

For a moment, we just drive, his body stiff behind the wheel when every other time I've been in a car with him, he's been relaxed, as if the car is just an extension of himself.

"You know what," I say, "never mind. It's not my business, anyway."

"Bree..."

I shift a bit so I'm looking at him more directly. "I'm not being bitchy. I mean it. It's not my business."

"I'm not upset. "It's just that I've made my decision, and Damien understands it." His words are firm, and it's clear he's done with the subject.

"Right," I say. "Taking that off the table."

His shoulders drop a bit. "This project is important to me. Doing it on my own is important to me. And if Damien were to get involved, the media would jump all over that. It would become a Stark project, and while I love my father, the INX is my baby. Can you understand that?"

"Sure," I say, because I do get it. But at the same time, he's leveraging his personal assets to both fill the INX gap and to help me. I know he says he can afford it, but I also know that we're talking huge amounts of money. And if Ash's financial position flips, then that means that I'll be the girl who bankrupted Ashton Stone.

I'm not sure I could handle that.

I'm also sure that I won't survive if those videos get out, especially the one with Anne. So, I'm going to drop the subject and let Ash help me. Not just because I need the three million that he's offering, but also because I know that at this point there's no way he'd back out of helping me.

I just wish he'd let someone like Damien step in to help him.

TWENTY-SIX

By the time we're back inside the Vegas city limits, our conversation has shifted to the mundane details of getting to the airport in the morning. "I'll keep the McLaren garaged here," Ash decides. "We'll take a taxi to the airport, then take the Stark International Gulfstream to Austin."

"It's here?"

"I asked Grayson to fly her here in the morning. Damien's always said the fleet's at my disposal. Figure I've got to take my dad at his word."

"Have you used it before?"

He shakes his head, and I hide a smile, glad to see this evidence that their relationship really is growing stronger.

"We'll board about ten, we'll land at Bergstrom and be in downtown Austin before two."

"Is that where you live? One of the condos downtown?" I've been to Austin a couple of times for the South by Southwest festival, and it's one of my favorite towns. Plus, I've fallen in love with Tex-Mex food, so even despite the circumstances, I'm glad to be seeing the city again. And I'm very curious to see where Ashton Stone lives. Considering he's a young tech-oriented guy, I figure one of the high-rise condos in that city fits him perfectly, if not stereotypically.

He surprises me by shaking his head. "I've got a house on Hudson Bend. On Lake Travis," he adds in response to my questioning look. "That's where I live."

"That sounds amazing."

"It is. But it's also in the middle of a major remodel, so, yes. We'll be staying downtown. At my condo," he adds with a grin.

"But you don't live there?"

"I use it for guests," he says. "And I crash there when I stay too late at the office."

"Which is downtown," I guess, and he nods.

"Home or office or just a hang-out, I'm looking forward to seeing it all." I lace my voice with a tease, but it's true. I want to know everything there is to know about Ash, and that includes how and where he lives.

"We probably won't have time to see the house on this trip," he tells me. "But we'll come back once the remodel is finished."

He says the words casually, but their impact on me is anything but. "Oh," I say, hoping I sound just as cool and collected. "That sounds like a great plan."

He catches my eye, then takes my hand. Slowly, he lifts it to his lips, his eyes never leaving mine. Then he kisses my fingers and releases my hand. And even though we're not on the plane yet, in that moment, I feel like I'm flying.

"Hopefully Noah will have some information for us by the time we land," he says, the words bringing me back down to earth.

"Noah Carter?" My head is spinning. "What information? Noah—"

"Is not in law enforcement—not officially, anyway. And he won't say a word to Damien."

I don't know Noah well, but he's a friend of Damien's,

and I know enough to know that he's consulted with law enforcement on a number of major crimes. "Ash, I can't risk—"

He reaches across the console and takes my hand. "He isn't paid by or actively consulting with any law enforcement agency. But he is a whiz with tech. And he knows I need fast help with a blackmail attempt. He doesn't know who or what. He has no other information. But I wanted him prepared for when you agreed to let me bring him in."

"He's not in yet?"

"Right now, he's only meeting us for drinks as my friend."

"And you're so sure I'm going to agree to let him help that you're only mentioning this now?" I hear my voice rising in fear. It doesn't sound like Ash has broken any of the blackmailer's rules, but I'm still worried. What if Noah doesn't understand and pulls in a cop? Or has someone on the team who's also on the Stark Security payroll, and investigative company founded by Damien after the kidnapping.

Except I know Noah wouldn't do either of those things. And that's when I realize what's scaring me. It's not who Noah is, it's what he'll be doing.

What if he sees the images of me?

I shiver, then hug myself, shaking my head slowly. "You should have asked me first."

He reaches over and puts his hand on mine. "I'm sorry. I didn't mean to scare you or make it worse. I thought having Noah set up before we got there was a good idea. We're leaving LA, but we're flying into a safety net."

"I just—those videos." I swallow as I blink back tears. "I don't want anyone to see."

"Oh, baby," he says, his shoulders drooping. "I'm so sorry. Of course, that worries you."

"I don't want anyone—"

"And no one will," he says firmly. "I can't think of a single reason why Noah or anyone else we call in to help will have to."

"You think we'll have more than Noah on the team?"

"I think we want to trace the money. And since that's outside my pay grade, we're going to rely on the most trustworthy and loyal help we can round up. Okay? "His voice is as gentle as the fingertip that strokes my cheek. "I'm sorry," he adds. "I thought I was giving you one less thing to think about. I wasn't trying to make it worse. I would never do that to you. I lo—"

He clears his throat. "I lost my head. But we're on the same page now."

I barely hear those last words. All I hear is what he didn't say: *love*.

Was that what he'd truly intended to say? Or am I only hearing something I want to hear?

Want to hear...

The thought echoes in my head, surreal and scary. And far too fast.

Or is it? I was attracted to Ash the first moment I saw him, back when he burst into the Stark home full of misplaced anger and a lust for revenge.

I've followed his career and I've listened in awe whenever anyone brings up his skill and intelligence. I've felt my heart squeeze when he sits on the floor to play with his younger siblings, and I happily accepted anytime he offered to join me in the playroom when I was drowning in kids.

Other than those first, horrible days when everyone's expectations and understandings were all screwed up, Ashton Stone has proven to be one hell of a guy.

He's even more so now, as far as I'm concerned. Yes, helping me helps his little sister, but he didn't know that when he first signed on.

I needed three million, and he pledged to get it for me.

At a price.

The little voice in my head is more accusation than warning. Because no matter what Ashton's motives were for demanding the deal we struck, at the end of the day, it proved two things beyond a shadow of a doubt: That he wants me, at least for now. And, so help me, that I want him, too.

"Bree?" The worry in his tone pulls me from my thoughts.

"Sorry. What?"

"Are we okay?"

I'm not sure if he means about the possible slip of his tongue until he continues with, "Noah isn't going to see those videos, and neither is anyone else who may end up helping us. I should have checked with you first, and I'm sorry I didn't. I thought I was lifting the burden, not making it heavier.

"I get that," I tell him. "Truly. I just—I freaked a little bit."

"I'm not going to blame you for that."

We drive in silence for a while, then at a stoplight, he turns to me. "Do you trust me?"

"I'm here, aren't I?"

"Do you trust me," he repeats, his voice serious enough to make my heart squeeze a little.

"Yes," I say. "Don't you know that?"

The light changes, but he meets my eyes before moving forward. "I'd like to get Noah started if it's okay with you."

This time my whole chest goes tight, and the feeling isn't warm and enticing as it was only moments ago. Instead, it's hard and a little terrifying.

I force myself to say, "Yes. If you think it's okay, then of course, it's okay."

He takes his eyes off the road long enough to meet and hold mine. If he can see my fear, he doesn't acknowledge it. He simply lifts my hand to his mouth and kisses my palm.

And right then, although nothing has really changed at all, everything changes. Because I know that I really do trust him. Wholly and completely. With my life. And—though I'm not sure he knows it or even wants it—also with my heart.

He tugs his hand from mine to shift gears again, and I wait for the feeling to dissipate. It doesn't. Somehow, someway, Ash has truly gotten under my skin. Or maybe he'd always been there, and this is the first time I've allowed myself to realize it.

I don't know.

All I'm certain of is that something has shifted inside me. I trust him, yes. But what I feel is a hell of a lot stronger than that.

"You said you kept the URL the first QR code sent you to, right?"

I turn in my seat. "Yeah. Why?"

"Do you have it with you?"

"It's in my notes app on my phone." I pull up the app while we're talking. "Why?"

He tells me to take his phone and open his email app. When I do, I see an email already composed to NCarter. The subject is "party details" and in the body, there's a web address.

"That's where the QR code we got at the hotel sent us," he says. "Now take yours, text it to my phone, then copy it into the email and hit send."

"Party details?"

"We're not breaking a rule by sending that info to Noah," he says, "but why take chances?"

I gape at him. "You think whoever is doing this to me is monitoring our emails?"

"Actually, I don't. But again, why—"

"Take chances," I finish. And I have to silently agree.

As soon as the email is sent, he reaches for my hand, and our fingers twine again. I know he'll have to let go the next time he needs to shift, but for the moment, I relish the connection. I'm about to ask him if he thinks that Noah will really be able to get any solid info from those URLs, when my phone rings.

"Aria," I say, glancing down at the phone in my lap as Ash pulls his hand away and puts it on the wheel, almost as if we're pre-teens caught kissing in the bleachers. The thought makes me smile, and I hear the brightness and humor in my voice as I answer my phone.

My smile fades with Aria's first words. "Are you okay?"

"As much as I can be under the circumstances."

Beside me, Ash mouths *what?*

I shake my head, my attention on Aria. "Why? What's wrong?"

"Oh. Um. Nothing," she says. "I mean, no more than we already know about. I just had one of my feelings."

Woo, I mouth to Ash, who bites back a grin. "What kind of feeling?" I ask Aria. "Something about me? About Ash?"

"No, no. Just, well, I mean, you're good, right? You're going to get the money in time to meet that bullshit deadline?"

"Absolutely."

"And he's..."

"What?"

"I don't know."

"You're being insanely cryptic, Ar."

"I know. Sorry. I just... I just want to know you're okay. That your, um, arrangement is working out. I mean, I'm assuming you agreed to the, um, terms?"

I grimace as I glance sideways to Ash. "It's working out great."

"Good. That's great. And you'll get the money in time?"

"Of course. I mean, Anne's his sister, remember?" Ash glances my way. I shrug.

"She clears her throat, and I can't help but feel like there's something she's not telling me.

"Come on, Aria. What's going on?"

"Nothing. Honest."

"You're weirding me out."

"O.M.G.," she says. "It's no big. I mean, I just saw some of the pictures. You two in Vegas."

"I told you that we're heading to Austin. And trust me when I say the photos weren't our idea."

"Where are you, anyway?"

"In the car. On some highway."

"Driving?"

"Ash is driving. Are you sure nothing's going on? You're freaking me out."

"No, no, no," she says. "I don't mean to, really. Sorry. I'm glad everything's on track. Really. I just called because I have gossip."

I wait for her to go on, and when she doesn't, I prod. "Well? Lay it on me? We're still a ways from the hotel."

Beside me, Ash mouths, *what?*

I shrug, then tap the mute button. "I think she's worried we're doing exactly the kind of thing we've been doing."

"Me taking unfair sexual advantage of your situation?"

I grin, loving that we're so much on the same page we can joke about it. "Pretty much."

"Keep her on pins and needles," he says, and I flash a thumbs-up as I unmute my phone. "Sorry, Ar," I say. "We hit a dead zone. I missed all of that."

"You remember that guy Kari was hot for?"

"The surfer dude? Marty something?"

"Martin Street," she says, and yes.

"What about him?" Considering the bullshit I'm currently living with, this probably shouldn't be something that grabs my attention. But right now, the chance to spend a few minutes feeling like a normal girl talking to her bestie about normal girl things sounds about as perfect as it gets.

"Looks like they broke up."

Okay, that is not my idea of worthy gossip. Maybe on a day when I'm not being blackmailed, but today? Not so much. And, honestly, after that bullshit interview Kari sprang on me, her dating life doesn't rate high on my Interesting Gossip list, anyway.

Still, I give Aria an A for effort and try to sound interested when I say, "Well, there's lots of surfers for her to pick from. I'm sure she'll find someone else in time."

"Yeah, well, guess who he's seeing now...."

"Um, you?"

"Oh, please. Like I want Kari's cast-offs." I'm about to guess again, but Aria can't hold it in and blurts out, "Maggie Fucking Bridge."

"No. Way." I am seriously gobsmacked.

"Way," Aria says.

"And they're *dating* dating?"

"Yeah. At least I think so. I saw them all cozy in one of the inside booths."

"Cozy? Like making out?"

"Whispering. Sitting on the same side of the table, practically all over each other, and whispering."

"Whoa." I'm usually not that into gossip, but I just can't picture Maggie with anyone, much less a sexy surfer dude. I mean, honestly. Who would want her?

"I know, right?" Aria says when I tell her as much.

"Is Kari totally wigging?"

"That's what makes it even more bizarre," Aria tells me. "Kari seems totally cool with it."

"Weird."

"Totally," she says. "She's probably only okay on the surface. I bet she's seething inside."

I second that, and we share a few more minutes of chitchat before I tell her that we've reached the hotel, and I end the call just as the bellman opens my door.

I grin as Ash takes my elbow and escorts me into the ornate lobby. "And that's why I have a roommate," I tell him. "Because Aria can't survive without someone to talk to."

"She reminds me of a guy I shared a dorm with my freshman year of college," he begins, and by the time we're halfway across the lobby I've let loose a very undignified snort of laughter. Which causes him to laugh, which starts me up all over again.

We're so engaged with amusing ourselves that it isn't until we're in the elevator and the doors are closing that I notice that, once again, folks are looking our direction, several pointing. Only this time, it seems to be everyone who's looking. And more than half of them are holding their phones up and aiming them in our direction. Apropos considering Aria called because she saw a photo just like the ones they're taking.

As the elevator doors slide shut, I sigh, thinking about how we've just run the kind of celebrity gauntlet that I imagine has become second nature to Ash.

And which— in my now-considered opinion— is way up there on the nuisance scale.

TWENTY-SEVEN

I'd put my phone in silent mode after the call from Aria, and the moment we're back in the suite and I reset it, the thing starts pinging like machine gun fire. A billion notifications, including one from Caleb. I don't bother listening to his voicemail. Instead, I just hit the button to call him back.

He answers before the first ring has even finished.

"Why did you do it?" he demands. "I offer you the money and you tell Aria you're turning me down so that you can strike a deal with the devil? It's a good thing your parents are out of the country. They probably haven't heard about this bullshit yet."

It has been a very long time since I've talked to Caleb, and I'd forgotten how much of a superior air he always puts on just because he's two years older than me and Aria.

"Caleb, it's been like a decade since we've even spoken. So cut me some slack. What the hell are you talking about?"

"Seriously? We're going to play that game?"

"Did you talk with Aria? Because I really do appreciate that you offered me the money. But there was a time issue, and we both know you couldn't have liquidated—"

"I called Aria. I got her voicemail. I figured she was yelling at you. I mean, what the hell, Brianna? I offer to cover you on this, and yet you willingly choose those kinds of strings."

I freeze, my stomach going queasy even before my head catches up. It's not until I see Ash standing in the doorway, a folder in his hand, and a murderous expression on his face, that I acknowledge the reality that's now slapping me in the face.

"I have to go," I tell Caleb. And then—even though I know he's going to go griping to Aria—I hang up on my best friend's cousin.

"What?" I demand, my stomach getting queasier and queasier as I stalk across the room toward Ash. Because even though I hope I'm wrong, I know what he's going to say.

As it turns out, he says nothing, just passes me the folder. Slowly, I open it. It's filled with printouts from various web publications. And each and every one of them includes a picture of Ash, a picture of me, and some sort of headline that makes clear that Ashton Stone is paying me three million dollars in exchange for my sexual favors.

So, yeah. Caleb knows.

My phone chimes in my hand, and I look down to see a notification of both a call and a text from Aria. I close my eyes and sigh, realizing that was the topic she'd been dancing around, wanting to know how I was handling the press, but not wanting to say anything in case I hadn't yet seen it.

I let the call go to voicemail. I'm really not in the mood to talk.

There is one thing Caleb got right—I'm very, very glad my parents are on a cruise ship somewhere in the vicinity of Greece.

With a shudder, I pass the folder back to Ash. My stomach is queasy, and I'm forcing myself not to throw up. "Your pictures look great," I say. "But you're famous enough they must have a good stockpile to choose from. All the photos of me are from after the kidnapping. Except one. I saw one that was taken at a Stark Children's Foundation benefit." I smirk, recognizing the irony.

"Bree." I hear the pain in his voice and try to turn away. He stops me with a hand to my shoulder, then takes the folder and tosses it onto a coffee table. "Are you okay?"

I want to snap at him. To tell him I am not even remotely okay, and, gee, why might that be? Answer: because I agreed to be Ash's sex toy so I could snag three million and protect my privacy.

Suddenly, I feel like I'm swimming in irony.

I take a breath, then force down that urge to snap. Instead, I start to pace the suite. I pause in the kitchen area, open one of the packets of Oreos, and start to eat as I walk. "This doesn't make any sense. Nobody knows except Aria, and she wouldn't—"

"Are you sure?" There's a harshness in his voice, and I whip around to face him.

"Hell, yes, I'm sure. She would *never* betray my trust. *Never.* "Don't you have any fucking friends?"

"I'm sorry," he says, looking genuinely contrite. "And yes, now I do. And none of them would betray me that way, either."

"*Now* you do?" Both the word and the tone capture my attention and dull my wrath.

He shrugs. "I grew up in pretty shitty circumstances. Not that many friends. Things changed for me in college. Before that?" He glances at me for only a second, but it's enough to see the pain in his eyes. "Before that, things were pretty damn bad."

"Ash, I'm sorry." I don't remember crossing the room, but my arms are around his waist and I'm looking up at him, wishing I could change his past or erase his pain.

He presses a kiss to my forehead. "We have more to worry

about than the tragic story of my life." With a finger, he tilts my chin up. "Especially since it's not so tragic anymore."

"Isn't it?" My mouth is suddenly dry and my heart's beating a little too fast.

His fingertips brush my shoulder. "I like to think I'm on my way to a happily ever after."

"Happy endings are good," I say, telling myself not to hope. That these are just words in the eye of a storm, and I can't expect them to mean anything. Especially since, once the storm passes, we'll be surrounded by rubble.

He cups my cheek with his palm, and his smile seems a little sad. He looks like he's about to say something else, but he's silent for so long I decide that I'm wrong. This is just a moment. One calm moment in the storm for us to share.

Then he speaks, and I realize the storm hasn't even started. "Our deal's off," he says, stepping back as an arctic wind cuts through me, turning my blood to ice.

"What are you talking about?" My mind is reeling. In my head, I'm shouting at him, but the words come out even and measured, so heavy with pain and betrayal that I have to push them past my numb lips. "You know there's no other way for me to get the money in time, and now you—"

"*No.* I'll get you your money. It's the rest of it." He tosses the folder onto the coffee table, and those horrible pages slide out, then flutter to the floor. "I'm not doing that to you. I'm not making real every vile thing they're saying in the press. Not now that I've seen—"

He turns away, then scrubs his hands over his face before looking at me. "I'm such a fucking asshole, and I'm so sorry. Bree, I'm so, so sorry. After everything you've been through...."

He shakes his head. "No, no, that's bullshit. I'm not dropping the terms because of what you went through. Because damn me all to hell, what kind of asshole puts those kinds of terms out there under any circumstances? *That,*" he says, pointing to the sea of printouts. "Every foul thing they call me in those papers, they are a thousand percent right. And I'm so damn sorry."

I'm so shocked I can only stand there as he takes a step toward me, then kisses my cheek. I watch as he turns, then goes into the smaller of the two bedrooms. For a moment, I simply stand there, telling myself how much I admire his integrity.

I wait for the flood of relief that our deal is over. That there are no longer any conditions to satisfy before he gives me the money.

Except there is no flood. No relief.

Instead, I feel empty.

More than that, I'm angry. So angry that I don't have a plan when I march across the suite toward his door, then burst inside. It's fury driving the show.

Fury that has me scanning the room, then finding him pacing by the door to the private balcony. Fury that zeroes in on that vile sheet of letterhead with the single QR code on it.

I'm across the room in seconds, and I yank it out of his hands, tearing the page in the process. I wave it in his face, my body so ahead of my mind that I don't even know what I'm doing or why I'm doing it. Only that it has to be done.

"*This.*" I ball up the sheet and toss it at him "Everything that fucking code leads to stems from Rory. Everything stems from some asshole who was torturing me. Who grabbed me because I had some connection to someone with money."

I have no idea where I'm going with this—not really. But the words keep flooding out as I storm back and forth in the room. Ash stands there, watching me as if I'm a bomb about to explode.

Except I think I already have.

"The money Nikki and Damien paid? That had nothing to

do with me. That was to get Anne back. I was only there in that dark, horrible room because otherwise I was a liability. And since I was there, I became some sick fuck's toy. Just the little doll he used to get his jollies."

I poke Ash hard in the chest. "Is that all you wanted from me, too? Just a good time with the broken girl?"

He takes a step back, his eyes as wide and shocked as if I'd just slapped his face. "Bree, god, no. You can't believe that."

"No? Well, guess what. That wasn't what I wanted either. To be some prick's little plaything. But whether I wanted it or not, the bastard used me. And all that bullshit about me being drugged and asleep is just that—bullshit. It's inside me," I say, smacking my fist against my chest. "It comes out in my dreams. It comes out all the damn time. I never knew why before, but now I do. Because Rory put it inside me, and it's colored my life for years."

I'm breathing hard, my throat raw from the horrible, high pitch of my voice. Everything I'm saying is true, and at the same time I have no idea what I'm going to say next. I've never said any of this aloud. I'm not even sure I realized the truth until I saw the tape.

But it's true. The torment I experienced has been hiding in my dreams. Creeping through my subconscious. Coloring my work, my imagination, my life.

And now that I understand—now that I know what happened to me—I feel like an elastic band pulled too taut. I've snapped, and I've been flung to the side, propelled by the violence of experiencing my own breaking point.

"I had no idea who my captor was—not then. And when I found out the truth, when I learned a guy I'd actually *dated* had done that to me, all I wanted was to hurt him. But I couldn't. I couldn't get to him. And then he was caught. And then he was killed, and I had nothing—*nothing*—to do with ending him."

I bend over, my hands on my knees as I suck in gallons of air. I know I've lost it. That I've jumped right into the deep end. I'm almost scared of myself. But at the same time, it feels good. So good. And I'm not done yet.

I straighten, still breathing hard. I allow myself one glance at Ash's face, then look away when I see compassion. I'm not ready for that. I'm not ready to be outside of this bubble.

"I wanted to hurt him," I whisper. "I wanted to so badly." It's all flooding out of me now, leaving my body cold and shaking. "But I couldn't. I had no power. Not when he had me in that room. Not afterwards," I add. "At least not until I helped catch him. And that felt good. But it wasn't what I wanted. Not the closure I needed. And then he was dead."

I draw in a breath, then another. "Now he's just a ghost. He can't hurt me. But I can't hurt him, either."

With a small sob, I sink down to sit on the edge of the bed. He sits beside me, and though he starts to reach for my hand, he pulls back. He's only inches from me, but he doesn't touch me.

Part of me is glad.

Another part wants his arm around me so that I can let out the rest of it. So that I can sob and sob until I'm hollow inside, all wrung out.

Because I'm not empty. Not yet.

"Bree..."

I close my eyes, almost undone by the pain and tenderness in his voice.

"I have a choice now," I say, twisting to look up at him. "Those things he did to me, he didn't give me a choice. He stole from me. I'm not ever letting anyone do that again."

"You shouldn't." Now, he takes my hand and I relish the way his fingers twine with mine.

"Don't you get it?" I continue as I shift on the bed to look at him more directly. "I have the choice now. When we made our deal, it was *my* decision. You may have come up with the terms, but it was *my* choice. *My decision.*"

I draw in a breath. "Yes, I need the money, but I could have found another way. But you were the first person I thought of when I needed help. And when you named your terms, I didn't run."

I lift my chin and meet his eyes. "I didn't run," I repeat, "because I wanted those terms. I chose you. And I still do, Ash. I still choose you. At least so long as you want me, too."

I wait, feeling small and vulnerable as I try to read his face. Those eyes that seem haunted by pain, but whether it's mine or his own, I don't know.

Then he reaches out and strokes my hair. "Oh, baby. Do you think I don't want you? I do. Desperately. Painfully. But…"

"What?" I press when the word hangs between us.

"I've seen the fear in your eyes. When you saw those images. When I first pushed this deal on you. It was a shit thing to do, and I can't forget that. Or forgive myself for it."

"There's nothing to forgive. I'm not afraid of you. And it wasn't a shit thing because you get it. You get *me*." I cup his face, his beard stubble scratchy against my palm. "Somehow you knew what I wanted. And needed. What I still need," I add, my voice so soft it's almost a whisper. "Your terms opened that door for me. Don't you see that?"

He doesn't answer right away, and fear grows in the silence. I'm terrified he's going to send me back to LA. That he's going to say I'm too fragile and that he'll still get the money and try to track my blackmailer, but that he's still pulling out of the physical part of our deal.

The silence lingers for so long, I'm about to speak up and beg him to kiss me. To keep me.

Then he squeezes my hand, and, very softly, he says, "The

bastard stole your control. And whoever is blackmailing you now is riding on that."

"I know."

He hooks a finger under my chin and turns my head so that I'm looking right in his eyes. "So take it back."

"That's what I'm trying to do."

The tiniest hint of a smile plays at the corners of his mouth. "Try harder."

I frown, not sure what he's getting at.

"Do what you want," he says. "Tell me what to do."

"Oh." A delicious tingle spreads up my body, and I want to tell him to kiss me. To take me hard and fast. But I can't quite manage to get the words out.

Gently, he brushes my hair away from my face. "Tell me," he murmurs as I feel my cheeks heat. "Anything you want."

"You," I say, so softly I doubt he can hear me. "Use me," I add, then peek up at his face, afraid he's going to think I'm crazy to ask for that after ranting about Rory stealing my control.

"Thank you," he says, and I must frown because he continues. "For trusting me. For surrendering to me."

Surrendering. Yes. And the fact that he understands I need to take control by giving control is the most potent of aphrodisiacs.

TWENTY-EIGHT

Use me.

The words seemed to dance around Ash. Teasing. Tempting.

He'd just had her at the track. Her body moving with his. Her hips rocking in his lap. Her eyes like fire as they'd locked with his.

She'd felt like a miracle in his arms. A sweet breeze caressing his skin. A raging fire, burning away his uncertainty. A sword killing his demons.

For a woman so soft, she had her sharp edges, and damned if she hadn't used that blade to cut through all his bullshit. All his fears. His regrets. She'd taken it all down to that warm and gooey center.

Need.

Desire.

Bree Bernstein had stolen his heart months ago.

Use her, she'd said?

Oh, yes, he would use her. He'd own her. He'd claim her. He'd break them both into a thousand pieces only to come back together stronger than ever.

He would make her his own, all the while knowing that he was already hers, and that she craved their connection—body and soul—as much as he did.

That was the real crux of it, wasn't it? They'd both proclaimed to be loners, and maybe they were. But only with the rest of the world. The truth was, neither one of them had ever been alone. They'd always had each other.

It had just taken a significant chunk of both their lifetimes to find that out.

"Yes," he whispered, grabbing her upper arms and pulling her to him. He kissed her long and deep, then pushed her back onto the mattress so that she looked up at him, laughing.

She was back in that dress again—they really should get her a new outfit, but he'd become attached to that wicked, wonderful dress. "Take it off," he ordered, then watched in awe as she tugged it down and shimmied out of it, leaving her naked on the spread.

"You're beautiful." The words were more than a whisper. They were a prayer. And she was the altar at which he would worship.

She rolled over onto her hands and knees, then crawled across the mattress toward him. "I'm nowhere near as pretty as you are."

He laughed. "Okay. I'll give you that one."

"Hey!" She grabbed one of the throw pillows and tossed it at him. He ducked, and when she grabbed another and started to throw, he caught her wrist instead. Then he tugged her toward him until she was naked on her knees, and he slid off the bed to stand in front of her.

"I like that," he said, then slowly traced a fingertip over her perfect skin. Gliding over hips, breasts. Watching the little shivers. The way her nipples puckered. The cadence of her breath. The tempo of her heart.

He cupped her neck with one hand and met her eyes, almost done in by the heat he saw there. A need that seemed to rival his own.

Then he slid his hand down to cup her between her legs. She gasped and started to close her eyes.

"No. Keep them open. Look at me."

She bit her lip, but she didn't argue, and as his fingers played with her slick core—as he thrust his fingers deep inside her—she kept her eyes fixed on his. Eyes that went dark with longing.

Eyes that seemed to see all the way into his soul.

And when he felt her core tighten around his fingers and her body shake, he saw wild pleasure and a greedy desire fill those eyes.

He knew it was desire for him.

Roughly, he pushed her back so that she fell against the mattress. Then he straddled her naked body, still fully dressed himself.

He held himself over her, his cock straining at his clothes as he teased kisses down her body.

He loved the taste of her. The soft noises she made. The feel of her skin against his lips. She was so wet. So needy.

And he was so hard. So wanting.

He could have kissed her for hours, but then she whispered his name. And that was his undoing.

He had to have her. Had to claim her and make her his own. And as she begged, he fumbled for his fly, then thrust inside her, already knowing she was wet and ready.

She made such wonderful sounds as he fucked her. The way she cried for more. The way she screamed his name when he took her to that precipice. That cliff where pleasure is so potent it borders on pain.

He wanted to make the pleasure last forever for both of

them, but he couldn't. She meant too much, and he couldn't hold back.

He exploded inside her, the climax so powerful it felt like he'd snuffed out the world. This was more than lust. More than their deal.

"You're mine," he whispered. Easing up so that he was holding himself over her. "It's not about the money. It's not about sex. It's not about the fact that I might die if I don't fuck you again soon. It's about us. You're mine, Bree."

"Yes," she whispered. "I'm yours." She reached up and slid her fingers into his hair. "I think I have been for a very long time."

For a moment, their eyes locked, then he fumbled out of his pants before entering her again, taking it as slowly as he could stand. Their locked gaze never wavered.

"Mine," he whispered. And again and again, until they exploded together, their atoms mingled, and the words were made real.

I curl up as close to Ash as humanly possible, reveling in the way his body feels against mine. Awed by how safe I feel in his embrace. "I can't decide if you wore me out or revved me up," I say, making him laugh.

"Both, I think," he says. "Only you're the one who wore me out."

"Let's share that trophy." I roll over so that I'm facing him, my leg thrown over his body so that I can soak in his warmth.

I rest my head on his chest, then sigh as he strokes my hair. It's not something I usually like, but for some reason when Ash plays with my hair, I want to close my eyes and just revel in the feel of it.

Sappy. I'm definitely sliding into the land of sappy.

And the truly crazy thing? I don't mind at all.

"Tomorrow we're getting you a new dress from one of the boutiques downstairs," he says.

"But Nikki's dress is just getting broken in."

"Don't tease, or you'll be stuck with it. I'm rather fond of the way you look in that thing."

I consider tossing out one more sarcastic comment but hold it back. The dress truly has seen better days. "Fair enough," I say. "And speaking of dresses, I need to text the girls at the Ripped Bodice to see if they have a security camera installed inside."

That's the bookstore you were signing at, right? I thought you already had."

"Meant to. Got sidetracked." Our evening in the stands wasn't what had erased that errand from my mind, but that's what pops into my head. I snuggle closer, and sigh. "Is it crazy that I feel so good right now?"

He shifts so that he's propped up on an elbow, his fingertips idly stroking my skin. "What do you mean?"

"Just that someone's blackmailing me, and there's a very good chance that no matter whether we pay or not those horrible pictures of me will end up all over social media."

"Baby, no—"

I press my finger to his lips, cutting him off. "I know you're going to do everything you can to make sure that doesn't happen. But it's still possible. But that's not even my point. I'm just saying that my life could flip completely upside down five minutes from now, but in this moment, I feel good."

I trace my fingertip down over his bare chest. "I feel good because of you." I hesitate, gathering courage. "Am I crazy?"

"Probably," he says, then brushes a kiss over my lips. "But at least we'll be crazy together, because I feel the exact same way."

"Yeah?" I'm smiling like a fifteen-year-old girl just asked to the prom by the senior jock.

"Yeah," he says, then nods at my phone. "Send that text in the morning. Right now, let's get some sleep."

I start to roll over, then pause. "Can I ask you one more thing?"

"Anything."

"That woman. The one in the video who jumped. Why did it hurt you to see that?"

I'm hurting him now, I realize, just by asking the question. "Never mind," I say. "You don't have to talk about it."

From the silence that hangs between us, I think he's going to take me up on that, but then he says, "Delia."

There's a long pause before he continues. "We dated for a while. She was a sweet girl. A little too quiet and shy, but we had fun, and I even congratulated myself for pulling her a bit out of her shell. I ended up breaking up with her, and it was just your normal breakup. But I guess she snapped. There was a place we used to go. A lookout on some cliffs, and she asked me to meet her there one day. Said she had a present for me."

He draws a breath, and I reach for his hand. "She told me she was pregnant." His voice is low. Flat. "Said I needed to take care of her. I told her it wasn't mine. But she got agitated. So angry. She called me all sorts of names, and I just lost it."

I swallow. "You pushed her?"

His eyes widen. "God, no. I told her I wasn't going to be harassed. That I'd had a vasectomy, so I knew it couldn't be mine."

"You lied?"

"I told her the truth. I had it done when I turned eighteen. My mother? That horrible aunt I lived with. Not to mention the lies I'd believed about Damien." He shakes his head. "Not the genetic pool I wanted for my kids." He brushes his fingers tenderly over my arm. "Problem?"

I meet his eyes, sure he's teasing. But he's serious. Something warm and fuzzy flips inside me. "I think that's great. You can always adopt." I swallow. "It's something I've thought about, too." I don't tell him that I thought about it after Rory. Back when I didn't think I'd ever want to be with a man again. Or if I did want, that I wouldn't be able to handle it.

I'm handling it just fine with Ash. So far, at least.

"What happened?"

"I left her there." His voice is flat, and he shuts his eyes. She left a voicemail for a friend. She said the baby was mine. She said I was vile and wouldn't help her."

"She jumped?"

"She did. It was a small story at the time. I was racing, so it got some press, but nothing major. Then as I got more well-known, the media dragged it up again and again. But nobody bothered to report that the baby wasn't mine. Or that she'd been seeing a psychiatrist and had stopped taking her meds. Then the story got told and retold and embellished, and I came out looking about as bad as a man can look."

"I'm so sorry you had to go through that."

"I'm sorry I didn't try to help her. She was trying to pull me into a problem that wasn't mine, and I turned away from her. I felt trapped and protected myself instead of trying to help her through it."

"You couldn't have known she would jump," I tell him, a bit awed that even though her lies tarnished his reputation, he still feels more compassion than anger. Especially since I know that once he gained fame racing, there'd been a steady flow of women who've monetized dates with him by selling stories to tabloids.

"It wasn't your fault," I say again. "She was broken. I know a little bit about that."

His smile is gentle as he twines my fingers with his. "You're stronger than you think," he says, then pulls me close for a long, sweet kiss. The kind that makes my head spin and my whole body sigh. I snuggle close. "How can you like me with all my flaws?"

"You see flaws. I see strength. Besides, I could ask you the same question."

I grin. "What makes you think I like you?"

We share a smile. Then a soft kiss. I'm tired, my body heavy with exhaustion, but Ash has fired my senses. I move closer pressing my breasts against his chest. My eyes looking into his. I feel bold. Sexy.

Reckless.

This is me, but at the same time, it isn't. It's need and hunger. Desire and lust.

Mostly, though, it's trust. "Ash." His name is a whisper on the air, barely escaping before my mouth closes over his. His arms tighten around me, one hand sliding down to cup my ass and press me closer. He's already hard, and the pressure of his cock makes me moan against his mouth. Makes me want and need. Makes desire so palpable it's like hunger, and right then, I am truly starving.

But the only thing I crave is Ash. It's like he's a miracle. A man who's come in and swept my fears away. Since Rory, there's been no one. I tried twice. Sweet guys. Gentle. But both times I ended up curled up in a ball and begging them to leave.

With Ash, I'll beg him to stay. He's like a drug to me. Cutting away my resistance. Making me wild, unabashed.

Hungry.

And every touch, every caress, every hard, deep thrust feeds that hunger until I am sated and satisfied.

Most of all, though, I'm safe in the circle of his arms. Here, my fears can't even get close.

"I didn't expect you," I murmur, already half-asleep.

"I know," he says, as he pulls the covers over us both. "I didn't expect you, either."

I fear it will take a while for sleep to creep up on me. I'm too afraid the dream will come. Rory. The kidnapping.

But all that comes is sweet oblivion, then a shaft of sunlight peeking through the drapes to push me gently into morning.

I roll toward Ash and snuggle closer, wondering if the dreams are simply giving me breathing room... or if Ash really is a man who can truly keep them at bay.

TWENTY-NINE

The Los Angeles area pretty much overflows with excellent bars, but as far as I'm concerned, none of them hold a candle to Austin's Driskill Hotel bar with its dark wood, lush lighting, incredible ceiling, and Texas-themed sculptures. It's friendly and comfortable, and it's been my favorite since the first time I went to South By Southwest when I was a sophomore in college.

I'd flown to Texas to meet up with an old high school boyfriend. He'd taken me to the Driskill for a drink, and then surprised me by having also booked a room in the famously haunted hotel. We didn't see any ghosts, but I did see a little bit of heaven that night.

Noah Carter has already claimed a table by the time we arrive, and I recognize him right away by his coppery red hair, green eyes, and friendly smile. What surprises me is that he recognizes me as well.

"It's so good to see you," he tells me, clasping my hand as Ash pulls a chair out for me. "I'm so sorry about the circumstances."

I thank him for the concern—and for the help. Ash brought me up to speed on the plane, so I know that Noah's optimistic about tracing the money to its ultimate destination once we transfer it tomorrow.

"Assuming the trace works, we'll be able to get it back, right?"

"We certainly hope so," Noah tells me as Ash squeezes my hand. "The bigger goal is to find the people behind all of this. Then the money situation will sort itself out."

I just nod. While I appreciate the thought, I'm still hoping that the money can be reclaimed. I hate knowing how much Ash is sacrificing for me. But at the same time, I really do love him for making the sacrifice.

Love.

That word has been popping into my head since last night. And even before last night, if I'm honest. And as I sit in this dark bar and listen to these two men discuss how this is all going to go down tomorrow, I can't help but face the truth—somewhere along the way, I fell in love with Ashton Stone. I'm not even sure if that fall started years ago or yesterday or just moments ago when he rested his palm on my thigh under the table.

It doesn't matter. I love him. And even though I haven't told him yet, it feels really, really, good.

"So how will this work?" I ask Noah, forcing my thoughts back to the practical. "And did you get anything from the URLs?"

Noah looks to Ash first, then shakes his head. "Nothing. Whoever set them up knew what they were doing. We're monitoring them, though. If they log-on, there's a good chance we can triangulate their location."

"Really? How?"

Noah and Ash exchange a look, and I roll my eyes. "Techno magic," I say.

Noah grins. "Something like that."

"Is it legal?"

"Do you really want me to answer that?"

I lean against Ash, who pulls me close. "I'm gonna go with no," I say, as Ash laughs, then kisses my forehead.

"It's actually the money that'll give us the best shot," Ash tells me. "Sucks to have to risk that much, but Noah has some tricks up his sleeve."

I turn to Noah, who looks smug. "Digital currency marking. It's like using a florescent marker on a hundred-dollar bill. We just do it digitally."

"That will work?"

"The marking, yes. Tracing it to the source..." He trails off with a shrug. "It's something my company's been developing for law enforcement."

I whip around to face Ash. "The rules—"

"Noah isn't law enforcement, remember? And this tech is still entirely his."

"Besides," Noah adds, "they will never spot the trace."

My stomach twists, but calms when Ash takes my hand, then leans over and whispers, "Trust me."

"Okay," I say. Because the truth is that I do.

With a smile to Noah, I scoop up some more salsa with a chip, then lean against Ash, determined to enjoy the evening.

Somehow, I manage to pull that off.

For the next hour, we don't even talk about the blackmail. Instead, I sip wine as I listen to Ash and Noah catch up. Noah talking about how proud he is of his wife, who's apparently a singer. And Ash sharing some info about the INX-20 in technospeak, so I have only the vaguest of takeaways.

"Sorry, Bree," Noah says as the waitress brings another round of drinks. "We haven't caught up in a while."

As I'm assuring him it's no problem, my phone screen flashes with an incoming call from Kari. "And now you can catch up some more," I tease as I stand. I head toward the exit into the hotel and park myself on the stair landing overlooking the ornate lobby. I know from experience that cellular reception sucks in the bar. Hopefully, I'll be able to better hear my friend out here.

"Guess what!" Her voice is so enthusiastic I can practically see her bouncing behind the counter at Upper Crust.

"I'm not even going to try. Knowing you it could be anything from global warming to new sandals."

"Not even close," she says. "Martin and I are coming to Vegas!"

"Martin? I thought—" I cut myself off, realizing that Aria had gotten it wrong when she said Martin had moved from Kari to Maggie.

"You thought what?"

"I had his name wrong," I lie. "I thought it was Marvin. But, listen, I hope you two have fun in Vegas. I'm kind of in the middle of a—"

"We were hoping to have drinks with you. You're there, right? I mean," she adds, lowering her voice, "I saw one of those nasty articles about you and Ashton Stone, and that he's paying you—well, anyway. I'm sure you know."

"I do." I try not to sound too cold. Kari can be pretty clueless, and she entirely lacks filters, but she's still a friend. "It's crazy the shit some of those tabloid reporters will think up. But we're not in Vegas, anymore. We're in Austin."

"Oh. Why?"

I like Kari well enough, but she's a gossip, so there is no way

I'm giving her even a hint of a clue as to why I'm really here. "Ash lives here. I told him it's one of my favorite cities, so he suggested we spend a few days here before going back to LA."

"So, things are good with you two?"

"They're great," I say, with real enthusiasm. Because despite all the hell swirling around us, the me-and-Ash part of the equation is truly fantastic.

"Well, I'm totally bummed we won't be seeing you, but I'm super-psyched that you two are getting along despite all that publicity bullshit."

"It's not fun," I tell her. "But we're doing okay."

"Oh! Oh! I forgot to tell you. I finished *Mystics at Dawn*. It is just as good as Bethany's first book."

I press my hand against my heart, only then realizing how nervous I am about book two in the series. It's still months from release, but considering how crazy my life has become, I've barely even thought about it. "I'm so, so glad to hear that," I tell Kari. "Your opinion means a lot."

She'd read an early manuscript of *Reveries* and had both pumped up my ego and given me some decent notes, so I'd offered her this book as well. "I still have one more round of revisions," I tell her. "Anything—wait. Hang on."

There's a commotion across the bar, and I peer in to see folks standing from the two and four-tops, craning their necks toward the far side of the bar that opens directly onto the street.

At first, I can't see a thing, then I see *her*. Kiki King. A multiple Grammy winner who I now remember lives in Austin.

"So sorry, but I have to go," I tell Kari. "We'll talk about the book later. Have fun in Vegas."

"Oh, I just—"

But my finger's already on the button to end the call, and now I hurry back toward our table, hoping I'll be able to catch another glimpse.

"You okay?" Ash asks, as I slide into my chair and start to crane my neck looking for her.

"I just saw Kiki King. I love her stuff. If she sits anywhere near us, do you think it would be totally inappropriate to ask for her autograph?"

Ash starts to answer, then just closes his mouth, looking so amused I give him a light slap on the arm. "Stop laughing at me. I don't fan girl often, but I really like her. I've seen her in concert twice already."

"I'm not laughing at you," he assures me. Then tilts his head up and says, "Hey, Kiki."

I spin around so fast I almost give myself whiplash, then feel my mouth drop open when Kiki Freaking King slides onto Noah's lap and gives him a kiss on the cheek.

That's when I remember that King is Kiki's stage name. Her real name is Kiki Porter Carter, and considering how long Noah has worked with Damien, I have no idea how I missed this little factoid about his wife's identity.

"Ash," she says with a huge smile. "I'd give you a hug, but I'm a little trapped."

"She's been gone for a week," Noah tells us all. "I'm not letting her off my lap for at least another five minutes."

"I love your work," I say as a man I recognize from parties at Nikki and Damien's house joins our group. A man with chestnut hair, broad shoulders, and hard assessing eyes. Media mogul Matthew Holt, who I happen to know is also Kiki's producer.

He also owns a sex club in Los Angeles, but I'm not sure that's public knowledge, and I'm certainly not going to mention it now.

He pauses, frowning as he looks at me. I'm about to introduce myself when he taps the side of his nose. "Bree, right? We've met at various Stark functions."

"Yes," I say, more than awed by the man's memory. Then again, he has his fingers in pretty much every entertainment pie, not to mention various other entrepreneurial ventures. It's probably fair to assume that men like that tend to remember random facts, stock prices, and the names of people they've met.

"Matthew, I'm about to drag Noah—and I assume Kiki by association—over to my condo. We have a few things to talk about in a less public venue. Care to join us?"

His eyes sweep the room, landing on a stunning woman standing next to the piano and scowling at her phone. "Actually," Matthew says, "I'm going to pass. I think I have a date." His mouth curves into a knowing smile. "And if it turns out I'm wrong, I'll give you a shout before I pop by."

"Fair enough," Ash says. "Drinks when we're both back in LA?"

"Absolutely." His eyes meet mine. "It will be nice to see you again, Bree."

"Oh," I say stupidly. Because I'm not sure if he's assuming there's more between Ash and me than there really is... or if he's expecting there will be by the time we meet again.

Ash's rooftop condo is absolutely stunning. Not only does it look out over Lady Bird Lake—which from what I can tell is really a river that that separates North and South Austin—but it also has a view of the Congress Avenue Bridge and the famous bats that live beneath it.

Or, at least, that's what Ash tells me. Apparently, they come out at sunset, and since we didn't get to the condo until almost midnight, we missed tonight's show.

"Tomorrow," he says as I stand on the patio and look across the river to the lights of South Austin. He brushes a kiss to my temple. "We'll sit out here with champagne, watch the bats fly into the sunset, and celebrate the fact that those prick blackmailers are in custody and won't ever bother you again."

"You really believe that?" He's standing behind me, his arms around my waist, and I twist to look up at him.

"How can I not? Have you seen my table?"

Despite the circumstances, I can't help but laugh. Noah has completely taken over the oval-shaped dining table. There are three computers, some sort of gizmo that looks like a Big Black Box, but which Noah swears is the heart of it all, a bazillion cords, and various other techno gadgets that I'm assured will help Noah trace the money Ash will be transferring on my behalf at two tomorrow, which is also noon Pacific time.

As Ash and Noah settle in to talk techno, Kiki and I take a bottle of wine out onto the patio, and, despite me having a serious fan girl moment, we have a reasonably normal time talking life, the universe, and men while we sip a very nice chardonnay.

"I'm so sorry you're going through this," Kiki says. "But Noah's the smartest man I know—don't tell Ash or Damien," she adds, making me laugh. "He'll track the money, and he'll find out who's behind this, and it will all be over."

"I hope so," I say. "I'd thought it was done when Rory was captured. Then it all came back months later when we learned that he wasn't the only one involved."

"And now this."

I nod. "Now this."

"As soon as it's over, you and Ash need to take a trip."

"That would be amazing," I tell her. "But..." I trail off with a shrug.

"But?"

"We—I mean, well, we kind of got thrown together. I needed help, and he stepped in, and that's great, but after?" I blink, fighting back tears. "I mean, I want...and I think...but how can I truly know?"

She tilts her head, the light of the moon glimmering off her hair. "Maybe you have the question backwards. How can you not know?"

I shake my head, clueless. "What do you mean?"

She leans forward, then lowers her voice. "I mean that he's in love with you. And unless my powers of observation have really started to tank, you're in love with him, too."

I pull my knees up and hug them, feeling all of twelve years old.

Her laugh is as musical as her singing voice. "Can I give you some totally unsolicited advice?"

"Um, okay?"

"Don't be scared to try."

I hug my knees tighter. "What do you mean?"

"You both have so much baggage. Noah and I did, too. Everyone does, I think. But with you two... I don't know that you actually have *more* baggage, but it's definitely heavier."

She shoots me a grimace. "Forgive the metaphor. I've been traveling a lot and living out of a suitcase. All I'm trying to say is that you both have reasons to bolt. You seem perfectly fine to me, but I'm guessing you still have issues from being kidnapped."

"Understatement."

She offers me a supportive smile. "And Ash has, well, Ash has the family from hell on one side, and a much kinder albeit unconventional family on the other. That boy was put through the wringer growing up, and it's a miracle he turned out sane. I think you're good for him. He probably thinks he's not good for you."

"What are you saying?"

She combs her fingers through her hair, then shrugs. "Honesty? I'm not really sure. I guess it's just that from where I'm sitting, it's obvious you both love each other. So fight for it if you have to. Because if there's one thing I've learned over the last few years with Noah, it's that love is the most important thing. And if you have to go to the mattresses for it, then that's what you do."

THIRTY

"I heard back from The Ripped Bodice," I tell Ash later that night after Noah and Kiki have left. Since I didn't want Leah or Bea to know about the blackmail scheme, I'd come up with the somewhat ridiculous story of how I wanted to have the souvenir footage for my digital scrapbook.

If they thought I was weird, they were kind enough not to say so. Unfortunately, there wasn't a security cam inside or outside. "So dead end there," I tell Ash as we're snuggled in bed together.

He turns on his side, tugging the sheet down as he does. "Noah thinks there may be another possibility." He traces his fingertip over my bare breasts as he talks.

"Oh?" I'm trying very hard to make my voice sound normal. "Like what?"

"He made some calls. There's an art gallery across the street, and the odds are good they have security cams. Depending on the angle and how often they record over the old video, we might get lucky."

"Lucky," I say, my voice dreamy. And not because of security cams. "Despite everything, I've felt pretty lucky lately."

"Have you?" His finger teases my nipple, and I bite my lower lip as I manage to make an affirmative noise.

"I feel pretty lucky myself these days."

I start to speak, freeze, then try again. "Kiki thinks we're good together."

"I've always liked that woman."

"I realized we never really worked out what happens after you transfer the money."

His fingers stop moving. "What do you mean?"

I roll over, then straddle him. We're both naked, and I'm sitting below his waist, his cock pressing against my rear.

"If you're planning on having a conversation, you need to know this position isn't exactly conducive."

"Good," I say, then bend forward to brush a kiss over his lips. "It occurred to me that we never talked about what would happen when you got your three million back."

"I might not," he says.

"You will. Did you see your kitchen table? No blackmailer's going to be a match for the power of that tech."

He chuckles. "I hope you're right." His eyes narrow, and he cocks his head. "Or maybe I don't."

I laugh. "It occurs to me that it's not just about the money. It's about the timing as well. You can get repaid the cash, but I still owe you for pulling this all together quickly enough that my secrets don't get splashed to the world."

A grin tugs at the corner of his mouth. "I couldn't have made a better argument myself."

"Once the videos got out, they'd be in the world forever. It's not like our bad guy can call them back."

"My three million is the gift that keeps on giving."

I nod. "And so..."

He puts his hands on my hips, and I rock against him,

sliding down with each thrust until my very wet core is sliding over his very hard cock.

"So, I think that means I owe you a debt that can't ever really be repaid."

"And you know what that means, Ms. Bernstein?"

"Tell me."

"You're mine," he whispers, cupping my head and pulling me down for a kiss. "You're just going to have to stay mine forever."

"Oh, hell yes," Noah says around eleven-forty-five the next morning. "Finally, a bit of luck. Luck being a somewhat loose and amorphous term," he adds, presumably so that I won't squeal and get my hopes too high.

We've all been up since before dawn, trying to solve the riddle of who I'm about to pay before we have to actually make the payment.

So far, there's been nothing, so Noah's announcement—whatever it's about—is definitely squeal-worthy.

I look between him and Ash, both of whom are sitting at the breakfast bar behind their open laptops. I'm standing in the kitchen sipping coffee. Kiki's on a plane to Manhattan where she's meeting with some Broadway producer about a part in a musical. I've apologized to Noah about eight thousand times, but he assured me that this is the way their life works, and if she gets the part, he'll move up there for the duration. "Trust me," he'd said earlier, "I don't need to be there for the audition. And she doesn't want me there right now anyway. Believe it or not, she still gets nervous about that stuff."

"Really?" That little bit of insight into a woman who lives her life in the spotlight makes me feel better. If she can be nervous about singing—which is what she does for a living then it's perfectly rational for me to be a wreck today as we try to find the low-life scum-puppies who are blackmailing me.

"So how are we lucky?" I ask now. "Did we catch the bad guy?"

"Getting closer. Look." Noah signals me to come stand behind him. Ash is already sitting next to him, and he stands now so that he can put his arms around my waist as we both look at Noah's monitor.

"What am I seeing?" It's a grainy, time-stamped video of a person—probably a man—crossing a street, then slipping into an alley and disappearing from view. He seems to be wearing a cap, so there's no way to tell if his hair is light or dark.

Ash gives my hand a squeeze. "He could very well be the guy who put that QR code card in your gift basket."

I twist around to look at him. "Wait. What? How?"

"The art gallery," Noah says. "This footage is from one of their exterior cameras."

The video is playing on a loop, and I watch more closely as the man—this time, I'm sure it's a man—crosses, pauses, and disappears into the dark. "The alley he turns into is the one behind the bookstore," Noah says.

The guy in the vid is wearing a white tee, and although it's grainy and there's no other person in the frame to compare him to, when I look at his shoulders in comparison to his hips, I have to think the shoulders are pretty broad.

"Agreed," Ash says, when I tell them as much, and Noah nods as well.

"Is there a front view of him?"

"I've got one more feed to check," Noah says. He taps some buttons, and the current video is replaced by another. It's the same action—the man crossing the street, then disappearing into the gray behind the Ripped Bodice—only this is from a different camera, so the angle is slightly different. Now, it's clear that he's wearing a ball cap, but unlike the first video that entirely hid his hair, this time a tuft sticks out at the side. The tape is black and white, but the tuft is light, so probably blond or very, very light brown.

"This is good, right? I mean, this could really help us find him."

The men exchange glances. "It's a start," Noah says. "But we don't have a face. It won't be easy."

"There's something familiar about him," I say, still staring at the screen and that tuft of hair. Those shoulders. The way he moves. *Something*. But I can't quite put my finger on it.

"Finger!" I say the word in the same moment that I see the truth. "Look. *Look*," I repeat, poking at the monitor. "See? He's twisting a ring."

I glance between the men, expecting grins and high-fives. Instead, they simply gape at me.

"Martin Street. He works at Upper Crust. I'm positive."

"Holy shit," Ash says, his voice low. "You two nailed him."

I'm giddy as I look between the men. "What do we do now? Send in a team, right? He can't possibly be the only one involved."

"We keep with the plan," Ash says. "We make sure you're right. We transfer the money. And we trace it."

I nod. Digital tracking. I still don't understand it, but I trust these men.

"You're sure about this?" Ash asks me, coming to my side and taking my hand. "There's always the chance he'll have time to release those videos. Or whoever's working with him will. Odds are good they're already cued up. It's just a matter of pushing a button and making them go live. You're strong, baby," he says, pulling me close. "But strong or not, you shouldn't have to live with those videos out in the world. Anne shouldn't have to, either."

"If I back away, they win by default," I say. "And I think Nikki and Damien would agree. Anne and I aren't the ones who did anything wrong." I manage a little shrug. "Do I want the videos released? No. Am I willing to risk it to catch the people who are doing this? Yes."

I bite my lip as I look at Ash. "Should I call and talk to Nikki and Damien?"

He shakes his head. "You know them well, just like you said. And so do I. Besides," he adds with a grim half-smile. "We're going to nail the fuckers, and those videos aren't going to see the light of day."

I squeeze his hand. "I believe you," I say. I mean it with all my heart, too. But the truth is, if I'm wrong—if those videos are released—I'll survive.

When this started, I wasn't strong enough. But I've learned a lot about myself these last few days with Ash. Now, I *am* strong enough.

"You're amazing," he says, then takes my hand and kisses my palm. "And we're going to take Martin and the rest of them down."

"Damn right, we are."

"Come on, then," Noah says, and Ash and I go sit with him at the table. I take my phone out and scan the code. A moment later, a site pops up. It flashes an animated graphic of fire from which a newly forged sword emerges. Then the words: *Remember the rules.*

Those words fade, and others pop up: *Beware the razor's edge.*

I must make a sound, because both Ash and Noah look at me, brows furrowed.

"Baby," Ash says, tucking my hair behind my ear. "You've gone completely pale. What is it?"

But I can't answer. Right now, I can barely stand.

"Bree." I hear the rising anxiety in his voice. "Bree, talk to me."

Somehow, I manage to form words. "It's a quote," I say. "From *Reveries*." I look between the two of them, their expressions making clear they don't understand. "My book. "They're quoting my book."

"Assholes," Ash whispers, his arm tightening around me as the quote disappears and transfer instructions pop up. "They just had to twist the knife. Are you okay?"

I nod, numb, as Noah starts working his magic. Ash kisses my cheek, then does whatever one does to set up a transfer of three million dollars from one account to the other.

But it's not necessary anymore. I'm certain I know where that money is going. All we're doing now is proving it.

As I hug myself, he looks to Noah. "Ready?"

Noah holds up a finger, taps something on his keyboard with his other hand, then says, "Now."

My entire body goes stiff, as if I'm preparing for some sort of explosion. But nothing feels different at all. It's over, though. That much I know. Because the instructions on my phone morph into a video of fireworks that fizzle out with a message in a curly-que font: *Thanks for playing!*

The sick fucks are actually having fun. And Kari—oh, god, Kari. I'd thought she was my friend. And the truth feels like a knife through my soul.

I hug myself as I start to pace, trying to keep the anger and betrayal from bursting out and splattering all over the room.

How could they do this? How could I not have seen this coming?

My mind is reeling, my thoughts going everywhere. But one

thing stands out from the melee—I want them caught. Imprisoned. Exposed. I want them to know just how *not* funny this whole thing is.

Because it's not about the money. Not anymore.

It's about the betrayal.

I don't realize I'm crying until I feel Ash's arms go around me. I turn into him, burying my face in his chest and simply sob as he leads me back to the table, pulls out a chair, and settles me on his lap.

For a few blissful moments, we sit like that, him stroking my hair and telling me that the ordeal is almost over while on the other side of the room, Noah's *tap, tap, tap* on the keyboard harmonizes with the drip and sizzle of the coffee maker. I tell myself I should say something, but saying it would make it real. And maybe Noah's trace will prove me wrong—oh, how I hope I'm wrong.

Then I hear Noah's low whisper of, "Oh, yeah, you fucker. We've got you now."

Ash sits up straighter, and though I try to stand—his legs must be numb—he just pulls me closer. "Tell us you have him."

"Marty Road," Noah says. "That's the holder of the receiving account. Pretty damn close to Martin Street, don't you think?"

My entire body sags. "It's him," I whisper. "It's him and Kari and Maggie."

Ash's brow furrows. "Bree?"

I draw a breath. "He's been hanging out with Kari and with Maggie. Kari's Rory's ex. She dated him before I did. And she's at the heart of all this."

Noah cocks his head. "How do you—"

"She's the one who introduced Rory to me," I say, cutting him off. "And we were close enough that I let her read the very first draft of *Reveries,* before I'd even started to edit it."

I keep going, feeling numb as I explain how that version included a lot of things that changed in later drafts, including a quote that Kari had loved: *Love is a blade; beware the razor's edge.*

No one else read that version of the manuscript. Not my agent. Not my editor. Not even Aria. And the line was completely different in the next draft. That second version stuck, and it's what's in the book: *Love is like a sword. Do not test the well-honed blade.*

As soon as I tell that to the men, Noah gets on the phone. I know he's calling the authorities, but it doesn't matter now. We know who was involved. We'll get those tapes before the friends-who-are-my-enemies can release them.

And as Ash's arms tighten around me, I let myself sob as the horror of my friend's betrayal crashes over me like waves in a storm.

"Hey," Ash whispers, drawing me from an uneasy sleep. I blink, then sit up, realizing that Ash must have moved me to the sofa after I'd cried myself to sleep.

"How long—"

"You had quite a nap," he says, handing me a mug of coffee. "Over five hours."

"Kari?"

"They just took her into custody. Maggie, too." He goes on to tell me that Noah coordinated with the authorities, and they pulled in Martin Street within an hour after the money hit his account. Then he ratted out Kari and Maggie and two other guys who'd helped with the tech surrounding both the videos and the money transfer.

"Bree?"

"What? Oh. Yes. I'm okay," I say, sitting up. "Numb. Disheartened. I don't really know Martin, but Maggie was just an obnoxious reporter. I never would have thought she'd do something like this. And Kari—" My breath hitches. "Kari was my friend."

"No," Ash says. "She wasn't."

He stands up, then bends over to pick me up. He cradles me in his arms as he carries me to his bedroom, then strips off my shoes and the sweatpants of his I'd put on this morning since I wasn't about to wear Nikki's dress for even one more day. He leaves me in an over-sized tee, then puts me in bed and pulls the covers up to my chin. I sigh, then curl up into a ball.

I want to protest that I just woke up, but the truth is I'm still drained. And when he climbs into bed from the other side and moves close enough to put his hand on my hip, I know that right now, this is exactly where I need to be.

We stay like that for at least two hours, half-sleeping, half-touching. I think we both want more, but we each feel fragile.

As for me, I feel exhausted, too. Not from sleep deprivation, though. Exhausted from life. From disappointment. From the loss of a friend, and from the withering loss of my own trust in myself. Because I never saw it coming. Not from Rory, who started it all. Not from Kari, who I believed was my friend. Not from Maggie, who I knew was reprehensible. Even knowing that, I was blind.

What the hell is wrong with me?

THIRTY-ONE

The day after the arrests starts with a flurry of phone calls and paperwork and calls from the press that we refer to Ash's public relations chief, a tall, fifty-something woman with a no-nonsense attitude that goes hand-in-hand with a Mama Bear kind of protectiveness. I immediately adore her, all the more so because she's not only handling comments for Ash and me, but she's very strongly stated her opinion that we should make no media comments at all. And that's a policy I'm very happy to get behind.

Noah stays around for the next two days until we're certain everything is wrapped up tight, then he hits the road, eager to get to Manhattan. I'm sad to see him go, but also glad that Ash and I will be alone. Since the moment we landed in Austin, we'd been swept up in a flurry of activity and people.

"Whatever will we do with ourselves?" he teases.

"I can't imagine," I say, returning his grin.

"I do have a meeting at five," he says. "You're welcome to come, but we're going to be talking engines. My feelings won't be hurt if you'd rather hang around the condo. Or explore Austin, for that matter."

"How long is your meeting?"

"Shouldn't be much more than an hour. I'm meeting at their office. With travel time, I expect I'll be back no later than seven."

"Why don't you show me a little bit of downtown, buy me lunch, and then we can come back here for some recreational activities before you head off to do the Big Shot Corporate Dude thing."

"Recreational?"

"You know. Tennis. Rugby. Really hot sex. Take your pick."

"I haven't played tennis in ages."

"Imagine what you could do with a racquet."

He laughs. "Now I'll be thinking that during my meeting."

"You're welcome." I lift a shoulder. "Has to be more scintillating than engine talk."

He brushes the pad of his thumb over my lips. "Definitely."

We agree not to talk about the kidnapping or the arrest, and my initial fear that the morning will be filled with gaps of awkward silence—after all, that's certainly been the focus of our lives and conversation for the last few days—turns out to be completely wrong.

Instead, we talk about everything and nothing. From the architecture of the buildings on Austin's famous Sixth Street, to the height of the capitol building at the end of Congress Avenue, to our favorite television shows, to which local speakeasy we're going to check out that evening.

Any stretches of silence that sneak into the day are the comfortable kind. The whole day, in fact, is the comfortable kind. And by the time we return to his condo after lunch, I'm certain that the way I've come to feel about Ash isn't because he's the man who saved me, but because he's the man who fits me, like that one final piece in an unfinished jigsaw puzzle. You can tell what the picture is without it, sure. But the puzzle's not complete until that piece fills the gap.

"What?" he asks as we return to the condo, and I realize I'm lingering in the open doorway, just soaking him in.

"Just—thank you," I say, because *you fill my gap* sounds a little pervy.

He raises one brow, a trick I envy. "And for what do I deserve your gratitude?"

I grin and lift my shoulders. "For today. For taking the time to show me around even though I already stole three of your days. And for those three days. And everything that with went them." I take a step closer and take his hands. "For saving me."

He lifts our joined hands, then then brushes his lips over my knuckles. "Anytime," he says, and though I know the words are partly a tease, I'm also certain that he means them.

"Ash?"

"Mmm?"

"You know that recreational activity we talked about?"

His eyes skim over me in a way that's as intimate as a caress. "I do."

I move to him, slide one arm around his neck, then cup my other hand over his package. "I don't really want to play tennis."

I feel his cock go hard as he lowers his mouth to mine and murmurs, "Baby, I am very glad to hear that."

"Since the first moment I saw you. You took my breath away," Ash says as we snuggle together on top of the bedspread.

"The *first* moment? Are you talking about the day you

crashed Nikki and Damien's ceremony? Or the day you first suggested your sex-for-services scheme with me?"

He chuckles. "The lady has a point. I definitely wasn't a Class A kinda dude."

"More like class Triple X," I tease. "But I wanted you, from the first moment, too." It's the truth, and I know he hears it in my voice.

"Interesting," he says with a sensual lilt as he traces his fingertip over my arm, bare in my short-sleeved tee. "I was an ass, and you wanted me anyway. Very, very interesting."

"I'm an enigma," I quip.

"I love a good enigma," he says, then rolls on top of me and closes his mouth over mine in a kiss that's wild and claiming.

I melt into his touch, my body responding. There's no hesitation, no worry. I'm his now, wholly and completely, my desire so potent I just might die if I can't have this man right here. Right now.

As if he can read my mind, he breaks the kiss, then eases back to meet my eyes. The corner of his mouth curves up in a wildly sexy half-smile, and he slides off the bed, then slowly strips. His shirt first, then his slacks. I watch, my breathing fast and my skin tingling as he reveals the lean, tight body I've come to know so well. He's completely exposed except for what's under his black briefs. And they aren't hiding much.

I swallow, then lift my face to his. He smirks, then urges me toward him. I crawl to the edge of the bed, and he slowly tugs my tee over my head. I let it fall to the floor, leaving my breasts bare.

"Ash," I whisper, but he presses a fingertip to my lips. Then he lifts me by the waist and tosses me back onto the mattress. I laugh, then reach out my hand for him. When he takes it, I tug and he topples onto me, his mouth immediately finding mine, his hands exploring my body over my remaining clothes until

I'm so turned on I have to fight to keep from begging him to rip my skirt off.

Because I don't want to rush this. I want to savor it.

This joy I've found.

This man I love.

I don't want to push and get to the part where I'm afraid.

Where I remember just how much Rory broke me.

He rolls over, taking me with him so that I'm straddling his waist. He's hard, and I can feel his cock pressing against my ass through his briefs. I slide back just a little, wanting to tease both him and me.

"You're mine," he says, those chocolate brown eyes meeting mine. "You'll always be mine."

"Yes," I whisper as he pulls me to him. As his mouth finds mine. As his teeth nip at my lower lip and I taste blood.

I pull back, startled, and that's when I remember—*eyes*.

Ash's eyes are blue, not brown.

And when the man beneath me grins, all I see are his bared fangs on Rory's face.

Rory.

I sit bolt upright, yanked out of the nightmare. Gasping, I suck in air, as I look around, frantically trying to get my bearings.

Ash's condo. Ash's bedroom.

There's no Ash, though, and a stab of panic cuts through me until I remember that he's at a meeting. That's when relief flows through me. I don't want him here. Not now.

Not while my thoughts are so scrambled and confused that I'm not even sure what I'm thinking or what this hard knot of fear in my belly is all about.

Slowly, I scoot back until I'm leaning against the headboard, the pillow clutched in my lap. I thought they were gone, these nightmares. I thought that Ash had galloped into my life on a white steed and vanquished the demons that have haunted my dreams for years. And if not Ash, then surely the arrests three days ago would have vanquished those dreams. Everyone involved in the kidnapping is dead. Everyone involved in the blackmail has been caught. Ash's money was credited back to his account.

I draw in a shaky breath.

I was wrong. So damn wrong.

Because this isn't about Ash. It isn't even about Rory or Kari. It's about me.

I'd slept with Rory. I'd trusted Kari.

Even Maggie. I'd never liked her, but I also never suspected the true depths of the bitch who hid underneath.

I can't trust my own judgment and now my subconscious is telling me to run. That Ash is wrong for me. Or we're moving too fast, or that he's going to hurt me somehow.

I don't know. And maybe that's the point.

Because until I can trust myself, how can I trust anyone else?

I realize that tears are streaming down my face and I brush them away with a violent sweep of my hand.

As much as I think I want to love Ash, I have to go.

Because first and foremost, I need to take care of me.

THIRTY-TWO

"Why are you avoiding me?" Aria demands when I finally answer her call. "I've left five messages. Ash is burning up my phone because he can't find you, and you left without saying a word."

"I left him a note," I say, blinking back tears.

"He told me. A note that said you couldn't do it. That you couldn't trust yourself. Bree, honey, what the hell is going on?"

"I needed space."

"I've seen the tabloid pictures of you two. There was like zero space between you, and you both look blissfully happy."

I was. We were. But I don't say that out loud.

"Come on, it's me. Tell me what's going on. I mapped you. I know you're in New York. But didn't you tell me just last night that you and Ash were going to head back to LA for a few days, then turn back around for Austin? Although why you were so excited to help renovate his house when there's so much work to do on this one is beyond me. Except it's not," she adds, "because *Ash.* So, what the hell happened?"

I pull my bare feet up onto the chaise in my parents' sitting area and hug my knees. "Plans change."

"Dammit, Bree, it's me."

"I just—I just want to be home when my parents get back from the cruise."

"Uh-huh. And they're not home for another three days."

"Yeah, well, my agent set up a signing in Manhattan, too."

"I know. You forwarded the text yesterday. That's almost a week away."

"I want to get situated. Clean the house for Mom and Dad. And I want to talk to talk to Daddy's doctors so I can research protocols.

"So, you have good reasons to be there."

"Well, yeah," I say.

"Except they're all stupid, too."

"What are you talking about?"

"Call him. Talk to him."

"I will," I say, covering the lie with a shrug.

"Dammit, Bree. Ash isn't Rory."

I cringe, my body going stiff. "I never said he was. And it's not about Ash. It's about me."

"See? There is something. This isn't about the cruise or a book signing. Come on, girl. It's me. Tell me what is going on in that very imaginative head of yours."

"Why is this such a big deal to you? When did you become such an Ash fan?"

"Oh, I dunno. Maybe when I talked to you and heard boatloads of happiness in your voice. When I saw the way he looks at you in all those tabloid pictures. And the way you look back at him. Hell, girl. You glow in those pics."

I scrub my palms over my face, then adjust my ear pod. "I used to be happy with Rory, remember? And I thought Kari was my friend. And even though I knew Maggie Bridge was trouble, I never saw this coming."

"That's totally different," Aria says.

"Except it's not." I taste salt and realize I'm crying. "I didn't really see any of them. So how the hell can I trust that Ash is what I think he is?"

"This has happened before, remember?" Her voice has turned gentle. "You had a scary dream, but you got past it. And then you fell in love with him."

Her words squeeze my heart. And the truth is, I want to believe that. I want to trust in what I feel. In what my heart knows.

Except I don't trust my heart. Not anymore.

I don't think I ever will again.

"I like you, Ash," Aria said, sitting across from him in a Burbank Starbucks. "I really, really do. But I can't tell you where she is." She held up a fist of solidarity. Sacred Girl Code."

He'd flown in that morning, assuming that Bree had gone home. So far, though, he hadn't found her. Thankfully, Aria had agreed to meet him, though she'd made clear that she wasn't promising to help and could only talk for a few minutes.

"She's making a mistake," he said.

Aria nodded. "Totally agree. I told you. I like you."

"Do you know where she is?"

"Yeah. Of course."

"If I guess, will you tell me?"

She bit her lower lip, then shook her head. A second later, her phone chimed. "That's my alarm. I need to run. I got booked as an extra today in a crowd scene."

"Sounds like fun."

She stood, started to reach for her phone, then froze. "So, listen. Would you mind hanging here for a bit while I hit the ladies room? Keep an eye on my purse and phone?"

"Not at all."

He'd expected her to hurry off. Instead, she lingered, fiddling with her phone. Then she put it on the table and smiled at him before heading to the restroom.

He didn't much think about it. At least not until a minute later when an alarm chimed, flashing a message that said Open Me - 5721.

With curiosity and hope fluttering in his chest, he picked up the phone, silenced the alarm, and tapped in the code.

The lock screen disappeared, leaving him staring at her locator app.

And right there was the button to locate "Bestie Bree."

"Aria," he whispered as he tapped the link. "I owe you one."

The dappled sun makes patterns on the walkway as I stroll through Central Park with my parents. They arrived yesterday, and today's a good day for my dad. He's telling me the story of how he and my mom met by the little lake with the toy sailboats. "And when you came along, we used to take you there," he says. "Do you remember?"

"Of course. I loved it there. Still do."

He pauses, then looks at me with a goofy grin. "Talia, Talia, it is so good to have you back."

A few steps ahead of us, my mother pauses, then turns to look back at us, her sad eyes betraying what she overheard and the smile she's forcing. "We should probably turn around and head home. It's almost time for lunch."

"Yes, yes," my father says, then takes my hand. "Come, Talia. You heard Mother."

I meet my mom's eyes, both of us knowing he wasn't referring to her, but to his own mother. And as for me, I'm his sister. My Aunt Talia.

"Come walk with me, Samuel," my mother says, and my father obediently turns and goes to her. I send her a small smile, then face forward as I blink back tears. I've been home a week now, and my father's decline has me feeling like I'm sliding down, too. I honestly don't know how my mom has coped.

I hang back a bit as they walk past me, trying to clear my head of sad thoughts. My dad. Ash.

Ash.

I miss him so much, but I know I made the right choice.

I know, because that's what I tell myself every night when I go to bed... and every morning when I wake up nightmare free.

Except...

I sigh, then relax, allowing the errant thought into my head. *Except I miss him.* Every night he visits my dreams, and sometimes he's Rory and sometimes he's not.

I want him—I do. But I fear that I don't really know him.

And I still don't trust my judgment.

I tell myself to stop it. I don't want to reach the house only to have my mom look at my face and see what's been weighing on me. She's been trying to help, but since my mom is all about stability, her idea of helping is to tell me not to think about Ash and to instead focus on my writing.

Which would be great if I was one of those writers who is inspired by emotional turmoil. I'd be cranking out the pages like crazy.

But that's not me.

I'm the kind of writer where my turmoil fills my brain, leaving very little room for stories, and forcing me to sneak out words when my otherwise overactive brain isn't looking.

Fortunately, I've managed to get enough writing done to

have a spicy excerpt from the upcoming book to read at the signing next week. Hopefully, readers will like it.

For that matter, hopefully readers will show up.

I roll my eyes at my torrent of negativity. The last time I remember truly smiling was when I was with Ash.

Stop it.

I pick up my pace and am close to catching up with my parents when my phone chimes an incoming message. I snatch it out of my back pocket, then sag a bit when I see that it's Aria.

Because, yeah, I was hoping it was Ash.

Turn around.

I frown at the message but do as it says. And when I do, there she is, arms outstretched as she flies down the path and gathers me in a hug.

"What are you doing here?" I ask after we quit bouncing up and down.

"Airline miles! Figured I'd come see you and my parents. I just knew you needed my smiling face."

"I do," I say, hugging her again. "I really do."

I tap out a quick text to tell my mom that I'll be lagging behind, then I grab Aria's hand and swing it as we stroll. "Everything's good," I say before she can ask. "And I haven't talked to Ash."

"What's Teresa saying?"

I scowl. "Wise stuff."

Aria rolls her hand in a *tell me* gesture.

"You know," I say. "That we've done a lot of work over the years. That I'm stronger than I think. That I need to trust myself and realize that sometimes a nightmare is a nightmare and not my subconscious whispering secrets."

"Sounds like good advice to me."

I shrug. She's not wrong. But knowing that and *knowing* that are two entirely different things.

"Oh!" She stops to dig in her giant tote bag. "Did you see this?"

She passes me a printout of an article. I start to skim it as we walk, then stop, standing still as I read every word in the article.

"Damien's invested in the INX-20?"

"That's what it says. Ash asked him to. Said he knows that Damien believes in the motor, and that he knows how much Damien admires all the work and research Ash has put into it. And when it became clear to Ash that he needed another investor, he wanted to go to the man who'd not only believed in the project from the beginning, but who'd given Ash a chance even when Ash hadn't extended the same courtesy."

"That's great," I say, fighting the urge to pull out my phone and text Ash. But what would I say? That I was proud of him seemed too pedantic. And that I missed him cut too close to the truth.

So instead, I say nothing at all. I just turn to Aria and tell her we should try and catch a show tonight. And though I can tell she wants to steer the conversation to Ash, because she's my bestie, she just falls into step beside me and suggests we go see *Wicked* for the eight millionth time.

THIRTY-THREE

Three days after Aria shows me the article about Damien investing in Ash's company, he shows up at the coffee shop where I'm writing. Or, more accurately, where I'm staring at my laptop screen and telling myself I should be writing.

Really, I'm thinking about Ash.

Which is why I about jump out of my skin when he slides into the seat across from me.

"Can we talk?"

I shake my head.

He doesn't argue. He just stands and goes away.

I frown, then try to focus on my book. But now I really can't. All I can think about is him.

The next day, he shows up at the coffee shop again. "Can we talk?"

I meet his eyes, tilt my head, and say, "No."

He leaves again.

Three more days. Three more times.

Then on the next day, instead of asking if we can talk, he slips an index card to me. I turn it over. *Can we pass notes?*

I can't help it. I laugh. And, damn me, I nod.

He passes me a note: *Why?*

I read the note, then close my eyes and take a deep breath. I tug the note toward myself, then write: *Because I'm not strong enough.*

What does that mean?

I start to write an answer, then just shake my head. "Rory," I say. "The bastard broke me."

"Broken things can be fixed. Think about who you're talking to. I've got more cracks in me than cheap pottery."

As he speaks, he reaches for my hand. I don't tug it away. I want him—I do. But I'd wanted Rory, too.

"I talked to Aria," he says. "You don't trust me?"

I grimace, wishing I could kick Aria's ass for not only talking to him, but for getting it wrong. "I don't trust *me*."

His brow furrows. "She told me about the nightmare. She told me that I turn into Rory."

I nod.

He meets my eyes, his voice soft as he says, "You do understand that dreams aren't reality."

I yank my hand back. "Don't," I snap. "Do not patronize me."

"I'm not. But it's the truth. I'm not Rory. I'm not a monster. And I'm not going to hurt you."

I blink, and a single tear snakes down my cheek. "I want to believe that," I say, so softly I doubt he can hear me. "I do believe it. Except…"

I trail off because how do I explain that my reality is as distorted as my father's. I believe in the Ash I touched and felt and kissed and fucked. And at the same time, I'm terrified that all of that will be ripped away to reveal something I never suspected. Never saw coming.

Except that I did see it coming in my dreams. And the only sane thing to do is stay away.

But I miss him. With every day that passes, I miss him more and more, and I have to remind myself of the dreams. Of Rory and Kari.

"Hey," he says, his voice gentle. "Talk to me."

"I don't trust myself." The words are barely a whisper, but I know he hears them.

He leans back in his chair, his brow forming a V over his nose as he studies me the same way I've seen him look at technical documents. Finally, he leans forward again, his elbows on the table and his eyes locked on mine. "You haven't pushed Aria away."

"What?"

"You've had this epiphany. This realization that you can't trust your own judgment. And yet Aria is right there. Hearing all your fears. Protecting all your secrets."

"What the hell?" I snap. "Are you trying to fuck with my friendship?"

"I'm just pointing out that she's still at your right hand."

"I've known her all my life."

He nods slowly. "So that's it? Aria and her parents and your parents? Those are your people now? Your only people?"

"Ash, I—" I cut myself off, not sure how to respond. He's messing with my head.

"Sometimes you trust, and you get hurt. Sometimes you trust, and it's wonderful."

I say nothing. He's right. But how the hell can I make that leap, especially when I know better than anyone how deep the hurt can go?

As if he's read my mind, he says, "The only way to move forward is to trust again. If you don't, Rory wins."

I open my mouth to answer, but only manage a small sob.

"Don't let him win, baby. Take a chance. We're worth it."

Tears are streaming down my face, and I brush them away with the back of my hand. "I'm a mess," I say. "Why the hell do you even want me?"

"Because you're kind and creative and funny and smart. Because you make me laugh. Because you make me hard. Because I wake up every morning alone, and the first thing I think is that I want you beside me. Because every day has been gray since you walked away. I want you, Bree. I want you because I love you."

I'm crying in earnest now, and I'm pretty sure everyone in the place is staring at me.

"I don't want the nightmares," I whisper, reaching for his hand.

He takes it. "They'll go away. I'll love you hard enough that they'll have no choice."

"Ash." I can barely make out his face through my tears, but I don't need to see him. I feel the love—and the truth of his words—in his hand.

Then before I know it, he's standing beside me and pulling me to my feet. Then I'm melting in his arms as his lips claim mine for a long, deep, perfect kiss.

I know I haven't been magically cured. I know that I'll still have nightmares.

But I also know that Ash will be there to hold me. To help me.

To love me.

I'm still crying when we break apart, but they're happy tears now. And I don't even mind that all around us, customers are snapping pics with their phones. This time, I'll buy the tabloids and print the Instagram snaps myself. Because this is a moment I will cherish forever.

"I love you," I whisper. "I don't want to ever be apart again."

"That's what I was hoping to hear," he says. "And I promise that not a day will go by when I don't show you just how much I love you, too."

EPILOGUE

Eighteen Months Later—(Manhattan)

"Come in, come in," my father says, stepping aside so Ash, Aria, her parents, and I can enter the brownstone I grew up in.

I give my dad the first hug, my arms tight around him as I revel in the way he's hugging me back. When we'd visited three months ago, he hadn't remembered my name, much less Ash's. This time, he extends his hand to Ash and says, "Good to see you again."

"You, too, sir," Ash says before glancing my way, the delight in his eyes as vibrant as what I'm feeling.

"He's doing so great," I say to my mom a few minutes later when she and I are putting the final touches on the dinner we're about to serve.

"The center's doing wonderful things with so many of the patients in the program," she tells me. "Your young man is a gift from God."

I grin. "Yeah, well, I like to think so." I'd insisted on returning the three million to Ash after the authorities extracted it from the Marty Road account. He'd absolutely refused to take it back. So we'd compromised and donated it to a Manhattan-based clinic that was doing groundbreaking work with Alzheimer's patients. The only caveat? My dad gets the treatments. No placebos. And while he's not miraculously turned back into the man he used to be, he has fewer bad days. And even those seem better.

"What can we do?" Aria asks, as she and my second mom join us in the kitchen. Soon enough, all the dishes are on the table, and we're settling in to celebrate Ash and me and our sixth month wedding anniversary.

"You know," my father says after my mother makes a toast, "I don't think I ever heard how you two met."

Ash and I exchange a glance. Dad's heard that story at least two times. But it's not a story I ever tire of hearing Ash tell.

He offers my mom a wink, then looks at my dad. "Well, sir. The truth is that I paid her a few million to go out with me. It was the only way I could get her attention."

My dad nods and chuckles. "And was she worth it?"

Ash squeezes my hand. "Sir, she was worth every single penny."

Later, after Aria's walked home with her parents and I've helped my mom with the dishes, Ash and I take a walk. Not just a stroll, though that would be lovely. No, tonight, I have a destination in mind, and we walk the twelve blocks to Fifth Avenue and the tree Ash had sponsored.

I bend down, then take the handkerchief Ash hands me to wipe a layer of dust off the plaque and the inscription: *Love is like a sword. Do not test the well-honed blade.*

"I love you," he'd said when he'd first brought me here. "Kari and Maggie and Martin brought us together, but they also tested that love. I'd say they felt the blade."

The analogy may not be perfect, but the bench is. So is the thought. And so is this man who loves me. Who helped me get free of the monsters that haunted me. Mostly, anyway. And on the few nights when one sneaks into my dreams, Ash is there to hold me. To help me fight it back.

And I know he always will be.

THE END

A NOTE FROM JK

I hope you enjoyed Ash and Bree's book!

Be sure to visit my website at www.jkenner.com to subscribe to my newsletter so you don't miss Aria and Matthew's story in *Wicked Fortune,* coming soon!

Curious about some of the events that came before or about the characters you met in the story?

You can learn about Bree's kidnapping in *Lost With Me,* a Nikki and Damien Stark novel.

Ash comes into Nikki & Damien's life in *Enchant Me.*

Noah is first introduced in the Dirtiest Trilogy, which begins with *Dirtiest Secret.* He gets his own book later, and you can meet him and Kiki in *Wicked Torture.*

And if you haven't yet met Damien and Nikki, be sure to grab

Release Me, the first in the *New York Times* bestselling Stark Saga.

EXCERPT: RELEASE ME

The first book in the sexy, emotionally charged Stark Saga—a romance between a powerful man who's never heard "no" and a fiery woman who says "yes" on her own terms...

ONE

A cool ocean breeze caresses my bare shoulders, and I shiver, wishing I'd taken my roommate's advice and brought a shawl with me tonight. I arrived in Los Angeles only four days ago, and I haven't yet adjusted to the concept of summer temperatures changing with the setting of the sun. In Dallas, June is hot, July is hotter, and August is hell.

Not so in California, at least not by the beach. LA Lesson Number One: Always carry a sweater if you'll be out after dark.

Of course, I could leave the balcony and go back inside to the party. Mingle with the millionaires. Chat up the celebrities. Gaze dutifully at the paintings. It is a gala art opening, after all, and my boss brought me here to meet and greet and charm and chat. Not to lust over the panorama that is coming alive in front of me. Bloodred clouds bursting against the pale orange sky. Blue-gray waves shimmering with dappled gold.

I press my hands against the balcony rail and lean forward, drawn to the intense, unreachable beauty of the setting sun. I regret that I didn't bring the battered Nikon I've had since high school. Not that it would have fit in my itty-bitty beaded purse.

And a bulky camera bag paired with a little black dress is a big, fat fashion no-no.

But this is my very first Pacific Ocean sunset, and I'm determined to document the moment. I pull out my iPhone and snap a picture.

"Almost makes the paintings inside seem redundant, doesn't it?" I recognize the throaty, feminine voice and turn to face Evelyn Dodge, retired actress turned agent turned patron of the arts—and my hostess for the evening.

"I'm so sorry. I know I must look like a giddy tourist, but we don't have sunsets like this in Dallas."

"Don't apologize," she says. "I pay for that view every month when I write the mortgage check. It damn well better be spectacular."

I laugh, immediately more at ease.

"Hiding out?"

"Excuse me?"

"You're Carl's new assistant, right?" she asks, referring to my boss of three days.

"Nikki Fairchild."

"I remember now. Nikki from Texas." She looks me up and down, and I wonder if she's disappointed that I don't have big hair and cowboy boots. "So who does he want you to charm?"

"Charm?" I repeat, as if I don't know exactly what she means.

She cocks a single brow. "Honey, the man would rather walk on burning coals than come to an art show. He's fishing for investors and you're the bait." She makes a rough noise in the back of her throat. "Don't worry. I won't press you to tell me who. And I don't blame you for hiding out. Carl's brilliant, but he's a bit of a prick."

"It's the brilliant part I signed on for," I say, and she barks out a laugh.

The truth is that she's right about me being the bait. "Wear a cocktail dress," Carl had said. "Something flirty."

Seriously? I mean, Seriously?

I should have told him to wear his own damn cocktail dress. But I didn't. Because I want this job. I fought to get this job. Carl's company, C-Squared Technologies, successfully launched three web-based products in the last eighteen months. That track record had caught the industry's eye, and Carl had been hailed as a man to watch.

More important from my perspective, that meant he was a man to learn from, and I'd prepared for the job interview with an intensity bordering on obsession. Landing the position had been a huge coup for me. So what if he wanted me to wear something flirty? It was a small price to pay.

Shit.

"I need to get back to being the bait," I say.

"Oh, hell. Now I've gone and made you feel either guilty or self-conscious. Don't be. Let them get liquored up in there first. You catch more flies with alcohol anyway. Trust me. I know."

She's holding a pack of cigarettes, and now she taps one out, then extends the pack to me. I shake my head. I love the smell of tobacco—it reminds me of my grandfather—but actually inhaling the smoke does nothing for me.

"I'm too old and set in my ways to quit," she says. "But God forbid I smoke in my own damn house. I swear, the mob would burn me in effigy. You're not going to start lecturing me on the dangers of secondhand smoke, are you?"

"No," I promise.

"Then how about a light?"

I hold up the itty-bitty purse. "One lipstick, a credit card, my driver's license, and my phone."

"No condom?"

"I didn't think it was that kind of party," I say dryly.

"I knew I liked you." She glances around the balcony. "What the hell kind of party am I throwing if I don't even have one goddamn candle on one goddamn table? Well, fuck it." She puts the unlit cigarette to her mouth and inhales, her eyes closed and her expression rapturous. I can't help but like her. She wears hardly any makeup, in stark contrast to all the other women here tonight, myself included, and her dress is more of a caftan, the batik pattern as interesting as the woman herself.

She's what my mother would call a brassy broad—loud, large, opinionated, and self-confident. My mother would hate her. I think she's awesome.

She drops the unlit cigarette onto the tile and grinds it with the toe of her shoe. Then she signals to one of the catering staff, a girl dressed all in black and carrying a tray of champagne glasses.

The girl fumbles for a minute with the sliding door that opens onto the balcony, and I imagine those flutes tumbling off, breaking against the hard tile, the scattered shards glittering like a wash of diamonds.

I picture myself bending to snatch up a broken stem. I see the raw edge cutting into the soft flesh at the base of my thumb as I squeeze. I watch myself clutching it tighter, drawing strength from the pain, the way some people might try to extract luck from a rabbit's foot.

The fantasy blurs with memory, jarring me with its potency. It's fast and powerful, and a little disturbing because I haven't needed the pain in a long time, and I don't understand why I'm thinking about it now, when I feel steady and in control.

I am fine, I think. *I am fine, I am fine, I am fine.*

"Take one, honey," Evelyn says easily, holding a flute out to me.

I hesitate, searching her face for signs that my mask has

slipped and she's caught a glimpse of my rawness. But her face is clear and genial.

"No, don't you argue," she adds, misinterpreting my hesitation. "I bought a dozen cases and I hate to see good alcohol go to waste. Hell no," she adds when the girl tries to hand her a flute. "I hate the stuff. Get me a vodka. Straight up. Chilled. Four olives. Hurry up, now. Do you want me to dry up like a leaf and float away?"

The girl shakes her head, looking a bit like a twitchy, frightened rabbit. Possibly one that had sacrificed his foot for someone else's good luck.

Evelyn's attention returns to me. "So how do you like LA? What have you seen? Where have you been? Have you bought a map of the stars yet? Dear God, tell me you're not getting sucked into all that tourist bullshit."

"Mostly I've seen miles of freeway and the inside of my apartment."

"Well, that's just sad. Makes me even more glad that Carl dragged your skinny ass all the way out here tonight."

I've put on fifteen welcome pounds since the years when my mother monitored every tiny thing that went in my mouth, and while I'm perfectly happy with my size-eight ass, I wouldn't describe it as skinny. I know Evelyn means it as a compliment, though, and so I smile. "I'm glad he brought me, too. The paintings really are amazing."

"Now don't do that—don't you go sliding into the polite-conversation routine. No, no," she says before I can protest. "I'm sure you mean it. Hell, the paintings are wonderful. But you're getting the flat-eyed look of a girl on her best behavior, and we can't have that. Not when I was getting to know the real you."

"Sorry," I say. "I swear I'm not fading away on you."

Because I genuinely like her, I don't tell her that she's wrong —she hasn't met the real Nikki Fairchild. She's met Social Nikki who, much like Malibu Barbie, comes with a complete set of accessories. In my case, it's not a bikini and a convertible. Instead, I have the Elizabeth Fairchild Guide for Social Gatherings.

My mother's big on rules. She claims it's her Southern upbringing. In my weaker moments, I agree. Mostly, I just think she's a controlling bitch. Since the first time she took me for tea at the Mansion at Turtle Creek in Dallas at age three, I have had the rules drilled into my head. How to walk, how to talk, how to dress. What to eat, how much to drink, what kinds of jokes to tell.

I have it all down, every trick, every nuance, and I wear my practiced pageant smile like armor against the world. The result being that I don't think I could truly be myself at a party even if my life depended on it.

This, however, is not something Evelyn needs to know.

"Where exactly are you living?" she asks.

"Studio City. I'm sharing a condo with my best friend from high school."

"Straight down the 101 for work and then back home again. No wonder you've only seen concrete. Didn't anyone tell you that you should have taken an apartment on the Westside?"

"Too pricey to go it alone," I admit, and I can tell that my admission surprises her. When I make the effort—like when I'm Social Nikki—I can't help but look like I come from money. Probably because I do. Come from it, that is. But that doesn't mean I brought it with me.

"How old are you?"

"Twenty-four."

Evelyn nods sagely, as if my age reveals some secret about me. "You'll be wanting a place of your own soon enough. You call me when you do and we'll find you someplace with a view.

Not as good as this one, of course, but we can manage something better than a freeway on-ramp."

"It's not that bad, I promise."

"Of course it's not," she says in a tone that says the exact opposite. "As for views," she continues, gesturing toward the now-dark ocean and the sky that's starting to bloom with stars, "you're welcome to come back anytime and share mine."

"I might take you up on that," I admit. "I'd love to bring a decent camera back here and take a shot or two."

"It's an open invitation. I'll provide the wine and you can provide the entertainment. A young woman loose in the city. Will it be a drama? A rom-com? Not a tragedy, I hope. I love a good cry as much as the next woman, but I like you. You need a happy ending."

I tense, but Evelyn doesn't know she's hit a nerve. That's why I moved to LA, after all. New life. New story. New Nikki.

I ramp up the Social Nikki smile and lift my champagne flute. "To happy endings. And to this amazing party. I think I've kept you from it long enough."

"Bullshit," she says. "I'm the one monopolizing you, and we both know it."

We slip back inside, the buzz of alcohol-fueled conversation replacing the soft calm of the ocean.

"The truth is, I'm a terrible hostess. I do what I want, talk to whoever I want, and if my guests feel slighted they can damn well deal with it."

I gape. I can almost hear my mother's cries of horror all the way from Dallas.

"Besides," she continues, "this party isn't supposed to be about me. I put together this little shindig to introduce Blaine and his art to the community. He's the one who should be doing the mingling, not me. I may be fucking him, but I'm not going to baby him."

Evelyn has completely destroyed my image of how a hostess for the not-to-be-missed social event of the weekend is supposed to behave, and I think I'm a little in love with her for that.

"I haven't met Blaine yet. That's him, right?" I point to a tall reed of a man. He is bald, but sports a red goatee. I'm pretty sure it's not his natural color. A small crowd hums around him, like bees drawing nectar from a flower. His outfit is certainly as bright as one.

"That's my little center of attention, all right," Evelyn says. "The man of the hour. Talented, isn't he?" Her hand sweeps out to indicate her massive living room. Every wall is covered with paintings. Except for a few benches, whatever furniture was once in the room has been removed and replaced with easels on which more paintings stand.

I suppose technically they are portraits. The models are nudes, but these aren't like anything you would see in a classical art book. There's something edgy about them. Something provocative and raw. I can tell that they are expertly conceived and carried out, and yet they disturb me, as if they reveal more about the person viewing the portrait than about the painter or the model.

As far as I can tell, I'm the only one with that reaction. Certainly the crowd around Blaine is glowing. I can hear the gushing praise from here.

"I picked a winner with that one," Evelyn says. "But let's see. Who do you want to meet? Rip Carrington and Lyle Tarpin? Those two are guaranteed drama, that's for damn sure, and your roommate will be jealous as hell if you chat them up."

"She will?"

Evelyn's brows arch up. "Rip and Lyle? They've been feuding for weeks." She narrows her eyes at me. "The fiasco about the new season of their sitcom? It's all over the Internet? You really don't know them?"

"Sorry," I say, feeling the need to apologize. "My school schedule was pretty intense. And I'm sure you can imagine what working for Carl is like."

Speaking of...

I glance around, but I don't see my boss anywhere.

"That is one serious gap in your education," Evelyn says. "Culture—and yes, pop culture counts—is just as important as— what did you say you studied?"

"I don't think I mentioned it. But I have a double major in electrical engineering and computer science."

"So you've got brains and beauty. See? That's something else we have in common. Gotta say, though, with an education like that, I don't see why you signed up to be Carl's secretary."

I laugh. "I'm not, I swear. Carl was looking for someone with tech experience to work with him on the business side of things, and I was looking for a job where I could learn the business side. Get my feet wet. I think he was a little hesitant to hire me at first—my skills definitely lean toward tech—but I convinced him I'm a fast learner."

She peers at me. "I smell ambition."

I lift a shoulder in a casual shrug. "It's Los Angeles. Isn't that what this town is all about?"

"Ha! Carl's lucky he's got you. It'll be interesting to see how long he keeps you. But let's see... who here would intrigue you...?"

She casts about the room, finally pointing to a fifty-something man holding court in a corner. "That's Charles Maynard," she says. "I've known Charlie for years. Intimidating as hell until you get to know him. But it's worth it. His clients are either celebrities with name recognition or power brokers with more money than God. Either way, he's got all the best stories."

"He's a lawyer?"

"With Bender, Twain & McGuire. Very prestigious firm."

"I know," I say, happy to show that I'm not entirely ignorant, despite not knowing Rip or Lyle. "One of my closest friends works for the firm. He started here but he's in their New York office now."

"Well, come on, then, Texas. I'll introduce you." We take one step in that direction, but then Evelyn stops me. Maynard has pulled out his phone, and is shouting instructions at someone. I catch a few well-placed curses and eye Evelyn sideways. She looks unconcerned "He's a pussycat at heart. Trust me, I've worked with him before. Back in my agenting days, we put together more celebrity biopic deals for our clients than I can count. And we fought to keep a few tell-alls off the screen, too." She shakes her head, as if reliving those glory days, then pats my arm. "Still, we'll wait 'til he calms down a bit. In the meantime, though..."

She trails off, and the corners of her mouth turn down in a frown as she scans the room again. "I don't think he's here yet, but—oh! Yes! Now there's someone you should meet. And if you want to talk views, the house he's building has one that makes my view look like, well, like yours." She points toward the entrance hall, but all I see are bobbing heads and haute couture. "He hardly ever accepts invitations, but we go way back," she says.

I still can't see who she's talking about, but then the crowd parts and I see the man in profile. Goose bumps rise on my arms, but I'm not cold. In fact, I'm suddenly very, very warm.

He's tall and so handsome that the word is almost an insult. But it's more than that. It's not his looks, it's his presence. He commands the room simply by being in it, and I realize that Evelyn and I aren't the only ones looking at him. The entire crowd has noticed his arrival. He must feel the weight of all those eyes, and yet the attention doesn't faze him at all. He smiles at the girl with the champagne, takes a glass, and begins to chat casually with a woman who approaches him, a simpering smile stretched across her face.

"Damn that girl," Evelyn says. "She never did bring me my vodka."

But I barely hear her. "Damien Stark," I say. My voice surprises me. It's little more than breath.

Evelyn's brows rise so high I notice the movement in my peripheral vision. "Well, how about that?" she says knowingly. "Looks like I guessed right."

"You did," I admit. "Mr. Stark is just the man I want to see."

TWO

"Damien Stark is the holy grail." That's what Carl told me earlier that evening. Right after "Damn, Nikki. You look hot."

I think he was expecting me to blush and smile and thank him for his kind words. When I didn't, he cleared his throat and got down to business. "You know who Stark is, right?"

"You saw my resume," I reminded him. "The fellowship?" I'd been the recipient of the Stark International Science Fellowship for four of my five years at the University of Texas, and those extra dollars every semester had made all the difference in the world to me. Of course, even without a fellowship, you'd have to be from Mars not to know about the man. Only thirty years old, the reclusive former tennis star had taken the millions he'd earned in prizes and endorsements and reinvented himself. His tennis days had been overshadowed by his new identity as an entrepreneur, and Stark's massive empire raked in billions every year.

"Right, right," Carl said, distracted. "Team April is presenting at Stark Applied Technology on Tuesday." At C-Squared, every product team is named after a month. With only twenty-three employees, though, the company has yet to tap into autumn or winter.

"That's fabulous," I said, and I meant it. Inventors, software developers, and eager new business owners practically wet themselves to get an interview with Damien Stark. That Carl had snagged just such an appointment was proof that my hoop-jumping to get this job had been worth it.

"Damn straight," Carl said. "We're showing off the beta version of the 3-D training software. Brian and Dave are on point with me," he added, referring to the two software developers who'd written most of the code for the product. Considering its applications in athletics and Stark Applied Technology's focus on athletic medicine and training, I had to guess that Carl was about to pitch another winner. "I want you at the meeting with us," he added, and I managed not to embarrass myself by doing a fist-pump in the air. "Right now, we're scheduled to meet with Preston Rhodes. Do you know who he is?"

"No."

"Nobody does. Because Rhodes is a nobody."

So Carl didn't have a meeting with Stark, after all. I, however, had a feeling I knew where this conversation was going.

"Pop quiz, Nikki. How does an up-and-coming genius like me get an in-person meeting with a powerhouse like Damien Stark?"

"Networking," I said. I wasn't an A-student for nothing.

"And that's why I hired you." He tapped his temple, even as his eyes roamed over my dress and lingered at my cleavage. At least he wasn't so gauche as to actually articulate the basic fact that he was hoping that my tits—rather than his product—would intrigue Stark enough that he'd attend the meeting personally. But honestly, I wasn't sure my girls were up to the task. I'm easy on the eyes, but I'm more the girl-next-door, America's-sweetheart type. And I happen to know that Stark goes for the runway supermodel type.

I learned that six years ago when he was still playing tennis and I was still chasing tiaras. He'd been the token celebrity judge at the Miss Tri-County Texas pageant, and though we'd barely exchanged a dozen words at the mid-pageant reception, the encounter was burned into my memory.

I'd parked myself near the buffet and was contemplating the tiny squares of cheesecake, wondering if my mother would smell it on my breath if I ate just one, when he walked up with the kind of bold self-assurance that can seem like arrogance on some men, but on Damien Stark it just seemed sexy as hell. He eyed me first, then the cheesecakes. Then he took two and popped them both in his mouth. He chewed, swallowed, then grinned at me. His unusual eyes, one amber and one almost completely black, seemed to dance with mirth.

I tried to come up with something clever to say and failed miserably. So I just stood there, my polite smile plastered across my face as I wondered if his kiss would give me all the taste and none of the calories.

Then he leaned closer, and my breath hitched as his proximity increased. "I think we're kindred spirits, Miss Fairchild."

"I'm sorry?" Was he talking about the cheesecake? Good God, I hadn't actually looked jealous when he'd eaten them, had I? The idea was appalling.

"Neither of us wants to be here," he explained. He tilted his head slightly toward a nearby emergency exit, and I was overcome by the sudden image of him grabbing my hand and taking off running. The clarity of the thought alarmed me. But the certainty that I'd go with him didn't scare me at all.

"I—oh," I mumbled.

His eyes crinkled with his smile, and he opened his mouth

to speak. I didn't learn what he had to say, though, because Carmela D'Amato swept over to join us, then linked her arm with his. "Damie, darling." Her Italian accent was as thick as her dark wavy hair. "Come. We should go, yes?" I've never been a big tabloid reader, but it's hard to avoid celebrity gossip when you're doing the pageant thing. So I'd seen the headlines and articles that paired the big-shot tennis star with the Italian supermodel.

"Miss Fairchild," he said with a parting nod, then turned to escort Carmela into the crowd and out of the building. I watched them leave, consoling myself with the thought that there was regret in his eyes as we parted ways. Regret and resignation.

There wasn't, of course. Why would there be? But that nice little fantasy got me through the rest of the pageant.

And I didn't say one word about the encounter to Carl. Some things are best played close to the vest. Including how much I'm looking forward to meeting Damien Stark again.

"Come on, Texas," Evelyn says, pulling me from my thoughts. "Let's go say howdy."

I feel a tap on my shoulder and turn to find Carl behind me. He sports the kind of grin that suggests he just got laid. I know better. He's just giddy with the anticipation of getting close to Damien Stark.

Well, me, too.

The crowd has shifted again, blocking my view of the man. I still haven't seen his face, just his profile, and now I can't even see that. Evelyn's leading the way, making forward progress through the crowd despite a few stops and starts to chat with her guests. We're on the move again when a barrel-chested man in a plaid sport coat shifts to the left, once again revealing Damien Stark.

He is even more magnificent now than he was six years ago.

The brashness of youth has been replaced by a mature confidence. He is Jason and Hercules and Perseus—a figure so strong and beautiful and heroic that the blood of the gods must flow through him, because how else could a being so fine exist in this world? His face consists of hard lines and angles that seem sculpted by light and shadows, making him appear both classically gorgeous and undeniably unique. His dark hair absorbs the light as completely as a raven's wing, but it is not nearly as smooth. Instead, it looks wind-tossed, as if he's spent the day at sea.

That hair in contrast with his black tailored trousers and starched white shirt give him a casual elegance, and it's easy to believe that this man is just as comfortable on a tennis court as he is in a boardroom.

His famous eyes capture my attention. They seem edgy and dangerous and full of dark promises. More important, they are watching me. Following me as I move toward him.

I feel an odd sense of déjà vu as I move steadily across the floor, hyperaware of my body, my posture, the placement of my feet. Foolishly, I feel as if I'm a contestant all over again.

I keep my eyes forward, not looking at his face. I don't like the nervousness that has crept into my manner. The sense that he can see beneath the armor I wear along with my little black dress.

One step, then another.

I can't help it; I look straight at him. Our eyes lock, and I swear all the air is sucked from the room. It is my old fantasy come to life, and I am completely lost. The sense of déjà vu vanishes and there's nothing but this moment, electric and powerful. Sensual.

For all I know, I've gone spinning off into space. But no, I'm right there, floor beneath me, walls around me, and Damien Stark's eyes on mine. I see heat and purpose. And then I see nothing but raw, primal desire so intense I fear that I'll shatter under the force of it.

Carl takes my elbow, steadying me, and only then do I realize I'd started to stumble. "Are you okay?"

"New shoes. Thanks." I glance back at Stark, but his eyes have gone flat. His mouth is a thin line. Whatever that was—and what the hell was it?—the moment has passed.

By the time we reach Stark, I've almost convinced myself it was my imagination.

I barely process the words as Evelyn introduces Carl. My turn is next, and Carl presses his hand to my shoulder, pushing me subtly forward. His palm is sweating, and it feels clammy against my bare skin. I force myself not to shrug it off.

"Nikki is Carl's new assistant," Evelyn says.

I extend my hand. "Nikki Fairchild. It's a pleasure." I don't mention that we've met before. Now hardly seems the time to remind him that I once paraded before him in a bathing suit.

"Ms. Fairchild," he says, ignoring my hand. My stomach twists, but I'm not sure if it's from nerves, disappointment, or anger. He looks from Carl to Evelyn, pointedly avoiding my eyes. "You'll have to excuse me. There's something I need to attend to right away." And then he's gone, swallowed up into the crowd as effectively as a magician disappearing in a puff of smoke.

"What the fuck?" Carl says, summing up my sentiments exactly.

Uncharacteristically quiet, Evelyn simply gapes at me, her expressive mouth turned down into a frown.

But I don't need words to know what she's thinking. I can easily see that she's wondering the same thing I am: What just happened?

More important, what the hell did I do wrong?

THREE

My moment of mortification hangs over the three of us for what feels like an eternity. Then Carl takes my arm and begins to steer me away from Evelyn.

"Nikki?" Concern blooms in her eyes.

"I—it's okay," I say. I feel strangely numb and very confused. This is what I'd been looking forward to?

"I mean it, Nikki," Carl says, as soon as he's put some distance between us and our hostess. "What the fuck was that?"

"I don't know."

"Bullshit," he snaps. "Have you met before? Did you piss him off? Did you apply for a job with him before me? What the hell did you do, Nichole?"

I cringe against the use of my given name. "It's not me," I say, because I want that to be the truth. "He's famous. He's eccentric. He was rude, but it wasn't personal. How the hell could it have been?" I can hear my voice rising, and I force myself to tamp it down. To breathe.

I squeeze my left hand into a fist so tight my fingernails cut into my palm. I focus on the pain, on the simple process of breathing. I need to be cool. I need to be calm. I can't let the Social Nikki facade slip away.

Beside me, Carl runs his fingers through his hair and sucks in a noisy breath. "I need a drink. Come on."

"I'm fine, thanks." I am a long way from fine, but what I want right then is to be alone. Or as alone as I can be in a room full of people.

I can see that he wants to argue. I can also see that he hasn't yet decided what he's going to do. Approach Stark again? Leave the party and pretend it never happened? "Fine," he growls. He stalks off, and I can hear his muttered "Shit," as he disappears into the crowd.

I exhale, the tension in my shoulders slipping away. I head toward the balcony, but stop once I see that my private spot has been discovered. At least eight people mingle there, chatting and smiling. I am not in a chatty, smiley mood.

I veer toward one of the freestanding easels and stare blankly at the painting. It depicts a nude woman kneeling on a hard tile floor. Her arms are raised above her head, her wrists bound by a red ribbon.

The ribbon is attached to a chain that rises vertically out of the painting, and there is tension in her arms, as if she's tugging downward, trying to get free. Her stomach is smooth, her back arched so that the lines of her rib cage show. Her breasts are small, and the erect nipples and tight brown areolae glow under the artist's skill.

Her face is not so prominent. It's tilted away, shrouded in gray. I'm left with the impression that the model is ashamed of her arousal. That she would break free if she could. But she can't.

She's trapped there, her pleasure and her shame on display for all the world.

My own skin prickles and I realize that this girl and I have something in common. I'd felt a sensual power crash over me, and I'd reveled in it.

Then Stark had shut it off, as quickly as if he'd flipped a switch. And like that model I was left feeling awkward and ashamed.

Well, fuck him. That twit on the canvas might be embarrassed, but I wasn't going to be. I'd seen the heat in his eyes, and it had turned me on. Period. End of story. Time to move on.

I look hard at the woman on the canvas. She's weak. I don't like her, and I don't like the painting.

I start to move away, my own confidence restored—and I collide with none other than Damien Stark himself.

Well, shit.

His hand slides against my waist in an effort to steady me. I back away quickly, but not before my mind processes the feel of him. He's lean and hard, and I'm uncomfortably aware of the places where my body collided with his. My palm. My breasts. The curve of my waist tingles from the lingering shock of his touch.

"Ms. Fairchild." He's looking straight at me, his eyes neither flat nor cold. I realize that I have stopped breathing.

I clear my throat and flash a polite smile. The kind that quietly says "Fuck off."

"I owe you an apology."

Oh.

"Yes," I say, surprised. "You do."

I wait, but he says nothing else. Instead, he turns his attention to the painting. "It's an interesting image. But you would have made a much better model."

What the...?

"That's the worst apology I've ever heard."

He indicates the model's face. "She's weak," he says, and I forget all about the apology. I'm too intrigued by the way his words echo my earlier thoughts. "I suppose some people might be drawn to the contrast. Desire and shame. But I prefer something bolder. A more confident sensuality."

He looks at me as he says this last, and I'm not sure if he's finally apologizing for snubbing me, complimenting my composure, or being completely inappropriate. I decide to consider his words a compliment and go from there. It may not be the safest approach, but it's the most flattering.

"I'm delighted you think so," I say. "But I'm not the model type."

He takes a step back and with slow deliberation looks me up and down. His inspection seems to last for hours, though it must take only seconds. The air between us crackles, and I want to move toward him, to close the gap between us again. But I stay rooted to the spot.

He lingers for a moment on my lips before finally lifting his head to meet my eyes, and that is when I move. I can't help it. I'm drawn in by the force and pressure of the tempest building in those damnable eyes.

"No," he says simply.

At first I'm confused, thinking that he's protesting my proximity. Then I realize he's responding to my comment about not being the model type.

"You are," he continues. "But not like this—splashed across a canvas for all the world to see, belonging to no one and everyone." His head tilts slightly to the left, as if he's trying out a new perspective on me. "No," he murmurs again, but this time he doesn't elaborate.

I am not prone to blushing, and I'm mortified to realize that my cheeks are burning. For someone who just a few moments ago mentally told this man to fuck off, I am doing a piss-poor job of keeping the upper hand. "I was hoping to have the chance to talk to you this evening," I say.

His brow lifts ever so slightly, giving him an expression of polite amusement. "Oh?"

"I'm one of your fellowship recipients. I wanted to say thank you."

He doesn't say a word.

I soldier on. "I worked my way through college, so the fellowship helped tremendously. I don't think I could have graduated with two degrees if it hadn't been for the financial help. So thank you." I still don't mention the pageant. As far as I'm concerned, Damien Stark and I are deep in the land of the do-over.

"And what are you doing now that you've left the hallowed halls of academia?"

He speaks so formally that I know he's teasing me. I ignore it and answer the question seriously. "I joined the team at C-Squared," I say. "I'm Carl Rosenfeld's new assistant." Evelyn already told him this, but I assume he hadn't been paying attention.

"I see."

The way he says it suggests he doesn't see at all. "Is that a problem?"

"Two degrees. A straight-A average. Glowing recommendations from all your professors. Acceptance to Ph.D. programs at both MIT and Cal Tech."

I stare at him, baffled. The Stark International Fellowship Committee awards thirty fellowships each year. How the hell can he possibly know so much about my academic career?

"I merely find it interesting that you ended up not leading a product development team but doing gruntwork as the owner's assistant."

"I—" I don't know what to say. I'm still spinning from the surreal nature of this inquisition.

"Are you sleeping with your boss, Ms. Fairchild?"

"*What?*"

"I'm sorry. Was the question unclear? I asked if you were fucking Carl Rosenfeld."

"I—no." I blurt the answer out, because I can't let that image linger for longer than a second. Immediately, though, I regret speaking. What I should have done was slap his face. What the hell kind of question is that?

"Good," he says, so crisply and firmly and with such intensity that any thought I have of verbally bitch-slapping him vanishes completely. My thoughts, in fact, have taken a sharp left turn and I am undeniably, unwelcomely turned on. I glare at the woman in the portrait, hating her even more, and not particularly pleased with Damien Stark or myself. I suppose we have something in common, though. At the moment, we're both picturing me out of my little black dress.

Shit.

He doesn't even try to hide his amusement. "I believe I've shocked you, Ms. Fairchild."

"Hell yes, you've shocked me. What did you expect?"

He doesn't answer, just tilts his head back and laughs. It's as if a mask has slipped away, allowing me a glimpse of the real man hidden beneath. I smile, liking that we have this one small thing in common.

"Can anyone join this party?" It's Carl, and I want desperately to say no.

"How nice to see you again, Mr. Rosenfeld," Stark says. The mask is firmly back in place.

Carl glances at me, and I can see the question in his eyes. "Excuse me," I say. "I need to run to the ladies' room."

I escape to the cool elegance of Evelyn's powder room. She's thoughtfully provided mouthwash and hairspray and even disposable mascara wands. There is a lavender-scented salt scrub on the stone vanity, and I put a spoonful in my hands, then close my eyes and rub, imagining that I'm sloughing off the shell of myself to reveal something bright and shiny and new.

I rinse my hands in warm water, then caress my skin with my fingertips. My hands are soft now. Slick and sensual.

I meet my eyes in the mirror. "No," I whisper, but my hand slides down to brush the hem of my dress just below my knee. It's fitted at the bodice and waist, but the skirt is flared, designed to present an enticing little swish when you move.

My fingers dance across my knee, then trail lazily up my inner thigh. I meet my gaze in the mirror, then close my eyes. It's Stark's face I want to see. His eyes I imagine watching me from that mirror.

There's a sensuality in the way my fingers slowly graze my own skin. A lazy eroticism that some other time could build to something hot and explosive. But that's not where I'm going— that's what I'm destroying.

I stop when I feel it—the jagged, raised tissue of the five-year-old scar that mars the once-perfect flesh of my inner thigh. I press my fingertips to it, remembering the pain that punctuated that particular wound. That had been the weekend that my sister, Ashley, had died, and I'd just about crumbled under the weight of my grief.

But that's the past, and I close my eyes tight, my body hot, the scar throbbing beneath my hand.

This time when I open my eyes, all I see is myself. Nikki Fairchild, back in control.

I wrap my restored confidence around me like a blanket and return to the party. Both men look at me as I approach. Stark's face is unreadable, but Carl isn't even trying to hide his joy. He looks like a six-year-old on Christmas morning. "Say your goodbyes, Nikki. We're heading out. Lots to do. Lots to do."

"What? Now?" I don't bother to hide my confusion.

"Turns out Mr. Stark's going to be out of town on Tuesday, so we're pushing the meeting to tomorrow."

"Saturday?"

"Is that a problem?" Stark asks me.

"No, of course not, but—"

"He's attending personally," Carl says. "Personally," he repeats, as if I could have missed it the first time.

"Right. I'll just find Evelyn and say goodnight." I start to move away, but Stark's voice draws me back.

"I'd like Ms. Fairchild to stay."

"What?" Carl speaks, expressing my thought.

"The house I'm building is almost complete. I came here to find a painting for a particular room. I'd like a feminine perspective. I'll see her home safely, of course."

"Oh." Carl looks like he's going to protest, then thinks better of it. "She'll be happy to help."

The hell she will. It's one thing to wear the dress. It's another to completely skip the presentation rehearsal because a self-absorbed bazillionaire snaps his fingers and says jump. No matter how hot said bazillionaire might be.

But Carl cuts me off before I can form a coherent reply. "We'll speak tomorrow morning," he tells me. "The meeting's at two."

And then he's gone and I'm left seething beside a very smug Damien Stark.

"Who the hell do you think you are?"

"I know exactly who I am, Ms. Fairchild. Do you?"

"Maybe the better question is, who the hell do you think I am?"

"Are you attracted to me?"

"I—what?" I say, verbally stumbling. His words have knocked me off center, and I struggle to regain my balance. "That is so not the issue."

The corner of his mouth twitches, and I realize I've revealed too much.

"I'm Carl's assistant," I say firmly and slowly. "Not yours. And my job description does not include decorating your goddamn house." I'm not shouting, but my voice is as taut as a wire and my body even more so.

Stark, damn him, appears not only perfectly at ease, but also completely amused. "If your job duties include helping your boss find capital, then you may want to reconsider how you play the game. Insulting potential investors is probably not the best approach."

A cold stab of fear that I've screwed this up cuts through me. "Maybe not," I say. "But if you're going to withhold your money because I didn't roll over and flounce my skirts for you, then you're not the man the press makes you out to be. The Damien Stark I've read about invests in quality. Not in friendships or relationships or because he thinks some poor little inventor needs the deal. The Damien Stark I admire focuses on talent and talent alone. Or is that just public relations?"

I stand straight, ready to endure whatever verbal lashes he'll whip back at me. I'm not prepared for the response I get.

Stark laughs.

"You're right," he says. "I'm not going to invest in C-Squared because I met Carl at a party any more than I'd invest in it because you're in my bed."

"Oh." Once again, my cheeks heat. Once again, he's knocked me off balance.

"I do, however, want you."

My mouth is dry. I have to swallow before I can speak. "To help you pick a painting?"

"Yes," he confirms. "For now."

I force myself not to wonder about later. "Why?"

"Because I need an honest opinion. Most women on my arm

say what they think will make me happy, not what they actually mean."

"But I'm not on your arm, Mr. Stark." I let the words hang for a moment. Then I deliberately turn my back and walk away. I can feel him watching me, but I neither stop nor turn around. Slowly, I smile. I even add a little swing to my step. This is my moment of triumph and I intend to savor it.

Except victory isn't as delicious as I expected. In fact, it's a little bitter. Because secretly—oh, so secretly—I can't help but wonder what it would be like to be the girl on Damien Stark's arm.

FOUR

I cross the entire room before I pause, my heart pounding wildly in my chest. Fifty-five steps. I counted every one of them, and now that there's no place left to go I am simply standing still, staring at one of Blaine's paintings. Another nude, this one lying on her side across a stark white bed, only the foreground in focus. The rest of the room—walls, furniture—are nothing more than the blurred gray suggestions of shapes.

The woman's skin is pale, as if she's never seen the sun. But her face suggests otherwise. It reflects so much ecstasy that it seems to glow.

There is only one splash of color on the entire canvas—a long red ribbon. It is tied loosely around the woman's neck, then extends between her heavy breasts to trail down even farther. It slides between her legs, then continues, the image fading into the background before meeting the edge of the canvas. There's a tautness to the ribbon, though, and it's clear what story the artist is telling; her lover is there, just off the canvas, and he's holding the ribbon, making it slide over her, making her writhe against it in a desperate need to find the pleasure that he's teasing her with.

I swallow, imagining the sensation of that cool, smooth satin stroking me between my legs. Making me hot, making me come...

And in my fantasy, it's Damien Stark who is holding that ribbon.

This is not good.

I ease away from the painting toward the bar, which is the only place in the entire room where I'm not bombarded by erotic imagery. Honestly, I need the break. Erotic art doesn't usually make me melt. Except, of course, it's not the art that's making me hot.

I do, however, want you.

What had he meant by that?

More to the point, what do I want him to mean by that? Which, of course, is a bullshit question. I know what I want. The same thing I wanted six years ago. I also know it will never happen. And even the fantasy is a very bad idea.

I scan the room, telling myself I'm only looking over the art. Apparently this is my night for self-deception. I'm looking for Stark, but when I find him, I wish that I hadn't bothered. He's standing next to a tall, lithe woman with short dark hair. She looks like Audrey Hepburn in Sabrina, vibrant and beautiful. Her small features are alight with pleasure, and as she laughs she reaches out and touches him in a casual, intimate gesture. My stomach hurts just watching them. Good God, I don't even know this man. Can I really be jealous?

I consider the possibility, and in the spirit of tonight's theme, I deceive myself once more. Not jealousy—anger. I'm pissed that Stark could so cavalierly flirt with me even though he's obviously enthralled by another woman—a beautiful, charming, radiant woman.

"More champagne?" The bartender holds out a flute.

Tempting. Very tempting, but I shake my head. I don't need to get drunk. I need to get out of here.

More guests arrive, and the room overflows with people. I look for Stark again, but he has disappeared into the crowd. Audrey Hepburn is nowhere in sight, either. I'm sure wherever they are, they're having a dandy time.

I sandwich myself between a wall and a hallway cordoned off with a velvet rope. Presumably it leads to the rest of Evelyn's house. Right now, it's the closest thing to privacy I have.

I take out my phone, hit speed dial, and wait for Jamie to answer.

"You will so not believe this," she says, skipping all the preliminaries. "I just did the nasty with Douglas."

"Oh my God, Jamie. Why?" Okay, that came out before I had the chance to think about it, and while this revelation about Douglas is not good news, I'm grateful to be dragged so forcefully into Jamie's problems. Mine can wait.

Douglas is our next-door neighbor, and his bedroom shares a wall with mine. Even though it's only been four days, I have a pretty good idea of how often he gets laid. The idea that my best friend is another ticky mark on his bedpost does not thrill me.

Of course, from Jamie's perspective, he's a mark on her bedpost.

"We were by the pool drinking wine, and then we got in the hot tub and then..." She trails off, leaving "and then" to my imagination.

"He's still there? Or are you at his place?"

"God, no. I sent him home an hour ago."

"Jamie..."

"What? I just needed to burn some energy. Trust me, it's good. I'm so mellow now you wouldn't even believe."

I frown. Like a girl who collects stray puppies, Jamie brings home a lot of men. She doesn't, however, keep them around.

Not even until morning. As her roommate, I find that convenient. There's nothing quite like meeting an unshaved, unshowered, half-naked man staring into your refrigerator at three in the morning. As her friend, however, I worry.

She, in turn, worries about me for precisely the opposite reason. I've never brought a man home, much less kicked him out. As far as Jamie is concerned, that makes me subnormal.

This, however, isn't the time to get into it with my best friend. But Douglas? She had to go and pick Douglas? "Am I going to have to avert my eyes every time I see him in the complex?"

"He's cool," she says. "No big deal."

I close my eyes and shake my head. The mere thought of being naked like that—emotionally and physically—overwhelms me. Not a big deal? The hell it's not.

"How about you? Did you actually manage to form words this time?"

I scowl. As my best friend since forever, Jamie knows a few too many of my secrets. I'd told her all about my ambiguous encounter with uber-hottie Damien Stark at the pageant reception. Her reaction had been typical Jamie—if I'd just opened my mouth and formed actual words, he would have ditched Carmela and had his way with me. I'd told her she was insane, but her words had been like tinder to my smoldering fantasy.

"I talked to him," I admit now.

"Oh, really?" Her voice rises with interest.

"And he's coming to the presentation."

"And...?"

I have to laugh. "That's it, Jamie. That was the point."

"Oh. Well, okay, then. No, seriously, that's fabulous, Nik. You totally rocked it."

When she puts it that way, I have to agree.

"So what's he like now?"

I consider the question. It's not an easy one to answer. "He's... intense." Hot. Sexy. Surprising. Disturbing. No, it's not Stark that's disturbing—it's my reaction to him.

"Intense?" Jamie parrots. "Like that's a revelation? I mean, the guy owns half the known universe. I hardly think he'd be all warm and fuzzy. More like dark and dangerous."

I frown. Somehow, Jamie has summed up Damien Stark perfectly.

"Anything else to report? How are the paintings? I won't ask if you've seen any celebrities. Any celebrity younger than Cary Grant, and you're clueless. I mean, you could probably trip over Bradley Cooper and not even know it."

"Actually, Rip and Lyle are here, and they're being civil to each other despite their feud. It'll be interesting to see if the show gets picked up for another season."

The silence at the other end of the line tells me I have scored big with that one, and I make a mental note to thank Evelyn. It's not easy to surprise my roommate.

"You bitch," she finally says. "If you don't come back with Rip Carrington's autograph, I am so finding a new best friend."

"I'll try," I promise. "Actually, you could come here. I kind of need a ride."

"Because Carl keeled over and died from surprise when Stark said he'd do the meeting?"

"Sort of. He left to go prep. The meeting's been bumped to tomorrow."

"And you're still at the party, why?"

"Stark wanted me to stay."

"Oh, did he?"

"It's not like that. He's looking to buy a painting. He wanted a female perspective."

"And since you're the only female at the party..."

I remember Audrey Hepburn and feel confused. I'm most

definitely not the only female at the party. So what is Stark's game?

"I just need a ride," I snap, unfairly taking my irritation out on Jamie. "Can you come get me?"

"You're serious? Carl left you stranded in Malibu? That's like an hour away. He didn't even offer to reimburse cab fare?"

I hesitate a fraction of a second too long.

"What?" she demands.

"It's just that—well, Stark said he'd make sure I got home."

"And what? His Ferrari's not good enough for you? You'd rather ride in my ten-year-old Corolla?"

She has a point. It's Stark's fault I'm still here. Why should I inconvenience one of my friends—or fork over a buttload of money for cab fare—when he already said he'd get me home? Am I really that nervous about being alone with him?

Yes, actually, I am. Which is ridiculous. Elizabeth Fairchild's daughter does not get nervous around men. Elizabeth Fairchild's daughter wraps men around her little finger. I may have spent my whole life trying to escape from under my mother's thumb, but that doesn't mean she didn't manage to drill her lessons in deep.

"You're right," I say, even though the idea of Damien Stark wrapped around any woman's finger remains a little fuzzy. "I'll see you at home."

"If I'm asleep, wake me up. I want to hear everything."

"There's nothing to tell," I say.

"Liar," she chides, then clicks off.

I slide my phone into my purse and head back to the bar—now I want that champagne. I stand there holding my glass as I glance around the room. This time, I see Stark right away. Him and Audrey Hepburn. He's smiling, she's laughing, and I'm working myself up into quite a temper. I mean, he's the reason I'm stranded here, and yet he hasn't made any effort to speak to me again, to apologize for the whole "be my decorating wench" fiasco, or to arrange a ride for me. If I have to call a cab I am absolutely going to send a bill to Stark International.

Evelyn passes by, arm in arm with a man with hair so white he reminds me of Colonel Sanders. She pats him on the arm, murmurs something, then disengages herself. The colonel marches on as Evelyn eases up next to me. "Having a nice time?"

"Of course," I say.

She snorts.

"I know," I say. "I'm a terrible liar."

"Hell, honey, you weren't even putting any effort into that one."

"I'm sorry. I'm just..." I trail off and tuck a loose strand of hair behind my ear. I'd curled it and pinned it up in a chignon. A few loose curls are supposed to hang free and frame my face. Right now, the damn thing is just annoying me.

"He's inscrutable," Evelyn says.

"Who?"

She nods toward Damien, and I look in that direction. He's still talking with Audrey Hepburn, but I'm struck by the certainty that he had been watching me only moments earlier. I have nothing to base that on, though, and I'm frustrated, not knowing if the thought is wishful thinking or paranoia.

"Inscrutable?" I repeat.

"He's a hard man to figure out," Evelyn says. "I've known him since he was a boy—his father signed me to represent him when some damn breakfast cereal wanted his face on their television spots. As if Damien Stark with a sugar high was the way we wanted to go. No, I landed the boy some damn good endorsements, helped make him a goddamned household name. But most days I don't think I know him at all."

"Why not?"

"I told you, Texas. Inscrutable." She draws out each syllable, then punctuates the word with a shake of her head. " 'Course I don't fault him, not with the shit that was piled onto that poor kid. Who wouldn't end up a little bit damaged?"

"You mean the fame? That must have been hard. He was so young." Stark won the Junior Grand Slam at fifteen, and that had pushed him into the stratosphere. But the press had latched onto him long before that. With his good looks and working-class background, he'd been plucked out of the flurry of hopefuls as the tennis circuit's golden boy.

"No, no." Evelyn waves her hand as if dismissing the thought. "Damien knows how to handle the press. He's damn good at protecting his secrets, always has been." She eyes me, then laughs, as if to suggest she was only joking. But I don't think so. "Oh, honey, listen to me ramble. No, Damien Stark is just one of those dark, quiet types. He's like an iceberg, Texas. The deep parts are well hidden and what you do see is hard and a little bit cold."

She chuckles, amused at her own joke, then waves at someone who's caught her attention. I glance toward Damien, looking for evidence of the wounded child that Evelyn has recalled, but all I see is unerring strength and self-confidence. Am I seeing a mask? Or am I really looking at the man?

"What I'm trying to say," Evelyn continues, "is that you shouldn't take it personally. The way he acted, I mean. I doubt he meant to be rude. He was probably just off in his head and didn't even realize what he was doing."

I, of course, have moved past the snub at our meeting, but Evelyn doesn't realize that. My current issues with Damien Stark are wide and varied—ranging from the simple problem of a ride home to more complicated emotions that I'm not inclined to analyze.

"You were right about Rip and Lyle," I say, because she

keeps looking in Stark's direction, and I want to head off any suggestion that we edge our way into that conversation. "My roommate is in awe that I'm in the same room with them."

"Well, come on, then. I'll introduce you."

The two stars—both polished and shined within an inch of their lives—are perfectly polite and perfectly dull. I have nothing to say to them. I don't even know what their show is about. Evelyn can't seem to wrap her head around the possibility that anyone could either not care or not know about all things Hollywood. She seems to think I'm merely being coy and is about to leave me alone with these two.

Social Nikki would smile and make polite small talk. But Social Nikki is getting a bit frayed around the edges, and instead, I reach out, snagging a bit of Evelyn's sleeve before she escapes too far. She looks back at me, her brows raised in question. I have nothing to say. Panic bubbles in me; Social Nikki has completely left the building.

And then I see it—my excuse. My salvation. It's so unexpected—so completely out of place—that I half wonder if I'm not hallucinating. "That man," I say, pointing to a skinny twenty-something with long, wavy hair and wire-framed glasses. He looks like he belongs at Woodstock, not an art show, and I hold my breath, expecting the apparition to vanish. "Is that Orlando McKee?"

"You know Orlando?" she asks, then answers her own question. "Of course. The friend who works for Charles. But where did you two meet?" She nods goodbye to Lyle and Rip, who could care less about our departure; they're back to arguing between themselves and smiling brightly at the women who sidle in close for a snapshot.

"We grew up together," I explain as Evelyn steers me through the throng.

The truth is our families lived next door to each other until

Ollie went off to college, and even though he's two years older than me, we were inseparable until Ollie turned twelve and was shipped off to boarding school in Austin. I had been beside myself with envy.

I haven't seen Ollie for years, but he's the kind of friend that you don't need to talk to every day. Months can go by, and then he'll call me out of the blue, and we pick up the conversation like it had never stopped. He and Jamie are my closest friends in the world and I am beyond giddy that he's here, right when I need him so desperately.

We're close now, but he hasn't noticed us. He's talking about some television show with another guy, this one in jeans and a sport coat over a pale pink button-down. Very California. Ollie's hands are moving, because that's the way he talks, and when he flails one hand my direction, he glances that way out of reflex. I see the moment that realization hits him. He freezes, his hand drops, and he turns to face me, his arms going out wide.

"Nikki? My God, you look amazing." He pulls me into a tight Ollie hug, then pushes me back, his hands on my shoulders as he looks me up and down.

"Do I pass inspection?"

"When have you not?"

"Why aren't you in New York?"

"The firm transferred me back last week. I was going to call you this weekend. I couldn't remember when you were moving out here." He pulls me into another spontaneous hug, and I'm grinning so wide my mouth is starting to hurt. "Damn, it's good to see you."

"I take it you two know each other," the guy in jeans says drolly.

"Sorry," Ollie says. "Nikki, this is Jeff. We work together at Bender, Twain & McGuire."

"What he means is that I work for him," Jeff says. "I'm a

summer associate. Orlando is a third year now, and they love him there. I think Maynard's about ready to make him a partner."

"Very funny," Ollie says, but he looks pleased.

"Look at you," I say. "My little guppy's grown into a full-fledged shark."

"Ah-ah. You know the rules. For every lawyer joke you make, I get to make two dumb blonde jokes."

"I take it back."

"Come on, Jeff," Evelyn says. "Let's let these two catch up. We'll go find our own trouble to get into."

It would be polite to tell them not to bother, but neither one of us does. We're too wrapped up in reminiscing, and I'm too happy to have Ollie beside me.

We talk about everything and nothing as we head for the door, taking our conversation outside by silent agreement. I'm completely absorbed, warmed by memories and Ollie's familiar face. But as we reach the door, I turn back and look at the room. I'm not sure why I do. Maybe it's just a reflex, but I think it's something more. I think I'm looking for someone. For him.

Sure enough, my eyes find Damien Stark right away. He's no longer with Audrey Hepburn. Now he's talking with a short, balding man. He's focused and attentive. But his head lifts and his eyes find me.

And in that singular moment, I know that if he asked me to blow off my friend and stay in the room with him, I would do it.

Damn him, and damn me, but I would stay with Damien Stark.

Grab Your Copy Now
books2read.com/JK-RM

ALSO BY J. KENNER

For all of JK's Stark World and other titles, please visit www.jkenner.com

The Stark Saga

He'd pay any price to have her...

release me

claim me

complete me

take me (novella)

have me (novella)

play my game (novella)

seduce me (novella)

unwrap me (novella)

deepest kiss (novella)

entice me (novella)

anchor me

hold me (novella)

please me (novella)

lost with me

damien

indulge me (novella)

delight me (novella & bonus content)

cherish me (novella)

embrace me (novella)

enchant me

interview with the billionaire

The Fallen Saint Series

His touch is her sin. Her love is his salvation

My Fallen Saint

My Beautiful Sin

My Cruel Salvation

Sinner's Game

Charismatic. Dangerous. Sexy as hell. Meet the elite team of Stark Security.

Shattered With You

Shadows Of You

(free prequel to Broken With You)

Broken With You

Ruined With You

Wrecked With You

Destroyed With You

Memories of You

Ravaged With You

Hidden With You

Charmed By You

Tangled With You

Entwined With You

Craved By You

The Steele Books/Stark International:

He was the only man who made her feel alive.

Say My Name

On My Knees

Under My Skin

Take My Dare (includes short story Steal My Heart)

Stark International Novellas:

Meet Jamie & Ryan-so hot it sizzles.

Tame Me

Tempt Me

Tease Me

Touch Me

S.I.N. Trilogy:

It was wrong for them to be together…

…but harder to stay apart.

Dirtiest Secret

Hottest Mess

Sweetest Taboo

Most Wanted:

Three powerful, dangerous men.

Three sensual, seductive women.

Wanted

Heated

Ignited

Man of the Month

Who's your man of the month...?

Down On Me

Hold On Tight

Need You Now

Start Me Up

Get It On

In Your Eyes

Turn Me On

Shake It Up

All Night Long

In Too Deep

Light My Fire

Walk The Line

Royal Cocktail (bonus book)

*Bar Bites: A Man of the Month Cookbook(by J. Kenner & Suzanne M. Johnson)

Blackwell-Lyon:

Heat, humor & a hint of danger

Lovely Little Liar

Pretty Little Player

Sexy Little Sinner

Tempting Little Tease

Rising Storm:

Writing as Julie Kenner

Small town drama

Rising Storm: Tempest Rising

Rising Storm: Quiet Storm

PARANORMAL

Demon Hunting Soccer Mom

Like Buffy... grown up!

Paranormal women's fiction

Carpe Demon

California Demon

Demons Are Forever

Deja Demon

The Demon You Know (short story)

Demon Ex Machina

Pax Demonica

Day of the Demon

How To Train Your Demon

The Dark Pleasures Series:

Billionaire immortal romance

Caress of Darkness

Find Me In Darkness

Find Me In Pleasure

Find Me In Passion

Caress of Pleasure

ALSO BY J. KENNER

For all of JK's Stark World and other titles, please visit www.jkenner.com

The Stark Saga

He'd pay any price to have her...

release me

claim me

complete me

take me (novella)

have me (novella)

play my game (novella)

seduce me (novella)

unwrap me (novella)

deepest kiss (novella)

entice me (novella)

anchor me

hold me (novella)

please me (novella)

lost with me

damien

indulge me (novella)

delight me (novella & bonus content)

cherish me (novella)

embrace me (novella)

enchant me

interview with the billionaire

The Fallen Saint Series

His touch is her sin. Her love is his salvation

My Fallen Saint

My Beautiful Sin

My Cruel Salvation

Sinner's Game

Charismatic. Dangerous. Sexy as hell. Meet the elite team of Stark Security.

Shattered With You

Shadows Of You

(free prequel to Broken With You)

Broken With You

Ruined With You

Wrecked With You

Destroyed With You

Memories of You

Ravaged With You

Hidden With You

Charmed By You

Tangled With You

Entwined With You

Craved By You

The Steele Books/Stark International:

He was the only man who made her feel alive.

Say My Name

On My Knees

Under My Skin

Take My Dare (includes short story Steal My Heart)

Stark International Novellas:

Meet Jamie & Ryan-so hot it sizzles.

Tame Me

Tempt Me

Tease Me

Touch Me

S.I.N. Trilogy:

It was wrong for them to be together...

...but harder to stay apart.

Dirtiest Secret

Hottest Mess

Sweetest Taboo

Most Wanted:

Three powerful, dangerous men.

Three sensual, seductive women.

Wanted

Heated

Ignited

Man of the Month

Who's your man of the month...?

Down On Me

Hold On Tight

Need You Now

Start Me Up

Get It On

In Your Eyes

Turn Me On

Shake It Up

All Night Long

In Too Deep

Light My Fire

Walk The Line

Royal Cocktail (bonus book)

*Bar Bites: A Man of the Month Cookbook(by J. Kenner & Suzanne M. Johnson)

Blackwell-Lyon:

Heat, humor & a hint of danger

Lovely Little Liar

Pretty Little Player

Sexy Little Sinner

Tempting Little Tease

Rising Storm:

Writing as Julie Kenner

Small town drama

Rising Storm: Tempest Rising

Rising Storm: Quiet Storm

PARANORMAL

Demon Hunting Soccer Mom

Like Buffy... grown up!

Paranormal women's fiction

Carpe Demon

California Demon

Demons Are Forever

Deja Demon

The Demon You Know (short story)

Demon Ex Machina

Pax Demonica

Day of the Demon

How To Train Your Demon

The Dark Pleasures Series:

Billionaire immortal romance

Caress of Darkness

Find Me In Darkness

Find Me In Pleasure

Find Me In Passion

Caress of Pleasure

ABOUT THE AUTHOR

J. Kenner (aka Julie Kenner) is the *New York Times*, *USA Today*, *Publishers Weekly*, *Wall Street Journal* and #1 International bestselling author of over one hundred novels, novellas and short stories in a variety of genres.

JK has been praised by *Publishers Weekly* as an author with a "flair for dialogue and eccentric characterizations" and by *RT Bookclub* for having "cornered the market on sinfully attractive, dominant antiheroes and the women who swoon for them." A five-time finalist for Romance Writers of America's prestigious RITA award, JK took home the first RITA trophy awarded in the category of erotic romance in 2014 for her novel, *Claim Me* (book 2 of her Stark Trilogy) and the RITA trophy for *Wicked Dirty* in the same category in 2017.

In her previous career as an attorney, JK worked as a lawyer in Southern California and Texas. She currently lives in Central Texas, with her husband, two daughters, and two rather spastic cats.

Stay in touch! Text JKenner to 21000 to subscribe to JK's text alerts.

www.jkenner.com

Milton Keynes UK
Ingram Content Group UK Ltd.
UKHW030305050924
447823UK00004B/284

9 781648 397066